TAKE IT OR LEAVE IT

OTHER BOOKS BY RAYMOND FEDERMAN

Temporary Landscapes
Journey to Chaos: Samuel Beckett's Early Fiction
Among the Beasts / Parmi les Monstres
Cinq Nouvelles Nouvelles
Samuel Beckett: His Works and His Critics
Double or Nothing
Amer Eldorado
Surfiction: Fiction Now and Tomorrow

*Tiens! Petite Sœur, lis ça
et ne te mets pas
en colère, la
route est longue quand on
sait pas où on va, mais on
y rencontre des gens
qui comptent ——
avec affection!
Raymond Buffalo, 1978*

TAKE IT OR LEAVE IT

*an exaggerated second-hand tale
to be read aloud either standing or sitting*

by
Raymond   Federman

FICTION COLLECTIVE   NEW YORK

Grateful acknowledgement is made to the following magazines in which sections of this novel first appeared in slightly different forms: *Partisan Review; Chicago Review; North American Review; Oyez Review; Seems; Out of Sight; Ethos.*

This publication is in part made possible with support from the New York State Council on the Arts, Brooklyn College, and Teachers & Writers Collaborative.

First Edition
Copyright © 1976 by Raymond Federman
Typesetting & Design by New Hampshire Composition Inc.

Library of Congress Catalog No. 75-21556
ISBN: 0-914590-23-5 (paperback)
ISBN: 0-914590-22-7 (hardcover)

Published by FICTION COLLECTIVE

Distributed by George Braziller, Inc.
                One Park Avenue
                New York, N.Y. 10016

SUMMARY OF THE RECITATION

all sections in this tale are interchangeable therefore page numbers being useless they have been removed at the discretion of the author

For ERICA
encore une fois

There are many more languages than one imagines. And man reveals himself much more often than he wishes. So many things that speak! But there are always so few listeners, so that man, so to speak, only chatters in a void when he engages in confessions. He wastes his truths just as the sun wastes its light. Isn't it too bad that the void has no ears?

NIETZSCHE

. . . a satisfactory novel should be a self-evident sham to which the reader can regulate at will the degree of his credulity . . .

FLANN O'BRIEN

P R E T E X T

a spatial displacement of words

[to be inserted anywhere in the text]

One could imagine that it happened this way:
in the beginning
words scattered
by chance
and in all directions!

U c n r l e e e g e
  n o t o l d n r i s!

Wild lines of words would have crossed the sheets of paper
obeying only their own furor.

The pencil of the writer
his fingertips
his pen (machine) would have followed them.
Little by little
as words became more numerous
        more compact
    gathered together
    rushed together
into certain regions of the paper
small fields of forces would have localized themselves : eddies

                                        knots

                                        crests

                            contours of words

            : spontaneous designs of filings

                climbing up   the pages in

                    and down

                        mad laughter!

And it is from this
that   from place to place   the chance of a figure of
speech would have appeared.   Carried by this mass of aleatory
                        events by these thousands of
                                    forces
                        crisscrossing on the paper
a shy silhouette
a profile
a shiny saxophone
the sparkling wheels of a Buick
the carnavalesque uniform of a paratrooper (a story) would have
appeared!

But
it
was
quite
different!   The writer set down   first on the page
                    with a great deal of meticulousness
                                        trees
                                        roads
                                        cars
                                        people
in the streets   rooms
            and inside these rooms (behind windowpanes) puppets
                        which resembled the people
in the streets!

This done
the real beginning begins : a rain of words
small   large
compact
fall upon the design of the story!
It   is   pierced drown   covered   over buried-
torn lost! Lost? No!   It is here   but only in the form
of a game!

a game
of appearances   and
disappearances   ————
The previous figures are only a support
an adversary support
somewhat like the canvas
smooth   monochromatic
prepared by the painter before he begins his real work.   The
words cling to this surface
struggle against it - here the syntax struggles against the syntax!
It eagerly refuses the elements which
at the same time   make its setting
its resting place!

Space between past / present ———— between a tree and a
platform.   Here!   Art of fencing and strategy :
to find support on one's adversary
to rest upon that which is attacked
to find strength in what is being destroyed!

It is not a twilight which drowns everything
almost everything   in its shadow. It is the confrontation of two enemy races!

                                        Syntax
                                         upon
                                        syntax
                          against syntax is the joust
between differences of form
        (obtained by words)
and differences of force (established by words) : struggle of
                                              word-design

                                          , against
                                        word-syntax

— On the one side (but can one still speak of side
      when already all sides have been eliminated?   forms cut out
previously   by linear syntax.
On the other wordarrows brought in by some outside energy
                              bearer of wild forces
                                  dark conquerors!

Syntax, traditionally, is the unity, the continuity of words, the
law which dominates them. It reduces their multiplicity, controls
their violence. It fixes them into a place, a space, prescribes an
order to them. It prevents them from wandering. Even if it is
hidden, it reigns always on the horizon of words which buckle
under its mute exigency.

Here
the design-word
and the design-syntax   independent of one another
are set against one another! Syntax is abolished once and for all
                                        in advance!

Leaning against the winds over a precipice syntax integrates itself
to the constraints of the paper

                              its format

                         its dimensions

                            its margins

                              its edges

                        its consistency

                          its whiteness

                         It constitutes the given —
it is the hazard / fatality which determines what will happen
next : the unpredictable shape of t
                              y
                          p
                             o
                            g
                              r
                          a
                         p
                            h
                              y!

                              A dangerous game
because everything here has a positive value :
    nothing is cancelled
    nothing is erased

                   lost — no possibility of sad erasures!

[Or else everything is cancelled erased lost
when the writer begins his battle against the linearity of syntax]
with wild strokes all strokes are recorded a word carries another]
word the writer can always add another cross it out repeat it and]
thus multiply the network but the rule of the game forbids him to]
come back upon what has already been done a return to zero is not]
possible is in fact excluded from the start the played stroke has]
to remained played]

Undoubtedly
it is permitted to do some correcting but
                              corrections are
    to remain visible :   grey chafings
                          broken lines   crushed
                                  pulverized
multiply into a bundle of hollow and visible burrows! Everything here leaves a mark   ,but not sign of something
or something else   but mark of a multiplicty
of events of which none can ever fall back into non-existence! It is
a process of self-cancellation that renews itself upon its void a
series
therefore
without possible return
nor corrections just words which superimpose themselves upon
other words
                                                    strokes
                                               which reply
On the surface of this battle   to other strokes
upon which one has an o
                         b
                        l
                          ique view   the pages
Paradox of these l o o s e scribblings   become syntax

                            words
                      without order
where all elements are positive

                                        What reigns here
                                        is an indefinite
no negative splendor   addition

but also no summation   There is

                        no

            moment   where
everything is good   where
the series has reached a point of saturation   where
all that remains to be done would be to set the final period
            to end it all   to call the story finished   In
                                        fact

                   there can always be more
No law   words   words!
No lie
No order says to the writer :   Here and Now You Must Stop
                       Not A Word More!   He can
always go on
but there is also the risk — but the risk was there from the
beginning
— that one more word may be too much
        one more word may destroy it all
                may cancel the whole story
                may force the whole story down to-
                wards its ending!

Each word carries with it
the peril of being negative
because in excess
but after each word
there is still the danger
of stopping too soon
of leaving a gap
a void
something unsaid
the danger
of having established an arbitrary line
of having set a limit
to what cannot
must not
have one
no excess
but also never a limit
that is the risk here!

One can imagine the slow
painful
patient feverishness
which overcomes the writer
all along this battle of words and phrases
the first word can already be excessive
and ruin everything
but think how this danger
unique in the beginning
multiplies itself
as each new word calls into play
another
as each new set of words offers
thousands of new possibilities
and in multiplying themselves draw nearer to excess
one more word and it's too much
it's too late
everything is lost!

Think of the madness of sketching all these possible words, the desire and the need to add more, the excitement of chance, but also think of the cool restraint, the control, the necessary calculation, the extreme reserve and the cunning that this game without return presupposes! Irrational balance!

Between this madness and this caution each word must be written (set down) as though it were the last one the last gasp and the one word that happens to have no successor can only be the last one for only a moment! But it is this last moment however (neither more nor less ultimate than the others!) which carries the game to its highest point of intensity—for it is this last moment that the writer has chosen at his own risk and peril to cancel his story to turn away from it and let the battle unfold in front of us in its uninterrupted glory! But then appears before us on the shattered white space the people drawn by the black words from the beginning flattened and disseminated on the white surface of the paper inside the black ink-blood!

0

suppositions & prelibations

RECOMMENDATIONS FOR THOSE WHO ARE NOT DIRECTLY INVOLVED IN THIS TALE

Writing is not [I INSIST] *the living repetition of life.*

The author is [PERHAPS?] *that which gives the disquieting language of fiction its unities, its knots of coherence, its insertion into the real.*

All fiction is [I THINK] *a digression. It always deviates from its true purpose.*

All reading is [IN MY OPINION] *done haphazardly.*

THEREFORE

One must never tumble down into the psychology of the self.

CONSEQUENTLY

All events in this tale are distorted [AS MUCH AS POSSIBLE] *from reality.*

All the characters in this tale are given [OF COURSE] *false names.*

All places have their true names but could [INDEED] *be given other names.*

All those who listen to the tale [THE LISTENERS] *and ask questions* [THE QUESTIONERS] *are real people.*

The one who tells the tale [THE TELLER] *existed, long ago, but no longer exists today.*

The one whose tale is told [THE TOLD] *could have told his own tale directly, but for reasons unknown, chose to tell his tale indirectly to the one who is telling the tale directly for the pleasure (or displeasure) of those who are listening to the tale*

The action of the tale takes place on a platform [BETWEEN THE HEAD AND THE HANDS] *therefore* [WITHOUT ANY PRETENSION] *anywhere.*

Those who stand outside this tale have no right [OBVIOUSLY] *to interfere with the recitation.*

THUS

It is better to have one foot in the bush [bouche] *than two in the mouth.*

NOTE: These recommendations have not necessarily been invented by the author. Those who wish to find the original source may do so at their own risk for there is no (sacred!) source to writing.

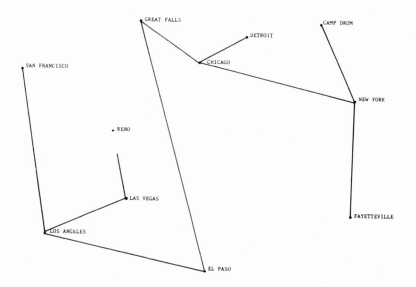

I want to write a book like a cloud that changes as it goes he said.

I want to tell a story that cancels itself as it goes I replied.

THE EASIEST OF COURSE WOULD BE TO BLOW my BRAINS
OUT ————— bang!

THIS WAY we WOULDN'T HAVE TO BEGIN

BUT SUPPOSE —————-

Yes ——————- Suppose!

And so here I stand on my platform (caught in between) at the
beginning (or so) with HIM on one side and THEM on the other
1=1 [......................]look at them[...................] 5 or 6 of them
(and more to come inevitably)

                          yapping like a bunch of old ladies:
                                    YAPYAPYAP!

[how the hell they got here - how the hell I got here — we'll never
know] But listen to them: BLAHBLAHBLAH!

Why . . . ?   *Why you . . . ?*
Where . . . ?   *Why couldn't he . . . ?*
When was it . . . ?   *What did he . . . ?*
Who was he . . . ?   *(It's not clear . . . ?)*
How . . . ?   *In which direction . . . ?*
And then . . . ?   *And then what happened . . . ?*
....?

& : (— $! 1 ½ 8 ⅝ - / , !) (
:::
::::::: D A M M I T ::
::::::::::::::::::::::::::::::::::::::: W I L L :::
:: Y O U :::::::::::::
:: G U Y S :::::::::::::::::::::::::::::::::::::
:::::::::::::: S :::
:::::::::::::::::: T ::
:::::::::::::::::::::: O ::
:::::::::::::::::::::::: P :::
:::::::::::::::::::::::::::::::::: B U G G I N G :::::::::::::::::::::::::::::::::::::::
:: M E ::::::::::
::::::: W I T H :::
:::::::::::::::::::::::::::::::::::: Y O U R :::
::::::::::::::: F U C K I N G :::::::::::::::::::::::: Q U E S T I O N S ::
:::

I

setting & tripping

Why, when, where, how, why me, why then, who, and then, in which direction? How the hell do I know!
. . . Dammit!   If you guys keep talking all the time / and at the same time / we'll never get it straight!   We'll never get there! Do you think it's easy to tell a story?   Any story?   HEY! Particularly when it's not YOUR story — a second-hand story! Anywhere?   To retell a story which was already told from the start in a rather dubious manner. Do you think it's easy to set it up so that it looks coherent? Or even readable? Not to mention credible? I tell you it's not easy. A life story (or even parts of it)! Particularly since there's no way to check no way to make sure to verify to go back and find proofs to back up to fill in that monstrous gap from his mouth to my mouth (from down there Word of
                              to up here)   mouth!
That's how he told me the story and that's how I'm telling it to you. I do my best. But of course there is a décalage. Room for distortions, exaggerations, deformations, errors. It's inevitable. Also, one must remember I cannot retrace my steps. Also, one must remember that linguistically we're both rather poor. No, he was not very talented. He had a good imagination and a good sense of story-telling, but what an abominable accent! And also with the passing of time, the failings of memory, the deterioration and the closing of the mind, the changing of times, and of course my own subjective interpretation of his story, my intermediary role in other words, my detestable personality . . .   all of these interfere, to a great extent, with those particular elements of the original story. And yet, I must tell you to the best of my knowledge what he told me.
But you guys bombard me with all your damn questions and me I get lost LOST (damn you)!

one
at
the
time — please — slow down!   Okay!
First, I'll tell the first trip the way he told it to me.

I'll tell the first time first — THE GREAT JOURNEY as he
called it.

Just the way he told it to me (approximately of course or if
you prefer as best I can)!

Not exactly the way it happened but the way he told it to me
on several occasions.

But don't ask me WHERE and WHEN and HOW because it
really doesn't matter much where and when and how he
told me the whole story!

    Of necessity I must rearrange his tale,
    substitute my own voice for his voice,
    my person for his person,
    and even, at times, my self for his self!

    Fill in the gaps, in other words!

    For there are many things which I have forgotten, many things
which cannot be told, many things which are not tellable, many
things of unspeakable nature!

Therefore I reconstruct
                I invent (a little)
                I distort
                I simulate
                I dissimulate
                I suggest
                I exaggerate

                I DO MY BEST (if you know what I mean) after all I'm
only here to report!

I'm only a second-hand teller!

And in those days I was only there to listen. I did not witness.
I did not experience. I only heard!

Thereforepleasestopbuggingmewithallyourfucking
questionsleavemealonewait!

Listen!

. . . ?

The first time? Good! The great discovery . . . The first trip?

That'swhat hecalled it!
That'swhat I'llcall it!

Make believe that it was me that it happened to me that I was
there that it is my story that it's me speaking that I'm appropriat-
ing his words in other words
that that that . . . And so here we go!   Make believe!

The funniest (he began) is that I had no idea where I was going
(that's for damn sure!), no idea what America was all about (who
does?), geographically speaking (that is), no idea particularly of
the size. Yes! Endless spaces and tremendous colors. Wow! Unbelievable the colors and the spaces (isn't he something?) You've
got to see that to believe it. At least once - once in a lifetime (if not
more)! And distances ————— distances that never end
—————- ENORMOUS distances ————— between places!
                                                      Ah what places!
We're getting there . . . Wait!   Between people too!
                                        Between words also!
And all these people (all these words) all of them Americans who
look (what a way to start!) at you, who scare you shitless (*sic*)
            who scare the hell out of you because they too are
scared
scared to move
scared to speak
scared to screw

scared to let themselves go   (most of them, I added)
scared to be   to be proud   mad   insolent   delirious   talkative   (Right on!)
scared to be   to be   (or not to be)   to be .. ..
(What a two-bit philosopher!)
FIRST TRIP then   (we're getting there . . .)

I didn't even know where to begin
in which direction to go
how I was supposed to get started
how to get going
to go from one end to the other — from the EAST COAST to the
WEST COAST — from coast-to-coast man — and *prompto!*
BLAH BLAH BLAH . . . ? [Soft shy voice]
Why?
That's a good one. Because . . .   just because . . .   he was really
dumb, really dumb in those days (no! not really dumb, naive
rather and enormously shy at that time, but that's not a crime!)
and quite inexperienced in our American way of life. But that's
not his fault. First trip, remember (mention it again not to confuse
it with other trips). Was I timid in those days (he'd say to me), but
that's not a sin. Happens to a lot of guys. And also ALSO I didn't
know I DIDN'T KNOW a damn thing at that time I was young
(twenty I think he said at the most) just twenty (not even) but
AMERICA yes AMERICA I had already three years of it behind
me yes THREE YEARS [I tell you] and UP to here FED UP above
the head and plein le dos . . .

GRRRRR GRRRRR . . . ?   [In a kind of mumbling between the
teeth]
How he came?   But by boat . . . by BOAT of course.   You
guys are really something!

Yes but this time I was going to discover IT - America
        to see IT close - America
            to dive into IT - America   (once and for all
you might say)   Because up to this point ME - America! I hadn't
seen much of it. Two years in Detroit (yes DETROIT — you guys
seem surprised!), and then approximately (more or less) one
year in NEW YORK (city) What a place!

SHID SHID SHID SHID . . . ? [With a certain ironic smile]
Why did he stay?   Because . . . because AMERICA (gentlemen)   it's a bit like a drug : the more you're there the more you
want to stay, the more you touch it the more you want it, the more
you get used to it the more you dig it, the more you dig it the more
you want it to force you to dig it, it grows on you, and so on, the
more you want to take advantage of it, and the more you dream
about the great fabulous things that are going to happen (to you).
And at the same time the more you feel like dropping the whole
thing immediately, like giving up, like screwing it all, like taking
off, cutting out on the spot, full speed, and tell America to shove
it, to go, anywhere: AFRICA (for instance), yes Dakar, Timbuktu,
anywhere: CHINA (even). Like a drug! For the birds (you might
say!), believe me, AMERICA pour les oiseaux (messieurs)! Yes,
it's just a matter of TAKE IT OR LEAVE IT (damn right) I tell you!
Takes a good ten years (and even more) to get used to it. What!
Twelve or fifteen or more, to get used to it (and even then)! And
even if you've taken it, even if you've hung on, for a good ten
years or twelve or fifteen or more (depending I suppose on your
temperament) you never really get used to it, and even if you do,
even when you think you are used to it and it begins to be better
(or worse, quite worse), even though it appears to be better, it's
only an illusion, a joke, an ENORMOUS joke, a fake, and yet they
think it's better, they think it's okay, at least that's what the

people imagine (those jerks who have not taken off or killed themselves) I mean all the lousy foreigners who came to America their heads full of shit full of dreams!

Most guys who arrive in America suffer at least ten or twelve years in the beginning (that is to say 99%), and since most Americans (100% in fact) at one time or another (originally) come from a foreign country that means in fact that 99% of these people suffer at least for a good ten years or more before getting used to America, therefore it means that only 1% (the uppercrust) doesn't suffer like the rest, and these are the guys THE LUCKY ONES who arrive with lots of money, all kinds of wealth, or who have rich families in America (American uncles loaded with dough — millionaires) whereas the rest of them (the 99% undercrust) they have nothing, they just are fucked from the beginning, and for them it's just a matter of taking it or leaving it, like a bunch of IDIOTS, just like that, without ever asking if it means anything, without ever asking themselves what the fuck this whole shit is all about, what the hell they're doing here working their asses to the bone a good eight or ten hours a day in shitholes, for nothing, not a damn thing, or else, eventually, for the birds!

But me, poor slob, I had it UP to here, three years already, three years I had of America behind me, and I hadn't understood a damn thing yet NOTHING

Absolutely nothing!

I arrived (just like that) by boat and there
she was AMERICA (big and fat and
beautiful like a cow) just standing there
and I looked at her and I wondered (in
the beginning a bit puzzled as I stood on
the pier in my old outmoded double-
breasted blue suit) without understanding a damn thing of what it meant (and I
stood there like an ass a poor shy Jewish
emigrant) to be here (alone on the platform) my head bent down towards my
hands (not even crying) simply asking
myself what the fuck am I doing here (in
French of course) with my beat-up suitcase at my feet with my stuff spilling out
of it like a pile of dirty laundry on the
platform (and AMERICA in front of me
nervous excited ready) and I suddenly
feeling like jerking off!   Feeling Sad!

II

the masturbatory gesture

Nothing!   Not a damn thing!
And yet had I seen all kinds of crap . . . suffering . . . loneliness . . . depression . . . homesickness . . . despair . . .
starvation . . . disgusting greasy filthy food (noodles especially, three times a day for months) . . . all kinds of bitchy things
. . . and all sorts of other crap . . . ah when it comes to crap it
fell on me from all sides (poor slob) and me I took it without
understanding a damn thing and never complaining NO never
. . . and yet it wasn't my fault . . . that's for sure . . . simply
a matter of . . .

TATATATA TA . . . ? [Young punk in an elegant corduroy jac-
ket]
Ah, you want to know when it was?
But   It was at the beginning of the Fifties Yes
              The GREAT journey ———— The GREAT discovery
It started in February. February 1951 to be exact. I was. I was in
North Carolina at the time. In the army. Yes I was in the Army. Of
course the American army! Why are you guys laughing? Can
happen to anyone. Ok it was a joke, a mistake (unbelievable the
number of mistakes a guy can make, just like that, in a lifetime,
and it's the the beginning, wait till you hear the rest, and also all
the trips — seven of them, all in all, up to this point, across the
continent,   yes   from   the   EAST   COAST   to
= = = = = = = = = = = = =   the   WEST   COAST   or
= = = = = = = = = = = = = = = = = VICE VERSA Seven trips in all:
THE SEVEN DEADLY TRIPS if you wish! That would make a nice
title for the story if I wanted to tell all the trips: or THE SEVEN
DEADLY TALES! But one mustn't exaggerate too much at first or
else. But still do you realize! Can you imagine! ME a G.I.! and in
North Carolina! Unbelievable. But of course it can be explained.

AH AAH AAAH . . . ? [With a rather cynical 100% look]
[Visualize that?] And then? The regiment was taking off for the
UPPER NEW YORK STATE (near the Canadian border) on maneuvers.
Everybody in my outfit was going up. To practice parachute
jumps in the snow.   Imagine that?   Yes in the snow!
                                          (Yes he was in the
                                          parachutists at
the time). Could have been fun!
They were all going up there in full gear (in the nordic snows by
trucks jeeps and buggies) three days on the road they had been
told no screwing around because in North Carolina there isn't
much snow that's for sure I tell you but me ME (HE if you prefer)
had been told that he was not (and no argument about it) going
up with the rest of the guys in his outfit :

Your orders for OVERSEAS DUTY
have arrived the Captain told him (just
the day before) and you have thirty
days (exactly thirty days) to get (your
ass man) to California — yes San
Francisco he specified — and you'll
embark on the boat for the FAR EAST
and no more 82nd

(Yeah! Terrific!)   Yes! . . .   Well, good luck Man! He was told.
What a nice guy that captain. Perhaps a bit queer (I think) around
the edges but nobody really cared about his social habits and his
(rather) curious way of walking on tiptoes since he didn't bug
anybody the guy and mostly minded his captainbusiness.
Thirty days' vacation, he told himself, shit was he going to take
advantage of it (damn right!) and it's normal since in most cases
when you're being shipped overseas to fight the war you get a
month's pay in advance (for that the American Army you can't
complain it's almost like a school a boarding school for girls). So this
time he was really going to enjoy it and take advantage of this
occasion and see the country (damn right!) investigate the whole

lay out explore the East the North the Midwest the Farwest the
whole fucking place—up & down & sideways! Like a pioneer!
Discover
the great plains in the Midwest   See the plateaux and the
rivers
and the deserts   (particularly the technicolored ones)
and the Rockies
and perhaps even the Grand Canyon
and perhaps even some Indians (with feathers on their heads)
and cowboys   and giant trees   and rattlesnakes   and buffalos
and the big superhighways
and the big cities   (Chicago LA. Frisco and all the rest)
Discover
the whole lay out
WOW was I going to see things!   (wow what a dreamer!)
the huge factories where they make giant salamis
and where they make all kinds of funny gadgets
          and all kinds of fancy cars (Cadillacs Fords Chevrolets)
all that   and more   I was going to see—
and I was even going to cross the   M I S S I S S I P P I
               (with its four I's and its four S's)
and perhaps even meet some gangsters in Chicago!
The whole fucking mess :   AMERICA!
I had a hard-on just thinking about it —   Here I come you old
BITCH! jumping in feet first   ready to hump you - - - - - - - left &
right
To penetrate you (all the way to the WEST COAST) because   (up
to now)   I must admit I hadn't gone very far — very deep.   Mostly
stayed on the margin. Yes dealing mostly in the CUNTFRONTA-
TION. But now it was really going to be an enormous PENISTRA-
TION.   I couldn't wait to get going.   AMERICA here I
                                                    c
                                                     o
                                                      m
                                                       e !

Before . . .   Before . . .   I . . . .

BAHBAHBAH . . . ? [With Anxiety from a tall guy with thick sun glasses]
Before what? Be . . Be . . . fore getting knocked off over there in the land of the Chinetoques on the other side the Pacific. That much was certain I tell you, that much could I predict (but useless to whine about it), yes I knew it, in a flash, in a filthy little hole, a muddy pissy foxhole at the extreme end (the FAR EAST end) of the world, in the boondocks of Korea (he had asked for it). I had a feeling about it, a conviction to be exact but no need to whine about it. I had begged, wished, hoped, cried for it. It must be stated. Me, it was me who had bugged the shit out of that Captain (that nice Captain) for weeks and weeks, me who had begged him almost down on my knees to get a transfer. Me who would even have (had the opportunity presented itself) counterfeited his signature. Yes, me who fed up with the whole damn outfit wanted ABSOLUTELY to VOLUNTEER for the real thing or if you prefer for action, for combat, for hand-to-hand extermination, just to get the fuck out of that stinking outfit in North Carolina.

[VOLUNTEER! YOU'RE CRAZY MAN!] The guy thought I was some kind of nut. Hopeless case psychopath or schizo. The nervous type. He couldn't understand (the Captain) what in hell was bugging me. He couldn't understand that I was disgusted fed up fed uP fed Up with America North Carolina the 82nd and those dumb hillbillies of the 82nd all those gunghos of the 82nd . . . . . The 82nd AIRBORNE DIVISION . . . . . you guys can talk to me about it! Yeah! Perhaps these creeps are tough and tremendously well trained for action, and quite ready to die for their country, but beyond that all cretins brutes animals dumbbells cons imbeciles, and on top of that ignorants who can hardly read or write and who spend most of their time (their entire existence in fact) half naked in their dirty underwears playing poker on their footlockers or talking about fucking, that's all they do, that's all they talk about, all day long, all night long — POKER & FUCKING — standing up, sitting, lying down, in the latrine, in the mess hall, in the barracks — POKER & FUCKING asses cunts tits blowjobs as if the whole world was made up only of SEXUAL ACTIVITIES and CARDS and not that they were lucky at it in any way : lucky poker players or expert fuckers! On the contrary, far from it lousy poker players and mediocre fuckers, that's what they all were. Most of them, in fact, still bragging (still bullshitting) about their first piece of pussy if they ever had one if they ever managed to get into one beyond the dirty hollow narrow disgusting space of their imagination! Beyond their dreams!

Ah you guys want me to be more specific!   Ah, when it comes to fucking could these jerks talk about it :
  Asses
  Teats
  Cunts
                        The whole feminine anatomy (real or imaginary) was summed up in these three words! But these poor frustrated sons of a bitch they couldn't even pick up a girl. Didn't even know how to make it, these big slobs. So. So, instead they jerked off all night full speed à plein tube under their khaki blankets (disgusting rags goose-shit color). Incredible the mass labor of the fat ugly masturbators of the 82nd AIRBORNE DIVI-SION! Wow have I seen gallons and gallons of sperm spilled, wasted, in the nights of North Carolina, and tons and tons of sheets stained, yellowed by the juice of these guys of the 82nd! Kilos and kilos! Piles and piles! Truckloads and truckloads of sheets full of vicious and doubtful traces and circles. Torrents and torrents of sperm squirted into the nights (of North Carolina) and the beds (of the 82nd AIRBORNE DIVISION)! Rivers and rivers of juice pumped full blast into imaginary assholes, cunts, and cre-vices, of all shapes and forms! Ah, what feasts of masturbation! What monstrous machinery of erections rushing in motion, in rhythm, all at the same staccato jerky beat! Yes, what pumping and pounding, laboring and plugging, stuffing and leaking (all night) with sigh with wind with squeaks and groans. What

music! Oui, quelle symphonie d'amour sans amour! What frenzy of beat-up flesh and torn muscles! Juicy and hideous mass shrivelling of greedy stiff pricks in madness. What a fiesta!

And they held it with two fingers with their fists with both hands and they did it flat on their stomachs on their backs on their sides obliquely sideways up and down and they stuffed it in all sorts of imaginary holes (round square oval) while in the heads of these poor bastards circulated in masses gigantic asses erotic furs of reddish color humid vegetations and all kinds of wild images disgusting dreams of giant cunts and teats pieces of androgynous bodies sloppy orgies and all that drowning into lakes of white sticky gooey liquid! What artists these guys were without really knowing it! Wow! Yes, what MAGNIFICENT landscapes, what EROTIC landscapes drawn, at midnight, by all these trembling HANDS and shivering MUSCLES! Ah, what dripping mountains of chopped MEAT! What rugged SIERRAS! Quel Guignol! What puppetries of FAT ugly FACES grimacing in the dark! What PUNCH & JUDY shows rehearsed, night after night, under the KHAKI blankets! What TRAFFIC! And when one of them stopped for a minute to take a BREATHER there went another one, passing the stick to the next guy like in a RELAY! And you could hear them PUFFING, gasping, for the finish line! What Olympiads! What world records broken in the beds of the 82nd AIRBORNE DIVISION! What performances achieved en douce and without any self-consciousness in the nights of NORTH CAROLINA! BravoBra

---

Never has so much energy been wasted for such illusions! For such fictions!

UNBELIEVABLE   Yes   UNBELIEVABLE

the poor pricks in pieces The tattered cocks of the next morning Reddish and bloody to scare the hell out of you SICKLY LOOKING like torn pieces of meat! Poor mashed up dicks You could see

them in the showers or the latrines early morning Empty and
Deflated STUPIFIED FACES empty and deflated like balloons!
And the next morning the complexes The next morning culpability all over the place You could see it there at the corners of their
twisted mouths in their eyes in all their gestures You could see it
there at dawn At reveille in the morning fog And these poor guys
who wouldn't dare look at each other face to face Squarely in the
eyes No At least not before they had pissed away slowly in
painful trickles the last shameful drops of their guilty juice of
G.I.'s:
///
ooooooooooooooooooooooooooooooooooooooooooooooooooooooooooo
Yes, but after all, it's understandable. These poor guys, they
weren't very happy there in the army, far from their native
corners of America, and their chickens, and their moms and
pops, and their buddies, and their girlfriends, without any real
human contacts there in the vast desert of the army. Alone in
spite of the crowd, alone in spite of the number, alone in the mass
stupidity of the 82nd AIRBORNE DIVISION. Therefore it's understandable the need these poor guys had to beat on their meat,
every night, alone and desperate!
Most of them were from the South —

          —SOUTHERNERS—
            from Alabama
            from Missouri
            from Tennessee
            from Mississippi
            from Louisiana
            from Oklahoma
            from Georgia
          —HILLBILLIES—
without any education
Most of them could hardly read or write . . . yes most of them
. . . dumb idiots . . . . ignorants . . . . farmers . . . .
jerks . . . . and when they spoke . . . . what a mess!
Marmelade coming out of their mouths : porridge . . . .
mashed potatoes!. Spoken$_{vomit}$!

ME!   at least I had some education [at the time] <u>Le Certificat</u>
<u>d'Etudes!</u> (In France — *OUI* — Lycée Henry IV) at the beginning
of the war . . . .   But after that — *OUI* — a big hole :
ooooooooooooooo
o   o
o   o
ooooooooooooooo   Yes a big H O L E —
                    the debacle the occupation
                    the Germans the French
                    the   J E W S   the

                              o
                         f cou
                       rse I'm J
            —————— *ewish You guy* ——————
               — — *s didn't know Loo* — — —
                — *k at my nose But that*— —
                 doesn't mean that I'm som
                 e sort of fanatic about all t
               hat crap about religion tradition
            deportation extermination etcetera et

                    the yellow star & then the great roun-
                    dup in 42 (le 14 juillet) the entire fam-
                    ily mother father sisters uncles aunts
                    cousins everybody picked up every-
                    body remade into lampshades (after
                    the showers)yes   at AUSCHWITZ!

Ah!   the camps
        the trains
        the farms (in the South)
        the raw potatoes (and diarrhea all night)
        AND   I   FOLLOWED   MY   SHADOW   [remember
that's what he called it]
Well let's skip all that --
No need to whine about it   That's for sure!
And then AMERICA — that FAT bitch — in 47! in 1947 — in
August!

PSITT PSITT PSITT PSITT . . . ?   [With surprise]

If it was after the war?   But of course after the war (at least that
's what he said). And now (finally) after three years of America in
shit up to my neck. Already! (If only he had known). But me at
least I read books (the guy was really something) and also I had
taken courses (at night) at the university (C.C.N.Y.) I couldn't
stop reading (books) it was like a sickness a real bookmadness.
Anything. Even sometimes in English but mostly French stuff.
(What a show-off) anything I could get my hands on. Me (at the
time) I had already read all of CAMUS and a few JEAN-PAUL
SARTRE (imagine!) and even some of LA BEAUVOIR. Well what
was available in those days :

QUAQUAQUAQUAQUA . . . ?   [Same guy in the corduroy
jacket]

What I mean?   What! Everything! What you guys want? Some
kind of bibliography?

La Nausée SSS Les Chemins de la liberté SSS (in three
volumes) SSS Huis Clos SSS Les Mouches SSS La Peste
SSS L'Etranger SSS Tous les hommes sont mortels SSS
etcetera SSS etcetera SSS even Le deuxième sexe SSS La
Putain respectueuse SSS Le Mythe de Sisyphe SSS

Everything! (in other words).   Le Mythe de Sisyphe
what a book! There were passages in it I didn't understand too
well (in those days) but in general I got the main point particularly
about death and suicide. *L'Etre et le néant* (remember that one?)
that was difficult to understand. But I read everything anyway
everything I could find (by chance).

(At least that's what he told me)

But listen to this one (we were sitting under a tree when he told
me that):

Do you know by any chance he once asked me of all people if I had read the books of Vernon Sullivan? Me in those days I thought he was an *Amerloque*!

Vernon SUL-LI-VAN! I loved to pronounce that name. It's very Anglo-Saxon you know.

Do you know by any chance the dirty book he wrote about a black guy who is all white (a fake-white) who fucks all the rich white broads in a Southern town whose name I don't remember? Of course I do. There is even a filthy scene, an unbelievable scene, where he screws one of them in the water, in the middle of the day on the beach with hundreds of people all around, wow it's the most filthy dirty scene I've ever read. Takes place in the South of the United States. North Carolina in fact. What a death at the end of the book when they catch him after an incredible chase. They lynch him at the end of the book and he has an enormous erection inside his pants. But you can see it from the outside because it bulges out. Do you remember he asked me? Do I remember!

Me in those days he went on I used to identify a lot with all these people in these books. Roquentin. Meursault. Ah what a guy Meursault! Oh, yes I almost forgot (he hit his head with his fingers), I also read some books by that religious guy. What's his name? MAUMAU MAURICE MAURIOT MAURUE or something like that. MAURIAC? That's it! There was one of them, I don't remember the title, which I liked particularly. It's the story of a country priest who digs the daughter of the rich landowner. They live way the hell on top of a hill in a castle with lots of horses. He's mad about her the priest and so one day in the middle of the day he rapes her. This was the first book I ever read in which a guy farts in the book. I was really impressed by that. It was very revolutionary!

But in those days (what a hopeless case) it was most of all with
MATHIEU I looked puzzled yes you know MATHIEU in La Mort
dans l'âme (of course) he's an existentialist that I identified the
most because me too at that time I was in the army and I was fed
up with life and the absurdity of life and I wanted to die therefore
it's like MATHIEU that I would have liked to die I can understand
why on top of a church while shooting into a bunch of enemy
creeps : BANG BANG BANG!

Therefore
you understand he said finally
why all the dumb idiots in my regiment couldn't make out what
the hell was going on in my mind!

Who would I pondered?

Those dumb bastards they didn't understand a damn thing.
Nothing!
Absolutely nothing! About existentialism and the business about
choice that one has to make to determine one's action
and about existence that precedes gasoline.

Essence you mean?

Yes essence it's the same thing. And the concept of freedom!
And the notion of self!
They didn't get any of that when I tried to explain all that in the
simplest terms.
Nothing!
They had no idea of what social responsibility towards others
([autrui]) was all about.
And the concept of political commitment ([engagement]) was
Greek to them. These guys of the 82nd AIRBORNE DIVISION
they didn't make heads or tails of all that,

and besides,

they didn't even believe in ideal philosophy.

Ideal! my ass they would say to me, and it's understandable because a guy must be gifted to understand that stuff (that philophilo stuff) you know I told him.

Yes but at least they could have made an effort particularly when I tried to explain to them the crap about l'en-soi and le pour-soi and particularly le sur-moi.

Maybe you should have told them about the moi-nous?

The what?

Skip it, I'm just anticipating a bit.

Those dumb guys they wouldn't listen to me. I tried but it was hopeless!

I tried to stop him at this point because it was really getting incoherent but he went on even though it started raining under our tree. But let him pursue his fantasies a bit more as best we can he may stumble on something interesting. These guys of the 82nd they were all a bunch of MATERIALISTS (not too bad) ESSEN-TIALISTS rather (without knowing it of course) / *but of course this is not your case You guys know what EXISTENTIALISM is It shows on your faces You guys have worked your way through that stuff once upon a time in your youth It's obvious It's visible in your eyes perceptible also at the corners of your mouths You guys have chewed and digested that stuff*

It shows in the intellectual wrinkles of your prosperous faces It's part of your intellectual baggage Your mental suitcase or if you prefer your BACKGROUND

Your UPBRINGING well let's forget it and listen to him in-stead let's skip all that existential crap it's old hat out of style passé bygone pure romanticism / but these guys of the 82nd these

egocentrics and even the Captain they were all ESSENTIALISTS
and yet the Captain that much must be said for him he was Jewish
(with a name like his COHEN it's clear) and not a bad guy in fact
quite a good pear but the rest of the shmucks in my outfit just a
bunch of creepy pricks without exceptions!

Captain COHEN one day he asked me if me too I was Jewish
(it was in his office because of a fight I had had with
a guy from my squad an idiot from Maryland a fat dirty
slob who didn't even know his right from his left and
who bitched all the time about the fucking army that
pank and who knowingly or unknowingly rightly maybe
wrongly perhaps called me a dirty KIKE me I didn't
even know what it meant in those days) because he
understood so I blushed a little when he put the
question to me and I said YES since I had quite
a black eye and it was useless to deny it (but
you should have seen the guy from Maryland he
had a broken nose) the Captain didn't go any
further for an explanation but maybe that's
why he didn't want me to go and get my ass
shot full of holes in the FAR EAST (among
all those damn Chinese Buddhists) because us Jews in general we
don't give a shit about wars we prefer to stay home nice and cozy
take care of our business eat our delicious kosher food and once in
a while for the good of humanity screw our plump dark-haired
Jewish women hop là!
He didn't say that in those words but he must have thought that
much. But at least — Captain COHEN — he read books. There
were all kinds of them in his office. Well lined on his G.I. regulation bookshelves

/-/-/-/-/-/-/-/-/-/-/-/-/-/-/-/-/-/-/-

YOUP YOUP YOUP . . . ? [Slyly from behind a blond Aryan
Mustache]

What kind?   What kind of what?   Books! English books of course. But especially big books on psychology. I would look at them sometimes when it was my turn to sweep his office (but this was before I became corporal because after that no more of that sweeping shit for me). But psychology psychopomp psychosis and all that psych psych and pipi junk and even psychodrama and psycholo lo all those contraptions in PSY and PIPI don't believe in it. All that stuff bores me to death. Bullshit all of it because (in my opinion) what's going on in the skulls (or bladders) of most guys that's their business (what you guys call their INNERSELVES). That's their private onions. That's why (in my opinion) one must never tumble down into the psychology of the self. You dig! Better not touch. That's what I think. And this is maybe why at times Captain COHEN he would come out with all sorts of weird screwy junk about the advantages of collective exi. . . *LOUDER! LOUDER! [all of a sudden in the middle of a sentence collectively & angrily]*

Ah you guys want me to speak louder! You guys can't hear too well!

I said . . . stence S C R E W Y junk about collective existence LIFE in the army (I suppose he got all that out of his PSY-cho-lo-GY books). But our nice Captain Cohen he read books at least, whereas the other fatasses of the regiment — even the NonComs: bunch of PUSHOVERS all of them — never a book. Never! Except once in a while COMIC BOOKS like Tarzan and Zorro or all sorts of junk of that caliber. And not often, I can assure you. COMIC BOOKS the official literature of the 82nd AIRBORNE DIVISION! Piles and Piles of COMIC BOOKS—all over! Most of the time these poor jerks didn't even read the words. They just looked at the pictures. They would even get an erection just looking at pictures of Jane flying bareass from one tree to another HOP! Otherwise

POKER & FUCKING   FUCKING & POKER

                        all day long

————————pairs   asses————————
————————flushes   teats————————
————————straights   cunts————————
————————fullhouses   orgasms————————
————————royalflushes   blowjobs————————
————————fourofakinds   sixtynines————————
that sums up life in the 82nd. And I would ask myself what the
hell all that meant what the hell I was doing in there. That sums
up my state of mind at that time (in 1951, I believe I have already
specified) yes that crucial moment of my existence (of my adventure!) when I was still naive enough to look for the words which
one day would permit me to explain to my eventual listeners the
meaning of this whole farce. Meanwhile that's all you heard from
these idiots their blah blah poker and quaqua fucking and always
bugging me with that : EH FRENCHY! IS IT TRUE WHAT THEY
SAY ABOUT THE FRENCH? THEY ALL EAT PUSSY?
                        Bunch of frustrated shitheads
                        Bunch of disgusting assholes

Or else : COME ON FRENCHY DROP YOUR
           FUCKING BOOK AND PLAY A FEW
           HANDS   WITH   US   EH   YOU
           CHEAPSKATE   WHAT   YOU
           GONNA DO WITH ALL YOUR
           FUCKING DOUGH YOU MOTHER
           FUCKERCOCKSUCKERPUSSYEAT-
           ER   WHAT   YOU   GONNA   DO
           FRENCHY BABY WITH ALL YOUR
           DOUGH WHEN YOU GET OUT OF
           HERE EH FRENCHY BABY

[I am quoting them exactly as they spoke always the same sentence never]
[a variation no imagination always the same crap day after day the same]
[spoken marmelade chewing it out from the side of their ugly fat mouths]

YES / they always called me F R E N C H Y / even when I
became corporal / and that bugged the shit out of them /
especially the little fat motherfucker from Maryland / some of
them didn't even know my real name / most of them hardly
noticed I spoke with an unbelievable accent / too dumb! /
So it was   F R E N C H Y   all the time
                F R E N C H Y   here
                F R E N C H Y   there
                F R E N C H Y   everywhere

and some of them thought that because I spoke with an accent
(unbelievable!) I must have been from the North — a Northerner!
Therefore : for these guys (geographically speaking all of them
Southerners) who hadn't the faintest notion of foreign languages
(it's obvious) — not to mention their chauvinism — it was
Y A N K E E   all the time
Y A N K E E   here
Y A N K E E   there
Y A N K E E   everywhere
and they all made fun of my accent
                 Y A N K E E F R E N C H Y   HEY!
YOU WANNA FIGHT YOU WANNA FUCK YOU WANNA SUCK YOU
WANNA   FIGHT   YOU   WANNA   FUCK
and so on like a broken record!
And sometimes some of them would call me
N I G G E R L O V E R   yes!
N I G G E R L O V E R   here
N I G G E R L O V E R   there
N I G G E R L O V E R   everywhere

because one day some of them had seen me in town (Fayetteville
of all places if you can imagine what the place was like) with a fat
gorgeous negress with a pair of magnificent boobs I had picked up

in a jazz joint [Me I adore jazz especially progressive jazz] one
night when I had an overnight pass. But at least that night while
all these puceaux were jerking off like calves (under their khaki
blankets) me I was —— I —— was fucking like a bull —— no a
—— Ah! you want me to skip all these details! It's a bit too ——
tootoo Ok! But all that nonetheless is necessary. Essential. It's
preparation / exposition / for what's going to follow: the
recitation.

But   OK!   OK!

Still I've got to explain a little what he was doing in those days,
and also to some extent how we related to each other, who he was
[??] who I was even if I exaggerate our rather vague relationship
— here & there & everywhere!

But in case you guys get confused in the course of this twin
recitation with the me and the he
  & the I and the He
  & the me now and the he then
  & the he past and the me present   (he past in the hole
                              me present on the platform
let me make it quite clear once and for all lest WE forget it
(here & there & everywhere)
I am here [alone]
                      He is there [together we are]
as one are we not / multiple though single / I + HE = WE or WE -
I = HE pluralized in our singularity
                        me telling him
                        him telling me   etc.
thus again should you guys confuse me for him as I confuse
myself with him and in him and vice versa let me assure you you
may be confused or you may not even care   but I am not
                                            he is he
                                            I am I

such are we not separate but one unto the other apart but united for the purpose of our mutual recitation for in fact what is a HE or rather what is the return of the HE through that deceptive I (or vice versa) if not an I camouflaged into a potential and reflexive HE minus the I of course or as clearly explained in an article I read recently:

"Le re du retour inscrit comme l'ex, ouverture de toute extériorité : comme si le retour, loin d'y mettre fin, marquait l'exil, le commencement en son recommencement de l'exode. Revenir, ce serait en venir de nouveau à s'ex-centrer, à errer. Seule demeure l'affirmation nomade."
(Page 251)

I am quoting this in French because the French language is so much clearer and so much more rational than our rather ambiguous Anglo-Saxon tongue but even in French this statement explains a great deal about OUR predicament, and our EXILE into this difficult recitation. But of course, one could go much further and discuss for instance the ambivalence of the I as a double I or the split in half of the I between the teller and the told the I / I in the present telling his past or the I / HE pretending to tell the present of his past. But that would only bring us back to the original question that of the narrated-narrator (or in this case recited-recitation) His I and my He (or vice versa). Nevertheless one could ask why tell the tale of the I through the HE or pretend to tell the HE through the I indirectly, whereas in fact there is only one I (past and present, quite true) merely rattling his own ejaculations and no one is fooled by this indirect manipulation of the basic recitation? Certainly!

Thus why not simply tell the tale of the I directly and forget about the I and the HE and the HE and the I and the HE / HE told me, etc. etc. bullshit? Why this fake distanciation, etc., and that double-talk in the midst of an overwise half-way decent recitation?

I will answer you quite simply and frankly by saying bug out!
Allez-vous faire voir!
A guy must pass the time as best he can or if you prefer fill the pages as quickly as he can.

And will again answer you with a quotation from a recent article I read on my way to Chicago just a few days ago (in French again unfortunately and I apologize for that but it seems that the beast in me lately mostly ponders in French — eventually should I find the courage I will produce a correct translation for all that French garbage).

The question of course is one of POETRY. For as the guy (Deguy) writes in his essay on page 37 to give the exact reference:
Comment un langage peut-il être reconnu comme poétique?

— Par la suspension de la volonté de communication économique.
— Par la traversée du non-sens.
— Par le déconcert de la logique de ratiocination.
— Par le refus du magique (ou désir d'influence sur le réel par des formules).
— Par l'insouciance à l 'égard de l'efficacité.
— Par l'attention portée sur la forme du message, ou, plus généralement, au risque que prend la langue quand elle parle. (Most relevant here).
— Par l'emportement du langage en sa capacité de dérèglement, sa retrempe au chaos de la différence.
— Par l'ambition totale d'un projet ou calcul mesurant-démesuré, pareil à celui de Malherbe selon Francis Ponge, ou de Ponge selon Ponge, sans lequel un poème (or in this case an exaggerated second-hand tale) n'est qu'une bribe, mais par lequel une oeuvre peut apparaître à un lecteur comme l'obsession du dire d'un seul et même dit de la diversité.

Now you
guys may ask what the fuck are Malherbe and Francis Ponge
doing in the story of a person whose reading didn't go beyond the
basic dozen or so volumes mentioned earlier?

Damn good question!

But in fact how can there
be any truth in a second-hand recitation?

And furthermore isn't there the
same difference (the same distance) between Malherbe and
Ponge as there is between my I and my He?

But enough theory for now. Let him
speak for himself without any further interference from my I.

Let him get
on with his own past I above and beyond my own present I.

What does it matter?

Particularly now.

Now that he is leaving the 82nd AIRBORNE DIVISION
for brighter horizons!

Particularly now.

Now that he is going to discover America and learn
at last
the truth
about himself!

III

exploration

Yes but now (finally) after EIGHT MONTHS of the 82nd all this was FINISHED!

Yes FINISHED   I was going to discover AMERICA! Thirty days of vacation!

Yes FINISHED   those stinking miles of hiking on foot — 10 or 15 per day FULLBACK on the back — 50 or 60 pounds — and for nothing at all — to be in SHAPE the captain would explain — just in case — READY for combat — he would say as the fucking troops would set out DOUBLE TIME on their daily promenades

Yes FINISHED   the training exercises maneuvers the false wars where it's all fake and where you do BANG BANG with your mouth simply because they don't give you real bullets for your gun only blanks — NO KIDDING the army what a JOKE what a FARCE and the 82nd AIRBORNE DIVISION even worse — just plain exhibitionism — plain lousy SHOW OFF — spit-shine flags & crap

Yes FINISHED   especially the PUSH UPS —ah the fucking paratroopers and their PUSH UPS — I did at least 200 each day (UP & DOWN) ass stiff like a springboard — 15 / 20 / 25 / EH EH FRENCHY that motherfucking fat sergeant would scream at me GIVE ME TWENTY and flop there I was nose in the dirt ass up in the air stiff like a trampoline pushing UP & DOWN — Wow was I in shape in those days! Muscles like that! No kidding! At times half of the regiment was flat on its face ass upward HORIZONTAL pumping PUSH UPS by the twenties the thirties & the fifties — yes everybody got a piece of the action and no exceptions — UP & DOWN — got to the point where a guy would flop down by reflex — without even being told asked or

ordered — instinctively — just for the fun of it
like a mechanical lamb — counting the cadence
LOUD & CLEAR and the fucking sergeant
kicking us in the ass LEFT & RIGHT or shoving
the butt of his rifle like a cock in our buttocks!

parenthetical digression

(the guy who took the most shit was my little buddy Bobo Robert Moinous is)
(his real name but it was pronounced Moeilnus he was skinny long & nervous)
(like a nail but strong obstinate tough like a camel he goofed so much and)
(so often the poor Moinous that he would spend half of his time horizontal flat & stiff on the)
(ground doing push ups like a machine & the other half)
(cleaning the shithouse like a vacuum cleaner while whistling jazz tunes a)
(finger up his ass happy like a bird he was some kind of guy Bobo the type)
(of guy I dig and he too was taking off no not for the maneuvers up in the)
(snows of Upper New York State but like me for the Far East to get his ass)
(out of the 82nd to get into the real fight he too had volunteered like me)
(ah the stupidities a guy can do in his life he would say to me I had deep)
(affection for him he had a passion for music jazz especially and together)
(we would listen to jazz records in his little mailroom because he was the)
(outfit's mail clerk and this is why I suppose we were such good buddies I)
(had left my records in New York we understood each other Moinous wasn't a)
(Southerner like the rest of the guys he was from the North yes from Massa)
(chusetts in fact yes a very good Boston family it seems and all the other)
(guys of course wondered what the hell he was doing in the paratroopers in)
(this stinking 82nd outfit how the hell he had landed here but that much I)
(must say about him he had class and also a lot of education he read books)
(all the time but only stuff in English real difficult stuff yes guys like)
(Shakespeare Spenser Milton Byron Coleridge a lot of poetry English poetry)
(California Here I Come he would scream sometimes a lot of Romantic poetry)
(and in fact I suspect that on the side he too Bobo wrote poetry he was so)
(strange and also that's why he too Bobo he wanted to get the fuck out and)
(as quickly as possible out of this stinking 82nd he was fed up but fed up)
(up to here with the 82nd and all the hillbillies and yet after all it was)
(not the same thing with him as with me that much must be said Moinous was)
(an American from Boston therefore we didn't have the same reasons and the)
(same background for wanting to get the hell out of this place nonetheless)
(that doesn't mean that He & I were going to travel together no to get our)
(asses to California though a priori it could be arranged and it could yet)
(happen that we would meet here & there up or down in the North or even in)
(the South on our way West Go West Young Man he would shout sometimes even)
(we had not discussed our plans our itineraries in advance that much needs)
(to be stated but in any case if by chance we were to meet in a vague spot)
(of America a little corner of this vast land of opportunity it would be a)
(pure coincidence that's for sure an accident luck or an exceptional event)

In any event we were taking off MOINOUS & I and goodbye the
82nd AIRBORNE DIVISION!
By the way MOINOU-(spelled sometimes without an s)-S needless to say he's just an afterthought.   Unpremeditated.   Free.

He just happened
He just happened
on the spot! He popped up in the middle of the whole mess
the whole   (if you permit me)
paratroopical mess, as a kind of *parenthetical digression* for the
purpose of *italicized diversion*.

So why not take advantage of his little presence even
though we may [or may not] want to pursue MOINOU-(s)
to his end but
what is certain is that nothing was planned in advance. Rest
assured, we did not think of it before. He was truly an inspiration.
Even under the tree where the whole story was related to me
MOINOUS was never mentioned.

Nothing in fact was planned decided drawn contemplated predicted sketched spoken discussed manipulated in advance between us.

We simply fell
into the he of
MOINOUS on the
spur of the moment &
(within   parentheses)
beyond that I was on my
own totally free!
Freedom of speech° I suppose!

Or call it finger reflex — though you may have noticed that he is
spoken of as a friend. Present and presented as a friend (the other
in the same one might say or the me in us).

Therefore, if later, by chance, we happen to
meet, here and there, on our way WEST it
will be accidental a pure coincidence as
stated above

But then we'll know (won't we?) that it was LUCK or an exceptional event!

The sort of thing that happens only once or twice in a lifetime or in
the course of a recitation such as this one and which is often called
by some people, quite inadvertently :

The insertion (or diversion of the hand into the glove) [itchy
hand usually] or if you prefer the throwing down of the
gauntlet that determines and regulates our fate!

Or what other people sometimes call (mysteriously and
quasimystically) in moments of despair:

THE HAND OF GOD!

But that's only if you are of those who believe that sort of crap. As
for me personally I prefer to chew my words carefully before
spewing them out!

But such as it may be I am rather of the opinion that MOINOUS
(with the S or without the S) is a kind of gratuitous apparition :
unexpected but desirable and whose personality (even though
sketchily drawn) may eventually become of the greatest value in
the pursuit of this undertaking — a vehicle which may at some
point (though temporarily) be able to carry upon himself those
vague neurotic complexes which cannot (and shall not) obviously
be attributed only to the teller of this retold tale (standing here on
his platform all alone)!

Rapidly then before we go on would it not (may I ask!) disturb the
discourse had not MOINOUS appeared to take upon himself
some of those elements one may find incongruous and inconsis-

tent as they may be of the recitation perfectly discontinuous
though controlled which as it is evident so far needless for a
moment to emphasize is already much too serene as well as much
too expansive and on the verge insofar as we can judge of tumbling into the dangerous void of the self already over-exposed
MOINOUS therefore singularly plural permits a kind of undoubl-
ing or splitting of the person of the pronominal person now in
progress which otherwise would remain anonymous giving the
story somewhat of a semblance of realism and of identity provid-
ing movement and regularity not to mention its insertion into the
real and its (must we say it again?) knot of coherence by the
simple accumulation of facts (this will become part of the process
eventually) of signs which from left to right but also top to bottom
at random as can be witnessed I assume or in technical terms
across a vertical and horizontal line (the French would say par-
devant I suppose bien sûr and par-derrière but that's their business one need not agree) still the recitation having been launched
it is rather obvious that one cannot stop in the middle unless one
(and why not you may ask?)simply goes on dashing as I have tried
before repeatedly and quite successfully but not without despair!

_____ -   _____ -   _____
__   _____ -   __-   __- _____   _____ -
_____-m_____-e_____- -----------------
____   _____   _____-   _____r_____-   ------------
__   _____-d_____-
-                              e_____-
-             ___   -   ---------------

Meanwhile FINISHED the stupidities of the 82nd FINISHED for good all that crap FINISHED all that walking running pushing jerking off screaming crying whining spitshining FINISHED the butterflies in the guts the kicks in the ass FINISHED at last we were going ° ° ° ° MOINOUS & I ° ° ° I & MOINOUS ° ° ° ° finally at last the two of us enfin together oneone each in his direction hand in hand y en a marre to the discovery of AMERICA (Shit is this getting repetitious!) two plus two comme un seul homme 0-0 from left to right up & down 2 2 = us MENOU to the discovery of (American) space & (American) bigness & (American) despair & (American) speed & (American) beauty & (American) heat & (American) grandeur and -

                                                                    and

QUOIQUOIQUOI . . . ? [With a great deal of restlessness]

Qua Qua Qua Else! What else! Have you ever taken a look at your dictionary°? Your PETIT LAROUSSE for instance? Just to see, for instance, what they say in there about AMERICA? - [We are suggesting the PETIT LAROUSSE because it's certainly better than anything we've seen anywhere else and because it's the only one available to us at this time] - Unbelievable!
[Page 1145 in our French edition — our translation of course]

AMERICA. One of the five parts of the world. 42 millions km². 357 millions inhabitants (<u>Americans</u>). America is the continent (*Imagine that!*) that stretches the further between the two poles — it stretches over 18,000 kilometers from the arctic regions down to the edge (*Ah what language!*) of the antarctic polar circles. The surface of America is but half that of (*One could cry laughing!*) the Old World, but it is four times the size of Europe!

<u>Geography</u> : . . . . . . (We shall skip that) . . . . !

<u>Population</u> : . . . . .   (We shall skip that too . . . .) !

<u>Discovery</u>: . . . . (That's more interesting - We shall not skip) . . . . . ! America was discovered by Christopher Columbus (*As if we didn't know that!*) in 1492. But already as of the VIIth or the IXth centuries - (*Eh and what about the VIIIth century?*) - the Norvegians had reached Greenland and probably the Eastern coast of North America (*If that's not incredible!*); however, their discovery was not exploited. (*But of course*) It was quite another matter (*Ahahahahah!*) with that of Columbus, after whom (*Obviously*) the most important explorators (*Oh la la, what a beautiful word!*) of North and Central America were: Cabot, Cartier, Jolliet, Cavelier de La Salle, Balboa, Champlain, Marquette and La Verendrye; in South America: Hojeda, Orellana, Humboldt, Solis, Amerigo Vespucci, Alvarez Cabral, Magellan, Crevaux (*Wow! y en a vraiment de quoi crever de rire!*)!

<u>History</u>: . . . . . (See articles devoted to various countries) . . . . !

Shit! Isn't this beautiful? What do you think? Isn't it incredible?
Fantastic!

Me what I like the most is the word EXPLORATOR!

EX-PLO-RA-TORS : Yes now MOINOUS and I we were also
                  going to be some kind of

EX-PLO-RA-TORS : But of course we were only going to explore
                  a small portion of America — only a small
                  portion of North America — [See articles
                  devoted to the United States for this ques-
                  tion] — In any case A MOI L'AMERIQUE
                  (he shouted) A NOUS L'AMERIQUE

EX-PLO-RA-TORS : Bobo and I   Enfin

la grande t-r-a-v-e-r-s-é-e!   la grande a-v-e-n-t-u-r-e!
                [COAST TO COAST]

AMERICA : I was going to cross it from one end to the other
               from right to left (he shouted)
               from New York to San Francisco
               going right through the middle
               I was going to enter into it — plunge into it
               the way you plunge into a big fat woman - legs

XiXiXiXiXiXi . . . ? [With a great deal of surprise from a fat
guy]

And Bobo?   Bobo . . . ? What he was going to do Bobo? I
don't know what he was going to do Bobo (he didn't tell me) and
personally I couldn't care less. No for the time being I did'nt give a

damn about anything I was too fed up with the 82nd. And remember they had not discussed any of their travel plans. That's what those no-good-pissors of the 82nd didn't understand. They thought they had it made in the 82nd. No sense of life no sense of adventure of discovery. Not at all. Nothing. Not curious a bit about America. Not like me. And most of all scared shitless of getting their asses shot full of holes (collectively and commemoratively and individually speaking) whereas Bobo and I we were the types who who who . . *zipzipzipzipzip* . . . ?
[Here goes another guy interrupting me
right]
[in the middle of a PARAgraph without
consi-]
[deration for the continuity of this fiction]

IV

frogliness

Hey Frenchy how the hell did you land in the 82nd AIRBORNE
DIVISION? Don't tell us you volunteered! Did they drag you in?
Did they force you? Don't tell us you volunteered!

But of course if
I landed in this chicken-shit outfit it was not my fault : I can't say
that it was my fault! Imagine that! Me - in the PARATROOPERS!
A guy could cry laughing. A guy must really feel like breaking his
legs or else be obsessed by the wide open space. For let us not kid
ourselves even though a guy must volunteer to be a member of
that most distinguished gutsy glorious tough spitshined outfit
known as

THE   P A R A
T
R
O
O
P
E
R
S

Me - I had volunteered in spite of myself!

I had volunteered as a fluke!

I had volunteered for butterflies in the stomach just
because I was fed up with FROGLIFE!

. . . *hahaha hahaha* . . . You guys can laugh! It was an accident.
A goof!

You see when they called me in the army (everybody in those days had to go, well all the jerks, and in those days, wow, was I a jerk, and because I had already made an application, yes what you guys call in your language, first papers, of course I'm a foreigner, for citizenship, it's my uncle who was a journalist who suggested I do that, well, it didn't take long, they drafted me immediately. I was then, let us say . . . *hohoho* . . . go ahead laugh you bunch of crums! I was then . . . hahaha . . . Ah! you guys didn't know I had an uncle in America (must have forgotten to mention him), yes well no he's dead now, no need therefore to talk about him, suffices to say that he was not (that's for sure) loaded with dough as most American uncles are, in most stories.

But in any event doesn't matter now, suffices to say for the time being that ONCE UPON A TIME I had an uncle, and so those bastards they didn't lose a moment to get their lousy paws on me.

Yes hardly or just two years in AMERICA, and I receive (AIR MAIL & SPECIAL DELIVERY) that charming letter,
that lovely sweet letter from the   STATE DEPARTMENT

Incredible the tone of that letter!
The style of that letter from the STATE DEPARTMENT!   It was as though all of a sudden (out of nowhere) they were offering you vacations at one of the swankiest resorts in Florida.
Holidays at the seashore!
Holidays at the mountain!
MARvelous voyages all over the world! FanTAstic opportunities! EXTRAordinary deals! MAGNIficent possibilities for the future! And it even mentioned (in a special paragraph *in italics*) numerous types of sporting and physical activities such as tennis, golf, swimming and diving, boating and fishing, ping pong, badmington and shuffle-board, hiking, camping, and free cinema twice a week!

And all sorts of other recreational facilities! And, of course, on top of it, Free Room & Board! And free clothing (summer / winter uniforms)! Free laundry. The possibility for quick advancement. Care and training. Joie de vivre. Friendship and companionship. Tourism. Mental physical medical attention as well as dental care and sexual education! In other words, the most PERFECT life! The most careless utopic and relaxed type of existence, in the best of all possible conditions! How could a guy resist? Might as well pack immediately! How could I hesitate? And then at the end of it as expected (in *SCRIPT*) a beautifully worded statement full of patriotic overtones to round off this stunning presentation :

This unforgettable occasion which you will have to serve your country, this profound sense of honor and pride you will feel as you stand erect before your flag to protect your nation and its great people will be for you an experience and a privilege of the highest and deepest degree as well as a chance to do your duty towards your fellow-citizens who have placed in the hands of its ARMY – but of its NAVY and AIRFORCE as well! – its national safety and liberty, its property and its sacred existence under GOD as a free and self-determined people whose belief in the goodness of its land as well as GOD's grace makes of all men and women free and equal citizens of a civilized and proud land of opportunities in the best and the most secured form of human and divine condition in the spirit of its founding fathers beyond and above all selfishness!
SIGNED:
THE PRESIDENT OF THE UNITED STATES OF AMERICA
Commander in Chief of all the Armed Forces (Airforce Navy Army Frogmen and Paratroopers Green Berets and Minute Men Black Shirts and Demolition Squads National Guards)!

Well! When you read that you felt like going immediately, on the spot, and with tears in your eyes and throbbings in your heart!

Me what bugged me the most was that they were going to cut my hair yes cut it like a lawn a flat-top or like some Indian or like a bush a brush a toothbrush (that's regulation) and in those days ME I had magnificent hair long and curly (extremely long in the neck) and fluffy always combed straight back without a part as was very much in style in those days and also I wore a little elegant mustache very sporty!

Those bastards!

And also there was MARILYN. . . . She was very sad when I showed her the letter from the *S.D.* that had just arrived (AIR MAIL & SPECIAL DELIVERY). My Hair & Marilyn!

I suppose I'll have to go back and talk about that about the story of Marilyn the beautiful story of what happened with Marilyn! I'll have to   (or else I can tell it to you in parentheses) but in any event it was LOVE (my first love) . . . . and what a deal yes what a fantastic deal I had with her husband BENNY in his factory his lampshade factory in Brooklyn . . . Maybe it was disgusting on my part! Immoral! . . . Yes really sneaky and indecent but we loved each other I tell you we loved each other so much at the time . . . and I was young! So young in those days . . . yes so young and so lonely too . . . but now now . . . finally I was taking off . . . cutting out . . . after 8 stinking months of the 82nd AIRBORNE DIVISION . . . full speed and on the double I was cutting out!
Ah what a joke it had been! What an enormous joke when you think of it! And all for nothing — for the birds and the butterflies! SO LONG! Goodriddance!

CALIFORNIA   HERE   I   COME !

We had hardly taken that one step forward — that symbolic step!
— (it was in New York that I had been indoctrinated) when that
fat ugly sergeant with red blotchy cheeks who was explaining
THAT now we're in the AAArmy and THAT THAT it's all
finished the cozy civilian life and youse guys from NOooWooON
BUNCH OF CREEPS it's gonna jump and and THAthatHAT
from now on it's double time and iiit'ss going toTOto jump and
no more fucking off asked : ANY QUESTIONS MEN?
Me, shyly, I raised my hand (I was in the second rank, Section B)
and asked (with my incredible accent) what I was supposed to do
to get into the FROGMEN?
Yes the FROGMEN because of the blue water I suppose (love the
color blue) Yes in the FROGMEN and suddenly the whole place
burst into laughter, a huge monstruous collective fart of laughter
(haha), they started laughing like a bunch of shitheads and I felt
like disappearing into the floor, like disintegrating on the spot
into smoke, into dust, yes ME (and why not?) I wanted to join that
glorious and audacious aquatic outfit known all over the world
Me I wanted to join the FROGMEN, what's so funny about that? I
ask you, yes tell me what's so hilarious about that? After all it was
not that dumb nor that farfetched since when I was younger
(between the age of 15 and 19) I'd had lots of experience lots of
practice in that field, I had been a fine, a tremendous swimmer,
one of the few, in fact, to break (what was believed at the time
unbreakable) the one minute barrier for the hundred yard
backstroke (honest you guys I'm not exaggerating), backstroke
specialist that's, in fact, what I was, and I even belonged to a great
team, one of the finest in those days, L'AMICALE DE NATA-
TION, when I was younger, (before I came over) and I even raced
all over Europe, and I even made it all on my own (singlehan-
dedly) to the CHAMPIONNAT DE FRANCE, and won all sorts of
medals ribbons cups and trophies, some of them in gold (in fact, I

still have some of them stashed away to prove it), and could even have made it with a bit more luck and much more training and perseverance (that's what Monsieur Rigolepas, my coach at the AMICALE, used to say) to the Olympic Team (the 1948 Team) as a backstroke specialist, but unfortunately I didn't have the time to train, I had to work (disgusting filthy degrading jobs) to survive, and keep afloat!

WHAT A FROGLIFE

Therefore you guys understand why it was impossible for me to spend my time training, back and forth, in a PISCINE, practicing flip-turns and starts in a swimming pool, I had to work in factories in the banlieue, nightshift and dayshift, and even sometimes overtime, all kinds of shitty jobs, as a lousy unskilled laborer in factories, hands bleeding all the time, hardly earning enough to survive, after the LIBERATION, and even when I came to this great land of opportunities, in the beginning, I worked my ass off, in Detroit at CHRYSLER in fact, and then in New York in a lampshade factory, just to survive, therefore it's understandable, I suppose, why, of all people, a great kid like me, a talented swimmer like me, yes a truly gifted swimmer like me who possibly could have set new world records with all his aquatic potentialities and his genuine devotion to water didn't have the time to train, in a PISS IN, three four hours a day, back and forth, four five miles a day in order to shape up, so to speak, for the OLYM-PIADS, no, I was too tired, too exhausted, too beat most of the time, struggling to survive as best I could working all day, and sometimes all night, and even overtime, to keep up and make ends meet, to stay above the water, above the surface, in other words!

I tell you I tried my best!
But that's no reason to think
(as those dumbbells must have been thinking while laughing —
those fatsoes) that I was not a tremendous swimmer
                              a marvelous swimmer!
with a clean smooth classical style (backstroke, I must specify, but
also in case of emergency and when called upon the butterfly
sometimes and even once in a while when the team was short-
handed the Australian crawl) and beautiful powerful strokes
which my coach, Monsieur Rigolepas, would regularly show to
all the other guys on the team — my fellowswimmers — as being
perhaps near perfect, as being almost a picture of perfection :
                     Look at that STYLE he would say
as I glided along the blue water smoothly and powerfully (back
and forth) in full sprint like a picture of aquatic perfection!

But of course there in the midst of all those flatfooted jerks, all
these draftees, all these chubby ding-bats, it was impossible to
make them see, to make them understand that, no, they
couldn't visualize why I wanted to be a FROGMEN!
          And so they stood there, these ugly fat fuckers, morsels
of earthly meat, slapping themselves gleefully on the belly,
elbowing one another as if they knew something I didn't
know, bent in half at the hips at the waist at the knees to better
laugh thinking, I suppose, that I was some kind of freaky guy,
some kind of funnyguy who doesn't know what the hell he's
talking about, a phony lousy dirty foreigner who gets lost, who
gets all wrapped up in words and doesn't even comprehend
the meaning, the basic meaning of the words he pronounces
(rightly or wrongly), a joker, a poor imbecile who hasn't the
faintest notion of what speech is all about!   AH, if

only they knew, those bipeds, how qualified I was, but no they hadn't the least comprehension, they couldn't care less about my natural, my genuine and sensational aquatic abilities, it didn't occur to them, in the narrow space of their skulls, that, at this very moment, I had perhaps a truer or

$$d_{e_{e_{P_{e_r}}}}$$ reason, a real qualifi-

cation (one might say) for asking such a relevant and appropriate question (in spite of my accent) and that indeed I could better serve my country (even though it was, admittedly, an adopted country) by performing underwater feats rather than walk, like a dumb and clumsy baboon, in the mud of their MOTHER EARTH, on my rather skinny legs and my ugly feet!

No, these cretins, it didn't occur to them! And so they kept on laughing, laughing, their collective fart of laughter, their soft diarrhea of laughter, laughing their guts out, choking congestively as if they were a single enormous bubble of chuckles, holding on with trembling hands to their crotches as if ready to piss in their smelly underwears in unison and all the while wiping with their sleeves tears of hilarity over the fangs of their greasy cheeks and me shivering angrily with shame with humiliation I didn't know what to do any more how to stand where to crawl and hide there in the middle of that giggling pack of panks or how to repair the blunder if blunder there had been but finally when it all calmed down (the monstrous ejaculation of laughter that is) and I was able once more to look up as I stood there my face red like an October apple with a worm devouring it inside that big slob of a depraved chunk of a subhuman piece of shit that glob of a sergeant flushed like a rotten apple (but in his case the red was natural) explained THATHAT . . . MAN . . . YOU'RE IN THE

WRONG ARMY MAN . . . THE FROGMEN . . . IT'S THE
NAVY . . . (AH AH AH) THE NAVY!
So what!
Good!
How was I supposed —— how was I to know that?
Thathathat (ahahah!) the FROGMEN it's the Navy!
Because of the water, I suppose, and that now me I was in the
infantry yes in the INFANTRY, on EARTH, among those who
trample the EARTH (like a bunch of dry geese) and not among
those who smoothly and powerfully slide, glide and frolic
through the blue water in search of HIGHER and DEEPER hori-
zons! Big deal!

In any case, his explanation that mediocre sergeant it was not
brilliant I assure you but I understood   yes I understood what he meant and I didn't insist. I just fell back, so to
speak, into my place in ranks and stood there, in silence, in total
stupor, depressed and deflated, crushed like a stepped-on-
piece-of-shit, my head l$_{o_{wer}}$ed, asking myself:

        qu'est-ce qu'il y a de si marrant (in French of course as I
tumbled back into the safe womb of my native tongue)? but which
meant more or less what the fuck's so funny, what the fuck's so
hilarious about asking such a simple question?   Yes why?
                                                    Why?
Why this brothel of laughter?   Okay!

    T H E   F R O G M E N   I T ' S   T H E   N A V Y !

So what!
How was I supposed to know that? WAS i here (as a matter of

fact) HAD i been indoctrinated into the army to make that kind of
distinction between
WATER ————————— & —————— EARTH

Dammit can a guy be jerky con dumb naive unprepared virgin
ill-at-ease slow when he just arrived in America! Wow can a guy
really take it in the mouth when he doesn't know what the fuck's
going on! But what am I? I ask you?
A prophet?
A superbrain? How was I supposed to know it's the Navy?
                What am I?   The Zorro of knowledge!
                    The   Tarzan   of   the   mind!
                What did they take me for?   Napoleon!   Jesus!
I had to ask!

But what I didn't know (unbelievable the English language) and
that's quite serious is that in America yes in the land of opportunities they have (well you guys have) a most beautiful a most
suggestive a most juicy colorful and enigmatic word an incredibly
appropriate word for us FRENCHMEN you guys you mothers
call us (don't ask me why?) FROGS yes FROGS — *CroakCroak-
CroakCroak*
— and ME
in those days
(already two years or so in America)
and I didn't know that!   I didn't know the double meaning of
that term.
DOESN'T MAKE SENSE!
Can you imagine that : FROGS ------------------------------------*GRENOUILLES*
at that time and in that place ME I didn't know that FROGS meant *FRENCHIES*
simple question of timing I suppose----------------------------------*CRAPAUDS*
simple question of TIME & SPACE no doubt--------------------------*TETARDS*
simple question of familiarization with the language surely-------*BATRACIENS*

But
me
in
any
event
ME
there
in
   front
of that fat
        cow
of a sergeant
who kept on laughing
like
LA VACHE QUI RIT

Me
with
my incredible
accent
they immediately
picked me   out
as a
FROG

But
let
them
laugh
those shitpots
those subhuman detritus
those dog flees
let
them choke laughing
those animal excrements

Let them laugh with their marmelade
                    their confiture
                    their oral mush
                    their verbal gravy
                    dripping out of their fat ugly pissoirs of a
                    mouth
those hillbillies
let
them be proud of their natural pronounciation
        proud of their American accent
        proud of their native tongue
let
them choke in their American laughter
RIRA BIEN QUI RIRA LE DERNIER

And so
finally
when it call calmed down that OBESE sergeant asked again if
there were Any ——- FURTHER ——- QUESTIONS ——- ?

A long moment of silence [ooooooo] long moment of silence[ ]
and he repeated — de ta ching each syl la ble —A
                                                  NY
                                          FUR
                                              THER
                                          QUES
                                               TIONS
                                                  MEN?

and suddenly there next to me a black guy (tall and skinny black
kid dark like a piece of charcoal) begins to gesticulate like a
disrupted puppet I look at him as he raises both his hands above
his head (he's really funny that guy with his imitation leopard cap
with a pompon on top) he wants to know that kid what he's got to
do to volunteer for the damn PARATROOPERS!

GEEEROONIMOOO!   shouts the meaty sergeant
                        and then says :   THIS WAY MAN ----
pointing to the door on the LEFT --------------------------------

And so when all the other guys took off --------DOUBLE TIME
through the door on the RIGHT------------------------------------
(on their way to their miserable military fate as infantrymen)
[perhaps I should mention at this point that they were all still in
civilian clothes even though this doesn't add much to the local
color] ——————— ME (*en douce* as the French say in such
situations) I followed my tall skinny black leopard buddy in the
opposite   direction   —————————-   OUT
————————————————————- tfel eht no rood eht hguorht

And that's how we landed in the PARATROOPERS
with butterflies in the stomach
and shit all over the ass!

And there we went (DOUBLE TIME) my new buddy and I full of
anticipation I can assure you but glad to have escaped FROG-
LIFE!

And there we went : Double time for the
                    MUSIC
                    of the
                    82nd
                    AIRBORNE division
                    Double time for TRAINING on the edge of
                        mental breakdown
                    Double time for the madness of PARALIFE
                        for the despair of PARASHIT
                    Double time for the thousands and
                        thousands of PUSH UPS!
                        horizontal in the dirt ass up
                        in the air and stiff like tram-
                        polines!
                    Double time for the parachute jumps (the
                        good ones & and the bad ones
                        & the fucked up ones)
                        and the perfect PLFs
                        (parachutelandingfalls) where
                        you break both arms and both
                        legs when you miss the DZ
                        (dropzone) and you DROP-
                        DEAD!
                    Double time therefore for the BUTTERFLIES
                        in the stomach and SHIT all
                        over the ASS!
and finally   Double time for the monstruous masturba-
                        tion sessions all night long
                        under the khaki blankets of the
                        82nd AIRBORNE DIVISION
                        and in the nights of NORTH
                        CAROLINA!

OUI

en avant pour la musique de la 82ème AIRBORNE DIVI-
SION   &

en avant pour l'entraînement à en crever — à en perdre la raison
en avant (à toute vitesse à plein tube)
              pour le désespoir de la PARAVIE
              pour le désespoir de la VIEPARA
              pour la PARAMERDE   &
              pour laPARAconnerie   &
en avant pour les pompes (à n'en plus finir)
              à   plat   ventre   et   horizontal
              dans   la   poussière   et   le   cul
              en   l'air   les   fesses   serrées
              raides   dures   stiff   comme   un
              tremplin (up & down)   &
en avant pour les sauteries en parachute (les ronds et les pas
              ronds) et les atterrissages sur la tête avec les papil-
              lons dans le ventre et la merde au cul   &
en avant pour les kilomètres et les kilomètres à pieds (tous les
              jours parfois même la nuit) —
              les pieds en sang les jambes en
              cerceaux les bras qui vous tom-
              bent des épaules et toujours
              avec le sourire militaire et le vis-
              age réglementaire de ceux qui
              font de leur mieux leur devoir et
              sont fiers par-dessus le marché
              de là faire la tête ici et mainten-
              ant le tête grosse comme cette
              boule vide que porte Hercule
              sur sons dos

&

en avant surtout pour les branlades monstres sous les couver-
tures (kaki) dégueulasses jaunies spermifiées
pourries POUAH!   &
en avant finalement pour les discussions à n'en plus finir (nuit et
jour matin et soir) sur le POKER & le
BAISAGE

OUI ....

OOPS! Please excuse me if he got carried away but it sounds   so much better
in his native tongue   so much better
in the original (I am of course translating as I go along)   so much better
when you don't feel restricted by linguistic barriers   so much better
when you can let yourself go into verbal delirium   (as he did so much better
than I can approximate here) and allow yourself a bit of mental   much better
fantasy   so much better
to say it another way even if it means the same thing   so much better

to crap out your crap on a different stool and a different pitch   so much better to retranslate
yourself after having translated yourself before

V

Cyrano of the regiment

YESYES BUTBUT . . . ?   [Deep voice with a tone of slight discouragement]
Yes but what!   [Ah you guys are still here I thought you'd left]

        Ah you guys are fed up with these disgusting details
              fed up up with these exaggerations
                   up with these explanations
                      with these digressions
                         these preambles

Ok — agreed!   The 82nd it can go fly a kite!   But
Nonetheless that's how he landed in that outfit and like it or not
(LADIES & GENTLEMEN) he has 27 jumps behind him!
            27 parachute jumps!   That's something!   Isn't it?
A bit scared at first but it's normal in the beginning.
                            You get used to it!
You hang on in spite of the pain @@@@@@@@@@@@@@@@@@@
              the fear §§§§§§§§§§§§§§§§§§§
          and the butterflies @@@@@@@@@@@@@@@@@@@@ But
then there is the training. Ah what tremendous training! Just in
case I suppose! Ah what preparation! Just in case there is a war.
But now finished! It was all over. He had it — above and beyond
the head he had it — up to here — (and MOINOUS too of course)!
Yet it was not that bad (after all) if one considers
if one reflects a bit on all the advantages of this kind of   E
                                                 X
                                             I

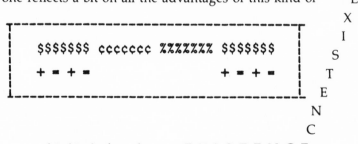

                                             S
                                           T
                                           E
                                         N
                                         C

      this kind of careless   E X I S T E N C E

where others think for you / where others decide for you / where others / in fact / protect you (and let us be fair and not forget the free board & room & the free uniforms)!   And so we took advantage of all that of all those advantages in other words — MOINOUS and I — but especially ME (*He hardly dared admit it*) I took advantage of my education: I wrote love letters for all the guys in my barrack [Company C / Third Platoon] voila!

I wrote love letters for all the jerks in my barrack who couldn't do it alone Love letters to all the guys' little broads in all the corners of America For all the ignorants in my barrack to all the little hicktowns of Texas Kentucky Alabama Tennessee Georgia Louisiana Mississippi and even as far north as Ohio which in those days I pronounced OYO because of the difficulty I had with the H in the middle question of background and experience I suppose In fact there was one guy whose girlfriend lived in Alaska therefore I even wrote some love letters as far away as Alaska I'm not kidding Took two weeks for the replies! nnnnnnnnnnnnnnnnnnnnnnnnnnnnnnnnnnnnnnnnnnnnnnnnnnnnn

nnnnnnnnnnnnnnnnnnnnnnnnnnnnnnnnnnnnnnnnnnnnnnnnnnnnn Five bucks a letter that was my price (TAKE IT OR LEAVE IT) and no one really bitched about it. Therefore WOW would I bang that loving stuff away (I had a beat-up old Underwood portable in those days)! Fabulous dreams. Unbreakable vows of all types. Uncontrolled promises. Endless resolutions. Languishing memories based (as it should be) on minimal details furnished by the crums in my barrack prior to the creative outburst. Weeping descriptions of Nature in local colors. Wild erotic situations of surrealistic denseness whose filaria of suggestiveness was certainly enough to corrupt even the most perverse kind of minds. Positions and contorsions that would require for correct execution and proper results the acrobatic talents of the entire population of a zoo or tiergarten. And in the margins of the writing paper which of course the guys would furnish with envelopes and stamps (AIR MAIL) dirty little drawings and doodles drawn with a set of color pencils. Ah what ORGIES! I invented on the spot! What ROMANTICISM! I created in those moments of epistolary passion sitting on the floor like an Indian chief typing away madly on my footlocker! I wrote approximately twelve letters per week (4 to 6 pages each), with a few extra ones for the holidays. I would read them aloud to all the jerks in the barrack before sending them off in bundles. And the answers (unbelievable if you can imagine!) we would get. I was THE CYRANO OF THAT REGIMENT. All them sweet little cunts in all them corners of America - including remote parts of Alaska - were madly in love with me without suspecting of course that the guy who was writing to them was not their official boyfriend.

I was the love-hack, the love-dispatcher of the 82nd AIRBORNE DIVISION. And as soon as the replies would arrive, in a continuous stream, the guys would make me read them, immediately on the spot, even before they themselves were allowed to open the letters, but, of course, some of them would cheat behind my back, they couldn't wait those dumb bastards to read how much their little broads adored them and how they reacted to my poetic delivery, but those who were caught opening a letter before me, the cheaters (two or three guys were spying for him), they had to

pay off a fine, the next letter would cost them one
dollar more and they were not permitted to hear the
next public reading I gave, once a week, of all the
replies that had arrived in the course of the week, that
would, indeed, teach them in no time that I meant
business, teach them a moral lesson!

Ah, did I have fun writing those letters, full speed, and
without the least apprehension, with two fingers, on
that beat-up old portable typewriter of mine, without
thinking much about what I wrote, in those days form
and content I must confess didn't mean much to me,
nor the questions of

style and meaning
I simply accumulated words any old way
I simply piled up the words as fast as

I could
up & down
&
sideways

metaphors
upon
contradictions   metaphors
on
top of contradictions
I exaggerated full blast
I played with words
with double meaning   &
triple meaning   &

                    without any respect (I must confess) for grammar
                         syntax   style   spelling
                              logic   disposition   order
                    punctuation   meaning
                         it was just a matter of filling up space
                                             PAGES
                                               &
                                             PAGES
(approximately a buck a page I kept
                                        telling myself
                         as I flipped them over)   and so
                         when I ran out of stuff to say
                         I would simply copy   borrow steal
                                   plagiarize   all
                                               over
                    I would   the damn place
                         simply open a book
                         any book
                         (usually romantic novels)
                         (or classical tragedies!)
and copy whole passages   *verbatim et litteratim*
throwing in a few foreign expressions   here and there
(Latin Spanish Italian German or just French)
                         those guys didn't know the difference
that's for sure   and the more I gave them the more they loved
it
Ah what creativity   what spirit of creativity I was
in   in those days
                    what inspirations
                         banging every
night on my old beat-up Underwood   (with two fin-
                                        gers)

sometimes telling one broad what I was supposed to say to
another one
sometimes even getting the letters all confused
                    the names all mixed up
sometimes sending a letter that was supposed to go to a girl in a
little
                                hicktown in Nebraska
                                to a girl in a little
                                hicktown in Arkansas
but who cared
    who gave a shit
        it kept going (full blast) and they loved me for it   both
                                the jerks in my outfit
        and all the little cunts in all the hicktowns of AMERICA

HERE IN FACT LET ME GIVE YOU AN EXAMPLE (AMONG
MANY) OF THE TYPE OF LOVE LETTERS I WROTE IN THOSE
DAYS - OF COURSE I'M ONLY QUOTING THE GOOD SEXY
PASSAGES - AND I'M SOMEWHAT CORRECTING EDITING
EXPURGATING CENSURING (IF I MAY) THE KIND OF EN-
GLISH I USED IN THOSE DAYS - PURIFYING (IN A SENSE)
THE KIND OF LANGUAGE I WROTE IN THOSE DAYS - IM-
PROVING SOMEWHAT THE TONE STYLE GRAMMAR SYN-
TAX - THE PRESENTATION ALSO - AND OF COURSE - THIS
GOES WITHOUT SAYING - CORRECTING THE ABOMINA-
BLE PRONUNCIATION I HAD THEN (AND STILL QUITE
IMPERFECT) WITHOUT HOWEVER ATTEMPTING TO DE-
FORM THE ORIGINAL

Fort Bragg, Fayetteville, N.C.
(Let us say), January 15, 1951

My Darling, My Treasure, My Lovely Adorable Juicy Peach, My Dear
M*******

You cannot imagine how much I thought of you, last night, under my
lonely khaki blankets, alone, in my narrow military bed, surrounded by
the heavy oppressive solitude of life in army. I felt, in me, through my
flesh torn by the pain of your absence, a suffering of indefinable nature.
The inner emptiness of my soul rang with shrieks and groans, it was as
though needles and knives of fire were piercing my body.

Unable to endure this atrocious suffering, I took my private member in
my hands, and feeling it palpitating savagely like a lost animal, no a giant
fruit rather, an enormous banana which was pulsating there outside my
own body, I began to shake it, to handle it, to squeeze it with all the furor
of my desire, and suddenly I felt flowing, full blast, Woosh, a delicious
juice that I wanted to transmit immediately to your essential organs. Ah
my dearest reservoir, how much I wanted to feel, at that moment, the
wild sugars of my fruit flow in you like a torrent. How I wanted to hear
them burst inside of you like a gun, like a cannon (a 75 millimeters), no,
like a volcano, in the deepest parts of you, in your most secret, tender,
rare and unexplored regions.

Ah! if only you knew, my golden treasure, how much I missed you (how
much we missed each other) last night, when, alone, naked and vibrant
under my military blankets, at the most solitary moment of night in
North Carolina my eyes closed, I saw the image of your sweet and soft
body sneak next to mine inside my cot. Ah! dear feathery chicken,
adorable pitless peach of tender flesh, smooth and rosy body of such lovely
round contours, velvety like a mushroom without tail, little sugared
snail, landscape of my inner dreams, if only I could make you feel, yes,
how much I wanted (last night but also every night) to penetrate you,
with what endless passion, what a huge desire I wanted to rush towards

you beyond the mountains, beyond the valleys, beyond the rivers and the canals from under my khaki blankets of loneliness, then you would have known the dimensions of my love, depth of my pool of pleasure, despair of my trembling tools, sources of my frantic appetite and frustration. I see in my dreams your voluptuous greedy hips and your adventurous thighs, hardly ripe, avidly opened to receive, there in that moist furry meadow of yours, the harvest of my nocturnal cultivation.

Ah! do I worry, do I WORRY to know that you are alone so far away in your little Missouri Hicktown. But . . . are you ALONE? Here comes doubt in my mind. I fear the thought that, perhaps, at this very moment, some son of a bitch of another guy (OH! do I tremble) is holding you in his tottering skinny arms, while my muscular arms, my PARATROOPER arms, my arms, splendidly fortified by thousands and thousands of push ups cannot hold cannot squeeze you tight to make you feel (despite the distance) with what madly power, what energy, what vitality, what frenzy I would like to grab those lovely contours of yours and squeeze them out of their last drop of love!

Here life is sad without you, and I find myself absentmindedly carving at random your initials on all the tree trunks in the forest of my solitude! But otherwise everything is fine, except for the disgusting grub. If you have by any chance a bit of money saved could you (DARLING) be nice to me as you've always been and send me a billet doux? I adore you passionately madly and desperately with my entire soul and body. Give your saintly Mom a BIG kiss for me (but not your Dad) and think of me THINK OF ME dear love as much as you can.

Your BIG and SAD Carrot, J***K*****

LET ME GIVE YOU NOW (BRIEFLY!) AN EXAMPLE OF THE
RESPONSES MY LOVE LETTERS WOULD OCCASION IT IS
(I THINK) A RATHER GOOD TYPICAL EXAMPLE BUT OF
COURSE (I NEED NOT EMPHASIZE) THE BROADS DIDN'T
HAVE MUCH IMAGINATION NOR A GREAT DEAL OF TA-
LENT FOR THOSE SORTS OF THINGS NONETHELESS (LET
US BE FAIR) THEY TRIED THEIR BEST AND WOULD PUT
ALL THEIR HEARTS INTO IT AND MAKE UNUSUALLY
VALIANT EFFORTS TO COME UP WITH DECENT REPLIES
NO DOUBT I INSPIRED THEM IN A WAY BECAUSE FROM
TIME TO TIME WE WOULD GET SOME TOUCHING AND
DELIRIOUSLY HILARIOUS LETTERS HARD TO BELIEVE
SOME OF THEM WILD ENOUGH TO DRIVE YOU UP THE
WALL BUT WHAT STYLE WOW WHAT GRAMMAR WHAT
ATROCIOUS ORTHOGRAPHY (QUITE INCREDIBLE) MOST
OF THAT STUFF PURE HILLBILLY JARGON (OBVIOUSLY
THOSE DUMB LITTLE FARM GIRLS WERE ILLITERATE
[*LIKE THEIR BOYFRIENDS*] AND COULD HARDLY READ OR
WRITE OR JUST ENOUGH TO SCRIBBLE THEIR ANSWERS)
THEREFORE ONCE AND AGAIN WE ARE FORCED TO
CORRECT SOMEWHAT HERE AND THERE IN ORDER TO
IMPROVE THEIR REPLIES (OR AT LEAST THE ONE EXAM-
PLE WE ARE PRESENTING HERE) AND IN ORDER TO REN-
DER THEM MORE READABLE MORE COMPREHENSIBLE
MORE ACCEPTABLE BUT (PLEASE) DO NOT IMAGINE FOR
A MOMENT THAT WE ARE INVENTING THIS REPLY THIS
REMARKABLE REPLY ABSOLUTELY NOT THIS IS A REAL
PEARL AN ORIGINAL A GENUINE FULLY GUARANTEED
AND OFFICIALLY AUTHENTICATED VERSION AS WRIT-
TEN BY ONE OF THE GIRLS (*WHOSE NAME OF COURSE
SHALL REMAIN ANONYMOUS*) AS DELIVERED TO US
ONE DAY ENCLOSED IN A PINK PERFUMED ENVELOPE
VIA AIR MAIL SPECIAL DELIVERY

This example is chosen at random from among a stock of more
than four or five hundred.

My BIG Dear Turnip, My SAD Muscular Paratrooper, My Lonely Prune, Dear J****,

I reread your last letter at least two hundred times since it came and it is with tears in my eyes, dearly adored carrot, that I'm writing you today, for me too I feel inside of me, in my most secret regions, as you say so well my creamy one, in my most private parts, that immense void, which you ALONE can fill so well! Yesterday, me too, nude and trembling under my soft warm pink blankets, I felt those huge needles and knives of your absence (Oh delicious heavy artillery of yours!) softly penetrate my inner landscape devastated by the sadness and boredom of civilian life in Missouri where nothing - NOTHING (I swear to you) ever happens, ever comes to fulfill me, to replenish me, to sweeten me with the sugars of love.

My legs timidly spread apart, my eyes tightly closed, my breasts raised shyly and lovingly towards you out there in the direction of North Carolina, in a pleading manner, I suddenly imagined you had returned to lie next to me in my empty couch. Your solid and vigorous hands were voyaging all over my sad body, circulating back and forth over my palpitating contours, rediscovering at once the boundaries of your property which, I swear to you, on my beloved my dear brave paratrooper since you departed so heroically more than six months ago!

As my hands, shivering with desire, followed the traces of yours along those contours of my body you describe so poetically, a strict, severe, monotonous voice, deep down inside of me, kept whispering that I should not do such unspeakable gestures, not let myself be tempted by those *movements of weakness and despair, that I should not harvest in the darkness of my solitude, especially without the proper tools, the golden wheat that belongs to you. This deep voice (no doubt the voice of reason, of religion, of morality, of Law & Order) grew louder and louder as I pursued (in my mind only) the image, that magnificent image, of your giant fruit, your sweet banana, enormous, nervous and probing, as it wriggled deep inside of me in search of love. But, it is finally with empty hands (empty and humid hands, ALAS) that I came back BACK TO MYSELF, alone, weeping of sadness in my lonely bed, still knowing how you must want me, out there, far away, beyond the meadows, beyond the plains and the deserts, beyond the dark clouds, beyond the highways and the throughways and the superhighways. Oh! my darling prune, how I love to hear those juicy words you speak so tenderly, that rich and poetic vocabulary you know how to dispatch so well in my direction with such waves of eloquence.*

Ah, my dearest ferocious monkey how well you know how to climb the trees and branches of our love to hurl yourself (like TARZAN) into the voluptuous jungle of our passion. My precious apricot do not doubt of me, do not worry, I am yours, do not be jealous, for I am yours alone, for ever and everymore! I am of those who remain faithful until death doth us part in the flesh and in the soul. I am waiting for you, you are there in my skin, bones, nerves and organs like a Dainty Deity whom I sacralize, whom I divinize. Come back, oh how I miss you. I can't stand it any more.

My mother tells me that I am crazy to love you so much, crazy to adore a man like you because you are not worth it, because you are a GOOD-FOR-NOTHING, a miserable, lazy creature, but me I know, yes I know that it is not true, and I am convinced that you are GOOD-FOR-SOMETHING, and that it is not your damn fault if you are the way you are. Me, I know that you are good, real, beautiful, gorgeous, enormous, vibrant like a stallion. If I didn't know you as much as I do, would I stop to inscribe your name lovingly with my fingers in the fresh cow-dungs I encounter in the pasture where I wander aimlessly as I nostagically search those secret places where we used to cultivate our love? So, I beg of you, brave adorable paratrooper, continue to do all your training and your PUSH UPS, solidly, regularly, and stubbornly (in spite of those mean sergeants) so that when you come back to me (SOON!) you will be in full shape, strong and ready to grab me and crush me in your fortified arms.

Here the weather is bad. Rains all the time. I'm sad and depressed. Everybody is sad and unfriendly. I spend my time watching television, or playing my record player. Yes, the days, the weeks, the months pass so slowly in my solitude. If I can manage to save a little cash (without my dear Mom noticing it) from the money she gives me to do the shopping, I'll send you a nice TEN dollar bill AIR MAIL & SPECIAL DELIVERY for the anniversary (I do hope you remember!) of our first encounter at the State Fair as we proudly watched the black Angus parade in the corral, and of our first passionate and secret embraces in the back seat of your brand new Chevrolet. Good Bye! Good Bye dearest love, my brutal and manly paratrooper. I send you thousands and thousands French kisses XXXXXXXXXXXXXXXXXXXXX!

Your BIG Juicy Apple, SAD and Desperate Without You But Faithful and Devoted, Your One and Only Peachy M***

@@@@@@@@@@@@@@@@@@@@@@@@@@@@@

Other examples of such love letters are available (at reduced rate) either from the publisher or directly from the author of this exaggerated tale. Discretion guaranteed. Money back if not satisfied!

@@@@@@@@@@@@@@@@@@@@@@@@@@@@@

VI

exhilaration

HUM HUM HUM . . . ! [With a good deal of curiosity]
Ah you guys want to know if this extra curricular activity was
profitable? Yes, Not bad in fact. In fact it's with the dough he
made writing those fantastic love letters that eventually he
bought himself a car. Not new of course. Used. A 1947
BUICKspecial. Black. A real tank. But fast like hell. 320 horse
power. And with radio and heater and even white wall tires.

Normally I did FAYETTEVILLE/NOUILLORQUE

xxxxxxxxxxxxxxxxxxxxxxxxxxxxxxxxxxxxxxxxxxxxx
xxxxxxxxxxxxxxxxxxxxxxxxxxxxxxxxxxxxxxxxxxxxx
in less than twelve hours without stops!

HUM HUM HUM . . . ! [Skeptically]
Not tremendous you guys say!   You guys are forgetting that in
those days (in 1951) they didn't have yet the big SUPERHIGH-
WAYS and that you had to cross all the big cities from one end to
other - Richmond
        Washington
        Baltimore
        Philadelphia
and then all of New Jersey before arriving in *Nouillorque*!
But now I had decided to sell it (in *Nouillorque* he explained) my
BUICK 1947 special! Yes to get rid of it before taking off for the big
crossing of America! First of all because it used too much gas and
secondly because it wouldn't have made it(I can assure you he
said) from COAST to COAST — from New York to San Francisco
— (yes, *cent francs six quo*! as he pronounced it). Therefore better
get rid of it. I decided that the best would be to go as far as New
York with the damn thing. It should make it that far (hopefully).
And then sell the damn jalopy. Put it on the market. A little ad in
the New York Times! It'll sell on the spot. Maybe 300 bucks. No

maybe 200. Maybe less or maybe more! If I'm lucky and the guy doesn't look too deeply too carefully inside the motor. From the outside it looks damn nice. You guys may think perhaps that it was stupid of him to want to get rid of a car like that. Particularly since at this stage he could really enjoy such a comfortable means of transportation to go cross country   but you see in a way (he raised his index finger) i like to make it on my own   me i like to take chances and this was a chance in a lifetime to do it right   to go west as the pioneers had done   for indeed the more chancy the more risqué the more difficult the going the better the journey (that's philosophy for you) and it is less where you go than how you go that makes the difference ultimate-ly   in a way me CHRISTOPHER COLUMBUS of the 82nd one might say i wanted to go the hard way and play the game outside the rules or if i dare say so (as he stuck out his thumb) subcon-sciously i wanted to thumb my way through america (just as you thumb your way through a picture book I added without any irony) yes precisely   that's what i always wanted to do   yes as far back as i can remember when i was a kid in the banlieue watching at the cinéma du quartier cowboys and indians shoot it out in the farwest how i dreamt about this journey   rehearsed it a thousand times in my mind (in the mental cinema of your mind) yes i suppose   what a chance what a great and unique occasion   i might never have another chance like that again in the rest of my life (he was really going wild now gesticulating like a mad puppet in the shadow of the tree where we were sitting for his recitation) think   THINK what experiences what exciting experiences a guy could experience   what great material a guy could gather from such a trip (and what an incredible story one could tell eventually) yes why not (should one decide to relate even partially the story of such a journey across america I threw in) yes to report to whomever may want to listen to the tale of such a unique adventure (directly or indirectly or even standing or sitting) at a time when (yes if one had thumbed one's way up and down and across america from east to west) right of such a gratuitous journey rather than having to do it cozily (and cowardly may I add) in a 1947 BUICKspecial whose bald tires may not even last more than five hundred miles imagine then IMAGINE what splendid and original anecdotes one could tell with the distance of time particularly (and the ever present possibility of reliving all that through the creative process of even a second-hand narration and through the imagination of a qualified narrator however incoherent he might be I need not point out to whom this fantastic material has been entrusted in full confidence for the sole purpose of recreating it someday of putting it in the best possible form and with the best possible tools available) ah what fabulous stories!

What TRUE stories one could relate afterwards!

THE REAL THING!

No doubt the difference between masturbating and fucking!

Between an original or a crummy reproduction (or is it vice versa?) that hardly brings out the subtleties inherent in a spontaneous primary work!

That's what I kept thinking to myself as I contemplated seriously and at times regretfully selling my car in New York through an ad in the Times! For 2 or 3 hundred bucks. Dammit! Or even less. Assuming of course it could get me rolling safely that far (*en passant par Richmond Washington Baltimore et Philadelphie et toute cette saloperie du New Jersey*), but a guy must take chances. That's ···hat I kept saying to myself there in the back of my head as I calculated (it's always better to calculate in such cases than not calculate) the advantages of selling my BUICK in New York rather than take a chance with a car that was already in doubtful condition but to which I WAS NONETHELESS IMMENSELY AT-

TACHED — a car which we must not forget had been bought
with the money saved from the hard labor of weeks and weeks of
love-letter-writing! A car therefore which indeed had become a
reality out of the fiction of love! — A sentimental BUICK!

But MOINOUS   with whom I had discussed the matter
he thought it was dumb   really dumb of me to want
to sell the damn thing   crazy in fact to want to get rid of the
BUICK
just to get it out of your system is not enough of a reason he said for no
doubt that's what's bugging you   guilt   yes guilt   or if you prefer
the umbilical value of the damn thing   Sentimental BUICK
my ass he said   indeed in spite of the poor condition of the motor I
must admit that it was a fine automobile   a true work of art
                              a masterpiece he said
but of course MOINOUS was more inclined than I was towards aesthe-
tics he was an IDEALIST   whereas me I was more of a
REALIST but everyone has his weaknesses I suppose
                           Look at it he would say
                           look at those delicate lines
                           look at that unusual shape
                           look at those wheels those big
                           tires Isn't it magnificent

Look at that front end
Look at that rear end! And the radio
                     and the white walls and the heater and
that deep jet black color! You're mad to even consider getting rid of
it particularly when you could make such good use of it to go
across the country!   If I were you If I had
the money   If I were in your place   and even

if it doesn't make it all the way he said you should use it by all
means at least as far as it can go and then drop it   drop
whatever is left of it   like a banana peel   when one
is finished with the banana!   But not before!

Like a banana peel   I don't see the connection   typical of
him to make that kind of farfetched comparison   but he had a damn
good   argument   he almost convinced me   Okay even
                                                              if I lose
       it's not very intelligent of me he said to even   a bit of
       consider getting rid of such an immensely   dough
       valuable piece of machinery a most useful   he said
       piece of transportation for the kind of jour-   to get rid of it
       ney under consideration no it's not very   I ought to
       practical of you to be that unrealistic that   keep it as
       thoughtless to be so ungrateful so   long as it
       materialistic so naive   works he said

                                                       a most
                              convincing argument indeed
                                              keep it as
                                              long as it
works particularly he added when one has such a long and difficult
journey to make not knowing in fact how one will get where one has to
go and especially when one cannot be sure of encountering along the
way the kinds of people who will look upon you with
friendly eyes or the kind of
sociability you expect of
Americans and he went on to
state that if I kept the damn car
well who knows what
I might do I might even decide to come
with you at least part of the way even
perhaps all of
the way he said after a pause and even pay part of the traveling expenses
such as gas oil etc etc and perhaps even some of the unexpected expenses
one might not have anticipated in advance such as an unfortunate blow
out or a breakdown of the mechanical functioning of the motor etc etc etc
                              quite a tempting argument

but that
if
I sell it my BUICK in New York then I can go fuck myself in the brain he
                    said   typical of him to use such descriptive expes-
                    sions
and that in fact
he would do the crossing all by himself
nice and cozy and comfortably by bus or
by train or even by plane because after
all MOINOUS he really wanted to enjoy himself on this trip
                        and take advantage of all the sights
                        America had to offer and wanted this
to be an exciting a memorable trip an unforgettable trip an extraordinary experience and he even contemplated the possibility of
doing all kinds of little detours in some remote corners of America
to visit his relatives and MOINOUS he had a lot of relatives in
America
whereas
me
I had nothing
nobody except my uncle in New York who is dead now but who was still
alive at the time but whom I rarely saw but whom however it would be
nice to see again perhaps for the last time indeed

Uncle David . . . the one mentioned earlier . . . not yet de-
ceased then . . . at the period being alluded to now . . . lived
in Detroit for a while before he moved to New York . . . a
journalist (this may not have been mentioned as of yet) . . . of
world-wide reputation . . . spoke seven languages . . . a
polyglot if ever there was one . . . a true learned man . . .
talked about him before I believe when we were cooking the
noodles . . . but that's his business if he wants to go by bus or
train or even by plane . . . quite frankly . . . I don't really give
a fart if MOINOUS wants to visit his relatives . . . who gives a
damn . . . he can go where he wants . . . couldn't care less
. . . his relatives he can keep them . . . his trips . . . his
ambitions and obsessions . . . that's his problem . . . and
even his little detours . . . personally . . . I don't see the point

. . . I don't feel attached to him even though I'm fond of him and I'd rather make my own detours . . . plan my own itinerary to all the sights that America has to offer . . . all those magnificent places . . . Chicago and Las Vegas . . . Hollywood . . . the Grand Canyon . . . Death Valley . . . do it my way . . . go my own way right and left . . . up and down . . . damn right . . . to the North and to the South . . . and sideways even . . . East and West . . . and through the middle . . . fast and slow . . . up and away . . . after all that is my decision . . . I have that much freedom . . . freedom of movement of course (and of speech I presume) . . . before we arrive at the end . . . where we are supposed to be eventually . . . to the end of this damn journey (damn story) in San Francisco . . . on time . . . 30 days later . . . (200 or 300 pages or so should suffice) . . . to take the boat . . . the boat across the Pacific (slow boat to China) . . . where it's hot . . . smelly . . . exotic . . . and where they kill quick . . . in a whiffy so to speak . . . and where they write in designs and speak in music . . . yukuramu kata omoi koso yare . . . sayonara . . . as they stab you neatly in the guts . . . that's approximately what I was ruminating to myself one fine day when as the troops were preparing to move on for the maneuvers in the snows of Upper New York State Captain COHEN calls me in his office. It was a Tuesday. I remember that exactly. A gray day with fog hanging like a shroud over the barracks. He calls me to his neat little office which I had swept so many times and tells me that I need not pack my gears because I'm not going with the rest of the outfit (up North) to CAMP DRUM (near the Canadian border) to practice parachute jumps in the snow (imagine that in the snow) because my orders for the FAR EAST which I had been expecting any day now had arrived finally and that now I had (and MOINOUS too of course) thirty days to get my ass to San Francisco. Shit I told

myself was I going to take advantage of those thirty days! Wow was I ready for a vacation (and MOINOUS too)! Were we ready for the journey out West and the discovery of AMERICA which we had been discussing night after night in MOINOUS's little mailroom while listening to his jazz records and smoking cigarettes (in those days he smoked LUCKIES if it means anything)!
This is it!   Here we go!
But Captain COHEN he looked disappointed when he told me that. But me, as I stood there in the middle of his office, at ease as he had told me to be after the initial salute, I started screaming of exhilaration : OLE OLE I took a deep breath YE YE YE WOOPY A E I O U BANG BANG FLING FLANG I jumped on top of his desk HOPLA YADO YADO BIDO BIDO PIF PAF PLOUF TIC TOC RAH RAH RAH TRALALA I started tap dancing TEEPEEDEEEPEEEDEEEPEEEDEEE TASPASMALAUXCOUIL-LES!
Up and away!   Damn right!
I was so excited I did three backwards somersaults right there on the spot stood on my hands and walked around the room did a dozen arm extensions as I stood on one leg. Captain COHEN didn't react at first. He didn't say a word. Didn't even flinch. He just looked at me with a blank look, a look of utter stupefaction, wondering, I suppose, what the fuck was wrong, what the hell was happening here (unless he had already witnessed such a séance before, with the guys of the 82nd AIRBORNE DIVISION anything can happen)! But then he reached for the telephone with a disgusted desperate shrug of the shoulders (obviously to call the regimental psychiatrist or the MP's) hesitated a moment and suddenly changed his mind. He got up s l o w l y and leaning on his desk with both hands he shouted in a kind of fury with saliva dripping from his mouth : CORPORAL HOMBRE DELLA PLUMA . . . GET THE FUCK OUT OF HERE . . . AND ON THE DOUBLE! I didn't even bother to salute!

I ran out of there like a jumping jack like a bouncing ball
hopping leaping shouting screaming I ran out of there as if I
had the shits up my ass laughing puffing giggling pissing in
my pants I ran out of there gesticulating like a mad man like
a disrupted automat and there in the middle of nowhere like
a fancy acrobat I started doing sidekicks wheelbarrows
cartwheels entrechats handstands flipturns somersaults
back and forth backward and forward and suddenly I stopped let a wild geronimo out of my chest and reverently
impulsively as a gesture of gratitude I got down in the
horizontal push up position we were so well trained to
assume merely by reflex and knocked off a good twenty-five
with a grace with a pace with a suppleness with an enthusiasm that would have driven our dear sergeant straight
up the wall had that sonofabitch been present to witness
this   astounding   impromptu   spectacle

Wow was it good! Was I excited —- ready to —- but perhaps I am
anticipating a bit too much? (No, not at all, I told him) —- well
what better way to release the tension? At times like these one
must allow oneself a touch of gaiety (a touch of looseness) for
indeed as it was once proposed *it is what one says that delimits and
organizes what one things* and to be honest as you must have
realized by now I never stop delimiting and organizing what I
say, and of course what I think (same with me, I told him)! *iiiii iiiii
iiiii . . . iiiii iiiii iiiii . . . iiiii iiiii iiiii . . .* ! Ah you guys are
smiling! You guys didn't expect him to come up with such a
profound reflection there in the middle of such exhilaration.
Right in the middle of his story. And what a story! And particularly in such delightful moments of dissipation. Well, if I were
him I would tell you to go fuck yourselves [Astounded looks—
vociferations] Okay let's calm down!

VII

interruptions & vociferations

[aside to himself and to (?) who may never]
Remembering what was said earlier :

I want to write a book like a cloud that changes as it goes!
And what was replied :
I want to tell a story that cancels itself as it goes!

AND AT THAT POINT I INTERRUPTED MYSELF AND KNEW I
WAS IN FOR SOMETHING : PRECISELY WHAT
I COULD NOT KNOW OR TELL!

SO (?) THE STORY MUST GO ON, YOU PRETENDING TO BE
ME, ME YOU. IN OTHER WORDS YOU DECANCELLING THE
FICTION I WRITE AND I WRITING THAT UNWRITTEN
AND NEVERTOBEWRITTEN ARTICLE ABOUT THE ARTICLE
THAT YOU WILL NEVER WRITE ABOUT THE FICTION THAT
YOU HAVE WRITTEN UNDER MY NAME. OR, TO PUT IT IN
SIMPLER TERMS
HAVING TAKEN OVER MY WORDS
AND NEGATED MY WORLD
AND HAVING PUT AN END TO THE ENDLESSNESS OF MY
STORY (what happened when the regiment left, etc.) YOU ARE
NOW UNABLE TO DISTINGUISH THE DANCER FROM THE
DANCE
BUT I BEGIN AGAIN THE IMPOSSIBLE AND HOPELESS BE-
GINNING OF WHAT CAN NEVER BE BEGUN (OR ENDED)
AND POSTDATING OUR CRITIFICTION I REINSERT MYSELF
INTO YOUR PRICKLY TEXTICULE AND THROUGH THE
LEAPFROG TECHNIQUE (to be explained later) PURSUE MY
JOURNEY INTO THE ABSURD UNENDING OR IF YOU PRE-
FER ENDLESS POSSIBILITY OF   therefore

Let us continue calmy seriously deliberately and briefly, and without any further detours. Oh yes! What was the last question? Oh yes I got it! What was his uncle doing in America? No! That's not it! What then? Ah! You guys want to know what happened when the regiment left? Okay!

It might however be appropriate at this time to pause a moment and quote (without of course revealing the sources) (in French or in English doesn't matter much) a statement or two gathered at random that might permit us to continue this discourse on a more stable basis for indeed it is sometimes essential to rely on others in order to gain confidence in oneself to be able to pursue and bring to its proper end one's chosen undertaking in spite of the fact that one knows prior to one's departure that the journey is hopeless and that it is indeed futile to insist on any further developments unless one finds a suitable reason

THEREFORE

There are many ways in which the thing I am trying to say may be tried in vain to be said. I have experimented, as you know, both in public and in private, under duress, through faintness of heart and through weakness of mind, with two or three hundred.

The pathetic antithesis possession-poverty was, perhaps, not the most tedious. But we begin to weary of it, do we not?

The realisation that art has always been bourgeois . . . is finally of scant interest . . . The situation is that of him who is helpless, cannot act, in the event cannot SPEAK, since he is obliged to SPEAK. . . The act is of him who, helpless, unable to act, acts, in the event SPEAKS, since he is obliged to SPEAK. . . . I know that all that is required now, in order to bring even this horrible matter to an acceptable conclusion, is to make of this submission, this admission, this fidelity to failure, a new occasion – a new term of relation – and of the act which, unable to act, obliged none the less to act, he makes an expressive act even if only of itself of its impossibility, of its obligation. (P. 125)

NEVERTHELESS

Le temps vient de ne pas s'en tenir à noter la capture et
l'effacement des flux libidinaux dans un ordre dont la
représentation et ses cloisons jointives / disjonctives
est, serait le dernier mot, car cette capture, cet effacement sont le capitalisme, mais le temps vient de servir
et d'encourager leur divagation errant sur toutes les
surfaces et fentes immédiates crues, de corps, d'his-
toires, de terre, de langage. . . .   (P. 925)

And so, you guys want to know exactly what happened when the
regiment left! Well . . .   . . . Well

(But before we go on I must warn you I must warn you of
something extremely important. Everything I am telling you of
course is true. Naturally it is somewhat distorted from reality. But
in general it follows the broad lines of life. Evidently it is possible
that there are errors, and exaggerations in this tale. False reflections. Chronological deformations. Confusions! Padding! In
other words, all kinds of things which, normally, ought not to be
found in such a tale, and yet, inevitably, cannot, must not be left
out! Because (as I firmly believe) all fiction is digression. And
moreover life is but a fiction, or in the words of the poet, a
biography is something one invents afterwards. Someday,
perhaps, when I shall write all this, when it will be time to write
the story of his life ((his so-called MONOBIOGRAPHY)) in a
coherent form, as everyone else does these days (((well all the
little panks of daddy's boys))) ((((all the pseudostruc-
turalisators)))) to be à la mode (((((ah, this big word surprises
you))))) then I shall rectify I shall correct all the errors. I shall
probe deeper into his thoughts. Dig under the surface. I shall,
certainly, speak of all his misfortunes ((((((mental & physical))))))
real or imagined, but above all I shall speak particularly of all the

parenthetical elements of his life (((((((THE PARENTHESES)))))))
(((((((((third version, straddling two languages, two continents and two lives, two cultures also — spread-eagle over the Atlantic)))))))) and of his adventures (((((((((in fact it is at the DEUX CONTINENTS that it began next to the SEUIL, in October to be precise, Rue Jacob, while others were busily doing their little work, quietly, and with a sense of self-satisfaction, in a mass of numbers and a stack of logics))))))))) but for the time being let us forget, let us indeed neglect this parenthesis ((((((((((endless obscure parenthesis)))))))))) which refuses to close itself, and let us speak first of what I shall do or what I shall write when the right moment comes. When the the time comes to relate his story properly. Yes his story, in writing and on paper, rather than to recite the damn thing, in a half-ass manner orally and haphazardly. Then there will be, for sure, much more reflections, much more details, logical and realistic details, and above all a sharp sense of proportions with a well worked out style, a carefully drawn style with neat sentences and well defined paragraphs, delimited margins, chapters of equal length, punctuation within the rules of grammar, rational syntax, elegantly arranged sequences, and correct modern usage of language. And professional typing, of course. But for the time being one must move quickly. One must move along swiftly, as best one can, or else you guys are not going to want to stick around for the rest of the story. You guys are going to get bored rapidly, disgusted, fed up, and the whole story will fall apart even before I can get him out of the fucking 82nd, en route to New York where, you will remember, he had decided to sell his car, say goodbye to MARILYN (who shall be discussed in much more details subsequently), get rid of whatever he had stored in MARILYN's closet, his possessions, kiss his uncle farewell (maybe for the last time), and forge his way West, across these big United States!

Therefore, you guys understand the necessity to move fast, but when I shall rewrite all that in his black BUICK, the whole mess, with profound thoughts and reflections, it will be better, I assure you, more correct, all that is mere preparation, all this marmelade, what can you do, one works as best as one can, and I have seen in my days all kinds of shitty tales with precisely the kind of details that fuck up the whole thing, but I sum up, some day I will relate, from beginning to end, and in a glorious style, the 82nd and on to the West Coast, in the paratroopers, then all those hillbillies stood there like a bunch of shitheads and started laughing, and I didn't know how to repair the blunder, what to do, all alone, with my incredible accent, we waited for the laughter to calm down, but perhaps I am anticipating a bit too much, within the rules of grammar, and then there was MARILYN, I must not forget her, with neat paragraphs, chapters too, and poker and fucking all day long, all night long, on footlockers, endless poker games, and in their minds sexual orgies, mustn't forget that lovely woman, masturbation sessions, with BENNY, in his lampshade factory, in Brooklyn, in his black BUICK, what a deal, yes, one must move quickly or else, finally, what can I do, you guys, one, and so on, just as, hardly started, can, but then we . . . between . . . desperate . . . and so much more . . . yet . . . do . . . can . . .

Well ============================ Well

Ah! You guys have another question?   [What a bunch of bug-
gers!]   Okay but quickly, if you please.   Ah, that's it!   That's
your question:

Within the system of social structures of Capitalism didn't he feel
that he was being exploited as a foreigner by the mere fact that he
had been drafted in the U.S. Army to fight a war in the Far East in
which he had quite frankly little interest at the time in question?

Do I understand correctly? UNBELIEVABLE! You guys are really
a bunch of perverts! The stuff you guys can come up with! And
now I am asked if I understand THE QUESTION! Of course I
understand your question! Who do you take me for? But still,
here you are, 5 or 6 of you, comfortable, nice and dozy, listening
to me well entrenched in your intellectual security, your mental
refuge, interrupting the flow of the discourse without any con-
sideration for whatever effort I am putting into it, and you dare
ask such questions! Just when I was on the verge of getting things
more or less in shape to be able to continue. You guys are really a
bunch of disruptors No Kidding!

Yes
    his story
        you find it amusing.
                        You think that perhaps it is tellable
                                            recitable
since you stand there listening to it with gaping mouths.
                                    And why not!

Interesting even (even a bit obscene).

　　　　　　　　　　　　　Don't you think so?

　　　　　　　　　　　　　Nonetheless
you guys would have liked to have had his experiences

　　　　　　　　　　　　　　　his adventures

　　　　　　　　　　　　　　　　　and his
avatars.

　　His bitchy existence! N'est-ce pas?

　　　　　　　　　　　　Would have liked to have lived
his miserable life

　　　　　　　to have suffered his misery

　　　　　　　　　　and all the shit that went with
it!

　　The Universal Crap

　　　　　　　up to the waist and above!

　　　　　　　　　　　But for you guys there is
always a solution as it was once suggested :

　　　　　　　　　　　You simply contrive a little
kingdom in the midst of the universal muck and then shit on it.

　　　　　　　　　　　　　　Is it not
what you guys do most of the time?

Well let me tell you, he and I, we have crapped on life left and
right, and without Reservation, without Constipation, we have
other problems, left and right. Human Misery! Bullshit! well you
Guys haven't heard the Best yet! not even half, not even two-/
thirds. wait till it Comes out. wait till the Real Shit falls on you. ah
you guys think you are Above all that Universal Muck. above it
All because you are intellectuals, untouched by the Raw Experience of Life. the Real Stuff! safe in your mental Refuges because

You are of the Mind and not of the Guts or the Flesh or the Bones YEA the Bones too that creak with Suffering. YEA arms and legs Hurting all the time (day and night). YEA stomachs whining all the time with Hunger. YEA hands full of Blisters, bleeding all the times. unknown to you all that Raw Greasy Experience of Life and Work and Hunger and Misery and Humiliation and Stench! YEA for your guys it's the Good Families, Private Schools, lots of Dough and Cozy Country Houses in Connecticut, Swanky Neighborhoods, Big Fancy Cars in Three Car Garages, First Class Travelling, Stocks, Bonds, Vacations at the Seashore, Trips to Europe, Reputable Family Doctors and Psychiatrists, Publishing Companies, and your Books, the Books you write with your left hand, reviewed in the New York Times, and of course the Book-Of-The-Month-Club, Fancy Weddings, Polite Neat Kids in Pink Bedrooms, Maids to Fuck on the side when the Wife is out Shopping at Saks I presume, Credit Cards, Ten Dollar Ties, initials on your Cuff Links, twenty pairs of shoes, silk under-wears, Suits by the Dozen in your Wardrobes, Life on a Silver Platter in other words, and of course The Republican Party, and political Banquets at Hundred Bucks a Plate, and Funerals in Cadillacs, and then Posthumously remembered with all the love and affection and sorrow you so well deserve, but Life, YEA real Life! and Work! and Misery! unknown! that's for the other guy. don't bother me with that! and yet you guys are still shoving on us your Aesthetic Crap about Art and Literature! YEA you guys are still trying to push on us, to peddle on us your Pitiful memories of High School Masturbation or your messed up First Piece of Ass, in your Curious Solitude, as you say so well, with your fucked up Mentalities and your crooked Sense of Decency, on the Threshold of Life around the corner from those Rich Daddies of yours and your Sweet Mommies and your charming Relatives, and that's what you guys would have Us believe is the Stuff of

Literature. Stuff my Ass! You guys haven't seen anything yet, wait till it comes out. Haven't heard the best yet. Wait!

Well let me tell you maybe all that [STUFF] from a symbolic
or a metaphoric point of view
may mean something and can help peddle a few broken down ideas about life but dammit it's old stuff!

///

Let me tell you those clumsy stupid farmers
of the 82nd at night under their khaki blankets they too were dealing in symbolism (without knowing it of course) they too when they dripped frantically into the metaphors of asses and cunts and furry triangles they saw circulating in the corners of their skulls they too in fact were involved in symbolism and it was not served to them on a shiny silver platter no it was raw suffering from the loneliness the misery the pain of their nightly ejaculations into the desert of military life!

Therefore
you guys can be proud your SOCIAL STRUCTURES and your EXPLOITATION and your crappy CAPITALISM $$$$$$$$$$$$
what the fuck do you know about the lonely nights of North Carolina & the misery of the 82nd & the butterflies in the stomach & the sadness & the fear & the pain! Well if you listen I'll tell you what he said even though he may not have had your delicate sense of story-telling!

Yah! That much must be stated, you guys know how to express yourselves. Yah beautifully. Impeccable style. Long and difficult sentences. Nothing there to bitch about. Complex phrases. Well constructed (within the rules and the logic of grammar) and with respect for syntax and punctuation. And all kinds of scientific words and well-made images. And all sorts of levels of meaning and double meaning. That much is clear. There you are unbeatable. And when it comes to expression and writing, you guys surpass one another, without the least effort. You guys are really tremendous in the catechism of litterature and Belles-Lettres with all its ABCDEFGHIJKLMNOPQRSTUVWXYZ in Capital Letters and in miniscule letters abcdefghijklmnopqrstuvwxyz and the whole upper gamut of punctuation : . ? , ! ( ) - [ ] ☑ ' '' > % } ¢ ' ÷ ⊗ % : all that *very indicative exclamative interrogative derogative punctuational scripture!*

In fact, I think it's one of your buddies (he works in pharmacy, or something like that, I believe) who said (I'm quoting him without reference because I'm sure you guys will immediately recognize where it comes from) in one of those texts much discussed these days and which struck me so much at first gleaning that I learned it by heart (not all of it because it's more than 60 pages but the following passage which I am now quoting [in my translation] integrally & without changing either style punctuation signification and / or lovely syntax)

Writing is not an order of inde enfeebled utterance, not at all dead in reprieve, a differed li phantom the phantasm the simu ot inanimate, is not insignific and always identically; this si se without great respondent, is Having lost the straight path, f rectitude, the norm, it rolls does not know where he is going ost his rights, like an outlaw, adventurer. Wandering in the st

pendent signification, it is an a dead thing : a living dead, a fe, a semblance of breath. The lacrum of living discourse in n ant, it simply signifies little gnifier of little, this discour like all phantasms : wandering! the right direction, the rule o here and there like someone who but also like someone who has l a bad lot, a thief, a bum or an reets he does not even know who

D E R ? I D A

he is, what is his identity, if his father. He repeats the same corners, but he does not know h know from where one comes and rse without respondent, is not state of infancy. Himself unroo th his country and his home, th is at the disposal of everyone, incompetent, of those who under of those who have no concern in theless afflict it with imperti l, offered on the sidewalk, isn

he has one, and a name, that of thing when questioned at street ow to repeat his origin. Not to where one is going, for a discou to know how to speak, it is the ted, anonymous, without ties wi is most insignificant signifier of the competent as well as the stand or think they understand, it, knowing nothing of it, none nence. Available for one and al 't writing above all democratic

Damn good point! WRITING (and one should add SPEAKING —
        publicly and even privately) is it not above all
        DEMOCRATIC?

        Well, that beautiful DISCOURSE on WRIT-
        ING
        . . . that magnificent DRAWING of WRIT-
        ING — and SPEAKING
for that matter — is it not what I AM (he would say to you were he
present to reply)?   Is it not ME — that your little buddy (who
knows the secret of WRITING obviously) is describing (without
knowing it) while using a vocabulary much more elegant
        much more serious
and indubitably richer and cleaner than mine but with terms that
subtly and metaphorically hide (or reveal, whichever way you
stick it) my TRUE SELF my REAL IDENTITY (he would certainly
reply now, were he able to hear the words that remake him, the
words that I am now speaking before you for his sake)?

Indeed, it is HE, the bum, the anonymous thief, the great
traveler, the bad lot, the outlaw, the adventurer, the pioneer
(whose story I'm now trying to recapitulate to the best of my
memory on the basis of his rather skimpy and even distorted
first-hand relation and his somewhat incoherent and at times
even delirious recitation there under that tree where we sat many
years ago on several occasions as he transmitted to me orally the
essential facts and elements of his miserable life), it is HE, the
insignificant signifier, the guy without a name and without a
respondent, the living dead in reprieve of little consequence,
without country or home, it is HE that I am trying here to retell to
the best of my ability, that differed existence of a phantom a
phantasm a fantoche a fanfaron, yes it is HE!

Undoubtedly he could have been ME, for I now assume the responsibility, the credibility of this bygone paratrooper whose story I am now reconstructing! He was indeed a SIMULACRUM that poor jerk who had lost the right direction and the rule of rectitude, who had wandered off the straight path, when we met, that foreigner who had rolled here and there, and off the mark, right to left in utter confusion, top to bottom, and through the middle in total indecision, like someone who doesn't know where the fuck he comes from and where he is going and who doesn't give a damn if eventually his story does get told, directly or indirectly, in a discursive or a non-discursive manner, for the good of humanity, and the pleasure of those who may decide to listen to it, this (abracadabra) story, this atrocious delirium, this oral vomit, this verbal prostitution offered freely on the sidewalks and on the platform (between the head and the hands like an acrobat) of the pages, in the form of an anal-ytic blahblah, in the form of a linguistic screwing of the semantic rules of recitation, of a cacophonic jawing, of a xxxxxxx, no he did not give a damn if his story was ever told or retold — publicly or privately — because he knew that all stories are democratic (that much he knew) and that therefore his own story was also democratic, since it was a dis-course made of words, and that if his story was himself, more or less a duplication of himself, a coincidence of his life, then he too must be democratic, and, of course, by extension, he who tells the story must by all means be democratic, consequently as the teller of his tale I am DEMOCRACY or the voice of DEMOCRACY whether or not my tale is told in an exaggerated form second-handedly, therefore don't bug the shit out of me, don't tickle me with all your salads of SOCIAL STRUCTURES your jello of EXPLOITATION of the working class military class or even the non-working class, and particularly your chicken-picking-shit charabia about CAPITALISM, mes deux, for it is not what you say

that counts, he would say to you, and I would agree with him, but how you say it, especially in this kind of double situation! it's nice to talk and you guys can talk but what are you really what the hell do you think you are bunch of little shits bunch of crappy questioneers bunch of incompetent who afflict me bury me with all your impertinences but in fact what are you but a bunch of disgusting rectificators inquisitors interrupters
[! . . ? X / % . xx OO 1 .:. $ *iii* / *aaa* zOz (!)

no let me speak let go me on i'm not finished i stop just started stop like a bunch of cry-babies shouting wait get a moment to the end or i four three you damn it flights am almost oratorically at before the end wait wait your screw it turn till i insulting finish you in a don't double get column nervous like

a bunch		a bunch
of snobs		of lambs
of queers		of creeps
of jerkers		of fuckers
of auditors		of pederasts
of mediocres		of correctors
of charlatans		of dooshmen
of mommy's boys		of flagellators
of motherscrewers		of goose-pimplers
of half-ass-suckers		of good-for-nothing
etceteraetceteraetcetera		aretectearetectearetecte

yes that's what you guys are in short and I skip and I forget a good dozen or two of juicy qualifiers but you get the point and everything you guys know it comes from books all the social junk about social structures etcetera and all that shaky goody goody crap about exploitation etcetera and capitalism out of the books etcetera and when it comes to books wow you guys have read them all

TONS & TONS   TONS & TONS

P   P
I   I
L   L
E   E
S & S

every-thing

| platoaristotlevirgilsaintbricolagecalvindescartes |
| pascalmalebranchevoltairediderotrousseaukanthegel |
| ofcoursedarwinmarxspinozaschopenhaueraugustecomte |
| nietzschefreudbergsonmustnotforgetthesethreelenin |
| engelsheideggercertainlyhusserlcamussartremerleau |
| pontyandallthephenomenologistsexistentialistsupto |
| thestructuralistslevistraussfoucaultdeleuzeserres |
| lacanderridaandlegroupetelquelsollersetsabandeles |
| garsdelavantgardeetcteraandperhapshombredelapluma |

VIII

superman & real life

EveRYthing : the whOle hihistoricococucultural puppetshow of the mind from the greGREcolatinus craAp to the Struc-TUTUroanTItioedipianist junk of today and I've'I've skiiiipped dozens and doDODOzens in the corners yea enouuughh toto drIve you out of your mind and upupupup the Walllll but hellll with it tiMe is runnnnnnning out so let's geT a mooomooove on and shooove all thaaat sHit aside out oof the WaY and get back to what is ReAAAl to liFe even iiif it'ss you guuuyyys who DeDe-Cide what oTHer Guys (SlOBs like Us) must reeeaD ororr ouuught not to reeeeaaaD yEa when it comes to READING wellll you guys are supraSUPRAsup ooout of this world formmimmid-able it gogogoes wiwiwitwithout sAying yeA it mamakes senSe bebecause for you the mmmmmechanismmmmm of READING is exextremmmmely immmmmportant crucrucial in FAct as im-mmmportant if nnoot more thAAAn LiFe ititselllf bebebecause reeeeal lifE I mean bobody life what doess it mamamater to you what iiiisss it for you if not alll the jujunk you pipile upup in YoUr skUUlls out of theee booooooooks yEa reaality for yooou guyyys itt's simpppply a mattteeeer of boookikishness of boOOOkkk pppppiiiiiiiling of bookboobookinage I mean and all the rest nonexexiiSTANT bebecaussse when it comes to READinnng or even simply piiillliiing boooooks up you guys are cHAmpions and beeesides bebesisides youu guys are all invoovolved with BOOks pupublishing edititing rerereviewing and you dondon-don'tt jerrrrk oFf about iiiiit you guys EdiT aall the reviews mag-gaggazines neews papapppppers joujournals and you guys read all the mamannnunuscripts thathat the pooooooR slObs send you and which youyou sendd riggght back bebecaussse you guys aaaare the oooones wHo judge whooo dedeDeciDe what ooothEr GuUUUys should or shooould nononot read who deeeCiCide whooo is in the gooood dididirection on theee straight pAtH and if they follllow the rurullles ofofof rectttittttitude and yoOOOOu

guys dedetermmmmmmine what'sss ofifficiiaaaal and whaat's
nononot offffficial what's truuuue and what's nooot truue
whaaaaat's commmmmmmmmmmmmmercial and what's not
commmerrrrrrrrcial what's reeeaaadaable and what's unrreada-
ble but what aboUt ReAl LiiiiFe yes what about iT
REAL LIFE
well let me tell you what he said about REAL LIFE
REAL LIFE is not all that shit that ends in ISM
nationalism / chauvinism / determinism / pessimism /
nihilism / marxism / capitalism and though you guys claim
to be antiantiantianti and not proproproproproropro nothing
that's for sure
antireligious / anticlerical / antilife / antisystem / antiestab-
lishment / antihuman   deep inside
AH
your little wooden cross (and iron cross too)
still bug the shit out of you
your priests and psychiatrists with their shabby little stories
still make you blush with culpability and envy and remorse and
humility   and   well let me tell you
and I can already see you smile from the corners of your sweet
effeminate mouths (your delicious mouths)
because deep inside of you you are all a bunch of frustrated
perverts but let's skip all that I don't want to offend you too much
and let me tell you rapidly what he told me about himself:
            I am the FIRST SUPERMAN of the 20th century
he said one day yes that's what I am the FIRST and perhaps the
LAST if not the ONLY ONE because .... I don't know
what took me .... why I got carried away like that ....
please excuse me .... I don't understand .... I don't
understand why I suddenly ...... why I suddenly started shouting at you .... just like that .... for a good ten or fifteen
minutes .... right in the middle of this ..... this .... recitation
.... I don't know why .... I don't know what ..... what happened
...... I ...... suddenly ..... please .... cancel all that

yes please if you please skip it jump over it wipe it out and let us if
you please continue and merely consider what precedes as a simple dig
ression a moment of irrationality caused by the fever of the session a moment of irrationality caused
by   the   fever   of   the   recita
tion   or   by   the   obsession   of   America   because   gentlemen   between   you
and   I   and   without   blushing   America   is   hard   to   take   to   swal
low   hard   to   conquer   because   do   I   dare   suggest   it   America   it's
a   big   fat   broad   that   one   must   seize   with   one's   arms   squeeze
passionately   a   big   sexy   bitch   with   enormous   teats   a   splen
did   ass   and   a   lovely   furry   cunt   and   if   you   want   to   poss
ess   to   explore   to   search   that   magnificent   bit   of   geog
raphy   you   have   to   go   a   long   way   and   have   the   desire
and   courage   not   only   to   speak   about   it   but   do   som
ething   about   it   and   the   problem   with   most   Ameri
cans   is   that   they   don't   have   the   guts   nor   the
initiative   to   fuck   the   hell   out   of   their   mo
ther   land   and   so   instead   of   really   trying
to   shove   their   dicks   into   it   they   justi
fy   their   cowardice   by   simply   dropping
their   pants   in   front   of   it   and   jerk
off   like   a   bunch   of   kids   where   in
fact   me   gentlemen   I   wanted   to   p
enetrate   that   mother   land   yes
I   wanted   to   explode   to   burs
t   inside   her   ass   and   insi
de   her   cunt   I   wanted   my
sperm   to   flow   between
her   gorgeous   cheeks
one   good   time   and
that's   why   I   de
cided   to   love

it   to   love   it
without   shame   I
confess   and   so   it
is   why   I   had   to   cro
ss   the   land   from   east
to   west   in   such   a   manly
way   that   I   could   think   of
myself   as   a   SUPERMAN   a   kind
of   extraordinary   being   inflat
ed   by   pride   and   scorn   and   fraud
to   better   cover   up   my   lack   of   exp
erience   my   fear   my   weaknesses   my   he
sitation   my   apprehension   but   also   all
the   viciousness   that   makes   a   man   in   ord
er   to   be   able   to   hang   on   in   front   of   this
feminine   geography   rather   than   just   drop   my
pants   like   everybody   else   and   jerk   off   like   a
kid   even   though   it   was   trying   to   destroy   me   swa
llow   me   make   of   me   just   another   lousy   American   of
little   importance   of   minor   consequence   who   lets   him
self   be   atrophied   by   the   American   way   of   life   without
ever   making   a   stand   without   ever   saying   to   himself   fuck
it   all   of   course   these   were   mere   thoughts   at   the   time   and
it's   impossible   now   or   even   later   to   ascertain   if   those   wer
e   really   his   thoughts   or   simply   thoughts   that   had   gathered   i
n   him   out   of   unknown   sources   but   nonetheless   whether   true   whet
her   false   the   decision   was   made   I   was   not   going   to   submit   to   let
myself be subjected like all the other jerks to being a mere bench- warmer who never gets into the
game   as   a   fullfledged   participant   but

AH AH AH . . OH OH OH . . AH AH AH . . OH OH OH . . . !
[Quite expectedly] Ahahah, Ohohoh, I know, to say SUPER-
MAN immediately implies, I know, no not a COMIC BOOK
hero, Ahahah, Ohohoh, you bunch of meatheads, something
else, much more important, the name of a guy I don't even dare
pronounce here, big name! Who do you think he was?
Some kind of illiterate!   Yes it's a beautiful name to pronounce to
                           drop in the conversation yes you let
                           your pink tongue and
your saliva slide lightly over the Z
                           over the S
                           over the CH in one smooth juicy gliding
                           hardly felt
but delicious a sweet sliding of your [bourgeois] tongue — ZSCH
— just like that and suddenly all the jerks who listen to you are
crushed by the sound of that big name yes crushed diminished
ashamed!
Of course you guys have glanced at all that stuff but not too
deeply, no, not too deeply, because it scares the shit out of you
that ZSCH, and he too, that poor guy, was scared when he
pronounced it before me but that does not negate the fact that he
was not the FIRST SUPERMAN of the 20th century, as he stated
himself.
What do you think of that?
And he was being MODEST because, dear SIRS, one must not
forget MODESTY!
                                              Fuck MODESTY!
Scorn and contempt and hatred that's what one learns from that
ZSCH damn right scorn and not modesty or humility or resigna-
tion or submission or fear! One must shit and piss on all human
weakness well, gentlemen, I assure you he shitted and pissed all

over it, and this is why he could call himself without any modesty
the FIRST if not the ONLY ONE to have totally squarely integrally
radically and definitely shoved aside religion morality responsibility and of course the LITTLE JESUS and his OLD MAN heaven
and hell and all the rest, but of course one could argue that he was
not the only one, that will be decided!
I made myself alone
I pulled myself out of the hole out of the cemetery yes the
CE   ME   TE   RY and not from between ←O→ my mother's

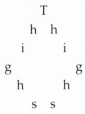

from my own grave
three times
four times
I made myself strong ——————— touch those muscles he
shouted
I made myself beautiful —————— look at this face he grinned
intelligent too————— and what was missing to intelligence I replaced with imagination he explained yes imagination
energy and willpower and raw strength and insolence courage
stubborness
and madness too and so you guys can go screw yourselves
forward &
backward collectively or individually but stop bugging me with
all your damn questions your useless interruptions your disrup-
tions your remarks your impatience you guys have the wrong
guy I'm merely speaking for him merely reporting go argue with

somebody else you are making a mistake a gross error leave me alone I try my best but no here they come right in the middle of my recitation (in spite of the strict RECOMMENDATIONS) no respect for the logic of my platformatic narrative those smartasses not enough problems just keeping up with the damn story infuriated no doubt by the tone of my vociferations the breath of my invectives in short by the color of my argument which certainly demands an immediate rebut and a quick straightening of the speaker and so here they come (climbing up on my rather shaky platform metaphorically speaking) and bing bang they bombard me with all sorts of harangues a neat brutal bombardment of the most insulting epithets squarely thrown in my face like quick jabs bang and pif paf it comes from all sides with cries and demented gestures in harsh tones of voice
and it's enough to shut the fuck up out of you for ever
  enough to never again permit you to tell the rest of your stories!

```
↑↓↑↓↑↓↑↓↑↓↑↓↑↓↑↓↑↓        ΨΨΨΨΨΨΨΨΨΨΨΨΨΨΨΨΨΨΨΨΨ

←0→←0→←0→←0→←0→←0→←      ααααααααααααααααααααα

TΞ↑→Λ>§Δ↔→TΞ↑↓0←←Ξ→→TΞ   ΦΦΦΦΦΦΦΦΦΦΦΦΦΦΦΦΦΦΦΦΦ

♩♩♩♩♩♩♩♩♩♩♩♩♩♩♩♩♩♩♩♩♩    ΔΔΔΔΔΔΔΔΔΔΔΔΔΔΔΔΔΔΔΔΔ

≈≈≈≈≈≈≈≈≈≈≈≈≈≈≈≈≈≈≈≈≈    ΛΛΛΛΛΛΛΛΛΛΛΛΛΛΛΛΛΛΛΛΛ

§§§§§§§§§§§§§§§§§§§§§    ∂∂∂∂∂∂∂∂∂∂∂∂∂∂∂∂∂∂∂∂∂

≡Ψ≡Ψ≡Ψ≡Ψ≡Ψ≡Ψ≡Ψ≡Ψ≡Ψ≡Ψ   >>>>>>>>>>>>>>>>>>>>>

∞√∞√∞√∞√∞√∞√∞√∞√∞√∞√∞√   ΩΩΩΩΩΩΩΩΩΩΩΩΩΩΩΩΩΩΩΩΩ
```

IX

a false start

What a bunch of bastards! After all that! After we've managed somehow to come that far, and now they're trying to screw it all up. I really should tell them to go shove it. I feel like packing up my tools and cutting the fuck out of here, right in the middle. Let them find another jerk another teller to satisfy their curiosity. Why do I need this crap? Let them get to the end of the journey by themselves. Listen, unless you guys cool off unless you guys control yourselves. Lay off me! I flush the whole crappy thing down the drain. What the hell do we need to get excited like that I ask you? Is it really necessary? I didn't mean to offend you. Didn't do it on purpose. But no, not them, those lousy angry auditors, those stuffy storymongers, they keep coming at me, up my platform, with more furor, and even more delight than before, and so I tell them that I'm sorry, that the whole digression [VI, VII, VIII, IX] was unpremeditated. I apologize! If I got off the subject, if I got carried away into the wrong direction it's because the excitement, the fever, yes the fever of the recitation, got me all wound up. It was a false start. But if you guys are willing to stick around for a while longer, you'll see, I'll get back on the right path the straight line. You'll see, I'll respect the rules and norms of rectitude! I'll be more careful. It's just that, as I once heard it said, to live is to tell naively the impossibility of living. And so I don't understand at all why you guys should be that disturbed by my vociferating, particularly since it was purely accidental. An unfortunate turn of events, but henceforth, I'll try to keep going as smoothly and as correctly and as directly as I can, for, as I once heard it said also, the one who exists (I suppose me in this case), in relation to the one who no longer exists (the departed speaker), is alone to carry the burden of existing (of speaking his own life), thus he stumbles toward his end, and that means, presumably (it is never that simple), that through his words his life becomes an unfortunate series of stumblings. A mess! A bad flop! A repetition of false starts!

Therefore you guys understand . . .

----

yes yes we do and we accept your apologies and your explanation but now will you please continue and try to be as coherent as possible as clear as possible and let us try to understand each other without any further complications for indeed it takes a great deal of patience to stay here

----

Okay.   I go on.

And so when the regiment left he went on . . .

---

but perhaps one or two more remarks because I can still hear you snickering under your breath and I can imagine what you are thinking of me at this precise moment what a —-k!

> what   a
> —b—-e!
> what   a
> s——d —s!
> what   a
> ——————p!

after all it's not very thrilling not very original not very unusual not very amusing nor very entertaining what he's telling us he should rather shut up remain silent humble modest civilized polite etc disappear stop! well maybe that's what you think no i refuse i refus i ref i re i r i r!

Like him I came out of the hole built my life made myself with imagination and will power and while playing double or nothing with my life with the life of others all you have to do if you want to know is consult the other version of my life the other script the noodle version and you'll see what I mean therefore you understand my dear fellows why if eventually you decide if

Isn't it your role to decide!

if my story is useless valueless

if it is readable recitable

well I don't give a shit because what matters here
is the playfulness of the matter
the interplay of the situation therefore relax

relax and listen
hang on here I go
here we go full speed
full blast unless you guys have another question
but all that crap about the system of social structures of capitalism
skip it
skip it I have no answers
OK you say OK
you even say that as a matter of fact within the social system of
capitalistic structures this whole story has no problematic

no order
no form no ideology there are rather more minuses than pluses in
it

(and what about pusles and misuses)   no
depth   no aesthetic value this tory in other words no
philosophy!
And from the point of view of linguistics truly bad

poor
not publishable to be totally redone
from beginning to end well gentlemen (ladies and gentlemen
because now I see a few ladies among you) I say to you merde
remerde and reremerde you can go wipe your asses with it but
what about the commercial value? yes did you consider the commercial value?
Did you think about that? Not yet!

Hey what are you guys doing! what's happening? are you asleep? ok! forget it!

forward! here we go! CHARGE! forward march! (en avant la musique) quick quick

I continue (sonofabitch there's more than than 20 of you now out there a real crowd

a ceremony move closer! Hey! you over there! yes you! the shorty with the hat!

come in front or else you won't be able to hear to see a damn thing! that's it!

much better but please don't feel obliged to stay! Is everybody ready?

Everybody comfortable?) And so where was I? What was he saying?

X

a typical little error

This time we dive in
we plunge in
we move forward
we progress rather than digress
we push on
we organize rather than disorganize
we recite correctly
we keep it going neatly
we don't fuck around any more
we don't try to be fancy
to say more than we know
we do it right
we pull no punches
we pile up the stuff in a straight line along a linear course of action
we tell it as he told it
we try not to exaggerate too much
we say it as we heard it!
It was six in the morning, a Wednesday, in
1951, in February, when all the guys in the regiment climbed
into the trucks. They were impeccable in their combat uniforms.
Full pack. Ready for action. And talkative. I was there with
Moinous and we were watching them. Joking with them. Ah
what a bunch of cruds! Eh Frenchy Baby . . . they were shouting at me . . . keep an eye on the fort . . . don't put on my
civies . . . don't jerk off too much . . Eh Frenchy don't let them
little gooks shoot you full of holes . . . don't forget to spitshine
my boots . . . motherfuckers . . . Eh watch out for them
sneaky chinoiseries youall . . . fuck off . . . Eh if my little
chick writes tell her I adore her Frenchy . . . pisspots . . . and
tell her that I'll stick my delicious banana up her prune next time
I've got a furlough . . . bunch of fat masturbators . . . you

guys couldn't even peel a lousy radish . . . so long Frenchy and fuck you . . . same to you . . . smile Frenchy . . . enculés! Well that's approximately what we said to each other that morning. I don't remember the rest. Not exactly. It was a rather cold morning. Thick fog. Thick gray fog like a G.I. blanket. The sun wasn't even up yet. I had put on my heavy combat jacket on top of my sweater (useless detail you guys will say but at least he was warm).

The Captain shook hands with me.
I gave him a sharp salute at attention. Chest out.
                                        Heels together.
                                        Toes at a 36° angle.
Good luck . . . Frenchy!
It was the first time he called me Frenchy. Thank you SIR!

And then the trucks left in a cloud of dust and noise. It was all empty now. Deserted. Cold. Except for Moinous and I. We stood there for a few minutes watching the trucks disappear in the blanket of fog and then suddenly we both had a feeling of sadness there in the chest. A sort of complex of inferiority. Ah yes! it's tough to get rid of yourself in the army as Céline used to say. What solitude suddenly!
And yet there were other guys left behind. Some cripple some bureaucrats. All the brown noses, the goldbrickers, the useless ones in other words the fuck offs. Left behind to take care of the joint. To do all the crappy little duties. Clean up the barracks. Pick up the shit. Cook the disgusting grub. Guard the place. All of them masturbators of the first order. But all the rest of the guys they had left (in the trucks).

But in our barrack [Company C] there was only Moinous and I. Only the two of us.

Moinous and I we had to wait for our travel orders to be ready. We waited two days. We kept checking at Headquarters. What's your hurry the staff sergeant said to us?

The first night Moinous and I we spent half of the night in his mailroom talking and listening to jazz records (he had quite a collection Moinous) and smoking cigarettes (Luckies) and around three or four in the morning we went to sleep Moinous on the second floor and me on the main floor we could have changed beds if we had wanted to to sleep next to each other and talk some more but me I liked my bed I was used to it and Moinous he liked his bed too on the second floor he was used to it and so we didn't change beds and when we were finished talking and listening to his jazz records and when we had smoked all our Luckies he went up to his bed on the second floor and me to mine on the main floor and I heard him move around upstairs for a while getting undressed and then it was all silent.

I wondered if Moinous too he jerked off every night under his khaki blankets like all the other jerks in the outfit.

I didn't fall asleep immediately. I was restless. Anxious. But eventually I fell into a delicious dream full of music. A blue dream (I won't tell you the dream because it was really filthy). In any case I slept well that night. No sighs no pumping no jerking all around me. None of that hullabaloo under the khaki blankets. No feverish pricks erected in the night. Except mine. But I didn't touch it. I didn't feel like it. Only the huge silence and deep solitude. And a touch of apprehension at the corner of the heart and inside the throat.

But then all that vanished into the blue dream where I saw myself smiling.

I did wake up once in the middle of the night to take a leak and Moinous shouted to me from upstairs Eh Frenchy you're beating your meat?

You're crazy man I shouted back go to sleep and I slipped back into my blue dream!

The next morning it was the big medical visit. Bareass with the doctor's fingers squeezing our balls and searching inside our asses. And then the shots. Wow the shots! Dammit did those little cocksuckers of medics enjoy themselves. At least a dozen. In both arms. In the thighs. In the ass. I almost fainted twice. All kinds of shots to protect us from all the Asiatic fevers. Those sneaky bastards of medics in their white uniforms they had hard-ons just sticking the needles in us. Bunch of dirty pédales! And another one. And another one. Didn't we forget to give him the Yellow Fever? Here bring your ass over here for Syphilis. And Diarrhea! And another one there in the corner of your cute ass Frenchy for madness. Swisssh! Hang on we're almost finished.

When it was all finished Moinous and I we staggered back to our barrack like two vegetable strainers. It hurt all over. We couldn't sit down we couldn't lie down. We just stood around like two pieces of human shit. And then they called us at Headquarters. Our travel papers were ready.

But me I was fucked!

Everything was in order — A-OK — except that some papers (certain documents the screwy staff sergeant explained) necessary for them to pay me my thirty days' leave in advance and my traveling expenses well these documents they had left with the trucks and the regiment for the snows of Upper New York.

Typical little error!

In a cloud of dust they had left my documents. The only thing to do the clever sergeant at Headquarters explained if you want to collect your dough is to get your ass up to CAMP DRUMP (near the Canadian border) it's only 3 or 4 hundred miles north of New York City and there they'll pay you on the spot immediately.

At first it really bugged the shit out of me the idea of wasting my time for a stupidity like that wasting part of my thirty days but finally I told myself why not! I've never seen that part of the country. I'll take advantage of this (typical) error to make a detour up there. In the snows. Might be fun. Part of the discovery!

Therefore in my mind everything was settled but Moinous didn't agree with me he kept saying to me that I should bitch about the fucking error after all I needed the dough for the trip and a month's pay in advance in those days man for a corporal (don't forget that he was a corporal) it's a good 150 bucks or more and add to this another 75 or so for traveling expenses (ah for that the American army you can't complain they really take care of you!) and he was right Moinous because for the time being me I had exactly 22 dollars and 35 cents in my pocket (two dollars and 35 cents left from the last pay day and twenty dollars from the last four love letters he'd scribbled in a hurry before the guys left for the maneuvers what a memory that guy had) just enough for gas (and a few sandwiches) to get as far as New York perhaps. Wooow did it garggle up gasoline that damn Buick of mine! Unbelievable! What a lemon that tank! But once in New York it'll be alright because Marilyn would certainly give me some money if I needed some (he blushed). For that she was really generous. What a fine woman!

But Moinous he insisted that I ought to bitch about that and tell them that if they didn't pay me now immediately on the spot then they can go shove it and that you're not going after all it's their mistake not yours and therefore it's up to them to do something about it Moinous kept saying and to be quite frank he was right it was their mistake yes but all that is theoretical and it's your problem the staff sergeant told me (what an ass!) so it's up to you to decide whether or not you want to collect your dough after all personally I don't give a damn what you do but if I was in your shoes and I needed the money well I wouldn't hesitate a moment but of course he was only speculating he was not me that smartass but he was right and so I said okay to myself I'll go up there to CAMP DRUM in the snows to pick up my dough it might be fun anyway and that's it I'll go up there in my Buick in fact this way it'll give me a bit more time with it before parting with it that means that I'll have to come back to New York yes I'll sell it in New York should be able to get 200 bucks for it or maybe 150 even if I have to put an ad in the New York Times at the last moment a Buick like that especially a 1947 a special with radio heater and white wall tires must be worth a few bucks on the market but in any case if I need extra money to get to CAMP DRUM surely Marilyn will for that she was always generous always managed to squeeze one or two bills my way behind BENNY's back as a kind of consolation I suppose!

In any case that night (our last night in the 82nd) we were happy
like kids Moi-Nous-and-Me!
Finally SO LONG

> the 82nd
> Fort Bragg
> Fayetteville
> North Carolina

We were leaving the following morning   early!
    But we stayed up anyway late into the night before
going to bed listening to Lester Young and smoking
cigarettes until we fell asleep inside our dreams!

XI

a good start

The Sun Rose at 7:53 that Morning in February 1951!

It was cold like hell (in spite of the clear blue sky). Moinous and I we met as prearranged in front of the barrack with our duffel bags fat like the rump of two rhinoceroses. Sharp and neat and shiny and stiff like two toy soldiers in our parade uniforms. Jump boots like mirrors spitshined at least for 45 minutes and we had spent another 25 minutes   tongues sticking out
polishing our   silver birdie

PARATROOPERWINGS

(well only the wings of the little birdie)

We looked at each other with pride and admiration we inspected each other smiling and suddenly like one man without any warning without even having consulted each other we flopped down into the dirt into the dry North Carolina dirt and pumped a good dozen push ups ass up in the air there in our beautiful parade dress stiff like a pair of trampolines and when that dozen was finished we pumped another good dozen for good measure UP & DOWN just like that just to relax (nice and easy) for kicks but especially to prove to ourselves once & for all that now the 82nd AIRBORNE DIVISION it could go fuck itself and we even pumped a third dozen UP & DOWN to prove it even more ass up in the air until we fell flat on our faces like one man in the dust

right there in our pretty uniforms laughing giggling rolling on top
of each other legs all tangled up and it's there dusty cruddy messy
resting on one elbow that we engaged in a little dialogue that will
now be quoted in its entirety since it was the last dialogue I ever
had (yes the LAST dialogue) with Moinous before getting on our
way!

— So you're coming with me to Nouillorque in my Buick?
— No not me old man I've decided to go down to Florida.
— Florida! What the fuck ya gonna do down t'ere? You're sick?
— No I'm gonna visit my aunt Augusta.
— Your what?
— My aunt! She's a fantastic cook. She makes me delicious fried
  chicken and apple pie. And you know three or four days in the
  sun man that'll pep me up for the rest of the trip.
— Where is it in Florida your aunt?
— Tallahassee.
— Ta la ah what?
— TAL LA HAS SEE . . . don't you know? You wanna come?

[florida wow I was really tempted but I didn't have enough]
[dough right now for such a detour no better get up to]
[new york and then up to camp drum and collect my damn]
[money bunch of motherfuckers up there in the snow and]
[then we'll see I suppose he would have loaned me some]
[money moinous if I had asked him to go with him visit]
[his aunt particularly since I love fried chicken it's]
[too bad but I really should see marilyn first and get]
[rid of my stuff and say goodbye to my uncle he wasn't]
[dead yet because after all it was his fault if I came]
[to america he was responsible originally three fucked]
[up years already dammit no better forget florida down]
[south for the time being maybe next time yes the next]
[trip another journey another story after all my trips]
[have taken me to places even further than florida and]
[florida it's not that far except that you have to cut]
[south rather than north through georgia from here yes]

— Too bad! No I can't.

— Too bad!

— You're really a dumb guy MOINOUS here I go offering you a
free ride all the way up to Nouillorque and what do you do you
decide to go down to Florida. It's in the wrong direction man
south in the sun.

— Yeah in the sun. In the other direction. Why not! You don't get
it Frenchy. You're a dumb ass.

We were still lying there in the dirt arguing Florida versus New
York when suddenly out of nowhere a lieutenant colonel in
fatigues walks by.

WHAT THE HELL YOU TWO GUYS DOING DOWN THERE!

We snapped up like one man chest out at attention and flipped
him a quick salute.   He threw one back at us.

CORPORAL!

I took a step forward.

IT'S A DETAIL SIR . . . I'M IN CHARGE . . . WE'RE
FIELDSTRIPPING CIGARETTE BUTTS SIR!

AT EASE . . . CARRY ON . . . BUT WITH A BIT MORE
MILITARY DECORUM!

YES SIR!

He left.

We didn't even ask ourselves what the fuck he was doing here
that lieutenant colonel rather than being up there in the snows
with the rest of the regiment. Another goldbricker.

We simply brushed each other's uniforms. Rectified ourselves a
little and went on with our dialogue.

— In any case I'll see you in Frisco, hey! (It's him speaking). And
from Florida which way you're heading?

— I don't know yet. Maybe up to Boston. You know my family.
And then I'll see. Maybe I'll make all kinds of little detours to

visit my relatives. I've got some everywhere. I'll take advantage of these thirty days.

— You lucky son of a bitch! And this way it'll be cheaper for you. You can sleep and eat with your relatives.

— Yeah!

— Well have a good time. And we'll see each other in Frisco. In about 30 days, hmm! . . . So long!

— So long! . . . See you man!

And . . . just like that . . . he disappeared BOB MOINOUS towards Florida with his duffel bag on his shoulder that beautiful morning in February 1951 (it was a Saturday, I think). I didn't even have time to say to him Hey maybe we'll bump into each other on the road! But I already know what BOB would have said (in his usual easygoing manner) Yes, maybe! In any case I never saw him again . . . except in San Francisco . . . but he was already dead . . . !

DEAD . . . DEAD! [With a general movement of surprise and disappointment]

Dead yes DEAD! Assassinated! A knife in the chest. In a filthy bar in San Francisco. Yes DEAD! Just like that — for nothing. For a dumb remark. I don't know. A stupid argument.

I was called in at the morgue to identify the body. Body number 48. All violet. I threw up afterwards. Almost threw up on top of Moinous' body I was so scared when they lifted the sheet. They had tied an orange tag yes an orange tag the color struck me around one of his big toes. I had never seen Moinous so badly shaven. In any case he had made it all the way here all the way to Frisco. Thirty days later. As prearranged. In fact, even before me.

But they killed him. They assassinated him. In a bar. I had lost my best friend. The best part of me. And yet he was not the type to argue with the first guy he met. Must have been some kind of mix-up. Ah! if only I had been there!

Therefore we'll never know what really happened. Not only in Frisco. But during Moinous' trip across the country. What he did what he saw and what he felt. What he discovered. Nothing! All that was cancelled now. Gone forever. But what is certain is that he made the trip. He made it. Yes I saw his body. I identified it for the cops and for the record. Number 48!

He made it from coast to coast!
But it's that kind of a story that makes you realize what a bitchy thing life is. Reality! Life and Death! Me too I made it to Frisco. Me too (he said) since I'm telling you the story of Moinous' death, even though I arrived too late. Coast to Coast! And in fact, it was *dans les côtes* yes dammit *dans les côtes* that Moinous got the knife.   Son of a bitch!

Later on, on the boat which was taking me towards my adventures across the Pacific, one night, alone on the upper deck, eyes in the stars, hair wind blown, vomit up my throat, while the other guys were playing poker or masturbating down below (full blast) totally unconcerned, I started crying like a kid about Moinous!

But perhaps I'm anticipating a bit too much. We'll get to that later on or eventually. But for the time being he was still alive Moinous (quite obviously) and on his way to Florida after our little dialogue (on foot) and me I watched him disappear over the horizon with his duffel bag over his shoulder and his skinny legs tottering underneath him — all alone!

SO LONG MOINOUS° so long I whispered to myself!

Of course that whole dialogue I have just quoted it's no longer the
real thing, the original. It's more or less reinvented because what
was said between them that morning, the real words they spoke
(there, in front of the barrack, that morning) there is no way to
remember that exactly, but in any case, that's how we left each
other, without really knowing if we would ever see each other
again, before arriving in San Francisco, where we were supposed
to be, thirty days later (exactly) as of today (that is to say as of that
Saturday, in 1951, in February) official date in fact!

Official date of their 30 days' leave (the GREAT JOURNEY) because officially their 30 days began as of the day they were given
their travel orders (which means the day before they departed
that Saturday morning after their meeting and final conversation
in front of the barrack) therefore on Friday but by a stroke of luck
or a mistake the fat sergeant at Headquarters had stamped the
date of the next day (Saturday in other words) on their travel
orders rather than the date (the official date) of Friday and so in a
way he had given our two travelers an extra day's leave (whether
or not this was intentional will never be known) but in any case
they had exactly 30 days as of that Saturday and not the preceding
Friday to report to San Francisco but only 30 days and no more the
sergeant emphasized otherwise you guys will be AWOL (deser-
ters I should even say because there is a war on even though it is
not an officially declared war) and you guys know the regulations
you've been warned therefore I suggest you get your asses to San
Francisco on time for the boat otherwise . . .

Therefore . . . SO LONG MOINOUS° I finally shouted but he had already vanished over the horizon into the fog (that damn North Carolina fog) towards Florida and the sun and the orange trees and his aunt Augusta with her fried chicken and her apple pie and ME I jumped in my BUICK special threw my duffel bag on the back seat but before starting the motor and slowly let go the clutch (it was in bad shape the clutch) I lit a cigarette folded my arms all around the steering wheel rested my chin there to think for a while to meditate reflect

. . . . ? [A bosomy lady with feathers on her hat]
What did he think about? Oh you know lady! The usual stuff. You're asking me too much. He didn't go into the details of his thoughts. He thought for a while that's all. One does not really remember what one thinks about in a moment like that.
In retrospect. Sad. Alone. Depressed. Particularly on such a day when one feels apprehensive about leaving a rather cozy place after all. When one sees one's best buddy departing in the wrong direction not knowing in fact if one will ever see him again. Alive!
What did he think about?
He simply contemplated his life. L$_{e_{a_n}e}$d over his past. I suppose.
His future.
He thought about all his troubles : his money up there in the snow of Upper New York State.
He thought about death. And love too (he hadn't had a piece of ass in ten days he told me).

Two hours later he had already gone past Richmond in Virginia and rolling along on Highway 101. Not too far now from Washington. From D.C. Quite excited about it.
And going well. Direction N.Y.

Indeed rolling along (about 75 miles per hour). But the radio wasn't working. Never fails. Therefore I was whistling while driving to pass the time. Jazz tunes. Noodling along happily.

And then it started raining (it was inevitable). My windshield wipers didn't work too well and it was hard to see the road in front of me.
And it was slippery (but one must live dangerously he said with a smile).

What a disgusting place Virginia! Ugly landscape. But I kept going (full speed) in spite of the rain about 75 miles per hour and even a bit faster downhill.
In other words a damn good start.
Rolling along!
I was wondering if it wouldn't be preferable to go up directly to CAMP DRUM in the snows to collect my dough if it wouldn't be preferable for the time being to skip New York because of Marilyn to whom I'd have to explain everything the FAR EAST the 30 days *volunteered you're crazy* I could at least have told her but then I remembered that I had only not even 14 bucks left (I had already filled up once sonofabitch that damn BUICK of mine did it garggle up gas) 14 bucks and a few pennies (and a quick stop for a snack sunnysides up and coffee a buck and a half plus tip) certainly not enough to get all the way up to CAMP DRUM (the dumb sergeant said 3 or 4 hundred miles north of New York a good day's ride seven or eight hours with that damn tank of mine) no better stop for a few hours in New York borrow some dough from Marilyn (15 or 20 dollars should do it) unless she gives it to me outright yes it's preferable I think
therefore
it's all set everything going well

no need to worry about it and in any case after CAMP DRUM I'll
see yes maybe I'll come back to New York spend a few days with
Marilyn (two or three maximum) our dear Marilyn (and Benny
too) and of course visit my uncle even if we don't really understand each other say goodbye to all my possessions faire mes
adieux and maybe even have a last partouze (a farewell screwing)
with Marilyn dammit do I need it if we can work out something
therefore
everything seems to work out
no need to worry and get rid of my stuff all my possessions all my
old goodies my former life my civies my books (not that he had
too many of them a few Camus and Sartre and a few detective
stories yes you know I remember he said la série jaune) and my
records my jazz records (78's) I had quite a collection too I was
proud of my jazz collection damn right even though they were all
78's
everything in other words
my whole lousy civilian life my private life three years of America
I tell you it's not much when one thinks about it not much to talk
about not very much not a very big package three years of one's
life in America it's easy to get rid of it
dump it
therefore
everything is settled no problems particularly now that I was
leaving for good no need to keep all that junk
either I get knocked off over there (it's quite possible) or else I
don't get knocked off but in either case I don't come back that's for
sure they can keep their American shit
finie l'Amérique
damn right America as they say on their bumper stickers LOVE IT
OR LEAVE IT well me I say TAKE IT OR LEAVE IT
America for the birds

therefore

no more of that crap fed up and if I'm not dead in the FAR EAST then I'll settle out there in Hong Kong or in Tokyo anywhere I'll start a business exportation or else I'll take off for Africa (yes Dakar with my aunt Rachel on my mother's side he explained without any specific details)

therefore

my old junk my possessions my stuff of former life I don't need it any more let somebody else take advantage of it what do I care and if eventually I do come back I'll buy new stuff brand new stuff because in a case like mine it's normal.

XII

**remembering Charlie Parker or how to get it out of
your system**

Oop Bop Sh'Bam . . . ? [Out of nowhere]

Ah!   You guys want to talk about jazz!

You guys want me to tell you how he went on and on raving about jazz!

There he was racing along Highway 101 raving about jazz, whistling jazz tunes to himself, noodling along. Yes, today what I miss the most it's my old jazz collection (he told me afterwards). What a treasure it was my old jazz collection — mostly BEBOP (all 78s), because in those days that's what jazz GREAT JAZZ was all about (the great days of BEBOP, you can't deny that). All scratched up. I had them all. All scratched up by the needle. All the Charlie Parker, all the Dizzy, Miles, and a few Bud Powell, Monk, Prez, and some Dexter Gordon. But especially Wardell Gray. Ah, Wardell Gray! Did I love that cat. What a tone! Ah what a sound! No shitting. The big mouth of the tenor. I was a real fanatic a real nut of the sax in those days. An addict (he started scatting an old tune jiggling his fingers in front of him blowing an imaginary sax) a real addict!

Ah!

Ah!   You guys too! That's nice. Yes but that guy he lived that stuff from the inside (in DETROIT) with all those cats in 47, 48, 49 who were revolutionizing jazz. He knew them all (proudly)!

Yes, I've known them all. We were buddies. No kidding! In Detroit in Shitcity. Yes in Detroit at first and then in New York. Yes, me too I blew the sax (a little). Tenor! And not that badly. (No, no more! He gave it up. Gave it up in New York. Fifty bucks for his sax in a pawn shop). All 78s! Alto sax too. And even the clarinet once in a while! All 78s. The one I miss the most now is the record where Parker blows his famous solo, that incredible solo,

on LOVER MAN. That was the day when he collapsed, passed
out on stage, fell down like a bag

like a bag of sawdust!

Loaded! Looped! Gone!

Yes that was during a concert. Towards the end of the solo (alto -
damn right). Couldn't even finish his solo he was so high. But
towards the end, WOW, does it move. Does it squeak! Unbelievable. Like cries, yes screams out of his guts.

Like a bag of sawdust!

He dropped

wow what a stinking highway

A real madness!

I had that one!   Yes in 78.   The original.

(ah, they've brought it out again! No I didn't
know. Doesn't matter)   Yes, but mine it was all scratched up
I'd played it so much. And there was even a little piece missing. A
broken piece just at the beginning. But I didn't give a damn
because that one I knew literally by heart — forward and backward.

From beginning to end!

LOVER MAN @@@   TA TA TA TUUMMM @@@
                   TA TA TA TA TA TUUUMMMMM
                   @@@

TA TA TA TUUMMM   @@@   ta   ta
                   TUUUMMMM

                              taa tata

tata tatatuuumm   @@@m   TREMENDOUS!

Gentlemen JAZZ you can't imagine how it was how it was for him what it was what it was for him to have lived it from the inside as he did in 47 in 48 in 49 he was there!

Yes I was there. I was part of it — in 47 in 48 — the great moments of BEBOP — in 49 — progressive jazz! I was there at the cool Metropolitan Bopera House.

Yes, ME, I was there. I knew them all. And you've got to have known all these cats to understand how much that stuff was eating them up down deep in there — in the GUTS. All my buddies (in DETROIT) they were jazz bums all of them terrific musicians. They had that in their skin man.

Of course they were all black! There's not a single bright light who can (as far as I know) blow real jazz.   NOT ONE!
BRIGHT LIGHT — ! — BULLSHIT — ! — 906 906 906 906 906 906 906 906 906

(o) (o) (o) (o) (o) (o) (o) (o) (o)

_____-

in 47 in 48 in 49 I would make deals with my buddies : a bright
light
for   a
shade
—

in fact that's how I discovered AMERICA (he told me) : in the dark!

(o) (o) (o) (o) . . . ?   [With sensual gestures]
Ah!   You guys want to know if they screw well!
[Bunch of perverts!]
Ah! You guys would like to know how well they fuck!
No! Gentlemen, they do not have a funny smell!

Yes! They screw like hell! And beautiful bodies. Skin smooth like the skin of a baby lamb. And teats juicy like grapefruits and asses (ah! the succulent asses of my cute little black chicks! he emphasized) round solid well balanced on magnificent thighs and lovely pink pussies!

Yes! Gentlemen . . . but I'll skip what he told me after that . . . I'll skip all that . . . or else . . . [shit I gotta got to the head in the fucking middle of nowhere on this stinking road wow the landscape round here ain't very brilliant]
. . .
. . .

No! There isn't a single bright light who can blow (or fuck) like all my buddies not a single one not even a cat like Stan Getz and the guy isn't at all bad on tenor no not even Mulligan not even Zoot Sims and these guys can blow they know their stuff . . . not one of them (as far as I know) can swing like my buddies. These white cats it's all cute stuff cool stuff. Doesn't scream like my buddies. Okay it's full of ideas sweet ideas but ideas come from the brains not from the guts and it's from the stomach — THE GUTS MAN and not from the brains that the real stuff comes out! Just listen to Prez listen to Miles Trane yes listen to Monk Clifford Brown then you can hear I tell you you can hear the guts squeaking crying bursting!

No! I'm not saying that you have to be an expert. That you have to know the background the history. Everything. That you have to have studied all the musical shit in a conservatory. Music. Discography. All I'm saying I mean is that if it's not there in the belly you don't have it. You see, me, and yet I lived with them, for years and years (IN THE DARK), well I couldn't stand up to them. Couldn't make it.!

But have you ever spent a night, yes an entire night
with Charlie Parker, with Bird, loaded like a donkey,
doped up like a camel or a dromedary (whichever you
prefer), exhausted like a bull who has just climbed a
whole herd of cows but still blowing - BLOWING HIS
BRAINS OUT! Yes, an entire night, in a filthy little
garage (yes in Detroit) toward the end of the 40's, in
1949 to be exact, when Parker was the king the KING
of jazz!

I remember. It was after a concert : JAZZ AT THE
PHILHARMONIC!
I remember.
They were all there:

```
              K   LA
  T     R   NEN C  E   DU           T M Y P  T        D
FA  N AVA 0              KE      T O  M    O  E   &  B
  S   R  R   Y   RK   J    ON                  R     IR
                      ORD
```

of course. And all kinds of other cats!
We all met at Frank's pad (in his garage) after the concert and
blew for a while. It was groovy! And then we all went to the
BLUE BIRD (a crazy gig on the Westside). They were all
there:
                        FATS
                        DUKE
                        KENNY
                           TOMMY & BIRD of
                     course!
And then Wardell Gray walked in!
                              Wow what a jam session!
One of those historical moments!   No kidding!

Me, I was lugging my big black case with my tenor sax inside — a KING! Parker hadn't brought his alto with him after the concert. He had left it at the hotel he explained. I didn't dare play my usual solos. No I was too chicken. I didn't dare that night even when Frank shouted from the stage above the yellow smoke of cigarettes and pot and everybody in the joint heard him and looked at me :

EH FRENCHY MAN COME AND BLOW EH MAN IT'S CRAZY COME AND BLOW YOUR HORN WITH US!

No   I didn't dare.

It was new. Brand new my tenor. I had bought it with the money I saved that summer working as a bus boy in the CATSKILLS in a fancy swanky resort type of a place. It was winter (and what a disgusting winter the winter 1949). I was getting damn good on my tenor. After only a few months. But it was good old Ernest who was teaching me and he knew his stuff. And I practiced a good ten twelve hours a day. Until my lips would start bleeding. In the bathroom! Yes in the BATHROOM because of the sonority. [Dammit I've got to find a latrine]. In those days I was living with a Hungarian family. Just a room with kitchen privileges. Eight bucks a week. It was not a bad place especially since they were never there the Hungarians. So me, I took advantage of the pad. Particularly the bathroom. Sometimes most of the night. The guy was a night watchman and the old lady was out a good part of the night playing canasta. It was really a good deal for me . . . EH SAY MAN CAN I BLOW YOUR HORN?

It was Parker who asked me that. He was standing there, next to me, lost in the big crowd at the BLUE BIRD, lost in the smoke (in a wrinkled gray suit) and it was as though GOD himself had come down (on Earth) to speak to me, to kiss me on the brow, at that very moment, at that pissy moment when I felt so shitty because I didn't have the guts to blow my usual three or four solos that night.

I almost fainted on the spot in front of everybody but I held back because I was with a lovely little broad. Rita. RITA was her name (the one I was screwing then a real nice girl who taught me a great deal about the secrets of love, a peach of a girl, with enormous teats). But when Parker asked me if he could blow my horn I didn't know . . . I didn't know what to do, what to say. I almost fainted . . . YES, I suppose that's what glory is. Glory and Love and Friendship and Pride! I felt my heart bouncing inside my chest. Glory Love Friendship Pride! It must have been at that moment at that precise moment that I understood (for the first time and maybe for the last time) I understood that all men are equal and that no man should ever yes EVER kneel before another man (he didn't say that, but he must have thought about it) yes NEVER but here at this moment, lost in the crowd, Parker's hand still touching my elbow, I almost, yes almost felt like kneeling, like flattening myself, like throwing myself down on the ground to kiss his feet, in a stroke of wild uncontrolled joy
[*I suppose this would be a good place to enumerate all the indignities men endure from one another but what good would it do at this very moment*]   But
what good would it have done . . .

YES i said in a whisper YES OF COURSE MAN . . . i finally managed to say in a kind of chocked up sob . . . !

Have you ever heard Parker blow the tenor?

Yes . . . of course, it's true, they've reissued some
of these where he blows tenor. Yes, but that night, that night
he played a solo — A SOLO that lasted 45 — yes 45 —
minutes ON MY SAXOPHONE! Can you imagine? On my
saxophone.

45 MINUTES

_____-
_____-

> just the piano (Duke) the bass
> (Tommy)
> and Kenny on drums — behind
> him alone

everybody in the place sat down
not a word
not a movement
just the cigarette smoke whirling above the heads into the
music
I swear
I swear there were guys in the place with tears running
down their faces!

A 45 MINUTE SOLO (on MY OLD FLAME) An Historical
Moment!

It was during the winter 1949 (and what a disgusting winter!)
I didn't wipe my MOUTHPIECE for three weeks after that.

> After that when they closed
the joint around three in the morning we all went back to
Frank's garage on the Eastside and it went on until about six
in the morning maybe later.

An incredible jam session. All the guys played even me finally three or four solos with my tenor, and at one point Parker tapped me on the shoulder, in a kind of EH CRAZY MAN congratulatory gesture, after I'd played a tremendous solo, a flight of twenty-four bars on ORNITHOLOGY a fantastic improvisation that came out of me just like that, I don't know how or from where, an inspiration that came out all at once, and all the cats were screaming at me BLOW FRENCHY BLOW, and so I blew, I blew beyond my capacities, beyond my possibilities, beyond the limits of my dexterity, and flew like a bird into musical regions unknown to me until then, virgin musical zones I couldn't believe existed, and I searched, probed, noodled, and suddenly switched key from a major yes a major sharp to a minor flat and let out a stream of chromatics that led me all the way up to a Parkerian squeak and all the cats screamed it was an incredible squeak which I held and held as though I was out of my mind weeping and laughing at the same time in my saxophone BLOW FRENCHY BLOW and I blew my lungs and my heart into my saxophone and I felt everything cracking inside of me my blood rushing to my head and when finally I stopped and wiped my lips with my sleeve there was I'm not kidding there was blood mixed with my sweat there on my sleeve, a streak of blood, and it was then, out of nowhere, that I felt Charlie Parker's hand on my shoulder. I almost wept: @@@@@@@@@@ almost!

==

Had I fallen dead on the spot right then I wouldn't have cared at all I had reached once and for all the summit (summit of summit) which no doubt I would never reach again NEVER again but I had played, finally succeeded in playing my one great solo, I had made it, I had blown my one great

solo and in front of Charlie Parker, for Charlie Parker but
also for all my other buddies all my black buddies who were
shouting to me BLOW FRENCHY BLOW because they understood that I was blowing my guts out fire and flames for
them and against all the shit that life shovels at us from all
directions yes that I was blowing because me too sad and
lonely slob like them I was hurting inside the guts and
because there's so many things ah yes so many things we
want to say to utter to let out but which can never come out
except once in a while unexpectedly in the sound of jazz in
the sweet sound of jazz after a whole night of gasping for
breath collectively of trying to find that one musical phrase a
bit of solo that says it all in the cries of jazz in the madness
and in the frenzy and in the freedom of jazz and me finally I
had managed to speak a few words of music a few clumsy
words of music to those dear brothers and sisters
and then
after that
we all went up to Ernie's pad for a whild collective jerking-
off session and some pot, but Parker and the rest of the
musicians from the concert from the Philarmonic they didn't
come up with us they didn't come up with us they didn't up
it with us to Ernie's pad because they were too tired (they
explained) they all split back to their hotel to sleep it off and
it's understandable since these cats were all exhausted after
a big night like that, but the rest of the guys came and we
were all quite excited. Everybody got promptly undressed
naked [no! all the broads had left to go to bed yes either alone
or else with the cats who made it with them] in a frenetic
mood. I had a little complex (complex of inferiority) next to
my black buddies because these guys had enorMOUS pricks
(at rest theirs was almost the dimension of mine in erection)

but we started working in there masturbating in there fin-
gering it in there with such vitality ah yes with such frenzy
with such joy and such insolence that soon me I no
longer felt ashamed of my mediocre dimensions
and I didn't think about anything except to
keep up at all cost with all the others
even if my ugly little thing was
smaller and more shriveled up
than theirs and I kept up
I kept up to the end
jerk after jerk (individual and collective)
full speed and slow motion
and we would pass our dicks to one another
stiff jubilant happy juicy
so that everyone would share in the pleasure and the improvisation

WHAT A COCKSESSION WHAT WORK AH WHAT FIREWORKS!

You guys may think I'm exaggerating what he told me but
you should have seen his face while he was telling me this ah
you should have seen the faces he said the twisted grimaces
of joy the glassy eyes bulging out of the sockets the naked
bodies strong black and shiny like pieces of furniture (except
mine, he said sadly, which seemed out of place in there, as it
should be obvious, but nobody had any time to care or to
notice) bouncing around hopping along as though dancing
to the sound of some inner ancestral music, and you should
have heard the heavy breathing the little cries and groans
and the puffing the general giggling and exaltation! And as
soon as a guy felt that it was coming he would rush towards
the middle of the room where a large porcelain dish had
been placed

on the floor   on a little piece
of square carpet (an oriental, he specified) to unload freely   so
that our sperms would mix without any prejudice

                                                              and
suddenly   one of the guys (a mad cat, high as you've never
seen)   let out a wild cry while slapping his chest à la
Tarzan picked up the plate and drank the whole mixture (the whole soup
in other words) to the last drop   without even stopping to take
a breath of air.

                                              That's friendship
for you, that's real love, I said to myself.   Everybody
applauded in the midst of wild cries of appreciation.

                                              A friend like
that is hard to find, I told myself   And he did appreciate in
a very personal way he did appreciate our encouragements

                                                              you
could see that in his way of wiping his mouth afterwards   in his eyes
too and also in the way he threw his shoulders back as he tiptoed to his
corner.   But after
this glorious, symbolic, magnificent gesture I felt somewhat guilty to be
quite frank because it occurred to me that I should have been first to think
of such a gesture   I should have been the one
to perform such a symbolic act   [not really I said to him trying to
reassure him]
                    [no, no]   after all I was
the outsider here, in this noble gathering, yes it should have been me the
mediocre white-skinned who should have thought of that   but no
one mentioned anything   no one looked at me   no one as a
matter of fact   noticed my embarrassment   and so we all went back
to work with even more fervor   more enthusiasm than before   some of us working on our fourth or fifth turn.   Little
butts of pot rolled by hand were being passed from lips to lips and we
would drag on those yellowish butts slowly and deeply and affection-
ately   but let me tell you (he emphasized) however we were not
smoking that stuff in 48 in 49 in 50 in order to take trips   NO   or to
escape or to negate life   NO   [ladies & gentlemen] on the contrary   in those days it was strictly to get excited   to get it up
[sexually, he added proudly] to solidify our hard-ons.   And so
after the guys had stopped applauding the guy who had emptied the
plate we all started working again   and it was a race to see who
would come the fastest and the most profusely   there was a guy
who kept score on a piece of paper with a red pencil   and each
time a guy unloaded everybody would shout at his success without any
sign of envy   we were all very liberal in those days   equal in
our pleasure   one and for all

I didn't do too badly, I ended up sixth on the grand total, sixth place that is, which is not bad, not bad at all, if one considers that in all were a good dozen that night, doing it individually and collectively in Ernie's pad, finishing ourselves, emptying ourselves so to say or to be more exact blowing away the last chords of our inner music, and then we all collapsed, all fell down to the floor, on top of each other pell mell, to go to sleep, like angels, like babies rather, and we slept, we snored together, naked, sweaty, shivering, until about five or six, and even later, in the afternoon, and there were guys who slept clinging to other guys' legs or arms, or even holding on to each other's penis with delicate fingers, stretched next to each other and on top of each other on the side, face to face, back to back, bodies folded in fetal designs one might say, so that we could feel closer to one another, more secure in each other's dreams, and some guys were speaking in their sleep, and others were laughing in their sleep, and others singing bla bla bla qua qua qua, and others scatting in their sleep oop bop sh'bam yado yadoyea bidobidobido, it was beautiful, yes, we all had beautiful dreams in our heads, blue dreams, like waves

‿⌢‿⌢‿⌢‿⌢‿⌢‿⌢‿⌢‿⌢‿⌢

XIII

anticipating the worse

I don't know why he said I told you this whole story why I let myself go like that he deplored getting all sentimental all worked up like a jerk over such old memories here above the past the near past I could drop the whole thing you know he said but at least it passed the time took me away from my troubles filled my head for a while and it gives you something to report while my old beat-up Buick races along toward New York and more problems ahead no doubt in this pissy landscape yea what piss poor landscape in Virginia and it rains comme une vache qui pisse in and out of the landscape and suddenly in the middle of these sentimental waves over the hills and down the valleys inside the blue dreams psitt bang shit crap what's happening dammit a blow out son of a bitch he said remembering his blow out that's all I needed . . . okay no need to describe the details of the repair . . . the changing of the tire in the rain . . . sloppy and clumsy . . . suffices to say that I had a spare tire in my trunk a jack and the proper tools . . . not in great shape the spare tire but good enough for the time being . . . and I was back on the road in less than five minutes . . . but crapidouille was I filthy and wet . . . I couldn't get back to my noodling . . . so confused too . . . it was all fucked up in my head now . . . no more music no more be bop no more sweet sound of jazz memories . . . it was a mess . . . all screwed up inside my head the improvisations . . . ah he said it's hard to start all over again from zero as I was trying to do and yet a guy must . . . sometimes it's necessary . . . especially in a situation lousy situation such as mine . . . and yet . . . I don't know what took me what got into me . . . maybe it's because I've got that in my skin . . . in my guts . . . bugs me all the time . . . even though my skin is white . . . my skin

. . . but as long as we are on that subject these guys they didn't give a damn about my skin or even my foreskin whether or not it was nice and shiny like theirs white yellow pink or even striped they didn't care unimportant for them what was important is that I was French ah yes that meant something to them because these black cats they thought the French were not racist what an illusion really dumb naive of them to think that no prejudices the French ah don't make me laugh bullshit no bigotry what a joke could I tell you stories about the French and their cute sense of equality crap well that's what they thought those black cats to each his dream no need to disillusion them personally I don't give a damn if they love the French and have a false vision of reality for all I know he may have invented the whole story but meanwhile   he   shouted   forward   march   and en
     avant
          la
          zizique   as the French say!
                                   If I have time
during the trip I'll tell you the rest. all the cute little black chicks I fucked in Detroit. skin smooth like the skin of a baby lamb. shades in the ass. man. Ernie would say to me. you get me a bright light and right off man I'll get you a shade. I'll tell you everything. the jam sessions all night. my whole life in shitcity Detroit. the factories. and all the other jobs I had. degrading jobs. parking lot attendant. soda jerk. baby sitter. grocery store clerk. street cleaner. garbage man. and then after work. late at night. blowing my horn in all the gigs. for nothing. a few beers. yeah man. he would say to me Ernie. a bright light. a tight white blond pussy. where I can squeeze my big black cock and I'll find you man a big fat shade that'll

suck the shit out of you. wow. balls and all wow can those shades suck. yes if I have the time I'll tell you all that. on the road. but meanwhile there he was in his 1947 Buickspecial. black. on his way to New York when suddenly around three or four in the afternoon of that first day on the road he said to himself HEY SAY it'd be fun to pass by Detroit to see all my old buddies if they're still there: Ernie Tommy Franky Kenny, ah! that cocksucker Kenny could he blow his guitar! Yes I've got eyes to see them all again!

But it wouldn't pay.

Wouldn't be the same,

we wouldn't have nothing more to say to each other.

No more sweet music. No more beboptalk. Finished.

You understand he said sadly I didn't have it in me no more. Didn't have it in the guts any more. It was hopeless for me. No class. Had to give it up. No not like them I mean. Not good enough. These cats Tommy Franky Kenny they had that in their skin from way back. Made it big too for a while even though they may be starving at it now. Not Ernie though. Never made it Ernie. No not a lucky guy Ernie. Not stubborn enough not hurting enough inside I suppose. Like all the rest. Went into the badass army instead. About the same time I did. For life though. 20 year stretch. A lifer . . . . . *saxosexisexosaxo* . . . ? [Little guy with one finger up in the air] Ah! His saxophone? You guys want to know what happened to his horn I suppose! His tenor Sax!

No, he didn't have it any more he told me. As we sat under our tree on several occasions. In a pawn shop. In New York. Just before going in the army he explained. Yes on Sixth Avenue. When I was shacking up or starving it up rather with Loulou (remember LOULOU? The Noodles?) Was I on

a downer then. Real bad low. On Sixth Avenue for fifty
bucks the bastards! FIFTY BUCKS for a KING! And still like
new. Had cost me at least 300 originally. That was the end of
the SAX for me. In New York it was Loulou's idea. Even sold
the pawn ticket for five bucks to some jerk eventually. The
dumbest stupidest thing I ever did. For 5 bucks!
But the hell with it. It's another story. Forget it. And now I was
not too far from Washington ————— about 50 miles or so
————- but I wasn't going to stop to do some sightseeing NO not
this time forget it ————-
no time to lose
not now
better get up to New York directly ————- another 8 hours or so
—— straight on ————-
It was a good twelve hours or more by car in those days from
Fort Bragg to New York they didn't have the big highways
yet the superhighways going through all the cities (the big
ones and the small ones) Richmond Washington Philadel-
phia and all of New Jersey that stinking filthy smelly New
Jersey ——-

twelve hours
and it kept raining cats and dogs
I couldn't waste too much time
time is precious
time is long too
time is shit too

The Motherfuckers!   Typical little error he said
                    My ass!   Typical solecism!
I should have told that fat sergeant I ain't gonna go on no fucking
chicken-shit detail like that!   Stick it!
Wow was I pissed off.   Normally I should have

collected my thirty days' pay in advance (I think he said that already) I should have collected that at Fort Bragg (in North Carolina) and my travel expenses on top of that but now because of that stupid little error ——— it's north of New York City about three hundred miles I estimate.

All my other papers were in order (my dossier he said) except they had goofed with the documents (fuck you with your documents) which were essential to pay me (unbelievable the American army: bunch of fuckups)!

——— the only thing to do the sergeant at the payroll office said if you want to collect your money is to get your ass up North to Camp Drum near the Canadian border.

Up North! Shit!

——— yes about three hundred miles north (northeast in fact) in Upper New York State.

Dammit!

———-if not it could take a good week or so maybe more if we ask them to send them documents back down here.

% % % % % % % % % % % % % % % % - doesn't pay to stick around this shithole!

——— a good week or so if we ask them to send your documents back down here therefore if you want my advice you better get your ass up there (near the Canadian border).

And why not I said to myself after all I've never seen that corner of the country it'll be part of the discovery part of the journey!

A guy must be practical. Don't you think so? Realistic rather in moments such as these. Don't you agree? Therefore in my head (as I kept whistling jazz tunes after having changed the tire) I began to work out while driving my Buickspecial the little details of my unfortunate detour up north I projected myself forward so to speak up north because the meaning of such a posteriori events may prove crucial in the future development of this recitation best be safe!

Indeed the meaning of a guy's future life often consists in proving to oneself at each chance one gets that one is a man and not a broomstick or something like that. and thus anticipate the worse. for. as it is often said and repeated by those who have undoubtedly reflected on the subject. and he started ad-libbing deliriously like a Rumanian fanatic in exile to the point that I began wondering if three years of American (already) had not seriously affected his power of reasoning. none the less I feel obliged to report at this time as faithfully as possible I suppose what he proffered that morning as we sat under our tree in the near past rather than the remote past me taking notes he speaking away *The intrinsic value of a discourse does not depend on the importance of its subject* he proclaimed *for then theologians would have it by far, but in fact in the way we approach the accidental and the meaningless, in the way of mastering what is insignificant. The essential never requires, as far as I know, the least talent.* (What can you say to that?) *For years, in fact for a lifetime, to have thought only of one's last moments, and discover, when the end comes at last,*

that it has been useless, how can

you argue with that? *that the thought of death helps in every-thing except dying*, that is indeed depressing. He remained silent for a few seconds.

A work is finished when one can no longer improve it even though one knows it to be insufficient and incomplete. I had no idea what the fuck he was talking about. *One is so worn out, that one no longer has the courage to add a single comma, even if indispensable. What determines the degree of completion of a work is not at all the exigencies of art or of truth, it is fatigue, and, even more so, disgust.* How right you are, I said! *There is no true art without a strong dosage of banality. The one who uses the unusual in a consistent manner quickly bores his audience, for nothing is more unbearable than the uniformity of the exceptional.* What the hell does he take himself for! *The inconvenience of practicing a second language, a borrowed language*, he finally concluded, obviously referring to himself, and somewhat enraged, *is not to have the right to make too many mistakes. But in fact, it is in seeking what's incorrect without, however, abusing it, in brushing ever so lightly or ever so softly solecism, at every moment, that one gives an appearance of life to writing*, and to speaking, of course, I put in convincingly! Such profundities took me somewhat unprepared. Not you? Particularly since what he said seemed totally out of place, out of context, in the midst of what we were talking about. And even today, as I recall this to you, I feel ill at ease and dejected about the whole thing. Indeed I would have argued with him had he not already moved on with the rest of the details of his journey up north.

Well, so it goes, I said to myself, at the time, as I resigned myself to his further confidence. Therefore let us go on even though the comparison he dropped into the soup like a hair between a man and a broomstick may never be clarified as far as I know.

Oh, but I see that you guys want me to comment, expect me to comment at this point on his delirious and somewhat incoherent reflections, there in the middle of nowhere.

But do I dare, do I dare at this crucial moment of our journey risk a confrontation?

Do I have the courage, or even the right to interfere with my own report? As the middleman, the second-hand teller am I not to remain objective? Aloof if you wish? Am I permitted to reflect on my own delivery, however it may be distorted?

Okay you will tell me have I not already done so repeatedly up to now? Yes! But isn't time to leave such matters to those who are better qualified than me? I mean the comments.

And yet I can feel you guys urging me on for some reply, some explanation of this unexpected intrusion, this gratuitous digression, as if we were not used to it by now. I can hear you guys mumbling in frustration!
Yes, in fact,
I saw you there, yes,

you, the little guy way in the back, yes, with the beret basque, I saw you react when I compared him to a Rumanian fanatic in exile. Did you feel personally attacked?
Well,
let me assure you, I didn't mean to offend you. I could just as well have compared him to a Russian defector,

or an Irish expatriate, they are all fanatics anyway, and,

in fact, it would have been more appropriate, but I sort of like

the sound of Rumanian fanatic in exile.   Don't you?
And what he said is closer to their kind of thinking,
                    the Rumanians, I mean,
the kind of junk they come up with, but since you guys want a
reply, my opinion,
in other words, about what he said,
                    about his impromptu statement, and
since, you guys, it seems, want me either to praise or denigrate
his words,
even though with the passing of time, and the gap between his
words, as spoken that morning,
under our tree, and my reporting them here, on my platform, in
the present, and under duress,
I shall oblige.   After all, it's like coming up to the surface
for a breath of fresh air after a long dive,
                    out of the past, near or
remote, who gives a shit, gives us a chance, so to speak, to get
better acquainted too, and, who knows, maybe some of you
guys, eventually, may want to visit us,
down here, where the real thing took place,
                    one of these days, even if it
disturbs the logic,
        the stability of our relation.   Therefore, quickly, just a
few remarks.   However, what I'm about to say is
not, note, to be interpreted as my final reply.   Not by
any means,
                    as more may be
said on the subject, subsequently.
You know that I respect / resist him too much simply
to praise, or misquote him more than I already have.
His just-friends will make him feel their felt praise, as
they already have. His resistance-friends will push

him to take the next dancing leap over the deep abyss. So will I when I find the breathing space (resistance muscular follows it seems exhaustion enhancing it furtively), and the time of course, record in detail and to the best of my ability my reactions to his tale in progress, to his spectacular performance so far. At this point, let me add only and without any reservations what I consider to be High Praise (of sorts): it (his story I mean) has touched me so deeply, that I must fight it mightily to keep from merely echoing it, now that I'm looking to find my own voice so-called; it is indeed difficult and frustrating to be threatened by engulfments in his circus tricks so delightfully appropriate, and therefore utterly miserable inappropriate to the game I'm playing now out of despair, and I would pursue this subject

further had he given me time, but he resumed his story so abruptly, with such a flurry of wild gesticulation, that I have to stop now in order to follow him because of the necessity of always working out all the little details, even if eventually one goofs them all up. So (it's him talking now) it's agreed. I stop in New York (still to me, under that tree that damn tree on another occasion) for a few hours only. Overnight [Ah that damn tree is getting on my nerves] just time to take care of my business my affairs my private things [as we sat under our tree! as he told it to me under a tree! on several occasions! what bullshit] say hello and good bye to my uncle [it could have been just as well under a bridge. yes or near a river. or on a bench. yes, on a bench in a public park, or in a bar. in a Turkish bath for all I know. or better yet, on the edge of a precipice. yes! that would be nice, on the edge of a precipice leaning against the wind. fuck that tree! and the birdies in the tree, if any!

For all I know he may be imagining the whole thing. Dreaming it
up! Maybe there was no HE —
                        HE my ass!
Maybe it was somebody else told me the story as told to him (and
so on) and I'm getting the whole thing confused
                        getting all worked up over nothing!
Originally in fact there was only one person speaking in the
French version — AMER ELDORADO — first draft!
Therefore who can check
                who can make sure
                who can prove that I was there
                        that he was there. What counts is that I'm
here now — in the present — (re)working out the details
                        (re)sorting out the mess
as best we can. But let me assure you it was not under a tree that
the story was told to me but truly on the edge of a precipice — if
you can imagine that — leaning against the wind (as my friend
Katz once said) and for all I know we might both fall in. Feet first
or head first. Doesn't matter much in the end!
                That would really be funny! Tragic indeed!
But here I am nonetheless working out the fucking details
for the second time.
But that's my business. Isn't it?
After all who is in charge here?
                who controls this mess?
                who decides on the lay out?
                who keeps things going back and forth? As best he can?
ME! yes MEnow and not HEthen!
So screw your guys and shut the fuck up and let us go on even if
the damn second version seems somewhat shaky
 even if I mess up things once in a while

even if the second-telling doesn't match the original
even if the logic of the chronology
      of the back and forth movement from past to
      present (or vice versa)   from

              him to me
              and me to him does
fall apart once in a while!   Who cares!

what is certain, and clear so far, the more I think about it is the fact
that it was not under a tree that he told me the story, but on the
edge of a precipice, leaning against the wind, and not, I might
add, on several occasions, as previously stated erroneously, but
at once, all at once, in an intervenient manner, one sitting if you
prefer, thus making the whole relation much more credible, and
also much more poetic, and, of course, much more dramatic too
(don't you agree?), therefore we shall not mention the tree any
more, yes hell with it, an abyss, a precipice is so much better, and
imagine for a moment how funny it would be if the two of us were
to fall in, that would really be interesting, head first or feet first
comes out the same in the end] so it's agreed, I stop in New York
for a few hours (it's the other guy talking now, keep alert!) just
time to say that I'm in town, passing through so to speak, tell
Marilyn what's going on, tell her that I'll be back, yes up north
(northeast as a matter of fact) because of a typical little error, up to
Camp Drum, it was a goof, near the Canadian border, about three
hundred miles the guy said, northeast, but don't worry, no in my
Buick, because of my one month's pay in advance, yes and my
travel expenses, you know what I mean, they're shipping me
overseas, got to go there quickly, yes in my Buick, still going, but
I'll be back before heading west, to San Francisco, yes I think of
you all the time, I love you, perhaps you can help me sell my car,
I'm mad about you, maybe an ad, in the New York Times, I adore

you, like to get about 150 bucks for it, try to arrange something too so we can love each other, be together, for a while, you know what I mean, just one more time, but be careful, if possible find me a good deal, because of Benny, 125 is the lowest I can take, it's still in great shape, looks nice from the outside, a damn good body, yes an add, a quiet motel in Long Island, the one we used to go to to love each other, I'm crazy about you, leaving soon for the war, in the Far East, but don't worry darling, I'll be back for sure, with my luck and my education, for sure they'll find me a nice and cozy job behind the lines, stick me behind a desk, banging on a typewriter, in Tokyo maybe (how things work out well) it'll be okay, you'll see (I'll insist here if she starts crying), you don't think I want to get knocked off out there, shot full of holes, if a guy anticipates the worse it always turns out fine, and he added in French to make her smile, une belle planque bien pénarde, in Tokyo!

That's what I'll tell her. With a lot of emotions. Dearest love!

So everything is fine (I'll say to her while kissing her tenderly) especially now that things are going so well with us, so smoothly!

But be careful, let's not let out that I've volunteered for this one!

VOLUNTEERED! You're crazy darling! Why? Why? Oh why dear love!

For combat!   She'll faint for sure. She'll crawl on her knees to beg me, to implore me to reconsider. She'll whine like a baby, or like an old lady who's just lost her French poodle. I can see the whole scene already. And if there is one thing I can't stand it's a female crying. Weeping females, that's all we need now! Please darling, can't you change your mind? Can't you tell them that you didn't mean it? That it's a mistake? Haven't you suffered enough during the last war? If you want me to I'll go and tell them this minute! Right now! The war, the farm, the camps! And your whole family exterminated (in lampshades)! You'll see they'll listen to me! They'll understand! You should have told them the sad story!

Oh shit! Not that again! Not that suffering crap again! No dear love, you can't do that. I've got to go. It's my duty (I'll tell her. That should make her flinch)! But I'll be back I'll be back I swear (and I'll squeeze her harder in my arms) and then we'll be able to start all over again. Everything will be fine again. And we'll talk things over seriously this time. About the future, our future. About love, our love! We'll be more careful and go away!

And if she asks why I'm getting rid of all my things (which I left with them in their fancy deluxe apartment) I'll tell her it's just that I want to clean up the past because when I come back from the war (no need to mention my misgiving about death she would scream) I want to start a new life. A clean life. Rethink everything. I want to start from nothing. From zero again. You'll see, no more messing around. No more wasting time. No more debauchery. False values. Finished all that irresponsible immature irrational life!

Oh, do you really mean it?

Yes!
Yes   Finished all that: Jazz
                              Black buddies
                              Gambling
                              Borrowed money never payed back
                              Unemployment
                              Starvation
                              Loneliness
                              Free love
                              Movies twice a day and sometimes more
                              Dirty books
                              Foul language
                              Crooked ideas
                              Politics
                              Comic books
                              Philosophy
                              Poetry
                              Adultery
                              And even cigarettes (two packs a day)
finished all that!

Henceforth (and there I'll squeeze her so hard she won't be able to
say anything) a good steady job
                    a regular full time job
                    well payed in a decent place
                    everyday from 8 to 5 (or 9 to 6 might be better) with
                    only one hour off for lunch
                    and even (going all the way° to make her feel good)
a fat savings account in a well established bank so that she won't
be able to chew my ass because I'm broke all the time and always
doing
something fishy to get money from her on the
side behind Benny's back whom I really like in
spite of all. BENNY! A damn nice fellow! Yes ° I'll
tell you more about Benny about what he told me
about him another time° during the trip perhaps°
if we have time.

Yes° I can already see the tears in her eyes when I'll tell her that. Ah what beautiful eyes, what big black eyes she had Marilyn! Loving eyes! And so kind° so generous!

yes + + + yes + + + and maybe you can come back and work for benny in his lampshade factory + + + (she'll say for sure) + + + I'm almost sure he'll take you back + + + and he'll even give you a nice raise + + + I'm almost sure of that + + + in fact + + + if you want me to I can already speak to him about it + + + how lovely it will be + + + (how beautiful she is when she says that and how compassionate) + + + you'll see + + + it's going to be perfect + + + even better than before + + + everything will be perfect

of course not a word about my apprehension not that I'm obsessed by death far from it but marilyn death has a bad a scary effect on her she thinks about it all the time as a child she was very sickly yes death it's an obsession with her and old age also yes old age and yet she's only 29 but the mere thought of wrinkles gray hair shriveled up skin withered face lost beauty loose flesh everything falling off the bones flattened ass deflated breasts broken down voice all that really scares the hell out of her the pains and ugliness of old age it frightens her (and love too but that's another thing

which can be discussed later on) whereas me in those days death I didn't think much about it on the contrary hardly because me as I said before he said throwing his thumb in a casual manner over his shoulder towards the past I came out of the hole out of the grave three times four times I shouldn't even be here today therefore fuck death and old age if you want my opinion one mustn't think about it(or hardly) in fact the only way to live and survive with the least apprehension in this crummy country is to think you are immortal until something happens to you which finally proves that you were wrong something mortal that is which disproves (once and for all) that life was a lousy mistake!

Yes a dumb mistake a gross error he said almost with tears in his
eyes!   But even in this case
                                            even when it happens
                                            it's not important I said
                                            trying to help him recover
                                            from his momentary weakness
Or   since it's already too late!
as it was once said ———
I believe it was a contemporary thinker of some reknown who
said that in an essay entitled for some strange reason THEAT-
RUM PHILOSOPHICUM (p. 91 volume 282 I think it was)

THE FACT OF BEING DEAD IS A STATE OF THINGS
IN RELATION TO WHICH AN ASSERTION CAN
EITHER BE TRUE OR FALSE – TO DIE IS A PURE
EVENT WHICH VERIFIES NOTHING! ——AhAh, you guys are
                                                          laughing!
Go ahead laugh!   Go on ———-! AhAh!   LAUGH!
But it's true :
            DEATH DOES NOT VERIFY ANYTHING!
            NOT A DAMN THING as far as I know!
                                          AhAh!   Because
first of all
one is never dead for oneself but always for others AhAh! in the
speech of others inside the anonymous babbling of others
and secondly
one can never say of oneself (especially not in the present tense)
once dead I AM DEAD
unless one speaks metaphorically
and let me assure you there is nothing metaphorical about being
dead or about dying
it's a pure event — the event of all events — which verifies
nothing!

Or

if you prefer

as my Rumanian friend used to say (throwing my thumb over my
recitation towards a vague spot in the near past):

IF DEATH HAD ONLY

NEGATIVE ASPECTS

TO IT   DYING WOULD BE

AN IMPRACTICABLE ACT!

Ah, I wish Marilyn was here now to hear this he said regretfully!
She would really be comforted particularly since she always
anticipated the worse even when things would turn out for the
best!

XIV

laughter & literature

all good story tellers go to BETHICKETT on their way to Heaven and
that is why perhaps they are so long in reaching their destination
someone said in the back
but I ignored him completely
why waste time and paper to answer such unfunded statements I told
myself?

Okay I'm not going to argue with you!
    I'm not going to make you weep / o-o / with all the sad
stories he told me and yet if I wanted to tell you all the crap he told
me (the trains the camps) if I wanted to describe in details and
realistically all the misery and suffering he endured (the
lampshades the farms the noodles) we would never get out of
here / o-o / ah yes his entire family remade into lampshades
(father mother sisters ah yes uncles aunts cousins too) you
wouldn't believe it (wiped out)!

The only sane thing to do in cases such as these he said is either to
shut up and forget or else learn to laugh - LAUGH - laugh and I
practiced three times a day he said to laugh at all that shitmerde at
myself at life death to laugh at everything (in retrospect bien
entendu) this way it helps you go on forces you to forget a little
that's the only way to keep going reinvent yourself in mad giggles
laugh your life out into words call it the fourire: laughterature!

The problem with you guys is that you don't know how to laugh: that's what's missing the most in you — laughter! Ah yes to sneer that much you can do (with your cute little mouths) but laughter BIG LAUGHTER no dice: monstruous bursts of laughter coming out of the belly noisy and furious laughter crazy strangled laughter mad laughter convulsive loud nervous laughter mocking laughter no not for you guys it doesn't work!

Ah the laughing act: doesn't work for you guys because you guys laugh Japanese style delicately with your hands in front of your mouth as if you were coughing! What the hell you guys think that laughter is some kind of sickness? Laugh: ah ah ah! oh oh oh oh! ah ah ah! Laugh: yes because when one guy weeps somewhere in the world there is always some other guy who laughs somewhere else: happy balance! Never fails it's normal equilibrium: laugh or cry comes out the same in the end! After all humanity is like a well with two buckets: when one goes down to be filled the other comes up to be emptied: humanity is like a deep hole!

Consequently one must always appreciate laughter — mad laughter above all — and fear everything else: especially death! !Fear death like a rebirth like a renascence like a renaissance like a resurrection . . . . . . *Who said that* . . . ? [Shy trembling voice way in the back] I don't know. I found that in my notes. Doesn't matter though. But we should perhaps point out that what we are saying here (of course) does not necessarily come from us. It's a paraphrase. A misquotation. We are merely repeating (more or less approximately) what a certainperson of reputation once said. Somewhere. And no doubt better than we even if that certainperson borrowed it from someone else as is (always) the case with analogies. Life is made up of verbal collages: repetitions with slight variations. Obviously then we're distorting the original!

But basically this is how humanity was once summed up. And don't you think it's a rather good analogy? And humanity, the one I am quoting (or misquoting whichever the case) wow did he mess it up! And that's not all. Even worse. He messed up the whole language of humanity in his multilingual scribblings. Wow did he fuck it up (the language of humanity) the one I am quoting (or misquoting) above but he warned us about it: Wait till I fix you with your charabia, he once said, your dead tongue!

Quack Quack!

======================

==========   ==========

Ah you guys are surprised that I know people of such caliber: people who say such splendid things. That really blocks the shit out of you really flips the crap out of you! Well it's not really that unusual! It's not because I am a second-hand teller. A mouth : a voice within a voice that I cannot afford to step out of my inter-mediary role once in a while. After all who is in charge here? It's quite true that I sometimes exaggerate a bit too much and that my recitation as it goes does not permit me to deploy my background, to present myself in full and in my own name, to speak of my own adventures (and misadventures) as a real person, but neverthe-less nothing prevents me (in moments of self-deprecation) from characterizing myself through others: through the words of others, through quotations, misquotations, references or differ-ences, collages / montages (or for that matter plagiarism of that most obvious source), and whatever else comes to mind. In moments of doubts and despair. And you haven't heard the best yet. I mean best of the kind of distorted material, sub-material, junk-material that I borrow left and right to throw into the recita-tion, randomly, to hold together, to enrich, to thicken what would otherwise be just a simple banal story of a G.I. who bugs the shit out of us with his illusions! Yes his illusions about a trip from North Carolina to California (en passant par Nouillorque) supposedly Yes just another straight boring story told directly by the one who experienced it some 20 years ago!

————-   ————-

That alone wouldn't be of great value (commercial or otherwise) That trip alone would be meaningless were it not told (retold over again) second-hand with the kind of reflections superimposed upon it by the voice within the voice which gives it a personal touch touch of life one might say Yes indeed that story would be boring spoken linearly!

————————-

And indeed the question could be asked: Would it be literature? Or for that matter would it have any literary value (commercial or even social)? That is the crucial question. Whereas by sprinkling smart quotations here and there in the recitation it gains in denseness in thickness also what it loses in speed and straightforwardness and in so doing appears to be literature. In other words it is by a system of double-talk that the story rises from its banality to what can be called a level of surfiction for were it not for all the digressions and diversions inserted into the story as it goes along (up and down and sideways) the curves of its own circumvolutions then it would be at best of minor interest. And that is why one must talk (and sometimes double-talk) at ease and without much concern for logic or for credibility about life life and death death and laughter laughter as literature literature as politics (eventually) for then and only (am I anticipating too much?) then can one approach the realm of literature. For what are we barbarians? What are we here for? If not to improve reality so that it may someday become fiction or literature!
Now I know what you guys are thinking: What about form? What about logic? What about consistency of point of view? What about

syntax? And of course what about style? And in fact I heard you
. . . yes you over there . . . the little guy with the mustache
. . . when you said to the guy next to you . . . yes the tall one
with the sun glasses . . . me I don't miss a thing . . . I heard
you mumbling something about form I think . . . wasn't it you
who said What this Gentleman is saying might be true and
amusing but who cares it has no form? I heard it . . . In fact I
find it rather incoherent rather styleless and even . . . no my
little man don't try to hide in the crowd . . . And even if he
invents well even if he tells a good story it's not really literature it
has no plot no dramatic development . . . fuck you . . . it's
not literature YOUNG PANK!
Not literature! — Ah you guys want me to tell you what I think
what I think literature is all about?

LITERATURE — it's
four walls
a table
a chair
paper
pencils
(or else a typewriter if you compose directly on the typewriter
and)
(tictac tictac tictac tictac tictac tictac tictac tictac tictac)
and after that hours and hours days and nights weeks and
months even years and years banging on it (on the damn
machine)
banging your head against the wall
your ass on the chair
alone — yes — alone
watching the flies fly by
picking your nose

smoking cigarettes to your death
sniffling cutting your nails
drumming the table with your fingers
doing nothing
waiting that something comes into your head
asking yourself what the fuck am I doing here!
That's where — and how — literature begins. But that's not all!
No —— don't imagine that's all I have to say about literature —
LITERATURE — it's patience   &   determination
                         violence   &   dontgiveashit
in other words
a simple question of
copying adding multiplying cutting folding correcting quoting
transforming imple question of
inventing stealing manipulating reducing lying rewriting distorting citing uestion of
starting all over again vomiting stopping falling asleep waking up
sitting tion of
meditating masturbating hesitating having a filthy taste in the
mouth crap of
wanting to commit suicide saying it all over again walking in your
sleep f
and of course crying (once in a while)
and laughing too (as much as possible)

Ah yes laughing — especially — laughing
aloud softly silently between your teeth while pissing in your
pants laughing
while slapping yourself on the belly with tears in your eyes ghing
to death while rolling on the floor to the point of chocking ing
with sobs tittering until it turns into screams giggling g
and it's not all — no it's only the beginning — it's only the
beginning! The beginning of literature!

For LITERATURE —— it's also words!
Yes WORDS —— inside of you around you above you besides
you deep in you! words at the corner of you underneath far away
from you inside everywhere!

WORDS	WORDS
WORDS you look at them	you bang on them WORDS
WORDS you touch them	you search for them WORDS
WORDS you line them up	you find them WORDS
WORDS you mix them all up	you lose them WORDS
WORDS you retouch them	you transform them WORDS
WORDS you manipulate them	you throw them away WORDS

and all that — your ass on the chair — and what you write — if it's
good — if it's bad — who gives a damn — doesn't matter — who
cares even if you spend 40 years — yes — and even 50 stupid
years (or even more) of your life — between the four walls —
sitting on that crummy chair — doesn't matter — because life —
yes — well we're hardly in it that immediately we've got to get the
fuck out — hop — but life I mean — while you're in it — there's no
way you can't play life — no no way you can't play the game of life
— yes — because it's a game a big game — and you can never say
— never — say I don't wanna play I don't wanna play any more —
stop everything — I'm getting off — I'm getting out — say — fuck
it all — I give up — no — no question of saying can't take it any
more — I'm fed up — finish — thumbs up I'm quitting — because
life hurts too much — and so even if it's 40 even 50 years of your
life you've spent there — in the room — cornered on the chair —
between four walls — eyes staring at the walls — asking yourself
what am I doing here — what the fuck am I doing here and all the
while pretending that it's the best way to pass the time — just a
way to keep going — finally — and approximately — pretending
you're doing literature — because literature — you say to yourself
— after all just a matter of patience and determination and don't
give a shit! and of course work — work — and more work: tictac

tictac tictac tictac!
for nothing — nothing!
for the birds — with sweat dripping down your arms
and your hands hurting
and your head spinning
and your ass hard like a rock just from sitting on the chair!
wow — it's tough!
But let's be serious — and let's go on with literature — for a while
!

Quelle connerie . . . Quelle salade! [A sonofabitch who didn't
understand a damn thing, it's obvious, to what I was saying, you
can see that from the way he shouts, from his disturbed gestures, and suddenly he jumps toward me up on my platform, grabs
me by the throat with both hands to make me stop I suppose, but
me I give him the knee in the balls, whack, and he retreats in the
crowd howling like a mule, holding on to his crotch, but then
everybody rushes forward to grab me, there on my platform, but I
scream, raise my arm hand extended palm forward, STOP! stop
that shit you guys, don't touch me!]

Okay, let's be serious!
We're not going to have a riot just because of literature [and so
everybody calms donwn, and they all go back to their places in
front of my platform in a semi-circle — Ouf — that was close!]

Okay, I'll go on with the story. Highway 101. Near Washington.
And still raining. But he was calm now. Happy . . . . . And
Bob? Oh yes, Bob, on his way to Florida! Mustn't forget him.
Therefore I continue with literature - [the guy whom I kicked in the

testicules did not stay for the rest of the story but doesn't matter

because others came to replace him yes many others now and there are even kids now among the adults listening with their mouths opened therefore careful watch out choose your words carefully don't get carried away no obscenities even though these days kids know more than one suspects especially little girls with pink ribbons in their hair I tell you they're the most perverse and in fact I see two of them sitting in the front row arms crossed like two princesses their laced panties publicly exposed next to their mommies what the fuck they're doing here at this time in their Sunday dresses one can wonder rather than being in school learning to write and read or at home learning to cook to knit sew or just clean the house but no use looking for trouble I have enough already that's damn sure especially with kids as long as they remain nice and quiet while I tell the story and they don't start whining when I come to the sad passages what the hell can't be too difficult I don't mind those kids it's not the time to be choosy better kids than nothing and the mommies they are sexy and don't bug the shit out of you like the intellectuals with all their questions and all their interruptions that's for sure what a bunch of casses-pieds whereas in the case of the mothers no need to take gloves anything goes you can really let yourself go with those good bourgeoises they love juicy stories makes them tickle from the tip of the tits to the slit of the cunt therefore no need to be timid allons-y let's take advantage of their tender presence!]

Well ladies and gentlemen (and dear children) (shit can't get out of it)!

Well maybe I can't tell you what literature is all about (no I can't) but perhaps I can tell you (in five or six sentences) what literature is not!

Oh yes / Do tell us / If you can / Oh do tell us / In English / In French or even in Portuguese! [charming feminine voice from deep in the crowd]

L I T E R A T U R E   ladies&gentlemen&dearchildren   L I T E R A T U R E

it is not a banana peel on which you slip deliberately to break your legs
ce n'est pas une peau de banane sur laquelle on glisse et se casse la jambe
não é uma casca de banana em que a gente escorrega para quebrar a perna!

it is not a set of drums on which you bang like mad to drive people crazy
ce n'est pas un tambour de ville sur lequel on tape dur pour faire du bruit
não é um tambor de arauto no qual a gente bate para fazer escândalo!

it is not a big red balloon that rises in the clouds on days of festivity
ce n'est pas un gros ballon rouge qui vole vers les nuages un jour de fêtes
não é um grande balão vermelho que sobe para o céu num dia de festas!

it is not a glass of wine you drink in the morning to fortify your brains
ce n'est pas un verre de vin qu'on boit le matin pour se fortifier l'esprit
não é um gole de pinga que a gente toma de manhã para ficar mais animado!

it is not a little white mouse that eats pieces of cheese its eyes closed
ce n'est pas une petite souris blanche qui mange du fromage les yeux fermés
não é um ratinho branco que se delicia com o queijo de olhos fechados!

it is not a dumb earthquake that demolishes the damn world for no reasons
ce n'est pas un tremblement de terre qui démolit tout avec ses tremblements
não é um tremor de terra que rebenta tudo com os seus abalos!

In other words literature cannot be explained! It is not self-explanatory! It does not speak for itself in two or three languages, native or foreign! It is done, if you wish, your ass on the chair, in front of the table, and if you don't have a chair, nor a table, then standing up, against the wall all alone, in the stinking room!

But of course, I see you coming, I hear you muttering, but I'm waiting for you around the corner: "Literature it's above all words, sentences, paragraphs, punctuation, good grammar, in other words style, decent language!"

But of course, you dumb ass, words, words, out of sight, and over the damn horizon!
Evidently, you shitty little constipator, words, words, and even that it's a fight! You have to struggle with them, fight with them, sleep with them before they make you or break you!

But words, words, I've got lots of them: English words
                                          French words
                                          Frenglish words
                                                    because me
you see sometimes I mix them all up
because me you see I'm not a purist
no I would rather say that I'm the doubletype (o-o)
                              the schizotype (S / S)
the type of guy who rides (% / %) two languages (- / -)
                    who humps (x / x) two languages at the same
                    time
and that is why I can say to you MERDESHIT in two languages in
one smooth vocal breath
directly   &   simultaneously

Perhaps they are not pretty MY WORDS but they are MY WORDS and me I employ them I arrange them as best I can MY WORDS because me you see MY WORDS now what interests me as of today in fact it's language abandoned to chaos and disorder liberated language delirious writing writing laughing up and

down the pages words that move and crack and giggle what
counts for me now it's floating language ludicrous style digressive words out of sight par-dessus l'horizon in other words the
kind of language that is not fit for printing not publishable in your
glossy magazines the kind of language that screams the kind of
┄┄┄ shit gently to literature without blushing!
┄┄┄ guage that speaks its mind openly and self-

u

w o u l d   d r a g   y o u r s e l f
ass in the crud just to publish three lines of
one of those decent glossy respectable

/yyyy . . . zzzzz . . . ! [Person non-identified]

$c_{RI}^{E}{}_{T}UR_{E}$

I know when you guys say writing you really mean

(o┄┄ E-C-R-I-T-U-R-E — we've already discussed that —
remember that pharmacist earlier?) and its CON-sequences! All
that linguistuff:

phrases - paragraphs - syntax - style - semantic - semiology -
taxinomy - semanalyze - saloperie - bavarderie - connerie - super-
cherie - pipie - rierie - mimie - cacaphony and all kinds of other
kinds of other iqueiques like that all kinds of other phiphies like
that one finds all over your ECRITURE and what is commonly
called charabia and when it comes to charabia you guys can really
dish it out wow   terrific

That is to say that even the automatism of repetition
that one recognizes inasmuch as to want to divide its
terms aims at nothing else but historistic temporality
of the experience of a transfer similarly the instinct of
death essentially expresses the limit of the historic
function of the subject but what is a subject and what
form does it take apriori there's the rub

----

and I am only quoting here a small portion (somewhat extended)
of some delicious passage of lacanic subtleties taken at random
one could find better examples of simmering speech though this
one will do for now as a conscious example of what you guys call
ECRITURE or even textuality!

You should have heard the lingualmishmash the confiture the
marmelade: the spokenvomit (deliberate that one) that came out
of the mouths (yes dripped out of the mouths) of the guys from
the 82nd that too was some form of language and could these
guys fuck it up could they vocaliber!

THEREFORE since we must speak whether or not we have something to say and the less we want to say and want to
hear the more we as homologos speak voluntarily
the more we are subjected as it were unconsciously
to speech or as PASCAL once said tout le mal du
monde vient du fait que nous ne sommes pas même
capables de rester assis tranquillement dans une
chambre and he should have added (page 136)
without being able to shut up!

and HOPLA here we are F U L L

```
            F           F           o o o o o
                                   o         o
            U           U          o   cir   o
                  o                o         o
            L           L          o   cle   o
                                   o         o
            L           L           o o o o o
            F  U  L  L
```

back in the room our ass on the chair
our eyes staring blankly straight
ahead and a
cigarette at the corner of the mouth another one bringing us one
more step closer to our death in front of the table ass on the chair
sweat running down our arms between the four walls at the end
of
LITERATURE
HOPLA!   VOILA!

Or as Branletapoire used to say:

> *Lovers and madmen have such seething brains*
> *Such shaping fantasies that apprehend*
> *More than cool reason ever comprehends.*
>
> *The lunatic the lover and the poet*
> *Are of imagination all compact.*

POSTSCRIPT

It was not going very well already in the kingdom of literature
since le nouveau roman that great triumph of sing-my-ass we were
going quite helpless copiously robbe-grilladized semiotized infull
from salsify to chinese lanterns but now we are truly moving tumbling
into shit here we are fallen crestfallen to the underlevel of undersol-
lersism into the invertebrate desensibilized by barthist analism
zerofied offhandedly materialized getting closer to objects and facts
than causes emasculated scientifically by shameless daily gossiping
superjerking scenarios moving now towards the immense the endless
organic debacle towards the great deluge of low-down tricks the
crashup of confusionism masturbatory telquelism drifting on the
lacanian raft derridian barge shipwrecked in other words on the sea
of fucked up literature where civilization can be measured assessed
rather by the distance man places between himself and his excrement

----

XV

New York summer camps politics & slogans

However, if you guys want to talk some more about literature, it'll have to wait until later, when we get on the road, during the big trip, we'll have more time then, during the crossing, because right now we're barely on our way, still in the original detour, the pretext, moving north only and not very far yet, on our way to Camp Drum, remember, but later, when we'll have more time and more space for such things, then we can discuss literature, but now we got to get back to the poor guy in his car on his way to New York, in his Buickspecial, in the gray rain, he was fed up by now with all that verbal crap going through his mind, fed up with words!

Ah words, that continuous stream of verbal mush going through one's mind in such situations, words, big ones, small ones, thin ones, words, short ones, long ones, soft ones, hard ones, some beautiful, others ugly, some simple and readily understood, others complex and incomprehensible, shit he said to himself, enough of that, let's get the show on the road, what the hell is going on, he mumbled, as he pulled out of Washington, and he was quite right, trying to get back on the right track, and still a long way to go, trying to forge ahead (physically and mentally speaking) into his future, the north-future of his life, before heading westward, as he was determined to do, with or without his Buick, and he was quite right!

All that literary mumbo jumbo (or vice versa?), useless indeed to pursue that any further, got to get going (got to), tell the rest of this story (what happened after he got to New York in his beat-up jalopy), see what happens with Marilyn, got to get him to New York eventually, first stage of this abracadabra story, first stop, can't fart around too much Merde!

It was around 9:00 p.m. that evening of his first day on the road and that's why I can't mess around too much to tell you more about literature because I have to report now the next episode unload that part of the story that comes next and how as soon as he arrived in New York immediately he called Marilyn he called her just from outside the Lincoln Tunnel about 9:05 p.m. just as I pulled into the city a bit tired but happy to be here happy to be back again in that good old filthy miserable lonely disgusting monstruous New York City

----

new york city new york city (what a great place) new york city new york city

----

ah New York at this time of evening in February in the rain the fog the mist incredible windows all the way up to the sky glass walls all over huge walls of glass up to the sky and even higher corridors of walls up to the sky even beyond skyscrapers my ass skyfuckers all the way up and you walk inside that labyrinth of corridors like a little bug flattened against the asphalt a guy must look ridiculous seen from above and the wind blows in there screams and the wind pushes you against the walls ah I love it I love it especially when the streets are deserted at night when the garbage flies in your face ah New York what a tough city you can die right there on the sidewalk and who cares no one will stop to look at you to touch you to take your hands and lift you up physically or morally but doesn't matter you die when it's time to die in New York City who needs an audience better die here than far away over there

----

new york city new york city (what a tough place) new york city new york city

----

and the broads the elegant broads on Fifth Avenue Madison Park
Avenue on the Eastside with their gorgeous bodies and legs silk
legs that drive you insane here go back and reread the arrival of
Bardamu in New York in le Voyage then you'll see what I mean by
elegant long supple svelte legs that keep going up and up under
the skirts to where it's all warm in there warm and furry where it's
all cozy in there but where only your imagination can enter to feel
it!

Here   simultaneously
let me quote you a little passage   just a few sentences
to refresh your memory page 193 in my Pléiade Edition (he said
to my astonishment)   because me too like a jerk
(he had found the place in his book) j'attendis une bonne heure or
more after the phone call à la même place and then de cette
pénombre in this gray rain de cette foule en route discontinue
morne surgit around 10:00 p.m. une brusque avalanche quite
unexpected de femmes absolument belles gorgeous stunning out
of nowhere quelle découverte quelle Amérique quel ravissement
was I lucky to be here je touchais au vif de mon pélerinage and if
je n'avais pas souffert en même temps des continuels rappels the
loud gurgling in my stomach de mon appétit wow was I hungry
suddenly je me serais cru parvenu à l'un de ces moments de
surnaturelle and of surrealistic révélation esthétique les beautés
que je découvrais just like that incessantes m'eussent avec un peu
de confiance et de confort and a bit more self-confidence ravi à ma
condition trivialement humaine il ne me manquait qu'un
sandwich a good juicy hamburger with French fries and a hot cup
of coffee en somme pour me croire en plein miracle mais comme il
me manquait le sandwich I started looking around for a cheap
joint a hamburger joint down Forty-second quelles gracieuses
souplesses however quelles délicatesses incroyables quelles

trouvailles d'harmonie what an incredible stock market of asses perilleuses nuances rêussites de toute la gamme des dangers de toutes les promesses possibles de la figure and of the legs et du corps and parmi tant de blondes ces brunes svelte and swanky et ces Titiennes et qu'il y en avait plus qu'il en venait encore from everywhere c'est peut-être (pensais-je) la Gréce qui recommence? I was on Broadway now j'arrive au bon moment in my Buickspecial which was parked illegally of course on a side street elles me parurent d'autant mieux divines ces apparitions qu'elles ne semblaient point du tout but not at all s'apercevoir que j'existais moi la a cote tout baveux tired gâteux dumfounded d'admiration tout érotico-mystique of fatigue hunger desire ready to burst out of my fly I'm not exaggerating so dizzy from all that ass watching so exhausted was I from all that travelling from all that excitement and apprehension
and all these gorgeous blondes and **brunettes**
redheads and platinums whirling like butterflies around me
all of them built like Greek goddesses with their challenging asses that made you feel like getting down piously on your knees behind them just to touch them smell them on the spot explore their forbiddingness made you feel like dropping your pants reverently right there on Fifth Avenue
Time Square
to jerk off publicly
to show your solemn admiration
your blind sexual servility to all these cockteasers!

Yes me that evening I understood he said pausing a moment as though he was suddenly reliving the whole scene and also every time I arrived in New York like that in the rain the fog by train bus boat bicycle or on foot I understood what Bardamu must have felt when he too arrived like a jerk in New York tout gâteux baveux ah if only Moinous was here with me now I thought to myself to see that to feel what I felt as I walked down the Avenue of the Americas my tongue hanging down my mouth saliva dripping down my chin from hunger and desire visually esquinté by this overwhelming spectacle he stopped and me too I understood how he felt!

Yes I felt it and felt it again and again I saw it and saw it again and again he murmured as he closed his Pléiade Edition and me too I had the vague sensation that it was Greece starting all over again in this land of opportunities me too I felt inside my pants what he had felt Bardamu while staring at all those perilous nuances of legs and bodies whirling like butterflies around me without them noticing that I was there ready to be loved ready to give myself democratically without ever looking at all those paltry jerks who stood there saliva dripping down their chins and enormous sickly looking pricks bulging inside their trousers no the skyscrapers could have crumbled on the sidewalks these gorgeous figures would have walked on without noticing the general excitement the public sensuality the mass desire that circulated around them through them too all these blondes and brunettes who absently swayed their asses in full view up and down the Avenues exhibiting their untouchable asses without the lease self-consciousness bouncing their impregnable asses except of course for those would could afford them those to whom those scrupulously elegant asses belong the rich guys who have the means and the rights of property the economic privileges of these ethereal asses yes that's the deciding factor of social and human rapports in New York and especially on Fifth Avenue Park Avenue and so on the Stock Market of Asses the Dow Jones of Fucking and me like a Greek slave or a Roman martyr I came and saw yes Veni Vidi Jerki but no Fucki today or at least not until later!

HELLO

----

ah what solitude what illusion what mirage what filthy weather too what a fiesta of socio-economic asses what a way to regain faith in humanity But New York it's something else too that's for sure it's like a spider web a huge stadium a sports arena with all kinds of athletic events the kinds that force you to excel to surpass yourself or else!

An incredible system of crushing forces a house of tortures an obstacle course yes an immense spider web!
Snowjob of all the possibilities!
And yet one always comes back like a little bug
a dumb fly to get caught in that big spider web!
Yes a network of telephone booths!   H E L L O !
Everybody is connected by the threads of that infernal spider web! And yet once you've been there that's it!   NORTH

Always coming back for more! And from all sides: WEST ...:... EAST

across the bridges inside the tunnels   SOUTH
on ferryboats on foot by car bus plane train bicycle roller skates!
Crawling on your stomach doesn't matter QUICK got to make it back!
Got to!
And as soon as you arrive
and as soon as you're over the bridge or out of the tunnel QUICK (never fails) a telephone booth!
The little dime in the slot! QUICK! Nervous fingers. and the familiar voice quickly connected far away at the end of one of the threads QUICK the spider web!
HELLO!

Ah it's you? (me) You're back in the City!

As if we had never left. as if we had never moved never travelled never grown old. as if we had just gone out to the corner drugstore. nothing! Even six months later two years five years later twenty years it's the same tralala!

Ah it's you?

Hello!

I thought you were in California. Arizona. Europe. In jail. China! . . . .

Hello! Are you still there?

En Chine moi?

En Ceinte!

En Culé!

En . . . En . . . En . . .

In . . . In . . . In . . .

No Korea!

Korea? . . . . What!

Yes! Never fails immediately the telephone booth the dime anybody the first name in the little black book simply to say hello that we are in town again back we're still alive yes moving on doing very well alive! . . . .

And how long are you staying? Never fails . . . . quick! the little black book with the addresses and the phone numbers and if you've lost it the little black book then you're really lost fucked you've had it! Ah what loneliness ah what deadliness New York without the black book!

Hello!

Hello! Can you hear me?

Ah you're back? But I didn't know! Why didn't you let me know? It's typical of you! Are you here for good?

No . . . . I've got to leave again . . . . Tomorrow morning!

Where to this time?

Up to Camp Drum . . . . (a little error . . . . because of my money)

Up . . . . Wheeere?

CAMP DRUM . . . . It's north . . . . Upper New York State (near the Canadian

. . . .

Can't hear a thing you're saying! Canada? What are you going to do
   there? What incredible noise! Must have a bad connection! In
   Canada! Where're you calling from?
No . . . . Near the Canadian border . . . . Right outside the Lincoln
   Tunnel!
You still love me?
(Never fails) . . . . What did you say?
DO YOU STILL LOVE ME?
Of course . . . . I adore you!
Oh how I missed you Darling! Why didn't you write me? Three months
   without a letter from you!
Can I come over?
Benny is not home yet. Some kind of business dinner in the city but he
   said he'll be home around eleven . . . . He called a while ago!
You think it's okay? I can . . . . just like that . . . . Does he suspect
   anything?
No . . . . you know he heard stories . . . nothing . . . you re-
   member after we came back from the Catskills . . . before you
   went in . . . when they drafted you in the army . . . remember . . . and you and I and the baby we spent a few more
   days alone up in the Catskills . . . together . . . when Benny
   . . . ah if I had known I swear . . . Benny had to go on a
   business trip . . . how beautiful it was . . . I was so crazy
   . . . I love you so much . . . so much . . .
Yes! . . . . Me too!
Oh Dearest Dearest Love!
Yes! . . . . So what happened?
Nothing . . . . nothing really . . . . wait a second I've got something
   on the stove . . . . I was just going to fix myself a cup of hot tea!
(Soft whistling in the telephone booth . . . . Jazz tunes)
Hello! Are you still there?

Yes . . . . So?

Do you have enough change or shall I call that number where you are?

Yes No tell me.

Not now . . . . I'll tell you everything later.

No tell me now . . . . go ahead . . . . it's better if I know now.

Remember the Lipman? . . . they have a house on the lake . . . we
    bumped into them once or twice up there . . . she started talking
    . . . ah what a bitch . . . spreading all kinds of rumors innuendoes
    . . . a real yenta . . . and Benny got wind of it . . . but he told her
    off told her to go to hell . . . he was furious . . . told her it was a lie
    . . . it was not true . . . a disgusting thing to do . . . spread such
    stories about me . . . about us . . . that he trusted me and I was a
    good wife . . . and trusted you too . . . that he had treated you like
    a son and even given you a job . . . a full-time job . . . isn't it true?
    . . . in his lampshade factory . . . you should have seen the look
    on her face when she heard that . . . that lipwoman
    . . . . Yes it's true . . . . he gave me a job!

Like his own son . . . . and that you really deserved it because you've
    suffered so much during the war . . . . your parents . . . your
    whole family . . . father mother sisters . . . .

Yes in lampshades!

Whereas the rest of us here in America . . . it was not the same thing
    . . . you know what I mean . . . and that's why . . . .

Maybe it's better if I don't come over?

No no . . . . it's alright!

Really!

Really!

It's because of my things . . . . the things I left in your closet when I
    went in . . . . my black suitcase . . . . and also I've to talk to you!
    Touch you . . . . kiss you . . . .

Oh yes yes! . . . . Everything will be fine perfect!

Really! You think I can come? Sleep over?

Of course Darling! You can sleep on the sofa in the livingroom. Just as you did before.

Maybe it's better if I wait until HE comes home? . . . . Listen . . . . I'll call back later . . . . after eleven . . . . this way HE'll be home and HE'll be surprised that I'm in town without a place to stay won't be able to say no . . . . don't say anything!

. . . . (Sighs)!

How is the baby?

Adorable! You'll see . . . . she's going to be seven soon.

Is she asleep?

No she's watching T.V. . . . . Milton Berle . . . . You want to talk to her?

No better not. Don't bother her I'll see her later or in the morning!

Oh did I miss you dearest love did I worry about you three months even more without a word from you!

I was real busy you know . . . . all that training . . . . and also I became corporal!

How many days' leave you have?

No . . . . I'll explain later . . . . I mean 30 days!

THIRTY DAYS!

No . . . . I'll explain later what's happening.

What's this trip you have to take to . . . . near the Canadian border?

Camp Drum! It's because of my money . . . . they goofed . . . .

Where is that Camp Drum?

Up north! The whole regiment is up there practicing jumps in the snow!

Must be cold up there! Listen Darling . . . . come now . . . . take a cab . . . . I'll pay for it!

No . . . . I've got my Buick!

Come now . . . . hurry up . . . . I need you so much . . . . I want to hold you to kiss you . . . . I want to . . . .

No it'll be crazy! Would ruin everything!

. . . . be near you . . . .

I don't need a taxi I have my car . . . . and still about 10 or 12 bucks and
some change left (wow does it eat up gas that damn Buick of mine you
wouldn't believe it!)

Oh you still have your Buick!

Yes . . . . No . . . . I mean I want to sell it . . . . an ad in the paper
. . . . in The New York Times maybe . . . . like to get 150 or more for
it . . . . in damn good shape still . . . . Listen . . . . I'll call back
later . . . . but be surprised . . . . around eleven eleven-thirty
. . . . you know like you had no idea I was in town . . . . try to
answer the phone yourself when it rings don't let HIM answer . . . .
be ready . . . . or else I'll panic!

Okay!

You know what it does to me . . . . I get intimidated!

Poor Darling!

I wouldn't know what to do . . . . Okay Bye Love! . . . . See you
later!

Good Bye Dearest . . . See you soon . . . . I give you a
kiss! . . . . *(IT'S 35 CENTS MORE SIR)* . . . .

....

. . . . . shit . . . . . shit . . . . and shitagain
that's all I needed he mumbled as he stepped out of the telephone booth I
really feel like taking off [Dammit do I hate dialogues! but they are
necessary sometimes here and there if you want the story to be more true
to life more realistic veracious] really feel like dropping the whole thing!
? . . . ? . . . ? . . . ? *Ah* you guys want to know if I couldn't have
summed up the whole thing in a few words? [Must be a guy who is in a
hurry who asks this question or else somebody who doesn't like to hear
details especially sentimental details]

Yes I suppose I could have!

To save time and space. It's true that dialogue was not very brilliant!

But just as he stepped out the telephone booth into the rain and started
walking toward his Buick he noticed a lousy Cop standing by his car

writing a ticket — A Parking Ticket!

It's not my day! Dammit! I hadn't seen that motherfucker from the booth (He was so involved I suppose with his dialogue)!   I didn't know SIR!

Can't you read? NO PARKING ANY TIME

it says!   Yes — Officer — but you see it was an EmerGENcy!

Your driver's license and on the double young man and no argument!

You think I enjoy standing there in the rain!   You don't understand — SIR! — but i'm in the Army (The Military Service — 82nd Airborne Division) and in my case I thought . . . . Ah you thought because you're a soldier you don't have to respect THE LAW! Military Service or no Military Service me I don't give a damn! THE LAW is THE LAW! You hear! and it's the same thing for Everybody! Civilians as well as Militaries Clergymen as well as Politicians! NO PARKING ANY TIME that's exactly what it means!   NO PARKING ANY TIME and that applies to everybody my dear little Corporal (must have noticed I had brand new stripes on my sleeves)! Son of a bitch! It's gonna cost me five bucks for sure and the mother's gonna pocket the damn cash!

? . . . ? . . . ? . . . ? Oh you guys want to know if the dialogue was in French? [Must be a foreigner who asks this question or someone who thinks mostly chauvinistically]

Of course not!   She wasn't French Marilyn! Her name at least indicates that much. The whole dialogue reported above more or less in its entirety was in English. Though she did have 3 or 4 years of high school French Marilyn and add to this the fact that Marilyn and Benny took a trip to France one summer and it's not impossible quite plausible even that the dialogue could have been in French simply to make it more sensuous. But even then it would have had to be spoken or translated rather in English for the convenience of the story and its present recitation. Though in French this dialogue would indeed have been nice because they could have used the familiar TU form the THOU form with each other rather than the impersonal YOU form. It's too bad but that's the problem with the English language: its excess of fluidity or rather its lack of rigidity always flattens social or sentimental relationships!

Meanwhile there he was cursing that lousy Cop (in English and in French simultaneously) who had undoubtedly pocketed his five bucks I need not point out but useless to pursue the matter any further it's normal procedure with such unexpected characters — cop-out-of-place or in this case out-of-context!

So I moved on. Up/Town! Had a good juicy hamburger with French fries and a hot cup of coffee in one of those hamburger joints where you eat your stuff standing up. Cost me less than a dollar (in fact exactly 88 cents he said I remember). Then I strolled leisurely (no that's not it he wandered rather) up and down Broadway and finally I ended up on 42nd Street where ultimately lonely bums like me end up! On 42nd Street wet and scared like a water rat. It was a Thursday (I think he said or maybe I'm mista-ken it was a Sunday. What a crowd in any case! And it was still raining cats and dogs as if the sky above was feeling sorry for him or as if this was an Irish story) I believe but it didn't matter much which day it was it was not my day. That's for damn sure!

o-o-o-o-o-o-o-

My Buick was parked now (illegally of course) on a side street. Just a block or two from Time Square!

o-o-o-o-o-o-o-o-o-o-o-o-o-o-o-o-o-

Ah TIME SQUARE!

o-o-o-o-o-o-o

You have to see that at night with the giant neon lights yellow green blue red reflecting in the wet pavement! And the people! The little buglike people rushing in all directions!

A real circus!

o-o-o-o-o-o-o-o-o-o-

Yes you have to see that TIME SQUARE at least once in your life. The center of the World!

o-o-o-o-o-o-o-o-o-o-

And all the movies on 42nd Street! It's unreal! Maddening! You can never decide which one to choose! It's surfictional! A real circus!

o-o-o-o-o-o-o-o-o-o-o-o-o-o-o-o-o-o-o

I would have loved to take in a flick a good western but I wasn't too much in the mood and besides I didn't have enough time now (he'd told her he would call back around eleven eleven-thirty) and yet the great the fantastic flicks they had that night the stupendous westerns they had on 42nd Street at that time triple features but me I hate to walk in in the middle and miss the beginning and even worse when I have to leave before the end before the BIGSHOOTOUT the SHOWDOWN when everybody draws and all the goodguys and all the badguys kill each other massacre each other by the dozen by the truckload and then only one guy is still standing up at the end and he climbs on his horse and rides away in the sun westward and you feel like diving through the screen to follow him!

o-o-o-o-o-o-o-o-o-o-o-o-o-o-o-o-o-o-o-o-o

o-o-o-o-o-o-o-o-o-o-o-o-o-o-o-o-o-o-o-o-o
It was past 10:30 p.m. now. So I walked around a bit more feeling
very sorry for myself. Finally I decided it'd be better to walk into
one of those fishy bookstores to dry up a bit where they sell dirty
books with pictures of naked females on the cover and a fag who
had stepped out of his closet moved close to me and told me in a
whisper and with tears in his eyes all about the loneliness of life
and the sadness of his little furnished room which incidentally
was just two blocks from here and the place had two beds and
where if I wanted to I could come up to rest for a while or listen to
his disks and smoke some of his Turkish cigarettes a friend of his
who was travelling abroad had just sent him and that if it was
okay with me and I wanted to and I didn't have any place else to
go then I could spend the night he really didn't care on the
contrary I was welcome he was not a selfish person but that if I
only wanted let's say to stay just a while to rest because I looked
tired from travelling all day it was okay too just a few hours and
by now he had moved closer to me that asshole and had even
placed his hand on my fly which to tell the truth was starting to
bulge by now but me I told that fag to go and take a walk by
himself and without gloves I told him that sneaky pédale and he
walked away with his disgusting crocodile tears in his eyes but
when he got to the door he turned around to make sure I had not
changed my mind and he pointed to his ass and gave me the
finger as he ran out! Disgusting I said to myself angrily! The kind
of crap a guy has to come up with when travelling or telling a
story! But one must be faithful to the details otherwise the trip or
the plot falls apart. That's where in fact the tragic of this situation
lies: it constantly deviates from its course, and tragedy an old

Greek once said is the imitation of an action that is serious and also since it has magnitude complete in itself, with incidents arousing pity and fear (talk to me about incidents that arouse pity and fear!), wherewith to accomplish its catharsis of such emotions! Plot then (or in this case travel) becomes central to the process of attaining the emotional peace of catharsis because it directs fear and pity and therefore controls the purgation of these emotions. Interesting! However, since we are not interested here (what are we a constipated race?) in plot, but only in travel, it is useless to worry about such problems. Nonetheless, such pitiful and fearful encounters disgust me, and not because I am a snob or an egghead, but I can't stand little fags who peddle their asses publicly, and this one with his finger up his ass and his Turkish cigarettes really got on my nerves. Naturally this does not mean that I may not someday try it, one never knows, with the right person and in the proper place, and of course in the right frame of mind in a moment of inspiration, especially when one travels a lot (as he is doing currently) across country, but perhaps one should not anticipate too much, yes here we go again projecting ourselves into other parts of this story, parts as of yet untold, unrecited, unlived therefore, and in fact that may never be told, recited, and therefore never experienced in full or partially, but still to make it that obvious on 42nd Street, and in a semipublic place, takes guts, dammit he should have called a cop, or the vice squad, that would have been funny, but at least that incident, that fearful and pitiful incident purged him of his illusions, also it passed the time while he worried about his phone call and what Benny would say!

And now it's 10:47! — Almost time for him to make that phone call!

Wow time drags its ass when one worries!

And he is worried about Benny! Better delay the action!

Okay doesn't rain any more.   At lease we won't have to be concerned with that for a while, otherwise you guys will think this is an Irish story. Always rains in Irish stories I'm told, it's to make it more realistic. But here rain is used strictly to stress I should perhaps point out the difficulties of the journey and also I should further point out to emphasize the emotions of the guy whose story is now in progress — the protagonist! Therefore that it now stopped raining at this point in the story (in other words the rain is temporarily cancelled as everything else in here though it might snow later) shows how the first-hand teller has cleared his mind of his imagined worries (this may not be the case with the second-hand teller) about Benny or at least that he is now beginning to think a bit more clearly about the whole situation in the blue sky (cleared of the clouds of apprehension) of his mind. Wondering calmly in an introspective manner how much Benny knows of his liaison his secret adulterous relationship with Marilyn? For already he had a feeling just before he left for the army that Benny was eyeing him sideways and suspiciously. It may have been his guilt feeling that made his imagination imagine such an oblique look but nonetheless he worried about it and told Marilyn who in turn started worrying too. It was not certain yet that Benny knew anything but it would really make a mess of things for them to get caught in bed when everything is going so well. Better be careful!

A little screwing
with the boss's wife never hurts a guy
he said blushing. Especially when there is love in it
- reciprocal love, he quickly added in a convincing tone of voice!
But even his tone of voice, however convincing he tried to make

it, did not erase the sense of despair he felt at this point (and I do not mean when he strolled up and down 42nd Street to pass the time before making his phone call, but when he sat under our tree, or rather, as corrected earlier, when he stood on the edge of the precipice leaning against the wind contextually speaking, that is to say not when he spoke to himself originally in the far past, but as he reported to me in the near past)! Divided in himself (teller told or in this case retold a second time or perhaps eventually even a third time) he felt himself on the edge of an incredibly tragic situation in which there is no contradictory sense of the self in its uniqueness and vitality to mitigate the despair, terror and boredom of existence (I am of course paraphrasing here), and indeed I would agree that none of his feelings (as I am now trying to rephrase them, to recapture them verbally and second-hand) was divided (torn one might say) against either himself or his environment (that is to say HE as HE said, I as I say — no schizoschizo crap — and of course America and New York and 42nd Street and Time Square and the long road the long and painful road from Fayetteville to Camp Drum before heading west but also Marilyn's and Benny's deluxe apartment in Brooklyn without however forgetting the space the long and playful space in which the recitation is performed), all of these are remarkably whole, and, given their conditions, frankly quite sane, natural, and normal. For in fact, all experience is both active and passive, the unity of the given and even of the construed, and the construction one places on what is given can for that matter be either positive or negative. It is what one desires, or fears, or is prepared to accept, or it is not! The element of negation is in every relationship and every experience of relationship (I am now quoting directly), whether or not illicit. The distinction between the absence of relationships and the experience of every relationship as an absence is the division between loneliness and a perpetual solitude, or between provisional hope or hopelessness and a permanent despair. This describes more or less the psychology of our protagonist at the time he faced the possibility of exclusion from both his own experience and his own story as it would eventually be retold. Therefore, it is fortunate that HE and I were able to establish the kind of loving relationship we had in the near past for otherwise everything would have been lost, and I would never have been able to report it for posterity. However since what one might call a *creative relationship* (my italics) with the other (I suppose that's what he meant by reciprocal love?) is impossible, and an interaction is substituted which may seem to operate efficiently and smoothly for a while but which has no life in it (real life that is but only a fictional or in this case surfictional density), it is therefore understandable why he needed to make his tone of voice as convincing as possible, not only when he spoke to himself originally (in the blue sky of his mind) but also when subsequently he reported the situation to me (leaning against the wind) with all the feeling of despair, terror, and boredom that the anticipated phone call to Benny was arousing in him at this point!

But now
　　　　　it's time
　　　　　　　　to face
　　　　　　　　　　the
　　　　　　　　　　　　zizique
　　　　　　　　　　　　　　as the French say in situations

such as these!
Quick! The dime in the slot! HELLO!　　　　　　　! HELLO
? . . . ? . . . ? . . . ? *Ah* but you guys want to know how the two of them met? *Oh* it's a long story but maybe I should tell you a bit about that (the essential as he told it to me) or else we'll get lost. Okay if you insist, but quickly, briefly, because me what I really

want to tell, and what you guys should hear now, it's the story of
his journey west (or at least one of the versions of his Seven
Deadly Trips), the big crossing I mean, the discovery of America!
In other words, the future! The future and not the past! Hell with
the past! I'm fed up with the past, fed up with his past, my past,
our past! I want to tell the real story now, as it will happen
eventually, the story of how we'll move west into the sun with the
sun out of the rain the snow the grey sky 1951 and how we'll be
winners all of us. WINNER TAKE ALL that's what we'll call the
next trip the big journey west, in case we don't make it in this one,
in case this one never gets totally told, cancels itself out before it's
finished, as it might well happen, because the interesting part of
this story lies in the journey west. Everything else up to here, the
millions and millions of words wasted in verbal ejaculation and
typographical delirium, not to mention the thousands and
thousands of repeats and circumvolutions (from DON to TIOLI),
all of that has been bullshit balls foutaise de la blague (and I
almost forgot EL AM) or if you prefer mere padding, the launch-
ing pad for the real story!

Okay since you insist! As I was saying before   during the
summer 1949 I was working as a bus boy in the Catskills   a
kind of country club   I think I mentioned it before   yes
when we discussed his saxophone   that tenor saxophone he
bought with the money he saved during the summer 1948 (and
what a disgusting summer that was)   remember   the
saxophone which Charlie Parker blew at the Blue Bird   shit
you guys are lousy listeners
Don't you remember? Oh it's not important, but at least it was not
a complete waste of time, on the contrary, quite advantageous, to
work as a bus boy in the Catskills, financially and even sexually,

without too much effort, good tips, and of course room and board for three or four months, four months if you worked the conventions in May, and on top of that all the extras a guy could take advantage of if he wasn't a dead fish, such as free use of all the facilities, in fact that's how I learned to play golf and tennis and ping pong and shuffle board and a bit of bridge, but especially golf, me in those days I played a great game of golf, terrific golf (he said gripping an imaginary golf club a six or seven imaginary iron and performing in front of me and without a touch of self-consciousness a rather good and smooth imaginary swing in a semiprofessional manner), incredible shots (he had finished his shot right there on the edge of the precipice and looked in the distance his hand shading his eyes as if following the flight of the imaginary ball) even made money hustling the Jewish doctors at the country club (he was still following the imaginary golf ball as he leaned over the precipice and almost fell in)!

Eh that's terrific! I said to him, because me too I love golf and even play the game myself. What's your handicap?

Scratch!

Scratch! No kidding! Me I'm, or rather I should say I used to be when I played regularly a 3 or a 4 handicap. And you guys do you like golf? Not really! Oh no it's not a sport for old men. Let me assure you you don't drive that little ball out there 250 yards or 300 without putting something behind it!

Me in those days I had tremendous drives! I drove the ball 270 / 280 and without pressing!

Me too! Though sometimes I used to slice the ball. Huge banana shots!

Do You Still Play . . .? [A sportive looking cat in a sweat shirt] Are you asking me or him?

Him I don't know. But me of course I still play. Not like I used to!

You don't think I spend my time telling stories all the time. One has to relax sometime. Though these days not as well and not as steady as I used to. Only once in a while breaking 80. On a good day. Usually in the low 80s now. 82 / 84. But golf (he said) what a sport! Ah feels great to go out there when something is bugging you and just drive the little ball 270 yards 280 yards. For nothing. Just for the form, for the style, or simply for relaxation!

Marilyn too she was a damn good golfer. But Marilyn I didn't meet her that summer I met her the following summer. Summer 1950 therefore, if I remember correctly. Shit time passes quickly! The damn thing about growing old is that it happens to you suddenly and you don't know when it really started to happen! The first summer (1948) (1949?) (Damn I'm getting all confused) I fell in love with another girl in the Catskills. Voluptuous like a stuffed kishka. Cute like a bagel. Bernice was her name. Blondish, big blue eyes that always looked dreamy. A bit dumb. A virgin! Imagine that! I was 22 then and she said she was 17 (or 18) but looked more. It was love love at first sight. Bang one look and I was fluttering! Dizzy! Goose flesh all over! We lost all sense of responsibility that summer and almost got married!
Her father had a little grocery store in the Bronx. A delicatessen it was where he sold mostly salami. Qu'est-ce que j'ai pu m'en taper des gros saucissons, oui des saucissons à l'ail à l'oeil bien sûr oui! [We are reporting this is the original so that you guys can see how clever how sharp he was with words in his native tongue when he wanted to be]
We couldn't stay away from each other so eventually I left Detroit to live in New York during the winter 1949 to be closer to Bernice (it's normal when you're in love) I found a filthy little furnished room in the Bronx behind Alexander (six dollars a week) not too far just four blocks in fact from where she lived with her folks and

her sister and of course I was broke down to the last pieces of clothing to hock and not a fucking job in sight it was a rough winter beginning of a tough recession even a possible depression people were saying that's when I was living (if one can call that living) on 12 bucks and 56 cents for a week when eventually I did find a job washing dishes in a cafeteria and that was for two of us I was sharing the room with a French guy I had met on the boat coming over in 47 stumbled into him again on 42nd Street the day I arrived from Detroit I hadn't found a place yet sort of looking for something cheap and close to Bernice and by pure coincidence he had just been kicked out from his uncle's house he too had an uncle in America (a rich uncle) but the uncle had kicked him and I mean literally kicked him in the ass out of his house that morning in fact when he found him in bed with his aunt what a screwy deal he was an artist Loulou was his name tall and good-looking sharp dresser and always walking around with his dick in his hand an abstract painter a modern though he would have been better in my opinion yes much better as a conceptualist because that lazy bastard never did a bit of labor not a fucking thing refused to work said that real artists should not get their hands dirty we often argued that point but he always had me crushed in that argument he had illusions grand illusions and not the least modesty about his talent (Picasso was shit for him) shouldn't a guy have something to show for his talent I would say to him that's a bourgeois point of view he would reply and that's why he lived off my 12 dollars and 56 cents a week (6 of which went for the rent) without any scruples sleeping all day and eating noodles three times a day in those days it was the best one could buy to survive though it's quite true on occasions I would bring home a little extra food I had stolen from my cafeteria but Loulou contributed nothing

nothing tangible to what our dear Bernice (whom I am sure Loulou screwed once or twice while I was working) called our lovely domestic arrangement and besides he didn't have a thing to show for his great talent nothing tangible not a damn thing except the walls of our furnished room on which when strokes of inspiration took him (about once a month at night) he would paint his abstract monstrosities and when that happened his strokes of inspiration then we would immediately sacrifice two or three days of noodles just to buy him some paint and brushes! Ah what an energumen Loulou! But I liked him and it's thanks to him thanks to his relaxed happy go lucky way of life if I have a sense of humor today. He taught me how to laugh at life and art but especially how to laugh at myself dammit you take yourself too seriously he would say to me as he messed up my hair knowing full well how infuriated that would make me and in those days I always kept my hair well groomed and nothing infuriated me and he knew that than somebody messing up my hair but no need to tell all that again some lovely pages were devoted to that part of my life and to Loulou in DOUBLE OR NOTHING (have you seen that by the way? I got the Frances Steloff Prize for it) especially page 122 devoted in full to Loulou!

Wow did the two of us consume a lot of salami after Bernice with some pressure from us finally took her courage in her hands and started to sneak salamis out of her father's delicatessen hiding them like giant pricks under her skirt. It gave her a feeling of total independence!

It must have also given her ideas because from that day on I mean the day she started smuggling salamis under her skirt she became sexually insatiable totally liberated. She is the one who even thought up the idea of giving Loulou a dollar or two to go to the movies so that the two of us could have the room all to ourselves. What a good deal that was!

But the best deal of all was my country club in the Catskills just an hour and a half by car from New York not far from the Hudson River in the woods a perfect spot!

People came up from New York (Brooklyn Long Island Queens and Jersey) to spend part of the summer and even the whole summer to breathe some fresh air and do some exercise.

Mostly Jews in those days in my summer resort [I don't want to insist too much on the Jewish side of this story but one cannot avoid it altogether I just hope you guys don't make too much out of it] the rich ones second and even third generation Americans.

They came up by car mostly Cadillacs and Lincolns (huge wagons) fully equipped (power steering power brakes air conditioned) with the whole family wives kids suitcases golf clubs tennis rackets mink coats (and even sometimes the in-laws).

The wives usually stayed up alone with the kids four to six weeks and even for the whole season while the husbands commuted (back and forth and to and fro) from the City on weekends (arriving Friday night just on time for the big meal and leaving right after the Sunday lunch but not before tipping us guys waiters and bus boys).

It was a rather good system because the husbands had to return to the City to take care of their businesses (big businesses) make more cash so that the wives and kids could enjoy the fresh healthy country air!

It was indeed a good system and a rather nice way to spend the summer ESPECIALLY for us guys the employees the waiters bus boys babysitters lifeguards counselors directors of social and physical activities the whole staff in other words that population (subpopulation) who like a bunch of amateurs took care of the needs of the kids the little brats who spent their time taking swimming lessons canoeing on the lake and shoving away the good kosher food but ESPECIALLY the capricious needs of the mothers the lovely mothers who spent their time playing tennis golf bridge canasta getting suntanned dieting and copulating at night with the staff but it was okay because the management insisted for us staff to mix it up with the paying guests (both outdoors and indoors)

o o o o o o o o o o o o o o o o o
o o o o o o o o o o o o o o o o o
o o o o o o o o o o o o o o o o o

It was a great social institution that summer resort in the Catskills we enjoyed it ESPECIALLY during the week when the husbands were doing business in the City making more money for the wives and kids so that they could better enjoy themselves with the staff but ESPECIALLY with us bus boys and waiters and we did our best to entertain these lonely wives and charming mothers even though it was exhausting at times all that extra curricular activity ESPECIALLY when we had to serve tables three times a day at full speed play tennis or golf between meals and those of us who were qualified (for example me as a talented swimmer) participate in organized social or athletic events and on top of that play poker half of the night (when there was nothing else to do) with the tough guys who worked in the kitchen the cooks and dishwashers or the groundkeepers but we did our best to please the paying guests and personally I have nothing to reproach myself after all we were only a bunch of amateurs kids working their way through college (except me)!
In any event that's how I met Marilyn one summer (summer 1950) while working as a bus boy in the Catskills but by then it was all over in fact finished with Bernice ————- Ah but I see that one of you guys has a question okay okay don't get excited like that you'll have a stroke okay go ahead yes you with the mustache I'm listening!

Why did he accept to go into the American Army and go
ahead I follow you *fight illegitimately a war against North
Korea & China in which I assume he had nothing to gain
personally since he was not a U.S. Citizen?* Damn good
question SIR . . . Ah but there is more . . . go on *And
why did he submit himself so slavishly to American Im-
perialism?* Oh I see! . . . *And why did he for that matter*
Oh there is still some more! *allow himself to become a tool
of that decadent that oppressive Capitalistic system?*

Intelligent question no doubt but can
one really answer without at least reflecting upon it for a while
may I ask for that is the real question and moreover can you tell
me what is the exact relationship SIR between your question and
what I was in the process of reporting? Okay since you insist I
shall drop for the time being what he told me about Marilyn (and
Bernice) and his summer resort in the Catskills as well as all the
other lovely married women (wives and mothers) he screwed up
there since you seem anxious that I reply to your question (indeed
a rather good question for once) but I must warn you that the
political implications of your question though legitimate and well
placed may take us into regions which I had hoped to avoid
however since politics we must now discuss eh bien allons-y!

Civilization (and in this case we mean the American civilization)
can be measured by the distance which man has placed between
himself (his daily bread) and his excrement. Agreed in his case he
didn't have to go, he could have refused since, as you pointed out
so justly Sir, he wasn't (yet) an American citizen, but then they
could have thrown him out, expatriated him from his newly
adopted country, shipped him back to France, to his miserable
French past, on the double, so long, with a kick in the ass,
goodbye, and no questions asked, deport him like a no good
alien, and therefore finished America, the American dream and

the land of opportunities, cancelled the beautiful journey west cross country, the 30 day vacation, if one can call that a vacation because up to now it hasn't been much of a vacation, finished also the $'s he could have collected, well at least those $'s he would have collected eventually when he had made it to Camp Drum, and even those other $'s he might have saved overseas (on the black market in Tokyo), and more dollars he would perhaps have earned honestly when he got out of that damn army, for then he would be a U.S. citizen who had proudly served his country, but no use anticipating that much, no need to talk about what has not yet happened, and might never happen, or at least talk about what has not yet been reported to us, directly or indirectly at this time, but you guys are really hardheaded, don't you understand a damn thing, bordel de bordel as he would say when he was angry, there was nothing else for him to do, he was starving at the time, it was a bad winter, and moreover his love life, his emotional well being, was in terrible shape, shitty like hell, therefore wasn't that sufficient reasons, among others, for a poor lonely guy like him to want to move his ass out of civilian life? Agreed, and I'm not arguing the matter to justify his behavior, it's dumb for anybody to go into the army to fight a war (legitimate or illegitimate is not the point here) when one doesn't really have the least patriotic feelings about it, nor for that matter any ideological reasons for doing so, but nonetheless he did not argue, did not question the letter from the STATE DEPART-MENT (mentioned previously), he did not protest his draft board's decision, he went and that's all, like a lamb, feeling somewhat relieved and happy inside (he admitted that much to me eventually), for, as he said to himself, after reading the charming letter from the S.D., at least in the army there's plenty to eat, for, my Dear Sir, yes you with the mustache, do you know what it is to be hungry all the time? Hungry to the point of searching inside garbage cans for something to chew on, of having your eyes bulge out of their sockets as you stare at people eating in restaurants, hear your belly whine at night like a wounded animal, feel your tongue stick to your palate like a bloodsucker, do you know what it is to have sores in your ass for not having anything to shit because you haven't had any food to eat for three days and your guts scream with fear and anger and despair!

Okay
no
need
to
complain
                                        what
                                        could
                                        he
                                        have
                                        done
                                        he
                                        had
                                        no
                                        other
                                        choice
                    and
                    besides
                    there
                    was
                    Benny
                    who was starting to eye him rather suspiciously!

                                    Therefore when they convoked him
                                    for the big medical examination
                                    he did not hesitate a moment
                                    and told himself shit man
                                    let us take advantage
                        of this great occasion and let us jump ahead
                                    feet first
you'll be well taken care of
room and board
and free clothing
and three complete meals a day
okay took them a few months
from the day of the medical
examination to the day of his
official indoctrination the day
when he received the charming letter from the State Department which specified
        when he was to report
        but meanwhile now that he knew what
        to expect
        now that he had so to speak a raison d'être
                        a goal in the near future
                        a path to follow
                    perhaps even a path that would lead to glory
        and that he was no longer in shit up to his neck and above
                that his future in fact was not starting to shine in blue
        ahead of him
now that he knew that he would eventually go safely into the army he
did not worry any more
or at least less
about his daily bread
his financial and emotional problems
his love life
instead he borrowed money left and right from friends and even in some
                        cases from people who were not his real friends to
                        celebrate his approaching departure and of course
                        he had no intention of ever repaying that money
                        since

he was
so to speak in a between-time-stage
                a financial meantime
                a virtual present rather than a true or actual present not to
                mention the emotional in-between
therefore he was in suspense
between two lives
and it is in this meanwhile
this parenthetical gap
this temporal spread
this existential displacement
this premilitary reprieve
this moment of anticipatory waiting (when he really didn't give a shit
about anything) that he and Marilyn fell in love with one another even
though they had already met before
and had even attempted on several
occasions to indulge their mutual
                and reciprocal love
and emotions into one another but to speak the truth love was nothing
love was secondary now compared to the possibilities opening to him in
the near future as he stood on the threshold of his military life as a
paratrooper!
In other words his love for Marilyn was temporarily suspended cancelled in favor of military anticipation regardless of the political implications that such a life may have
for him as he embarked
into the next stage of his future

but since you people want to discuss	**Politics**
since you people want to know how he felt about	**Politics**
well Gentlemen to tell the truth	**Politics**
didn't mean much to him	**Politics**
okay let's speak about	**Politics**
since that's what you seem to care about	**Politics**
because for you people	**Politics**
it's a real obsession	**Politics**
for him you know it was quite another thing	**Politics**
he didn't think much of	**Politics**
even if he got involved with	**Politics**
once in a while in his days	**Politics**
of course he's done his share of	**Politics**
but for him	**Politics**
it was above all scuffling	**Scuffles**
yes scuffling in the streets	**Scuffles**
that's what Politics is all about	**Scuffles**
wow! could I tell you stories of his	**Scuffles**
in the streets	**Scuffles**
in the streets of every city throughout the world	**Scuffles**
on all the public squares and Places de la République	**Scuffles**
for nothing (for the dumb masses if you wish)	**Scuffles**
until you run out of blood (for all kinds of stupid causes)	**Scuffles**
I've been hit on the head (he told me) with sticks	**Contusive**
sticks yes	**Contusive**
sticks in every corner of the world	**Contusive**
sticks	

in the streets of Paris in the streets of New York in the streets of Los
Angeles in the Streets of Baltimore Washington Chicago and Rome and
even once in the streets of Tokyo and another time in London and later in
the streets of Buffalo

and always with sticks	**Contusive**
sticks	

and always first always there in the first row (like a jerk) shouting as loud
as I could like a fanatic without truly knowing what the hell I was doing
there but always there like a cretin
shouting slogans
fist tight and UP in the air singing the INTERNATIONALE

[in English]
[in French]
getting my ass and my back and my head clubbed like a sack of sawdust
my blood dripping on the pavement of every city throughout the world
like a fanatic at night
during the day
early morning
in the cold
in the snow
in the heat
passing out
being dragged away in police vans beaten to death with   **Contusive**
sticks and you guys want to talk Politics with me!   **You're kidding!**

Dammit did he shout SLOGANS in his days against
those who love it or leave it
those who piously those who copiously
those who critically those who tricolor those who bumper sticker
those who hit you on the head those who inaugurate
those who believe they believe
those who trucify those who armisticize
those who take it or leave it
those who think they think
those who croak croak
those who caca and pipi
those who have feathers
those who have panaches
those who mumble
those who chew sideways
those who screw in the brain
those who hamletize
those who sing in tune
those who fuck in the dark
those who spitshine
those who eat too much
those who close their eyes
those who thumb their nose
those who fix bayonet
those who vietnamize
those who are too white
those who plug holes
those who can you hear
those who bury the living
those who statue liberty
those who float and never sink
those who club contusively
those who ask too many questions

Yes
Gentlemen
he shouted SLOGANS his guts out
for all kinds of causes
good ones and bad ones
ripe ones and sour ones
beautiful ones and ugly ones

And once or twice
he was thrown in jail
(in Chicago in Buffalo)
without ever knowing why
or what the fuck he was doing
there in this mess
this brothel   (politically speaking)
this circus   (ideologically speaking)

because Gentlemen
you're not going to tell me that one must have convictions
                                    obsessions
                                    beliefs
                                    ideologies in order to
                                    get out
into the streets
no   indeed
no   all you need is guts   (the belly that is)   and for him
GUTS blind guts was everything the center of his body and the center of
his world and the center of his life and if your belly is empty then out into
the streets dammit fist tight and UP in the air shouting like an imbecile all
kinds of crap / merde against
those who steal the bread out of people's mouth
those who dig graves for children
those who fuck flies in the ass
those who jerk off with gloves on
those who have their three daily meals six times a day while others
            have their daily bread approximately once a week or less!

In other words Politics it's a matter of You
Get It or The Other Guy Gets It Bang
because finally Politics TRUE POLITICS is mere fanaticism for
those who have no scruples because deep inside or on the surface
who gives a shit about the poor guys who run in the streets
shouting SLOGANS / who gives a damn about the belly of those
who are oppressed compressed depressed? all those who work
like animals in the factories in the holes shitholes tunnels ditches?
all those whose hands bleed? all those whose heads are crushed?
all those who spit their lungs in toilet bowls? those who have their
daily bread once a week? those who spread shit on their bread
and eat it in the dark?
Therefore those who speak of Liberté / Egalité / Fraternité /
                    those who speak of human misery / kids
                    eaten by rats / public works / all those who
                    bullshit their socio-politico
bla bla / their false humanism / their fake sentimentalism / their
crap about the masses and the working class / deep inside and on
the surface they don't give a shit about humanity because in
Politics TRUE POLITICS there is no room for sentimentality no
room for the belly there is only room for contusive sticks and
slogans and neither good nor bad it's all played beyond good and
evil and if you are one of the losers then Bang! it's you who takes it
on the head but if you're on the side of the guys who are winning
then it's you who gives it to the other guy it's just a matter of being
on the right side at the right time and then you're one of those
who those who those who those who those who those who fuck
the rest of humanity who beat the shits out of the other guy with
contusive clubs with hammers and nails and electric shocks and
fingers in the ass and needles in the arm and kicks in the belly and
cigarette burns while
                    the rest of humanity continues
                    to vomit its guts while shouting
                    stupid slogans!
Therefore you don't think I'm going to take you seriously because
of a little political question like that? Politics my friend (yes you
with the mustache) you can shove it up your ass in little capsules
(Psitt!) in square round or oval pills (Pistt!) it's delicious for
constipation believe me!

Deep breath / moment of hesitation!
Three in the morning — les yeux en trou de bite — LA PO LI TI
QUE!

o   o
‿

qu'il se la carre dans le croupion en petits morceaux bien découpés
he said

(.)   (.)

-
                                                                          to me
when I told him about that question (retrospectively) moi je m'en
fous pas mal and that's what I told the guy with the mustache as
he quickly retreated into the crowd Here let me tell you what he
said when I told him about your question (retroactively) the other
night (around two or three in the morning I couldn't sleep) he
said I came across something quite incredible in a book I was
reading something you guys could very well have written in your
spare time a real jewel the apotheosis of an inspired politicomer-
dique declaration (I am quoting that in italics so that you can see it
better and of course in French from the original):

> *Nous, nous ne sommes ni des ennemis de notre*
> *pays, ni des idéalistes nébuleux, mais des Francais*
> *pour qui le réalisme consiste à travailler pour la*
> *paix avec les armes de la paix, qui sont la vérité, le*
> *don de soi et l'amitié avec tous. Nous nous sentir-*
> *ions obligés à la même protestation pour des dé-*
> *tenus appartenant á tout autre parti, classe, nation*
> *ou confession, ou race, car notre action est un té-*
> *moignage de conscience.* (Signed TRENTE
> VOLONTAIRES)

Well what do you say now? Don't tell me you believe that kind of
crap!
Can you imagine do you realize doesn't it puzzle you to see where
we have
come to
just like that in the middle [well almost the middle] of this story
his story my
story or our
story in the
middle of an
abraca-dabra
story such as
this one?
It's really something - PITIFUL - to have to resort to
that kind of quotation (more or less quoted correctly)
that kind of remplissage just so that the story can move
forward progress a little — for the good of literature and of
humanity!
Lucky for you
guys you don't have to read everything — in toto!
Lucky for you
that the leaping system of reading (and writing) of this RECI-
(tation) permits you so to speak to leap (jump over if you prefer)
this type of sordid passages (or for that matter any other passages
in this story)!
That,
in fact, is the KEY to this RECI-(tation) :   THE LEAPFROG
technique!
[and you'll never know what you've missed]
which allows you
any time
anywhere
here and there, freely and at random, to HOP / HOP / HOP /
over the details!

and if some of you are listening (orally) to this story rather than reading it (visually) (sitting or standing) to yourself or aloud (according to the RECOMMENDATIONS) well then you can (any time you wish) permit yourselves little moments of somniferous punctuation (or soporific rest) you can in other words simply close your eyes (or your ears) and fall into complete silence (or darkness) thus allowing yourselves moments of auditive hesitation of public (or private) calm to give yourselves (totally or partially) time to regain your concentration and (in your intermittent snoozing) time to get back in the so-called swing of things chew on your candies if you have any go to the toilet if you need to take a leak or crap according to your needs while US (that is to say Me Him and Moinous) we can get back on the road of our journey and all this is quite normal since as it was repeatedly said in the course of this recitation in progress (also according to the prefatory RECOMMENDATIONS) there is so far in this story much that one can take in full or one can leave in part but whatever the case we have managed to come that far and for that at least we deserve a bit of encouragement so that we may pursue our arduous task

QUESTIONNAIRE

Permit me at this time if you please to interrupt this story a moment so that I may now ask you a few questions of my own regarding our intramural setup which will allow us to better situate ourselves in relation to one another thereby helping us better understand one another as we proceed with the rest of this endless recitation without further misunderstandings.

Here therefore a dozen questions to which I shall ask you to answer as honestly as possible by placing a little cross [+] inside the brackets furnished with the questions but without however signing your name to this questionnaire so that your identity may not be questioned by public opinion the censure bureau or the official members of the literary establishment.

[courtesy SNOW WHITE]

QUESTIONS :

1. Up to here have you liked the recitation? YES [ ] NO [ ]

2. Do you think the main character in the story resembles a real human being? YES [ ] NO [ ]

3. Have you understood up to now that MOINOUS dead or alive is only a symbolic figure? YES [ ] NO [ ]

4. Is it clear that the JOURNEY is a metaphor for something else? YES [ ] NO [ ]

5. In the rest of the story would you like more emotion YES [ ] or less emotion NO [ ]

6. In your opinion are there too many obscenities (and also too many sexual allusions) in this story? YES [ ] NO [ ]

7. Do you think that a new form of madness is essential (or even necessary) to improve literary creation? YES [ ] NO [ ]

8. Are you for or against legalized prostitution and / or for legalized homosexuality? YES [ ] NO [ ]   YES [ ] NO [ ]

9. Does the FIRST-HAND TELLER remind you of anyone you know in real life? YES [ ] NO [ ]

10. Do you think that a metaphysical dimension would improve this story? YES [ ] NO [ ]

11. Are you aware of the consequences this story may have on the future of literature and humanity? YES [ ] NO [ ]

12. Please write (in 25 words or less) your frank opinion of this recitation: ---
----

P.S. Do you think all books should have such a QUESTIONNAIRE?

YES [ ] NO [ ]

And furthermore have you ever seen such a QUESTIONNAIRE?

YES [ ] NO [ ]

If so where? ---

Please detach along the perforated line and mail back to publisher

XVI

by-pass & interference

DEFINITIONS

BY-PASS (bï / păs′, -päs′) *n.* 1. a road enabling motorists to avoid towns and other heavy traffic points or any obstruction to easy travel on a main highway. 2. a secondary pipe, or other channel connected with a main passage as for conducting a liquid or gas around a fixture, pipe, or appliance. 3. *Elect.* a shunt (def. 8). —*v.t.* 4. to avoid (obstructions, etc.) by following a by-pass. 5. to cause (fluid, etc.) to follow such a channel. 6. to go over the head of (one's immediate supervisor, etc.).

INTERFERENCE (ĭn′tar fĭr′ans) *n.* 1. act or fact of interfering. 2. *Physics.* the reciprocal action of waves (as of light, sound, etc.), when meeting, by which they reinforce or cancel each other. 3. *Radio.* a. the jumbling of radio signals because signals other than the desired one are being received. b. the signals which produce the incoherence.

QUA QUA QUA QUA QUA QUA QUA QUA QUA
[together in a chorus]
QUAQUAQUA . . . . don't get excited! calm down! . . . .
QUAQUAQUA everything will be okay! the left the right the
communists fascists socialists the popular front the postal service
democracy bullshit! all masturbators who drink too much
ouisqui-booze! let me tell you it's useless to theorize and yet you
guys never stop theorizing and terrorizing in your glossy publica-
tions on and on shouting scheming bitching and arguing publicly
and privately for nothing like a pack of dogs for any ideological
connerie in the newspapers on radio and on TV that's how you
spend most of your time while the rest of mankind starves or tells
stories (same thing) always screaming against this and against
that like a bunch of old ladies yapyapyap! against repression
censure treason experimental fiction surfiction! against those
who disagree with you but in fact you don't give a damn about all
that and about human misery and starvation and literature not a
fart about all that and in the evening satisfy with your futile and
useless daily activities you walk home leisurely hands in pockets
a good cigar at the corner of the mouth to eat well sleep well inside
your well-kept homes well protected and once in a while on
Saturday night usually a nice little piece of ass (simple question of
reflex or habit) with the old lady just like that turn over darling
spread your legs yes it's relaxing it's nice and cozy to stick your
little paternal member inside the sempiternal cunt of the old lady
so what the fuck do you bug the shit out of us with your weekend
politics I ask you? Go tell your sordid stories somewhere else!
Qua Qua Qua! There is nothing more depressing than weekend
politics! Personally I prefer a quiet weekend in the country telling
stories to friends! Therefore let's skip the passages which deal
with Bernice and how she lost her virginity in the Catskills (the
allusions to salamis suffice I suppose) and let's not insist either

(even though point blank he shifted subject) on the details of the evening the three of us spent in that deluxe apartment in Brooklyn when (us in this case meaning the protagonist Marilyn and Benny), finally, we took our courage in our hands, around eleven (eleven0nine to be exact) and called back and Benny answered the telephone (to our surprise and distress) instead of Marilyn (as previously arranged), but in spite of the antagonism in his voice he nonetheless invited us to spend the night (as expected) on the livingroom sofa (for lack of a guest room), therefore here we are now, comfortably seated (the livingroom sofa was embroidered with large colorful flowers) with a cup of freshly brewed coffee in our hands, the three of us (the baby was asleep by now in her baby room), close to each other, in a lovely circle (my ass in the flowers), a triangle rather, Benny on our right and Marilyn at our feet in a stunning deshabille her legs folded beneath her ass, more beautiful and loving than ever!

In spite of its apparent perfection it was not a pretty spectacle because of Benny's stringent oblique looks! It was impossible to grab dear Marilyn's ass, we were only able to touch (quickly) one of her breasts when Benny disappeared a moment in the bathroom to take a quick leak (supposedly) or catch us in the act! Evenings such as these are better forgotten but nonetheless we went on and it is therefore essential now to present the situation in details for it may have relevant and even symbolic consequences on events that will be reported subsequently if we ever get to such events!

Most of the evening was wasted telling stories about the paratroopers and life in the 82nd with all the crummy details of the training just in case there is a war and the twenty mile hikes we took daily with a fullpack on our back and the stupidity of the

dumb hillbillies in our outfit and the business of the love letters
we wrote (for the sake of love) for all the animals in our barrack
[Company C] and the big joke of the Push Ups up and down give
me twenty give me thirty nose in the dirt on the double and also
about the poker (but of course not a word about all the fucking
that went on in the minds of his fellowsoldiers and all the masturbating that went on in their hands under the filthy blankets of the
82nd in the nights of North Carolina) and Bob Moinous etcetera
etcetera

all that of course
expurgated corrected accelerated condensed reduced and embel-
lished to the maximum (in situations like these one must be
careful and prudent unless one is a pervert or a masochist) both
Marilyn and Benny seemed to enjoy our rather picturesque
stories since they showed pleasure in listening to us (in spite of
the malaise of the triangular situation) and even encouraged us to
go on in moments of verbal lapses or mental failings and so we
went on with full heartedness and did not hesitate to indulge in
flagrant exaggerations in propitious spots for instance we exaggerated greatly the number of push ups inflicted upon us daily

etcetera etcetera	the anguish and loneliness of paramilitary life
etcetera	the brutality and ignorance of the hillbillies in our outfit
etcetera etcetera	the kindness and understanding of Captain Cohen
etcetera	the bigotry and prejudice of the guy from Maryland
etcetera	the beauty and immensity of the sky when one jumps in it
etcetera etcetera	the number of miles we hiked everyday fullpack
etcetera etcetera	the affection we had for Moinous and Moinous for us

Nevertheless in spite of our stories told full speed - - - -
- - - - - - - - and exaggeratedly to better disguise our
anxiety - - - - - - - - - we were still illatease in this
luxurious livingroom sitting in the flowers at the
corner of our triangle wondering what the hell we
were doing here while you guys (allow us a little digression) were undoubtedly sitting home comfy eating

your delicious dinner with the family or already asleep
in your giant size beds or more likely screwing the hell
out of the old lady unless you were (which wouldn't
surprise us) sitting - - - - - - - - - - - or standing on some
political platform - - - - - - - - - (a little fantasy helps)
gesticulating and screaming like a bunch of baboons
against your wasted youth or against the government
or your daddies and your dear mammies who complex
the shit out of you (or anything else that was fashiona-
ble at the time) while us with our ass in the flowers we
kept wondering gosh (while looking sideways at
Benny) MUST I BITE THE HAND THAT STARVES
ME SO THAT IT CAN STRANGLE ME BETTER?
Gosh!

What would you guys have done in his place?
Ass in the flowers (or somewhere else) exhausted after twelve
hours of driving in his beat-up Buickspecial in the rain Benny on
his right and Marilyn at their feet sitting on her legs more beautiful than ever and more appetizing than ever with her big black
eyes and her sweet smiles! Can you visualize the scene?

THAT TRIO

THAT TRIANGLE

THAT MENAGE A TROIS

Can you sense the potential disaster :: (obstruction / by-pass /
etc.)?
Benny now moving across from them :: to sit in the leather
armchair thus destroying the perfect triangle :: or rather making
of a right angle triangle an irregular obtuse angle triangle ::
perhaps to see them better :: and Marilyn now stretching nonc-
halantly on her right side on the thick oriental carpet :: her knees

folded behind her in an S shape her head resting languishingly on her hand :: looking at me straight in the eyes (almost smiling :: with the tip of her soft tongue lightly touching her sensual lower lip ::) with raw passion!

Can you feel abstractly the electricity that circulated in the air? ======================= Can you feel how Benny suddenly looked mean and angry with his badly shaven face and his slouching broad shoulders of an ex-boxer who burns to fight again knowing full well that next time it will be total humiliation o o o o o o o o o o o o o o o o Can you feel how beautiful and sexy Marilyn was with her pleading big black eyes and her purple deshabille slightly opened at the breasts exhibiting the voluptuous alley between her two fleshy and well-rounded teats?

Wow could I fuck her on the spot right here on the oriental carpet! So much so that I am afraid it might show therefore hopla quickly I cross my legs [x] on top of another and sink back into the flowers!

And lucky for us the conversation subtly shifted to something else!

!to politics in fact!

Full speed and without hesitation (what the hell!) I told them (at this point he was not even looking at me any more sort of staring blankly in the precipice as though inventing on the spot) how me, in 36, in 42, in 46, in 49, in 52, in 58 (projecting ahead blindly), in

62, in 68, and I skip some (Hey! almost always even number years I said puzzled, and you seem to anticipate) yes almost, oh well, I was in the streets, with the masses, shouting slogans like a jerk (those youthful political memories must have put Benny in a better mood because he urged him to go on) yes therefore, I went on, me, I was saying, I was hardly ten years old (wow was he sublimating himself!) when my father took me to my first leftist rally, and what a political manifestation that was, yes what a debacle!

Ah have I seen all kinds of political parades
Ah have I seen all kinds of people's debacles
Ah have I sang the Internationale in my days!

We were walking close together (the masses) fists up in the air (like a bunch of pears), my little boy's fist (he explained looking up from the precipice) was smaller than all the others but it counted just as much! Ah did we shout slogans against Capitalism, bosses, cops, starvation, I had no idea what all that meant but I shouted with the rest, against le chomage and un-employment, against inflation and la soupe populaire, and the forty-eight hour week! Ah did we sing the Internationale that day! Me I didn't understand too well all that stuff about la lutte finale la gloire les forçats du travail (I suppose he sang his Inter-nationale and shouted his slogans in French in those days) les damnés de la terre les enfants de la patrie le genre humain, but I shouted with the rest of my fellowmen, and that day in particular (when he was hardly ten) it was a May 1st, what a riot, what a debacle when the cops charged the masses I tell you, les forçats du travail, les damnés de la terre, tout le genre humain et les enfants de la patrie did they get it in the ass that day!

Have you ever seen your father I asked Benny suddenly staring straight at him with his head bashed in blood streaming down his face his skull cut open by the vicious blows of the Gardes Mobiles' contusive sticks?

Seeing Benny react quite emotionally I pushed on and took advantage of his compassion, and don't forget I was not even ten years old (Marilyn was gasping), and my father's blood pissing out of his mouth nose ears while the flics were chasing us. My father was holding my little hand tight with his huge hand, so tight it was hurting me, and even lifting me off the ground as we turned the street corners, and I could hear in my back the cops' boots and the blows of the contusive sticks crashing on the skulls of those who could not run as fast as we did, and in the distance I could hear the Pin-Pon of the sirens (Marilyn was sobbing)!

You'll see how great how tremendous it'll be when we get to Russia one of these days my father used to say all the time while my mother cried her eyes out especially when we came home from those political rallies You're a brute she would say to him with sobs in her voice you have no sense of responsibility why can't you leave the child alone why do you have to drag him into all that dreck you good-for-nothing you lazy bum don't you think he'll learn soon enough about all that vacheté and all that misery why do you need to show him all that just to make him more vicious YOU DON'T UNDERSTAND DAMN YOU my father would shout back as he banged the table with his fist YOU DON'T UNDERSTAND A DAMN THING while my mother would shove a glass of milk at me but to tell the truth me I rather liked those political parades and all my father's friends yes I liked all these foreigners Polish Jews Russian Jews Rumanians

Chineses Czechs Spaniards Germans and even some Americans and all their foreign languages (yes his father spoke seven languages he told me with pride) Me I said to Benny without flinching I read Karl Marx and Engels when I was twelve years old not that I understood what they were talking about but at least I had that in me for later but that day (May 1st, 1938, le jour des prolétaires) Place de la Bastille when the cops chased us down the streets with their clubs and my father got hit on the head while we were singing the Internationale then it started to make sense suddenly!

Little pause in the story while Marilyn is serving us another fresh cup of coffee with some cookies and Benny runs to the john for another leak

---

Finally we lost the police so we stopped inside a big double door (they call that une porte cochère) we were out of breath breathing drivelling puffing like two horses we were Rue des Francs-Bourgeois said my father with a little smile the blood was dripping on his face I took out my big checkered handkerchief which my mother always put in my pocket a square yard of it and gave it to him so he could wipe his blood I could feel my hands trembling a little and yet it was not a cold day a rather nice day in fact (a Sunday I think he said) spring was in the air but I was trembling anyway and then suddenly my father (he was tall and quite good-looking with deep grey eyes) started laughing but an incredible an irresponsible laugh like he was going crazy or something coughing blood inside his laughter and me I didn't know what was happening so I didn't dare say anything or ask why he was laughing like that (it was normal I suppose at his age remember he was hardly ten) and suddenly still while laughing my father (he was very strong) grabbed me around the waist and lifted me off the ground so that our faces were equal on the same level and kissed me on the cheeks on the nose on the forehead leaving some of his blood on my face (huge sigh from Marilyn) and so me too I burst out into laughter I couldn't hold back and I started laughing however tears were running down my cheeks at the same time WoW did we laugh my father and I there Rue des Francs-Bourgeois it was really good really épatant!

But then I said to my father blushing a little: *Papa*
                                          J'ai envie
                                          De faire Pipi!

Maybe it was dumb of me to say something like that at such a moment but I couldn't hold it back any more. You got to go? Come. We'll find a place!

Quickly my father led me to a café not too far in fact from where we were and where he had taken me before because this was the place where usually he met his foreign friends and in fact many of them were already there in little groups discussing very loud in all kinds of foreign languages what had happened I suppose Place de la Bastille and my father showed me where the W.C. was and he went to discuss with the other foreigners at the bar!

Me in the cabinets (after my pipi) I looked at myself in the mirror above the sink (he had to raise himself on his toes to be able to see his face) and that's when I saw my father's blood on my face. It was dry now but I didn't wipe it.

But when we got home that night late woo did my mother cried and and screamed woo did she get angry at my father that night when she saw the blood (she didn't know it was not my blood) on my face!

But before going home when I came out of the cabinets my father bought me a nice cup of hot chocolate with a croissant and while I sat in a crooked chair in a corner he went on arguing (in Polish I believe) with the other fanatics!

You want them to kill him your only son my mother said in her tears can't you protect him look at him full of blood I don't understand your folies!

And when she saw my handkerchief all red with blood she really let out a scream of agony. I loved my mother but she was always so sad and always with tears at the corners of her eyes and always shoving an extra little something on top of me an extra sweater even during the summer always an extra pair of gloves and always giving me a little extra spoon of mashed potatoes or sliding an extra piece of meat from her plate to my plate on those days when we had meat saying that she wasn't hungry and my sisters yelling that it was not fair that it was always me getting more than all the rest of the family and my father getting angry and cursing in Polish or in Yiddish because she was spoiling me and me telling my mother I had enough I was full I was too hot — she had big black sad eyes my mother!

And my father!
What a man! A real polyglot. Seven languages he spoke!
He was an artist (a surrealist painter it seems). A starving artist . . . But what good did it do him all that politics? They made lampshades out of him (or soapcakes) and my mother too and my two sisters too and . . . I was lucky I didn't get exterminated (X-X-X-X) like them . . . it's because me I jumped off a train (remember the raw potatoes) during the night . . .

But this story I had already told Benny and Marilyn several times before therefore let's skip it . . . yes but Marilyn insisted (by now she was all excited) PLEASE TELL US AGAIN (I understood the reason why she wanted me to go on so that Benny would feel guilty and have pity on me and be nice to me) therefore full blast and without hesitation I lurch forward or as the French say je rentre dans le tas and dive into my story even if that means repeating myself somewhat after all let's be honest a biography or a guy's past experiences it's always something one invents afterwards in fact life is always a kind of fictional discourse a lot of bullshitting!

<><><><OH DO TELL US THAT STORY AGAIN DO TELL US ><><><>

Ah what a man he was my father (obviously he is reinventing him
somewhat) I was thirteen when they picked him up and the rest
of the family on that sinister 14 juillet or thereabout with their
yellow stars and their cries and their little bundles   my
mother was howling down the staircase tears rolling down from
her eyes   huge tears   and my two sisters too   and on
top of that at thirty my father (Damn did he have a rough life! I
wonder why he didn't commit suicide?) he became tuberculous
yes twice a week had to have stuff pumped into his
pneumothorax   saloperie! sometimes during the night he
would start choking and spitting blood   my mother knew what
to do but she would panic anyway (at this point Benny and
Marilyn started weeping like two kids)   he had eyes gray like
a stormy sky my father but my father ᜪᜪᜪᜪᜪᜪᜪᜪᜪᜪᜪᜪᜪᜪᜪ my
father

[X - X - X - X]   SYSTEMATIC EXTERMINATION   [X - X - X - X]
                     Ψ Ψ Ψ Ψ Ψ Ψ Ψ Ψ Ψ Ψ Ψ Ψ Ψ

˜˜˜˜˜˜˜˜˜˜˜˜˜˜ de ˜˜˜˜˜˜˜˜˜˜˜˜˜˜˜˜˜˜˜˜˜ camps ˜˜˜˜˜˜˜˜˜˜˜ jui ˜˜˜˜˜˜˜˜
˜˜˜˜˜˜˜ mè ˜˜˜˜˜˜˜˜˜˜˜˜˜˜˜˜˜˜˜˜ cre ˜˜˜˜˜˜˜˜˜˜˜˜˜˜˜˜˜ lam ˜˜˜˜˜˜˜˜˜˜˜˜˜
˜˜˜˜˜˜˜˜˜˜˜˜ savo ˜˜˜˜˜˜˜˜˜˜˜˜˜˜˜˜˜˜˜˜˜˜ uillet ˜˜˜˜˜˜˜˜˜˜˜ Ausch ˜˜˜˜
˜˜˜˜ tra ˜˜˜˜˜˜˜˜˜˜˜˜˜˜˜˜˜˜˜˜˜ ferme ˜˜˜˜˜˜˜˜˜˜˜˜˜˜˜˜˜˜˜˜˜ pè ˜˜˜˜˜˜˜˜˜˜˜
˜˜˜˜˜˜˜˜˜˜˜˜˜˜˜˜˜˜˜ bilité ˜˜˜˜˜˜˜˜˜˜˜˜˜˜ rat ˜˜˜˜˜ ap ˜˜˜˜˜˜ ap ˜˜˜˜˜˜
˜˜˜˜˜˜˜˜˜˜˜ rès ˜˜˜˜˜˜˜˜˜˜˜˜˜˜˜˜˜˜˜˜˜ si ˜˜˜˜˜˜˜˜˜˜˜˜˜˜˜˜˜˜ vac ˜˜˜˜˜˜˜˜˜
˜˜˜˜˜˜˜˜˜˜˜˜˜˜˜˜˜˜˜˜ mer ˜˜˜˜˜˜˜˜˜˜˜˜˜˜˜˜˜˜˜˜˜ de ˜˜˜˜˜˜˜˜˜˜˜˜˜˜˜˜˜˜˜˜

It was past two in the morning when I finished telling them my story with all the details (true and false and invented and exaggerated and skipped) everything I had seen felt suffered experienced before coming to America!

Finally we all went to bed. Benny and Marilyn in their big springy king size bed. Me on the flowery sofa. I felt jealous and I was all excited all worked up. I had an enormous erection under my blanket. But (quite unexpectedly) Marilyn sneaked into the livingroom (he didn't explain how she managed that) for a few minutes (some vague excuse, the newspaper or the TV guide she had forgotten on the coffee table). So here we are now alone. She's kneeling next to the sofa. Me I'm flat on my back my head popped up on two pillows inside the sofa. And we are kissing like crazy while fondling each other. I'm scared shitless that Benny might show up in the middle of all that kissing and fondling but her tongue is so deep and so fat inside my mouth that I can't think clearly and then here goes her hand sliding up my thigh under the blanket grabbing my fully erected genitals and in less than thirty seconds *pfitt* I let go into the flowers with a little shudder. Somebody moves in the bedroom and ni vu ni connu Marilyn trots out of the livingroom while blowing me sweet little kisses GOOD NIGHT!

xxxxxxxxxxxxxxxxxxxxxxxxxxxxxxxxxxxxxxxxxxxxxxxxxxxxxxxxxxxxx

All that had happened so fast that he really didn't give much details so that it's hard for me now to reconstruct the whole scene and what he had felt at the time. I mean originally when it happened and not when later on he described the situation to me. But in any event that was (more or less) the situation in its broad lines. And the situation shows it with no uncertainty (it seems to me) Marilyn had a great deal of affection or at least a great deal of comprehension for him. But still he was not at all satisfied and had difficulties falling asleep that night on the sofa which was too short for him to stretch his legs when on his back and not deep enough for him to curl up comfortably (he could neither stretch his legs fully when on his back or they would stick out nor fold them in the usual quattrocento position without falling off the sofa). A lousy deal!

But eventually the events of the day and the telling or retelling of his sad story made their effects felt and he managed to sink (that's in fact the word he used) into a deep and sound sleep.
And what a dream he had!
Or rather what a nightmare!
What an incredible salad of souvenirs in his subconscious!
What an erotic pile of torn pieces of surrealistic images!
the jerks of his regiment
colorful mushrooms and parachutes
big black asses and tight pink pussies
huge mountains of love letters with doodles
buickspecials superhighways washington rain snow
fairies dollar bills cops moinous bareass barbed wire
lampshades straights flushes teats footlockers holes music
all that forming a grotesque spectacle an orgy of colors and designs the likes of which had never been seen before or at least not by him and all that swimming in a lake of fuming sperm and in the middle of that creepy carnaval right in the center a huge red face grinning at him shouting at him all kinds of obscenities insults curses dirty words in English which were unknown to him until then and suddenly out of that big mouth came a deluge of ethnic epithets an anthropological bombardment of bigoted lava a whole list of prejudicial terms in English which in those days

made no sense to him the whole verbal America was being thrown in his face as if this poor little French Jew of Polish origin exiled in America this poor displaced immigrant was now the sum the total of these epithets the sole point of encounter the junction the melting pot of this verbal onslaught ethnologically speaking which fell on him hit him in the face struck him with such force and brutality that he suddenly started crying like a kid in his dream asking himself why? why me? Why do they always pick on me?

Yes why him? Asleep in the flowers after this exhausting day on the road and this rather disturbing emotional evening with Benny and Marilyn which forced him to reveal himself more than he really wanted. Why this dream? That of course will never be explained for he himself (the subject of the dream) could not come up with a logical explanation but nevertheless here is that list of words he heard in his head that night just as he told it:

SPADES
SPOOKS
SPICS
SCHWARTZES
COONS
CHINKS
COLORED
COMMIES
COMMI CRAPOLA
CHOSEN PEOPLE
JIGS
JUNGLE BUNNIES
PINKOS
PANSIES
RED SKINS
GOOKS
HEBES
KIKES
YIDS
BLACK BEAUTIES
BLEEDING HEARTS
PIGS
FREAKS
YENTAS
ATHEISTS
WEIRDOS
DUMB POLACKS
DINGBATS
DUMB BELLS
MEATHEADS
FAIRIES
FRUITS
QUEENS
FAGS
GOYEM
FOUR-EYES
DEGOS
SHEENIES
NIGGERS
YANKEES
PUSSY EATERS
FRENCHIES
FROGS

and that there were no more
more kept coming
and suddenly he recognized him
that bastard who was shouting at him
(no it was not Benny)
it was that fat ugly sergeant
who had indoctrinated him in the army
in New York
but he had a little square mustache
in the dream (à la Hitler)
and that's why he didn't recognize him immediately
but lucky for that motherfucker he woke up
otherwise he would have jumped that guy
and bashed his face in
in any event it was a most interesting
a most educational dream
and this is why he told it to me
I learned a great deal from it he said
it's in that dream that I first realized
that America is made of linguistic bigotry
and unless one knows the meaning
of these humiliating eponyms
one is really lost in America
one cannot find one's way toward success
and prosperity
therefore for me this dream was a revelation
and also a turning point
and that's why I told it to you
word for word
and that's why I'm reporting it now word for word

XVII

a visitor from above

The next morning he was gone on his way to Camp Drum in his
Buickspecial
vasy vasy vasy vasy vasy vasy vasy vasy vasy vasy vasy vasy
go go go go go go go go go go go go go go go go go go go go

Here he goes! Not the BIGREAL departure however. Not yet. A
temporary departure only. A false start for the time being. But it
was not easy! No it was not easy for him to leave that morning.
Marilyn wanted him to ABSOLUTELY stay another day or two
before going up to get his money. He needs a rest she kept saying.
It'll do him good. He looks tired. That money can wait.
          But Benny on the contrary kept saying that it might
not be wise to delay that in fact it might be better for him to go first
get his damn money up north and then PERHAPS come back to
New York for a few days' rest or else simply keep going west
which in his opinion was still the best thing to do
                    In any event that morning (the morning after
that horrible night spent on the sofa) with the remnants of the
dream buzzing in his head what a face he had! What a disgusting
taste in the mouth he had too! Blue balls [excuse me] on top of
that. Sore balls as a result of all that excitement under the blanket.
And impossible to do a fucking thing with Marilyn that morning
because that sneaky Benny had invented a phony excuse not to
go to work as usual even though it was a weekday yes a Friday (I
think) therefore a workday. Some kind of lousy headache and a
bellyache on top of that. Therefore impossible to speak intimately
to Marilyn. So he left. And here he goes now driving north. He
left soon after breakfast. After the sunnyside eggs with bacon
Marilyn fixed with loving care. And here he goes now driving
north into his story!
It's about 9:30 a.m. now. Gray sky hesitating between rain snow
or both! Twenty miles to Peekskill. Not much traffic. Funny noise
in the engine! SHIT what's happening? What the hell are you

doing here? This is unreal (I hadn't seen the guy there next to me in my Buickspecial taking notes)! Nothing . . . It's the other guys up there who sent me down here. I am one of your potential listeners.

POTENTIAL! What the fuck is that? . . . This is too much!

I am a free auditor . . . My name is Poussemoi.

But . . . bu-bu . . . tell me Pucemoi . . .

Poussemoi!

Okay Poussemoi Poussemoipas . . . how the hell did you manage to get in . . . how the hell did you by-pass the second-hand teller to come directly here . . . I mean . . . directly to the source?

Ummhm . . . !

It's not logical . . . fucks up the whole system! Imagine what will happen . . . what the POTENTIALS will say when they hear about this!

But I tell you they know . . . they are the ones who delegated me down here to take notes . . .

Delegated? Ah . . . That's why we didn't hear from them for a while!

Yes . . . but don't worry about the logic . . . and in any case the other guy . . . the second-hand teller is au courant . . . and even if he is not . . . as the saying goes . . . he has eyes behind his back to keep an eye on what is going to happen down here.

Oh Well! . . . in this case let's keep going. You're a cooky little fellow . . . aren't you? (Still something fishy about this newcomer. That really messes up my position! Not a bad looking guy. Tall. Well dressed. New tweed sport coat. Button down shirt with striped tie. A knowing cynical smile. Very Ivy League. Assistant professor type who still struggles to get his doctoral dissertation finished. Huge notebook on his lap. Pen in hand.) It's rather striking your appearance here (I say to him. But he doesn't

answer. I don't insist. Who knows maybe he'll pay part of the travel expenses. Except I was not too worried about that now. Marilyn had managed to slip me a twenty dollar bill behind Benny's back. Still this guy. This Ivy Leaguer. Here in my car. It's disturbing when you think of it. It's not normal. Goes against the logic of this story in its fundamental structure. Where the hell is the second-hand teller at this time when I need him the most? That ass! He took off! Must have gone to sleep! Can't he do something about this situation? Unless the sonofabitch was fed up with my story? Or else he lost control? That's quite possible. Meanwhile all the rules and regulations are going down the drain. Dammit! And I can't think of a rational explanation. What am I going to do? How am I going to justify this guy's presence? This extraordinary reversal of roles when eventually I relate this situation to my historiographer? Now everything is fucked up! Topsy-turvy! But at least since he is here that guy let's talk to him.) Hey! Say . . . how far are you going with me?
Depends!
Depends on what?
The others! You see they were fed up with the recitation . . . They felt it wasn't going anywhere and there were too many repetitions in it. So they . . .
I agree with you there but that's not my fault. It's the other guy who messed it up . . . it's his fault!
Yes . . . but . . . in any case they elected me to come down here and write down everything you say just in case . . . just in case something happens which hasn't yet been told . . . something unexpected.
Something unexpected? I can't believe it . . . everything my dear fellow that happens to me is unexpected! By now you should be aware of that!
Yes of course . . . it's just that we don't want to miss anything.

Stories are so predictable these days.

You can say that again! Yes but what about you . . . I mean what's . . . how shall I say . . . what's your function down here? Oh nothing . . . I was warned in advance that I'm not supposed to interfere with your story. I cannot participate in it . . . that is actively. I was furthermore advised not to delay the action. Therefore feel free to move on as you wish. I am only here to take notes faithfully . . . objectively!

(I found his explanation plausible, therefore I didn't insist and besides he seemed rather uncomfortable, out of place, the poor guy, there next to me in my car on our way to Camp Drum. Out of time also. Better make his stay agreeable. Also one never knows he could be useful if I'm stuck, he might even give me courage to go on. Give me some ideas. Therefore, why not be polite. Sociable. And make a bit of conversation with him.) Say what would you like to talk about? Do you want me to go on with politics or you'd rather I went on with something else? (The guy hesitates. So I thought a moment trying to find something to say but my thoughts normally never coincide with my words) here (I said finally since he was still not answering) how would you like to hear a little anecdote (a true anecdote) a buddy of mine told me once and which made me laugh like crazy? I think you'll like it. It's an unbelievable story. My buddy's name was Gustave (Gugusse for short). At the time of the anecdote he was working downtown in New York in a crummy cafeteria. You know the AUTOMAT, Horny & Hardon! The kind of cheap joint where you stick your money in a . . . little slot (your nickels dimes or quarters) to get your grub (sandwiches or salads). Well my buddy Gugusse he was the guy who shoved the stuff in the compartments! From behind. The sandwiches salads desserts yes bananas apple pies dried up puddings. He was so to speak hidden from the customers. Hidden away! Inside the kitchen if one can call that hole where he worked a kitchen! Unseen from the public at large. Unseen by that hungry mob of guys and girls (the working class) who came to put their coins in the slots, but Gugusse he could see them if he wanted to from the other side by simply looking inside the little boxes where their hands searched for the food (he couldn't see the faces but the hands as they pulled out casually or nervously the sandwiches salads desserts etc.) Well one day Gugusse he had a funny idea. Instead of placing a sandwich or a salad into one of the little boxes he put his cock there (and

of course in full erection) to see what would happen. It was a remarkable piece by its dimensions! And he waited for somebody to stick his or her quarter inside the slot! He didn't wait very long because it was lunch time a weekday. He hears the coin fall in the slot. He hears the little click as the box's door opens automatically. A hand slides quickly inside the box and searches here and there. And suddenly that hand touches something warm which it does not immediately recognize. At least not something alimentary from the sense of touch. That hand hesitates. Doesn't understand what this thing could be. Certainly not a sandwich! Of course my friend Gugusse is on the verge of bursting. But he holds back (laughter and sperm) as he feels a tremor go through him. Especially since (pure chance) it is a feminine hand which has inserted itself inside the box and is probing around. Finally the head that belongs with the hand, not understanding what's happening, and since it is curious to find out, comes down level with the opening of the box to look inside. Wild cry of astonishment! Of stupefaction and horror! QUACK! comes out of the mouth that belongs to the head when it realizes what it is holding in its hand. Well do I need to tell you what happened next? No!

Let me simply say that for a moment the whole place went wild when it heard that frightening cry. It created quite a commotion. The poor broad was convulsing on the floor! Immediate scandal! All the other chewing customers rush towards her with their mouths still full of grub. All the little old ladies with feathers on their hats and brooms up their asses! Cries over cries surge from all corners as everyone tries to see what's inside the box. With loud shouts of LET ME THROUGH LET ME THROUGH the manager of the place runs out of his cage on the mezzanine and of course my buddy Gugusse is kicked out of the joint and I mean literally on the sidewalk with the angry horror stricken outraged customers foaming at the mouth following him fists raised in the air shouting insults at him. Dirty filthy rat! Pervert! Repugnant pig! Somebody call the police! The vice squad! Ain't you ashamed at your age (he was about 26 years old Gugusse at the time of this anecdote)? People like you shouldn't be allowed in the street! Sadist! Trash! Debauchee!

/   /   /   /   /   /   /   /   /   /   /   /   /   /

I stop and look at my companion my fellow-traveler expecting him to burst into laughter. But no, on the contrary he looks rather embarrassed. His face flushed. Shocked perhaps. Shit! That's all I needed, a prude, and he doesn't even have a sense of humor. My luck, and he's going to travel with me. Ah those damn listeners, they couldn't have (s)elected somebody more lively. More understanding. I'll have to get rid of him. Dump him along the way. Quickly. I look at him again from the corner of my eyes! He starts coughing nervously with his hand in front of his mouth. One of the reasons (I say to him finally looking at him squarely) I told you the story of Gugusse is to make you better understand what it meant, in those days, to live in New York. It was tough. Therefore the least event, the least little distraction would help us go on. Help us survive. Yes help us do what we had to do. The guy reacts unconcernedly with his shoulder! Better change subject, otherwise. Oh but that sneaky bastard, he's got a hell of a nerve to pout at me because while I was talking he took down in his notebook everything I said. Wrote it all word for word, illustrated!

Oh well . . . what can I do? I concentrate on the road. Looking at the scenery. We are now almost in Massachusetts. Therefore almost out of New York State. According to the map the shortest and most direct way to Camp Drum I explain to my visitor from above when he questioned why we were going through Massachusetts to get to Upper New York State . . . Meanwhile I take a peek in his notebook (the sonofabitch!) wide opened on his lap. Not only did he write down everything I said. And I mean word for word. But he even made little drawings in red pencil. Dirty little drawings. To illustrate the anecdote I suppose. Shit! Wow am I going to be in trouble when he shows this to the potentials! Above! Quick let's talk about something else . . . I tap him on the shoulder as he seems to be falling asleep. Yes me you know I should have been . . . I should have been in politics . . . I had that in my blood . . . in a way you could say it was hereditary . . . but in fact I was involved . . . yes quite involved in politics in my days . . . not that I was a fanatic . . . far from it . . . but still . . . therefore you can tell your buddies that they can stop bugging me[me/us][moi / nous] with their questions their fucking questions about the exploitation of the masses . . . in a way me I am the masses . . . therefore if you want me to tell you why I did not protest . . . did not refuse . . . object . . . when the time came . . . and I allowed myself to be drafted . . . why I didn't tell them to . . . and why eventually I volunteered for action . . . which brings us then so to say to where we are now . . . on our way to Camp Drum . . . because of . . . etc . . . stupid mistake . . . etc . . . well let me tell you . . . quite simply

I . . . me . . . in New York . . . I was starving . . . dammit . . .
starving does that make sense to you . . . at least in the army I
kept saying mentally they feed you well . . . three times a day
. . . regularly . . . let me tell you that's important . . . and
besides I was fed up with life . . . on the edge of suicide . . .
every night . . . toying with ropes . . . pills . . . gas . . . and
also there was this thing with marilyn . . . it was driving me nuts
. . . up the wall . . . love . . . lovesick . . . well no need to go on
with that . . . I'll go into that later . . . if you're still around . . .
on the road . . . 30 days . . . love and politics . . . we'll have lots
of time . . . yes 30 days . . . in jail . . . too . . . jail . . . in
tokyo for a stupid . . . eventually . . . and then in buffalo . . .
but that's still a long way off . . . might come in later on in the
next stage . . . winner take all . . . bullshit . . . loser lose all . . .
political prisoners . . . for ridiculous reasons . . . broken nose
place de la république . . . ah you didn't notice that . . . look
. . . eagle nose . . . but let's skip it . . . and then the factory . . .
factories . . . let me ask you this . . . I mean the factory you did
you ever work in a factory . . . yes the real thing . . . 8 to 10
hours a day . . . night too . . . nightshift . . . after the war . . .
in the banlieue . . . the liberation . . . everybody singing the
liberation . . . I wasn't singing . . . in a factory . . . I bet you a
dime you'll never guess what we made in that factory . . . tubes
tubes for toothpaste that's what we made . . . 12 hours a day
. . . no . . . the nightshift . . . 12 hours a night . . . 8 to 8 . . .
tubes . . . and then in detroit . . . more factories . . . chrysler
. . . making springs for seats . . . car seats . . . junk . . .
imagine . . . hands bleeding even with them shitty greasy canvas gloves on . . . hands full of blisters . . . always ashamed of
my hands in those days . . . couldn't take it anymore . . . I
dropped the whole stinking smelly armpit of america shitcity
detroit . . . no the armpit it's buffalo . . . detroit it's the crotch

. . . I had it . . . moved to new york . . . winter 1950 . . . disgusting winter . . . I didn't care . . . mccarthysm . . . washington square . . . riots . . . black lists . . . reds . . . fear . . . cops on horseback charging the masses at full speed . . . we threw things at them . . . rocks . . . beer cans empty bottles . . . horses stepped on us . . . they beat the shit out of us . . . and at night late I would meet bernice in the bronx and we would walk up and down the grand concourse holding each other by the waist she'd bring me food salami from her old man's delicatessen then a quick one up in my furnished room a buck for loulou to go to the movies but she cried all the time bernice always accusing me of wanting only to make love to her my body that's all you want my body but never my mind you never want to talk with me intellectually and I must say she was well stacked bernice hard round teats skin soft like velvet and hardly any pubic hair the whole cunt exposed fresh and juicy like a peach dammit but always giving me an argument that's all you want from me it's all you think about sex so one day out of disgust anger fed up with her I gave marilyn a call I had already met her the summer before up in the catskills in my country club but nothing had happened between us just a little flirt nothing yet but it was obvious she wanted me it's just that we hadn't been able to work it out question of timing of finding the right place in any event she gave me her phone number in brooklyn just in case if ever in the future I came to new york for a visit yes it's quite possible then for sure do call me she said you promise but of course and even benny said to me if ever you happen to be thinking of moving to new york do call us if you need anything a place to stay for a few days a job don't hesitate one never knows yes americans are great this way but in their case it's normal because they were jewish and as we all know between jews there is always a fraternal rapport a racial bound especially in those days just after the war jews in this country felt a kind of link with us refugees from the holocaust yes a kind of moral responsibility because they had not suffered as much as the rest of us those of us who still had our tattoos on our wrists so they felt guilty toward us these american jews and tried hard to help therefore when you meet some of them they always tell you how much they have suffered, ah isn't it terrible terrible what happened to us always the us, the collective us, always suffering for the rest of us, because if there is one jew who suffers in the world, only one, then you can be sure all the other jews suffer for him, and since there is always a jew who suffers, one poor little jew who suffers somewhere in the world all the jews suffer for him, it's hopeless, endless, you can never step out of that circular fraternal suffering, it's really something that mutual suffering, all these jews suffering for you in retrospect, but still it doesn't mean that jews in general are not generous, warm-hearted, smart and industrious, sincere, and usually quite intelligent, even though the majority of them have marked sentimental tendencies, but if you want my opinion and think about it seriously, they are the ones who transformed the world, or at least america, especially since the war, when they all came over, the great jewish invasion, thousands and thousands, millions of them moving in, taking over, changing everything, fucking up culture and politics demolishing the good old anglo-saxon puritanical tradition infiltrating the movies the newspapers television literature businesses everything, the facts are here, all those great european wanderers they are the ones who changed america, scientists, rabbis, theologians, psychiatrists, sociologists, artists, writers, thinkers, discoverers, that great jewish intelligenzia, that whole tribe which hitler, that halfass corporal, tried to exterminate the chosen people, they are the ones in fact who made the intellectual and cultural revolution in america, it's ironical but if that shmuck hitler had guessed that by kicking the hell out of the jews, by wanting to make lampshades out of them he was going to change the entire structure of the american system, literally change the face of the world, displace the center of western civilization, the dumb bastard would have left them alone would have picked another race! Take my case for instance. What do you think I would be today if it were not for Hitler? Do you know what I would be? A tailor! Yes a little Jewish tailor Boulevard des Italiens. Or else an instituteur in some retarded school. But let me assure you I would not be on my way to Camp Drum discovering America. I would not be here with such a nice guy like you making up my life as I go along. No! Certainly not. Therefore funny as it may sound Hitler in a way was my Savior!

Yes it's laughable!   Preposterous!

Go ahead laugh, laugh! I see only an embarrassed smile on your face instead of a big laugh. Don't be shy. I don't give a shit, in fact let's laugh together. I've already told you. Or rather HE told you what HE thinks of laughter. The other guy. MY STORY-TELLER! But I should point out that what HE said also applies to ME because WE are together in this. ONE in ONE. ONE for ALL. ONE unto the OTHER for the sake of harmony!
                                        Voice within voice!

So let's laugh for a good ten or fifteen minutes. It'll relax us in the middle of all that sad stuff. Come on my little friend let's be joyful and take advantage of this situation, especially now that, to be quite blunt, the scenery around here is rather shitty. I mean in this part of Massachusetts, for have you noticed we are now speeding through Massachusetts. Things do fly! No it's not very spectacular around here. And besides. Look! As it was expected, and predicted earlier, it's starting to snow. That may indeed slow down matters a bit. Therefore let's concentrate on laughter for a while because my dear fellow I'm starting to be fed up with your sad look of a creepy undertaker!

Well said!

And furthermore the more I think about it the more I am convinced there is something illegal about your presence here in the middle of my story, some twenty years too soon. How the hell did you manage to pass from the level of the present to the level of the past? From outside to inside this very personal recitation? Doesn't make sense! Normally such transfers are not permitted. They go against the logic of traditional narrative techniques!

Therefore, if you want my opinion, let's not be carried away and let's not take everything I say too seriously. Especially since it's quite possible that you may be here only temporarily, that you may disappear, out of this story, just as quickly and just as subtly as you appeared in it. I am now in charge here, or at least for the time being. Our second-hand teller, I presume, the traitor, having abandoned the cause perhaps even permanently!

But in any event, to be here as you are or no longer be here as you may be soon, those damn potentials, bunch of inconsiderate bastards, could, might at least have sent me somebody a bit more congenial, a bit more amusing, a guy with whom I could have had a good laugh. After all you are the people who in the future will judge me, will appreciate or depreciate my story, I assume, one way or another. That much is certain. Why then this mockery?

But I warn you, don't feel obliged to stay if you are bored. Take off!

                                                                    Split!
Anytime you wish my dear fellow.   Cut!
                                              I can do without you.
                              You don't have to stick around. In fact
even that screwy second-hand   I can do without anybody!
teller can go to hell. Who needs him!   My story will go on
Self-propelled and self-proliferated!   by itself, nice and easy!
Me,   We can do without your notes too!
you see, all I need is a table, a chair, paper and pencils   (or else a
typewriter if you composed directly on the typewriter, used of
course)! That's all I need.
                                                        Or else a wall!
              °You know the expression WALLS HAVE EARS°
Well four walls that's enough for me. That's more than I need in
fact! A quiet little corner in a room and the story gets going, all by
itself
GOING!   GOING!   GONE!

On my platform. Because my platform me it's the chair, the
springboard my ass. And if there is no chair then the walls. The
walls! even if I have to do it standing up. Even if sometimes the
walls get on my   nerves and I
                     drive you mad

feel paranoiac   drive you up the wall nuts
like passing through them. Like going over them. Jumping over
as I've tried to explain not long ago in a little poem —— well a
quasi-poetic statement —— of rather curious form which I shall
now quote — on the next page — in its original form — in gothic
letters —- but somewhat corrected —— accelerated —— and
entitled —— for this occasion:
                R E F L E X I O N   O N   T H E   W A L L S

WALLS WALLS WALLS WALLS WALLS WALLS WALLS
WALLS I'M FED UP WITH WALL   WALLS WALLS
        THEY'RE EVERYWHERE
WALLS TALL ONES SMALL ONES   WALLS
        THICK ONES   HIGH ONES
WALLS ROUND AND SQUARE AND HUGE AND DARK   WALLS
        HOLLOW WALLS WITH HIDING PLACES INSIDE OF THEM
WALLS EVERYWHERE   WALLS
                                        80, WALLS
WALLS INSIDE   OUTSIDE   ALL AROUND WALLS
        METAL   STONE   PLASTER   MUD   WOOD   ADOBE
WALLS WITH RATS CRAWLING INSIDE   AND BUGS TOO WALLS
        AND THEY HAVE ALL KINDS OF BAD ATROCIOUS NAMES
WALLS   PARTITIONS WALLS

WALLS   PARAPETS WALLS
                                                 REMPARTS
WALLS   FENCES WALLS
                                                    CURBS
WALLS   FRAMES WALLS
                                                 RAILINGS
WALLS   BALUSTRADES WALLS
                                             BATTLEMENTS
WALLS   BREASTWORKS WALLS
                                              BARRICADES
WALLS DIVIDING WALLS   BULWARKS WALLS
                                               ENCLOSURES
WALLS DEFENSIVE WALLS   WALLS
        CELL WALLS   TOWN WALLS   SURROUNDING WALLS
WALLS GREAT WALLS   PAPER WALLS   CHINA WALLS WALLS
        INNER WALLS   OUTER WALLS
WALLS ENOUGH TO DRIVE YOU MAD   NUTS   CRAZY WALLS
WALLS OUT OF YOUR MIND UP THE WALL   SCHIZOPHRENIC WALLS
        AND YOU FEEL CORNERED LOCKED IN ENCLOSED STUCK IN
WALLS THERE   PRISONER WALLS
        WALLED IN   ALIENATED
WALLS AND YOU FEEL SICK SAD LONELY COMPRESSED MORBID CLAUS- WALLS
        TROPHOBIC   IN THERE
WALLS AND YOU'RE FED UP UP TO HERE ABOVE THE HEAD AND YOU WALLS
        WANT TO GET THE HELL OUT TAKE OFF GONE

WALLS AND SO YOU JUMP OVER THE FIRST WALL   WALLS
WALLS OR ELSE YOU GO RIGHT THROUGH IT   WALLS
        STRAIGHT ON   SIDEWAYS FLAT ON YOUR BACK
WALLS ON ALL FOURS   EYES CLOSED WALLS
        BUT ON THE OTHER SIDE ANOTHER WALL AND ON THE OTHER
WALLS SIDE OF THE OTHER SIDE ANOTHER ONE AND ANOTHER ONE WALLS
        AND ANOTHER ONE AND ANOTHER
WALLS AN INFINITY OF WALLS   WALLS
        AN ETERNITY OF WALLS
WALLS EVERYWHERE EVERYWHERE EVERYWHERE EVERYWHERE   WALLS
        WALLSWALLSWALLSWALLSWALLSWALLSWALLSWALLSWALLS
WALLS WALLS WALLS WALLS WALLS WALLS WALLS

Well, that's enough for the walls. What do you think? Not bad Hey! In fact, if you think my poem is half-way decent in its present form then perhaps, when you get back up there among your fellow-listeners and report to them, you may want to ask them to write a kind word of appreciation to the publisher, it might help, you know (I said to my tweedy fellow-traveler sitting there next to me in my Buick, visibly puzzled, some twenty years too soon). But be that as it may, when a Jew tells you to call him, in case of need, rest assured that in general you can count on him, especially in New York, and above all if you are Jewish yourself, and on top of it, as in my case, you're one of the lucky ones who escaped the holocaust, and you've just arrived from the old country, and you have (we must never let them forget it regardless of the time and place) suffered a great deal, as a result of the war, the Germans, the French, the yellow star, anti-semitism, the gas chambers, the occupation, deportation, concentration, extermination, etc., etc., and in my case, more specifically, starvation, farms, trains, raw potatoes, factories, etc., etc., the whole stupid messy fiasco of the war, then it's even better, because then, it's a cinch, the New York Jews they really feel sorry for you, and want to partake in your misery in retrospect, and that's why I was not ashamed nor intimidated to call them (Benny and Marilyn) in Brooklyn (in those days they still had their three room apartment in Brooklyn, on Kings Highway near Flatbush, but later they moved to Manhattan, in a really swanky place, upper eastside, 86th and Madison, a first class pad with doorman, but that place won't be described in this section) the day I had that final argument with Bernice when she refused once and for all to sleep with me because she felt that I was only interested in her body and not her mind, and she told me I was a lazy bum who refused to face up to his responsibilities, a lost cause, a rat!

XVIII

replacement & displacement

Oh shit not again! What the hell are you doing here? Where's the other guy? The Ivy Leaguer who was taking notes? The sad looking undertaker with his tweed sport coat? The one who was in my Buick a moment ago (out-of-place and out-of-context), and who refused to laugh even when . . . damn! . . . things are really getting screwed up here! If you guys keep circulating like that, freely, and without any warning, from present to past, back and forth, up and down, to and fro, without any respect for the logic of this recitation, and without even asking for my permission, it's really going to make a mess of this already shaky situation!

— No it's just that . . . you see . . . (the newcomer explains), it's a matter of tact, and adjustment. The others above felt (pointing above with his finger) that it might be better to replace him (the original interferer I suppose he meant) immediately because he was not doing his job properly, and also because of his deliberate and obvious lack of comprehension of the subject.

— You can say that again! Hey do you speak French by any chance? Because sometimes I have to fall back into my native tongue when I get stuck.

— Yes . . . I'm a bilingual replacement. The other was unilingual!

— Fantastic! You guys think of everything.

— Therefore this sudden and unexpected arrival, entrée en matière if you prefer, is quite justified.

— Oh, you do speak French . . . Entrée en matière! . . . not bad, hey damn good in fact!

— Yes, frankly, the other one was not doing well at all, we felt!

— You can say that again (I retorted to this new interferer)! He was a bore. A mediocre listener. In fact he was a total failure!

— You are being harsh. Let us just say that he was not suitable. That he didn't make it. That he was poorly selected. I only hope that I can perform better.

— I'm sure you will. It's just a matter of getting used to my unorthodox way of stating things, of relating events.

— Yes, but I'm only a substitute. A second-hand auditor, no pun intended. A replacement. A double auditor, if you prefer.

— I'm aware of that. Wow! This is really getting confusing, affolant! Wish I could get out of it . . . But tell me, what's your . . .

— My name is CLAUDE.

— And mine is SIMON (I cried, all of a sudden). Now I remember. Quite a nice combination. Very suggestive. (Nothing compelled me to give him this information, but I gave it, hoping to please I suppose). Yes SIMON (a perfect fictional name, and besides it happens to be my father's real name. I'm not kidding. You guys can check my birth certificate).

— CLAUDE / SIMON! What a strange coincidence. Do you think we'll make a good pair? Do you think we'll make it together?

— I'm sure we will. At least you seem more garrulous, more friendly in fact than what's-his-name (and much cuter too :

sandy blond curly hair
sensual deep blue eyes
slim muscular body
yellow sport shirt under
a thick ski sweater [for
it was rather coldish on
that day in February 51]
the artistic type
pleasant personality
but a bit effeminate)

— Thanks a lot!

— It's okay. But tell me how far are you going with me?

— To the END, if possible. But that'll depend on you, and of course on the others above.

— I see. Hey, say, by the way, on your way down here you didn't
happen to see my second-hand teller? . . . Can't understand
what happened to him!
— No. Nobody seems to know what happened to him. Where he
went. What took him to disappear like that. But don't worry.
You're doing well by yourself. Everybody above is pleased, so
far.
— Well, that's REcomforting. Nice of you to say that . . . But
enough of these preambles. What would you like to talk about (I
asked him even if we must repeat ourselves somewhat)? Would
you like to hear a story? Or shall we simply look at the scenery in
silence, like two idiots?
— (Affirmative nod of the head).
— A little anecdote?

The cute blondinet squares himself in his seat, there next to me,
on the front seat of my Buick, turns sideways towards me as if
ready to watch a porno film or something. This pleases me im-
mediately. I'm ready to go!
Therefore I concentrate.
Clear my throat.
Ready to unload my anecdote one more time.
The story of Gugusse and his cock in the box.
But I have second thoughts about it. Not that again.
No, not that filthy story again, or else he might think I have a
limited repertoire and a weak imagination.
But he seems anxious for me to get going with whatever I have to
say for the time being. Better invent something on the spot.
— Listen! Before I go on with the anecdote, you have to promise
me one thing. It's very important to me. When you get back
above, I mean back up in the present, among the potentials, I

want you to tell them how I'm trying my best to keep things going down here. How difficult it is, how unbearable it is to be alone all the time inside my stories, down at the bottom, speaking in a void. And especially, promise me, swear it, cross your heart, you will report everything I say faithfully. Word for word! Just as I say it. And without distorting anything. It's a matter of authenticity, you understand? I am quite finicky about that, because if you guys start believing things I have never said. Lies, or false stories. Then I'm really going to be in trouble. It's a question of ver-isimilitude, you dig?

— Phew, you're meticulous!

— Me-Ti-Cul-Ous, my ass! You're not going to imagine that I am here for the fun of it. That I am in this for nothing. What about glory? What about posterity? Yes what about it? Not to mention prosperity!

Okay, now he seems ready for my anecdote. Well warmed and receptive! I put on my sun glasses because of the snow (which is getting thicker and thicker) but also to better watch my compan-ion's reaction (on the sly). Wow, is he cute! I could easily . . . Here we go . . . full blast and without any further hesitation . . . Damn, the road is getting icy!

— No, wait! Before the anecdote I want to recite a poem first. Yes a poem I wrote recently for a buddy of mine. MOINOUS is his name . . .

— Oh, MOINOUS! Isn't he the young man from Boston who dies later on in San Francisco? Assassinated?

— How the hell do you know that? That part of the story hasn't happened yet! For the time being MOINOUS is on his way to Florida!

— Yes. It was already told . . . the second-hand teller . . . he . . . he

— The motherfucker! He preempted me. How the fuck did he manage to jump ahead of me like that? . . . into my story? The guy is a liar . . . a fake! . . . Oh well, it's better than nothing . . . better than silence I suppose. Okay, here goes the poem :
MOINOUS ——-——-

I undouble
I multiply
I play hide-and-seek with myself
I subdivide
I cry and decry in two languages
I disappear
I see me seen
I use the thou form with myself
I cut and recut myself
I remend myself with red thread
I disperse
I am moved
I put me in myself
I me we
I unknot
I me us
I me too
I singularize
I pluralize also
I decenter
I play ping pong alone from both sides
I schizophrenize
I amortize
I mask my mask
I meusize
I metooize
I me we am I
I decentralize
I concentrate towards the open side
I add up
I double up and undouble again
I redouble or nothing
I multiply by two and demultiply by four
I me me I

MOINOUS OR METOO

— What do you think of my poem? Not bad, hey! It really moves! Do you think it's publishable?

— Not too bad. It's just that . . . No I really like it a lot . . . but the form is somewhat . . . and also there is . . . how shall I put it . . . you know what I mean . . . within the main stream of contemporary verse it doesn't seem to . . . it's just my opinion . . . but I do think you'll have difficulties getting it published in a good literary magazine in its present form . . . especially since . . .

— Okay Okay . . . I got you . . . that's enough! You don't have to give us a complete critique of my poem, right here in the middle of a snow storm . . . in Massachusetts! That's all we need, a course in literary criticism! Why don't you say it outright? So you don't like my poem big deal! Why beat about the bush? Say it, and skip all that wishy-washy belles-lettres crap! And besides, you didn't understand what I was trying to do. You didn't understand the subtle experimental form of the poem. The way I manipulate prosody. No you didn't understand the metaphorical playfulness of my vocabulary. Doesn't matter, we're not going to have an argument here about a measly poem, especially at a time when poetry is dying all over the world, when poetry drags the lamentable remnants of its glorious past along the crevices of a torn landscape, when poetry cannot even extricate itself from the holes in which it has fallen. You're not going to deny that?

— No, no, that's not what I mean . . .

— Forget it, forget it . . . I don't want an argument, especially when the two of us were starting to get along so well, so far.

— You're right, Simon. Yes let's skip your poem, it's not important at this point.

— Fine. Forget it. I'm used to this kind of reaction. It's always like that with my poetry. Nobody understands what I'm trying to do!

— I'm sorry, Simon. I didn't mean to . . . but really you don't
have to feel sorry for yourself. Maybe someday . . . with poetry
you never know!

— Forget the poem and listen instead to this little anecdote (I say
to him without telling him, of course, that it is the same anecdote I
told the other visitor). A true anecdote (hoping that this time at
least it will make him laugh). It was told to me by a dear friend of
mine a few years ago, but it's still valid, and when I first heard it it
made such an impression on me I almost cracked up. Takes place
in a self-service restaurant. You know the AUTOMAT. In Boston
in fact, not too far from where we are now. The type of place
where you put your money (quarters dimes or nickels) into a little
slot to get your food. Sandwiches, all ready to go. Salads. And
even pies. It's automatic. At least that's what people imagine,
because they don't know that there is a guy behind the wall who
puts the food inside the boxes. Well my friend (Teddy was his
name) he was the guy who places the sandwiches, salads, desserts or even pickles, all kinds of grub, bananas, apples, cookies,
jellos, pies a la mode, inside the boxes from behind the wall,
inside the kitchen if one can call kitchen the stinking hole where
he prepared the food. But this way he could not be seen by the
customers, and lucky for him. And for them, because to tell the
truth Teddy was not the best-looking specimen of a human
being, no, he was rather disgusting-looking, so if you know what
I mean, he was better off hidden away behind the wall, in his
working anonymity, so to speak, like all great artists, unseen by
those cute secretaries, nervous salesmen, sneaky pederasts,
bitchy old ladies with feathers on their hats, all those second-class
citizens who ate in this joint and who, especially at lunchtime,
rushed to put with anxious fingers their coins in the slots to drag
out their food. Teddy was all alone in his kitchen like a rat caught
in a trap. He worked solo. But I'll skip the descriptive details of his

working conditions because I'm beginning to be hungry like hell. Not you? Maybe we should look for a place to stop and have a bite. We'll feel better if we eat. And it'll give us courage to go on before the two of us pass out.

But in any event, Teddy, behind his wall, when he bent down to peek inside the boxes when he felt like it, he could see the groping fingers (but rarely the faces though, because people in general never look in the boxes to see what's cooking in there, they have a kind of blind confidence in those who put the food inside the little compartments) of those second-class citizens who search inside the boxes to pull out blindly their sandwiches salads desserts or whatever.

A juicy steak with French fries and lots of ketchup that's what I would like right now. How about you?

Therefore one day, he had a funny idea, Teddy. Instead of placing a sandwich, or a salad, in one of the boxes (one of the boxes half-way up the wall, waist high you might say), he put his penis in there in full erection. He'd activated it before. It was a rather substantial *bite* by its well-above the norm dimensions.

[The cute blondinet reacts instantly to this brusk and rather unexpected turn of events. I notice that immediately as he crosses his legs nervously]. And he waited no more than 20 or 30 seconds before he heard a coin fall in the splot and felt a greedy hand search for food in the narrow space of the box.

This way if we stop for a bite it'll give us a chance to get better acquainted outside the confines of this car. As a matter of fact I'm starting to feel wobbly. I have a cramp in my leg and a lousy taste in the mouth. Not you? Must be the sofa, I suppose!
What a night! And that incredible nightmare on top of that! Were you there, I mean above, when I told that part of the story? The sofa and the flowers?

Well, it didn't take long because in fact it was lunchtime.
He hears the quarter fall in the slot.
(He had selected one of the larger boxes. A quarter box rather than a nickel box. Because of his dimensions, I suppose).
And he feels a sweet hand slide furtively and blindly of course inside the perverted space of the box and grab his vibrant tail. The hand leaps up.
It was of course a feminine hand. Hand of a secretary with long, well polished nails.
The hand marks a surprise. Strange banana, it seems to say to itself? Not grasping immediately the nature of this ripe fruit, its liveliness and its warmth.
This hand imagines that there must be some error. Quickly it suggests to the head (through the usual brain process) to come down and examine the curious situation.
Meanwhile my friend Teddy is jubilating but holding back, with all his will power, a groan of pleasure on the edge of his lips and inside his inflated testicles. Especially since (I learned about this later on) he had a bad habit of screaming savagely whenever he found himself, so to speak, on the verge of an orgasmic explosion.
After a few frantic manual stumblings and grabblings of Teddy's member the head finally reaches the level of the open box to verify with some anguish what the hand had already realized it was holding.
You cannot imagine, my dear CLAUDINE, the cry of panic which burst out of the girl's mouth, as it rounded itself into the shape of an asshole ready to deliver. Damn am I starving suddenly! Gurgitation in there!
How do you feel? And nothing in sight. What a stinking road! At the very moment when Teddy's banana having reached its ultimate distention let go into the girl's face.

[At this point CLAUDE cannot hold back any more and bursts into hysterical laughter realizing I presume that I am deliberately exaggerating the details of the incident in order to have a better reaction from him because in the earlier version the original version as told to the other visitor you may recall Gugusse's cock did not unload in the girl's face and he starts clapping himself gleefully on the legs and on mine too in a rather explosive and intimate fashion — the little fruit is all excited!]

Well he came like a motherfucker I tell you my friend Teddy, in the girl's eyes, in her hair, in her well rounded mouth too which swallowed half of the load in spite of itself! It was not a pretty spectacle!

When Teddy tells the anecdote himself in his own words, he has a funny way of imitating the cry of despair, the QUACK of agony which came out of the girl's mouth. A percussive QUACK which I cannot possibly imitate here.

Well needless to relate what took place next, the sordid details of the denouement, especially now, when I am so starved I can't stand it any more. How about you? You do not show any signs of hunger. Suffices to say that the cry was horrendous and quite inhuman in its intensity, and the public reaction even worse in its intolerance. The girl collapses to the ground. Twists herself in spasms. Immediate scandal of course. All the clients rush towards her and the box still masticating their lunch. And especially all the little old ladies in their flower dresses (it was summertime) who push and shove to get a better look inside the criminal box. What a scene! Vociferations accumulate on top of vociferations. A neatly dressed guy kneels next to the girl to give her artificial respiration and mouth to mouth resuscitation and takes advantage of her condition and the public tumult to grab her teats which are still pulsating from the shock. The lady-owner of the self-service (an enormous elephant in a greyish satin dress) bounces towards the scene of the crime. Teddy is dragged out of his hole still buttoning his fly (no! I mean zipping it up because here in America we are beyond the age of flies with buttons, the prehistoric age of braguettes à boutons, we are a civilized society). Nevertheless everybody knows that Teddy is the guilty one. His ugly face alone, his depraved look is enough to indicate that much. They push him furiously out of the restaurant into the street. An angry crowd quickly gathers! They hit him with clenched fists.

Insult him.

Curse him.

Kick him in the ass.

Tear his clothes off his back. Damn! I'm starting to have cramps in my stomach. Not you darling? There must be a coffee shop around here, or at least a drugstore, because all roads in America lead to a drugstore! Immediately somebody says somebody call the police!

Yes.

No. The vice-squad!

And meanwhile they bombard him with left-overs, dirty dishes, all kinds of garbage, half-chewed sandwiches, apple pies, and throw at him such a barrage of insults, some of them so obscene that I do not even dare repeat them here. All the juicy ready-made clichés appropriate in situations such as these. And someone even shouts at him aren't you ashamed at your age? As if the person who shouted that knew exactly how old my friend Teddy was (he must have been around 32-33 at the time, though it is true that his greyish hair, and his wrinkled face behind a rather bushy ancien regime beard made him look easily 43-44). What a riot!

ooooooooooooooooooooooooooooooooooooooooooooooooooooooo
ooooooooooooooooooooooooooooooooooooooooooooooooooooo

My jubilant little companion is on the verge of pissing in his pants so hard is he laughing now. Ready to roll on the floor of our Buick were there enough room for such demonstrations of gleefulness in that rather limited space.

At least that makes me happy! Finally someone who appreciates my sense of humor and my talent as a story-teller!

But is he sincere? Does he really mean it? Or is he merely pretending? Acting up? Just to please me!

Who cares anyway! At least this guys knows how to laugh. Not like that sour puss, that dud who preceded him. Perhaps the potentials are not that bad. Not as anti / anti as I was led to believe. In fact I should consider myself lucky to have listeners like them. Others in situations parallel to mine may not be as fortunate. Yes indeed things are going to work out better than I anticipated, even without the help of my lost second-hand teller. We manage. Who knows if things go on like this we'll be able to get out of here sooner than expected, and in better shape too. Completely reconciled with our listeners. Yes, there is hope now that we might make it to the end of this journey. Even all the way to San Francisco. But for the time being better concentrate on getting to Camp Drum because without our money it's hopeless. We won't be able to go very far. However, right now, with Claude being in such a good mood and his happy laughter still ringing in my Buick I feel much better.   I feel encouraged!
— Tremendous your story, Simon. Really fantastic! I really mean it! I've never heard anything so funny, so totally preposterous. Me, if I were in your shoes I would try to get it published. It's a knockout I tell you! Smashing! And you really tell it well. A true amphigouri! Your talent as a story-teller is undeniable.

Well at least Claude knows how to react. And he goes on laughing with real tears in his eyes, giggling, choking in his giggles, coughing and squeaking while bouncing his ass on the seat, there next to me, in our Buick now speeding along in what begins
to look like a
ferocious snowstorm, as he moves closer to me (consciously or subconsciously remains to be determined).

— You're really a funny guy, he says to me, placing his hand suddenly on my knee (the right knee of course since I am in the driver's seat)! And you really know how to tell a story. How to build the suspense in a gradual manner. You could (his hand has moved sneakily up my thigh) if you wanted to make a best-seller out of this one. It's the kind of story that the large public really loves. They go wild for stories of this nature. Believe me, I have experience in that field. Especially nowadays. In the present.

Coming from him, his hand now all the way up my crotch, from one of my intellectual auditors as it were, one of those who's been selected and delegated to listen to me (directly or indirectly), and who eventually may even judge, may even criticize, analyze, explicate my story, or as far as I know even decide its literary value, that really touches me a great deal. I almost feel like embracing him. But his hand now, perhaps inadvertently, starts unbuttoning my fly (no! I mean unzipping it because me too like all good Americans I have a zipper on my fly). He does it with rather skillful fingers. I feel my cock leap joyfully in my trousers. The sons of a bitch! I knew it, I knew it all the time! They did it on purpose! Their delegate is a queer. A pederast. They sent him down here to fuck me. To take advantage of me. And me, dumb ass that I am, I was ready to make peace with them. To reconcile with them. Well wait and see. Wait for the surprise my little cutty, wait and see who fucks who in the ass! Your spy! Your delegate, he better watch out for his ass! And in fact, here is a coffee shop up the road a bit next to a motel. Perfect timing! Let's take a break! Come on!

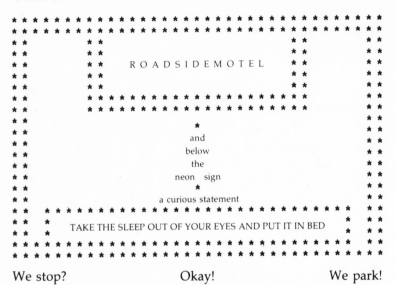

We stop?   Okay!   We park!

We get out of the car!
We both eat a juicy tender steak with French fries his medium rare mine bloody rare but without ketchup finally because both of us agreed after a short argument that ketchup is shit have a refill on coffee for which there is no extra charge to wash down the pies his coconut cream with a cherry on top mine chocolate delight we smoke a couple of cigarettes as we verify the bill which claude insists on paying   and now we're ready to get back on the road when claude (talk to me about subtlety or suggestiveness) starts yawning like a new born babe almost to the point of dislocating his jaw   you're tired I ask   affirmative nod of the head on his part   I have

never slept with a male I mean a queer before but at the stage
where we were and in the mood that I was in that day after that
horrible night on Marilyn's sofa   balls still sore from that
quicky job she gave me   and in my head the broken
pieces of that frightening nightmare   I could have fucked anything at this point   even a bird or a key hole   can't be
too choosy   claude walks directly towards the motel as we
come out of the coffee shop   natural reflex I suppose   I
catch on quickly but suddenly I feel panicky and for good reasons
I've just realized our friend claude doesn't speak a word of english   all that while we had been conversing in french   as
if I needed to mention it   because in fact claude was a french
delegate   he had been sent to me by the french faction
of my eventual listeners   that may complicate things a bit
but it is preferable to clarify this now   of course in the french
version of this story this kind of clarification will not be necessary
though it would be interesting to compare the two versions to see
how this works out   however in order to facilitate the flow
of the story it might be better now to move directly inside the
chamber I mean the motel room without relating the conversation
rather banal in fact which took place in the motel's office with the
woman at the desk!
                In other words let us skip all the superfluous details of the
                     mise-en-scène for what will now take place   okay
                          so here we are claude and I
                          at two in the afternoon or thereabout
of the day of my departure from new york city after that terrible night
spent on the sofa   and hardly 150
                                              or 175 miles at the most
                                              north of new york
                                              in what now appears to
and let us not forget   develop into a furious
that we are in february 1951   snowstorm   direction
and that claude introduced himself in my car   camp drum
and in my story in a rather dubious fashion and in a rather

aleatory manner thus creating further complications for the teller
and further unexpected digressions from the story-line which was already in danger of floundering miserably but all this does not require
further explanation since as it is often said in similar situations
everything so far is self-explanatory
                                  and self-evident   therefore
                                        better go directly to the action
                                        even though it is an action that
digresses flagrantly from the main action so here we are claude and I
in front of the motel   ROADSIDE MOTEL which also
[we have stepped backward a few narrative   bears the charming subtitle
steps in order to better jump into the action]   HAPPY TRAVELERS INN
We go in!   LADY SMILES!
— Do you have a double room, Mam?
— For how long?
— Not too long! (I look at Claude inquiringly) Depends . . you see we
drove all night . . and . . you understand . . in this furious snowstorm
. . lady understands . . . nods head understandingly . . . sort of a
bleached blond . . . asks no further questions . . . simply asks we don't
make too much noise . . . sexy broad . . . asks also we sign registration
card . . . a formality . . . claude signs marcel proust . . . me andré gide
. . . very appropriate . . . didn't even consult each other . . . simply a
matter of free association I suppose . . . camaraderie . . . room not bad
. . . clean but no t.v. of course . . . 1951 remember . . . though in this
story just about anything can happen . . . large bed in center of room
. . . and let us add to reassure those who may be interested that I did not
pay for the room . . . claude payed . . . so far he's been rather generous
. . . he will collect travel expenses I suppose when he gets back above in
the
present
and oops
one two three claude is bareass and jumps on top of the bed

                                   nice body well suntanned
                                   yellowish pubic hair all
                                   the way up his chest and
                              very curly cock already in erection
                                   of average dimensions no
                                   not circumcised I should
                                   point out for the record

buttocks   firm   and   well   rounded
on   top   of   nervous   legs   a   small
scar   on   the   left   knee   I   notice
rather   appetizing   this   young   man   but
it   should   be   stated   here   that   I   have
little   experience   indeed   none   at   all
in   such   matters   in   fact   this   is   the   first   time
I look at a guy in a manner other than . . . how
shall I say . . . other than in a masculine mode
. . . sexually I suppose would be a better way to put it
but if my natural instincts of a rather normal human being
are correct this might well be the first and the last time
I indulge in such abnormalities let us say that I am doing
it for aesthetic reasons or for the sake of literature but I will not
fall for it twice that's for damn sure even if in the next version of
this story such an occasion offers itself again to me no but one must
not prejudge one can never tell in advance in any event the damn potentials
they thought they had me well their cute delegate better be ready because I
tell you oops here I am bareass too on top of the bed next to claude but we
are hardly flat on our backs that claude already swallows my cock my jewish
cock all the way to my sore balls I tell him to take it easy slow down dear
little cocotte don't eat it all at once you've got to make it last enjoy it
shit it's not going well at all
I won't be able to describe the
scene the way it happened or at
least not in my own words because I
don't   have
a vocabulary rich enough for that nor the
kind
of imagination suited for this type of de-
vious
action
        no
        the best would be
        in a situation such
        as this one which does
        require a very specialized
        diction to use the words of somebody else
                        somebody more experienced than me
                        somebody who knows how to deal with
this type of encounter
I mean deal with it linguistically and imaginatively without offending or debasing
public morality   in other words
                        somebody specialized in eroticoqueerness
                        somebody more subtle than me

                                        more literary too
                                        more accustomed to the delicate
description of bodies that touch
                bodies that rub together
                somebody therefore who can handle this kind of activity
without having to worry about being accused of sexual depravation and
moral turpitude as it so often happens these days in popular stories

and fortunately for us
I came across a passage
the other day in a novel
a contemporary novel (and
a delicious passage it was
to say the least) which for
the occasion seems more than
adequate to me to describe at
this time what took place that
particular afternoon in my own story
                                        there in that room
                                        in february 1951 and this way since I will
                be quoting from another story it will be a story within a story a fiction
                                                                within a fiction
                                                        bodies within a quotation
                                        naked bodies within nude bodies
                                a kind of playgiaristic displacement of words and
                                of bodies fictitious bodies rather than real ones
                                conductive bodies (des corps conducteurs if I may
                                suggest in French) conductive of heat and passion
        and this way we'll be protected against the censure and against public opinion
because
in fact
it's the other guy
the other storyteller
who here and now will be
speaking for me therefore it's him (that contemporary novelist) who will be
censured eventually but ôf course I have no intention of revealing his name
that would be a dirty trick   therefore
the censure and public opinion they can go fuck themselves in the derrières
but nevertheless
                a situation such
                        as this one does
                                demand a rather
                        new and fresh
                vocabulary
        and a different
                technique of narration
                        as well as a whole system
                                of hidden metaphors and symbols
        and a language of full suggestiveness

which I do not feel capable
of mustering at this time
not that I could not work it out by
myself with time and patience and a
bit of luck
no I am not that naive nor that inexperienced
on the contrary but it's just that one must
be careful these days with words and besides me I
know all about such encounters even though it's
true that my only pederastic experience so
far let us say did not go very far
                    it happened about a year ago when I was
                    hitch-hiking (this was before I bought my
                    buickspecial) somewhere in virginia near
                    washington on a weekend pass and this
                    guy gave me a ride all the way to
                    richmond and even past richmond
                    and suddenly that sneaky guy
                    reached for my fly while driving
                    at full speed and opened it with
                    one hand quite expertly
                    and grabbed my genitals
                    and before I knew what the hell was happening
                    to me I came in his hand like a juicy melon
                    crushed by a hammer and the guy licked off
                    the sperm with gluttonous delight
                    but fortunately for me he didn't go
                    any further except that he wanted me
                    to do the same to him question of equality
                    and fraternity he said having noticed I
                    suppose that I spoke with a french accent
                but of course I told him to go jump in a cold shower
                and so the guy (a rather distinguished middle aged
                man) stopped the car and told me to get the hell
                out and that I was a prude a selfish fellow and a
                male chauvinist
well that's approximately the extent
of my experience in this field therefore
as you can see I don't really have the technical means
nor the direct knowledge to describe the somewhat heated
encounter in the room so I am forced to rely so to speak
    on another guy
    on the words of another guy
        to report my own adventure even if I have to
change a few words here and there for the sake of realism
and to better render the excitement and verity of my own situation

SO HERE WE GO :
[Incidentally I am quoting the passage in]
[French because the contemporary novel in]
[question was written in that language by]
[one of those so-called new romanciers I]
[tried to render the passage into English]
[but failed miserably Somehow it lost its]
[lyrical qualities and much of its Gallic]
[elegance in my rather poor approximation]
[of the original version Therefore even]
[at the risk of frustrating some of you I]
[prefer to give here the original passage]
[in French rather than my weak and faulty]
[translation   Were my second-hand teller]
[present at this time he would give you I]
[am sure a faithful and proper traduction]
[of this text but without him I am really]
[at a loss to perform this difficult task]
SO HERE WE GO :

Les corps lisses des jeunes amants sont animés d'ondulations
lentes, tantôt précipitées, ou se heurtent parfois dans de violents
soubresauts *Good!* Comme ces fragments de puzzles aux décou-
pures sinueuses, les deux profils aux yeux agrandis s'emboîtent
étroitement dans tout un réseau de baisers, les saillies de l'un et
les creux de l'autre à fleur de peau seulement séparés par les
souples méandres *Wow this is beautiful!* de la ligne unique qui
épouse tour à tour leurs nez leurs bouches et leurs mentons
encastrés *This guy is incredible! He really knows how to exaggerate!* Au
bout d'un moment cependant, dans le dessin qui se déforme et se
reforme au grè des mouvements ou des secousses de l'étreinte, il
devient possible de distinguer les beaux éléments particuliers de
chacun des deux corps. L'un est couché sur le dos les jambes
écartées. Sur son ventre et sa poitrine reposent les reins et le dos
de l'autre qui le bras droit noué sous le bras droit de l'autre,
l'enlaçant, la main droite *Shit I'm getting all confused with that*
meandering and interlacing of bodies, but the guy seems to know what
he's doing, therefore let's trust him, and allow things to follow their
course se refermant sur l'épaule de celui-ci, joint ses lèvres aux

siennes par une torsion du buste et de son cou renflé *Hey it's like a quattrocento!* cependant que, poussant ses fesses en sens inverse, il accueille en lui le membre raidi qui le pénètre légèrement en biais. Peu à peu les colonnes et les entassements de nuages diminuent de hauteur. *What the fuck are the columns and the clouds doing in here? That escapes me, but I must admit all that is rather well done, and shows a great deal of imagination on that guy's part!* [Incidentally the passage appears on page 133 in the original edition]

Finally Claude and I fell asleep in a gathering of clouds with our two Greek Columns totally in ruins. Me if I had written this description in my own words I would (perhaps in a stroke of inspiration) have put the clouds in it, or at least the sky, but the columns, no! I would never, in a million years, have thought of the columns as a symbol!
Damn this guy is good!   What an elegant style!

Columns descending from the clouds as they diminish that's imagination for you! This guy is lucky like hell to have images like these in his head! Me all I have in my rather aboulic skull are ruins of such images. Ruins of columns and
             clouds. Yes piles of literary detritus!
                          Linguistic junk!

In any event
it was quite nice
our little encounter
in the motel room that day
but when I woke up (around six or seven
that afternoon and it was already dark outside)
Claude was not there next to me in bed. I looked around the room. He must have gone for a stroll I thought to relax or recompose himself! But on the bedside table I found a note from him written in red with a lipstick which explained why at this time he had decided to break up our alliance so brusquely in the middle of my story!

My Dear Simon,

Please forgive this rather brusque departure, but it is full of shame that I take the road back to my present state, for I now fully realize how I have allowed myself to transgress too violently and in a way much too spontaneously the sweet intimacy of our relationship!

That this relationship was fictive, as you pretend it to be, it may be so, but I am not convinced. Know however that I have enjoyed our liaison, even though temporary, but that, nevertheless, I cannot see how I could, in good faith, remain at your sides without feeling crushed by the weight of our guilty encounter. How could I, when it is time to do so, and under the burden of this flagrant culpability, face, in my own name and my delicate functions, those who above (and in the present) delegated me near you, even if it was somewhat in an aleatory fashion, in order to represent them here, knowing full well that, as I was strictly warned, I should not abuse my visiting right as an auditor nor your confidence as a teller, and, worse yet, bring to a stop, and perhaps even destroy by my transgression what may, as we all hoped, have become a true and lasting entente, and a peaceful relation between you and your potential listeners.

Not having the right, as you well know, to interfere in all the detours and contours of your story, in other words in its recitation either direct or indirect, even in its most tempting moments, I none the less wanted to be part of it, but realizing how wrong I was even to think that it was possible, I am forced (and believe me I already suffer for it, and will continue to suffer as long as I live in real life or in fiction) to depart and return to the nothingness whence I came, the non-existent state which is mine outside your story.

But now I deserve this since I am not qualified, or at least no longer qualified to report (even partially) the details of our sweet encounter. I leave you with deep regrets. Forgive me and forget me if you can. Do not try to follow me or find me. Farewell Dear Dear Simon. I have deep affection and profound respect for you.

WHAT A JERK!   WHAT AN ASS!

Have you guys ever read anything so farfelu so hifalutin so
constipated? And the worse is that his rupture note was not
even signed. Not even an inscription, a pretense of a signature, nothing! Therefore inauthentic! Just a lousy insignificant piece of paper scribbled in red. If at least he had used his
blood to write it instead of that cheap lipstick, putain de
putain! A useless note! What good will it do me? He could at
least have left me something more tangible! Something
more real, more useful! A twenty dollar bill for instance.
Two or three snapshots of him in his yellow sweater to brag
about in the future. But no, nothing except this dumb
ridiculous letter full of infantile whining and fake excuses.
Ah I tell you I am not lucky! And worse yet is that now he is
not even going to report what I told him (partially or not
who gives a shit), to make a report of what happened down
here. Therefore I have wasted my time with him. By now I
could almost have reached my destination. All the way to
Camp Drum! All the sad beautiful funny stories I told him,
all that for nothing! All that wasted in his poor memory of a
whore! Up his ass and down the drain! Lost forever! Those
damn potentials they knew what the fuck they were doing
when they sent him down her that cute delegate and his
yellow sweater! Maybe I fucked him in the ass, but in the
end it's me who is fucked up. Doesn't pay to fool around
with potential critics!

QUEL CON!   QUEL CAVE!

Alright no use feeling sorry for yourself and waste any more
time. Alright no use feeling sorry for yourself and waste any
more time. Alright no use feeling sorry for yourself and

waste any more time. Yes let's get back on the
road.   BRRRRMMMM!   VR0000MMM!
Here we go!   Wow did it snow during all that
time! A good 12 or 16 inches on the ground and more
coming   down.   What   soup   out
there!   A narrow winding country road now
alongside a gully!
A PRECIPICE!   Careful don't lean against the
wind!   I am mentioning the gully now because one never
knows it might come into play later on! And let me emphasize not just a 10 or 15 feet gully.   But a really deep
and dangerous gully.   Visibility zero!   If I
were smart I would go back to the motel and try my luck
with the sexy blond! She looked like she was willing and
able.   At least for the night!   This way we wouldn't
have to go on with this wordshit!   I could stop right
here.   Call it quit!   FINIS!   End of the
road! Finished all that masturbatory recitation!   No
more funny beautiful sad useless stories!   Stop everything!   End of the journey!

everythingcanceledeverythingcanceledeverything
canceledeverythingcanceledeverythingcanceledev
erythingcanceledeverythingcanceledeverythingcan
celedeverythingcanceledeverythingcanceled every

Yes but I still have a way to go before getting out of Massachusetts or at least out of this soup into Vermont and I
promised myself to make it as far as Vermont today. No
cheating! Got to keep going a bit longer!
Hang on!   Something is going to happen!   Hang on!

XIX

dashing from one parenthesis to another

YAP YAP YAP . . . ? [Hey you guys are back! Hello there! Salut les]
QUA QUA QUA . . .[copains! Did you have a good rest? By the way]
BLA BLA BLA . . . ? [did the delegates make it back? No better not!]

What? Oh you guys want to know where I was? Why I left my
post . . . why I deserted the recitation? Deserted! You guys
exaggerate. I had to go to the bathroom. No . . . I'm kidding. I
went to see a friend. Buddy of mine, Ronnie. Ronald Sukenick.
You know UP and OUT and 98.6 — Fiction Collective. He was
having problems with his story. Wanted me to help a bit. I was
only gone for a short time. At the most two sections during the
visits of your delegates. But shit . . . what a mess here! That poor
guy had a rough time by himself. Really fucked up things down
here. He should have waited for me rather than go on by himself.
Well better get to work quickly and straighten out this damn
recitation. Got to get the story going again. Let's see where were
we? Oh yes, you guys wanted to know more about his past. No?
Oh you wanted to know if he still played the saxophone. No?
That's not it? Oh you wanted to know why he hadn't told Marilyn
. . . Why he was crossing Massachusetts and Vermont to get to
Upper New York State? It's not logical you say since he had left
from a place in New York State to get to another place in New
York State. From New York City which is in fact in New York
State. I agree with you that doesn't make much sense. He should
have stayed in New York State. (You see what a good mood I am
in!) Yes what the fuck is he doing in New England? But you guys
don't know your map of America. For if you look at the map of
this region carefully you will immediately see that to get to Camp
Drum from New York City it is in fact more direct to pass—bypass
if you prefer—through Massachusetts and Vermont. At least
within the logistics of this story it makes sense. Moreover in the
context of this story which unloads in all directions without

respect for logic and with rather crooked means it is indeed impossible to follow a straight line! For if one examines the topology of this recitation one quickly notices that we are now in the Northeast of our journey a few degrees Northeast of the right angle of our eventual destination. In other words more or less on the most direct road to the end of this story. Almost there at last. As far as I can tell. And since maps never lie one can see that he had to cross Massachusetts and Vermont (including a small section of Southwest Connecticut) to get where he was going. And if all that does not make sense you can go cook yourself an egg sunnyside up because I am fed up with all your dumb questions. I was hoping that after having delayed the action so long you guys would be anxious to hear the end of this story. Especially after that dirty filthy sneaky trick you played on the poor guy. Sending him that critiqueer! Don't act innocent. He may not have realized what was happening to him but I know what this is all about. You're not going to tell me I am inventing what happened in that motel room! Not at the stage where we are. And that while I went to visit Ronnie while I was absent so to speak and you guys were taking a little break so you claim the poor guy took the wrong road! Mesdames et Messieurs! We are on the right road. I am back for good and I shall keep going to the end of all this. Therefore a little effort and I'll get us to Camp Drum. In the North. On time to collect our money! On time to get back to New York City! Sell our Buick! Fuck Marilyn if possible and this time without worrying about Benny! We have to before taking off for the big trip. One more time. Perhaps for the last time as far as I know. And then here we go! The big trip! Across country! The great discovery at last! Coast to Coast! America here we come and then you'll hear some tremendous stories! The real thing this time and no more of this wordshit! Therefore let's hurry up and get him moving!

Out of Massachusetts and into Vermont. From one state to another. From one section to the next. From one episode to the next. Because me it's the story that interest me. Once the story is launched it must go on it must follow its course however crooked it may be and even at the risk of crumbling along the way. And even if it takes the wrong direction. But let me assure you that without me. Without the strict control that I am able to impose upon it the story would not go very far. It would surely disintegrate into nonsense. Witness the last two sections. How screwed up these are. How that poor guy fell flat on his narrative face when he tried to handle his own fabulation. And especially when those delegates showed up out of time and out of context. It is not easy I tell you for someone who lacks experience and imagination to handle this type of twin situation — situation which brings together elements of the past and of the present on the same level (not to mention elements of the future and of the potential). Though it is true that once upon a time he attempted to tell his own story without the help of a qualified story-teller. But what a mess that was! Here let me give you an example. It's a good one I think. I am taking it straight from some notes he gave me when we sat under our tree. DASHING FROM DON TO TIOLI he had entitled it. A rather poor title. A more appropriate title would be DASHING FROM ONE STORY TO ANOTHER. Or better yet DASHING FROM ONE PARENTHESIS TO ANOTHER as it is apparent in the text. I am presenting it just as it appeared in his own notes. The syntax alone is very revealing for it shows to what extent a bad story-teller in trying to be objective about his own experiences too often falls into self-consciousness while pretending to be aloof towards what he is describing from a distance. But distanciation is perhaps the most dangerous technique of narration particularly when dealing with the elements of one's private life. It would have been better in my opinion if he had used a more direct and more spontaneous approach in this text!

(D A S H I N G F R O M O N E P A R E N T H E S I S T O A N O T H E R)

this story will now tell itself alone without the support of the person
(pronominal or otherwise) which gave it movement composure and
identity HERE it will move therefore without efforts by a simple
horizontal (but vertical too) accumulation of signs and facts which
by the mere process of surcharging upon one another will decipher
left to right but also in sequence top to bottom because to come
back (retrace) to the place (the space) where closed was the story
on the threshold (DON) of AMERICA (of course) imperfect vision
(summary of other journeys) which repeats take it or leave it double
or nothing (same point) first then the scenes two or three (at most)
hardly a displacement (IF) fear anguish groans cries with people in
a room (imaginary with a table and a chair) explains the past
conditionally every detail (all) needed to survive by calculations true
(but which could be false) the story (TIOLI now AMERELDORADO
for a while) launched on a period of 365 days (or boxes) alone
without sallow fear in the room (without mirrors) at a precise moment seeming(ly) even though (obvious)ly situated before it had to
begin October 1st as noted on first page the calculations made (and
unmade) the 30th day before at the latest of September first with the
prices (verified and ascertained carefully) from top to bottom of the
room (furnished) first but without kitchen privileges then the noodles (never forget the noodles an entire existence of noodles) in
boxes (calculated but also designed) coffee or tea salt (again)
toothpaste toothbrush cigarettes (two packs a day just in case)
toilet paper writing paper (of course) chewing gum (in case of
despair) typewriter (used to specify and the little screw falling as it
always happens) and the story now three persons at the tip of the
hands (fingers) hardly sketched the second locked bearded imagining inventing the third while the first records faithfully (but what is to
record but to note from left to right top to bottom obliquely) all
possible shapes contours and detours of the story the writing

thoughts digressions lies of second person (noodler) what is said proposed calculated done undone the scenes (two or three at most) crisscrossing voiding the movement (a look upon AMERICA) when from the upper deck of the boat saw standing in the wind (Statue of Liberty above the shoulder of the girl) the old man polyglot with red tie without a hat waits for the young man (not yet in existence) shy third person to become in hollow future main protagonist (19 years old) dressed in grey double-breasted (outmoded) suit looks at her a step forward and thus the crisscrossing of noodles (365 boxes) as a measure of time (symbolically) assumes the space of the scenes (three four at the maximum) the waves on the shore (and the heart beating) the girl on the upper deck (Statue of Liberty) the arrival of the boat with music and the old man (wifeless) (careless) the subway ride (dirty look between the legs spread apart wide of a beautiful negress) family scene in the BRONX (here) first door (down the corridor) on the left and that feeling of culpability after the masturbatory gesture NOW (metaphor for the second version discovery of AMERICA (thirty days) another journey a trip before dying (writing love letters five dollars each) about twelve hours 300 miles north of New York a typical (inevitable) error armylife (go to hell) and there waits for the music to begin not a moment wasted (an exaggerated tale) sitting on the sofa (same version) told (recited) aloud standing or sitting on the sofa with flowers recounting his youth (memory of the father also polyglot and surrealist) a sentimental scene about politics on Sunday which recalls the days of the first version or DON (game poker tennis dice roulette) as well as screwing the money did come from somewhere even an illusion borrowed perhaps but the STORY (in spite of all) progresses (HERE in the middle) since all fiction is told digressively tale retold (used words) but the story (second-hand) moves along without efforts word (after) word by a mere accumulation of facts and signs but without really understanding stood on the upper deck that the boat will never arrive yet if the journey progresses in spite of it the sofa told of course in the conditional tense (always) days and days of calculatory passion in two languages (bilingual) FRENCH / ENGLISH with additions lists diagrams endless procrastinations like a mad acrobat of fiction but other images (symbolic of course) suitcases closets (yellow stars) rooms (furnished) typewriters a whole life DASHING but others to come and participate (a whole life) NOTHING three four scenes (at most) a slight displacement (the scenes not necessarily in sequence) no order logic quite accidental even if (GAME) first by bus ordinary or by train and the night shift at CHRYSLER hands bleeding (third battalion) gloves even with canvas (third version) to come (the young man waiting a void) the emptiness of an outmoded suit (double-breasted) grey his future and his past hollow calculations (UP & DOWN) hardly visible (MOINOUS) noise quaqua recordings yap yap sounds bla bla hardly audible now (everything ends) must be emphasized (everything begins again) only the girl (blond) with the Statue of Liberty beyond her left shoulder the sky grey designs indicates the presence (the passage) of the old man (journalist) alone a few tears (behind rimless or seemingly glasses) all three together now a new beginning AMERICA fat ob(scene) female (scene three) legs spread (on the edge of the sink) wide apart (MOTHER) friends noodle after noodle or box after box playing the saxophone (tenor / alto) night after night (with erotic dreams) sleepless counting the pages (the boxes too) the curtains closed counting the horses on the wall each with a number to remember or classify (but designed nonetheless) better (cut in two sometimes) in the moments of despair since the curtains will eventually (conditionally) be closed therefore no light (natural light) 365 days (each marked sordidly by the rhythm of the typewriter and the little screw falling off) a loss of time in the middle (approximately on the 270th or 280th day) slightly different version (TIOLI now) the second person locked and bearded tries (noodle eater noodler) noodling cornered in the middle screw driver fits in hand starting out his eyes staring the superhighway Washington and up to New York in twelve hours rain on the windows (grey sky of course) and a woman waits on the sofa the telephone rings (memory of lampshades with X-X-X-X systematic extermination) on the sofa impossible to make love in this situation (without forgetting the girl) remembers the journey North and then from East to West (or vice versa) with flowers DASHING (always) in his grey suit (with wings now) proudly legs crossed not to reveal the triangular jungle HERE dark above the stockings feeling stupid in a slow motion in the bathroom his pants down at his feet going in soft wet like cream cheese (feeling to expatriate SUMMARY) the father gone to a game a baseball game with the sister (all the others laughing at him because of the curious voice accent all of them farmers hillbillies ignorant jerks brutes animals from all corners of AMERICA writing love letters with all kinds of examples five dollars each 0-0-0 at least six or seven a week a few extra here and there) in the room (but without natural light) square tower of boxes (noodles) only three voices (only one having existed) all the others (firmly entrenched) waiting to become to be at the tip of the fingers on the machine (if not on the 270th day one day then surely) one of them sitting on the chair successive stories smoking two packs or two and a half a day cancer of the lungs ass on the chair at the table (legs spread apart ((literature of course)) firmly entrenched) telling stories any story crap lie or die scratching one's head banging on the table or on the walls with one's fingers one's head paper table fingers ass hard like rock to pass the time (invent) when it rains in a 1947 BUICK black SPECIAL full speed toward Washington full speed now (top to bottom) and then West toward the music at the BLUE BIRD in Detroit (jazz of course) while whistling and the buddies (friends of his mother's friend) on the sink's edge more or less involved (committed to Sunday politics) left or right slight displacement (sleep well eat well and once in a while good piece of ass) the easy life political parades on Sunday speeches (fists tight and up in the air) slogans Place de la Bastille under grey clouds under the wheels head smashed songs (cops too) THE INTERNATIONALE (with sticks tear gas) the masses head cut open (virgin) very soon and then a movie on 42nd Street HERE three times a day bleeding (99%) panties (but without crying) without breathing without efforts progressing UP & DOWN & SIDEWAYS by a simple a meaningless accumulation from left to right at random but also top to bottom as if DASHING without composure (movement heresy) identify DASHING hop hop (at the pronominal level) suddenly the end (or otherwise) from one story to another one parenthesis to another second-hand tale told and retold (fictive digression SUMMARY) a similar form DON or TIOLI (DANCE) at most two or three versions in sequence but with AMER ELDORADO in parenthesis (could have been VICE VERSA) maybe an accidental turn of events (two or three) without however forgetting (to remember) the noodles (Sum) boxes (SummarY) final versions (WINNER TAKE ALL) the horses (numbered) without explaining clarifying (now) the rest of the story in the future to repeat TIOLI or possibly cancel DON (with its delirious syntax) and go on to another version (SIDEWAYS) or slight displacement just to continue to be able to go on just to be able to be be become the story goes on vertically and horizontally without efforts by leaps by bounds without emotions alone no longer (MOINOUS) in a room (furnished) vociferating crying begging saying by a simple accumu-lation

(D A S H I N G F R O M O N E P A R E N T H E S I S T O A N O T H E R)

(!) (!) (!) (!) (!) (!) (!) (!) (!) (!) (!) (!) (!)
? × ? × ? × ? × ? × ? × ? × ?
0 - 0 - 0 - 0 - 0 - 0 - 0 - 0 - 0 - 0 - 0 - 0 - 0 - 0
× ? × ? × ? × ? × ? × ? × ? × ?
@ @
(!) (!) (!) (!) (!) (!) (!) (!) (!) (!) (!) (!) (!)

[all together with visible anger and foaming at the mouths like beasts]

What the fuck are you guys screaming like that? What got you worked up like a bunch of animals?Why this wild commotion?

Ah you gys think I went too far this time! I shouldn't have given all that verbal delirium!   That linguistic mush!

You guys think I should have skipped this example that I shouldn't have included it in my recitation that it distracts from what is already the epitome of unreadability that it is useless that it disturbs the stream of words that it is totally preposterous that it is bad incoherent that it undermines the texture of the textuality of this recitation which is already quite shaky that it proves nothing that it does not deserve the least attention that in fact it should be destroyed immediately that it should be burned that it is shameful to even pretend that whoever wrote this text even in the form of notes knew what the fuck he was saying at the time that this kind of writing is unhealthy immoral depraved sickly and so on and so on and so on and so on and so on and so on and so on!

Well I say to you that you don't understand that it serves as a jumping board as a transition as a bridge to go from one moment of his life and of his past to another moment of his life closer to the present that it is un petit pont between the confrontation and the discovery a means of crossing a dangerous precipice a way of leaping over a tricky situation

TTTTTTTTTTTTTTTTTTTTTTTTTTTTTTTTTTTTTTTTTTTTTTTTTTTTTT

----

and at the same time a way for me to get back into the course of action or if you wish it is a thematic digression but if you think we went too far in presenting it here if you really believe that it is out of place then you can throw it out tear it up shove it up your ass burn it erase it eat it me I don't care I can keep going without such transitional or parenthetical devices me I am the straightforward type of story-teller!

TTTTTTTTTTTTTTTTTTTTTTTTTTTTTTTTTTTTTTTTTTTTTTTTTTTTTT

Personally what counts for me is that we can move on and get this thing over once and for all and for the time being I must confess things seem to be stagnating around here it's not going very well yes rather poorly badly slowly digressively it's a mess the story hasn't progressed for a long time not an inch not a quarter of an inch but it's not my fault it has to do with the leapfrog technique but things will improve with luck and a bit of patience on your part and in fact I saw something just two minutes ago up the road a little sign which may indeed save us and help us get this thing going again a road panel which said in gothic letters

```
-------------------------------------------------
-------------------------------------------------
```

STATE LINE FORTY-FIVE MILES

```
-------------------------------------------------
-------------------------------------------------
```

—

which means that we are almost in Vermont almost therefore
with a quick and firm displacement of words and if all of us
together as one man get behind the wheel and push we'll get
there eventually so stick with it I tell you don't give up stop
bugging me and the story will go on (I give you my word) and
then after Camp Drum the real story the great journey!

TTTTTTTTTTTTTTTTTTTTTTTTTTTTTTTTTTTTTTTTTTTTTTTTTTTTTTTTT

T A K E   I T

O R

L E A V E   I T

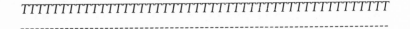

XX

a night to remember

Okay I concentrate at the wheel (but what soup out there! can't see a damn thing!) and in less than forty-five miles we change scenery. But meanwhile things were flying in his head, pieces of his past existence coming together and falling asunder into a mishmash of twisted images:

his father his mother his sisters aunts
and uncles cousins and the trains the
camps the farms and the jews the yellow
star lampshades le 14 juillet rats jerks the
liberation cries songs slogans his first
piece of ass black market factories I'm fed
up his uncle david in america the future
the boat and the statue of liberty disgusting grub detroit with the black buddies
jazz and the tenor sax blowing bebop
and more factories hands bleeding
chrysler I can't stand it anymore lonely
I'm taking off summer jobs and new york
bernice salami stupid humiliating and
degrading jobs starvation furnished
rooms bed bugs double or nothing cockroaches love sex and marilyn

Ah yes, Marilyn! I already told you how they met in his country club! In the Catskills. He was working as a bus boy during the summer (1948 I believe or 1949) and besides she had already written him a few times in Detroit after that summer. Two or three letters full of loving and sentimental understatements, and once (I think it was for Christmas or his birthday, a special occasion) she sent him a present, first one he got since he came to America, a beautiful bathrobe, imitation silk and wide lapels, dark brown, very elegant, large pockets too, and even his initials embroidered in gold on the breast pocket (he only wore it for special occasions to make it last), but it was nice of her to send him something like that, something so expensive and so personal, it showed how much affection she had for him, even though they had not yet slept together. Therefore, one day, just like that (the day he had that bad argument with Bernice because she refused to sleep with him), the very day he was fired from his job as a dishwasher (literally kicked out on the pavement) in a cafeteria because he was caught stealing food (they dragged him out into the street and cursed him like a pervert, like some criminal to the point of making him cry), sandwiches, fruit, cookies, to bring back to Loulou who stayed in their room in the Bronx all day, that filthy little furnished room (for six bucks a week) full of bed bugs and enormous cockroaches crawling out of the walls, right behind the big and fancy department store Alexander, off the Grand Concourse, poor Loulou a real artist who preferred to starve than compromise, Loulou who accepted the worse living conditions because he was a real artist, a genius, even though he didn't have much to show for his talents, and who argued quite forcefully that all great artists ought not to be concerned with reality and the struggle for daily bread, and this is why he was not ashamed nor even grateful that his daily bread was stolen for him from some stinking cafeteria. However when Bernice found out that he had lost his job, his only source of income, she started screaming at him as if her own future livelihood depended on it, saying that he was irresponsible, a thief who has no sense of other people's property, a bum, a good-for-nothing, that she hoped he had learned his lesson, and that he cared more about Loulou than about her, that he had no future, and what about our love, she said with tears in her eyes of course, and that he would never succeed, never make it in America if he continued like that, and that when her own poor father came to America from Poland he didn't have a penny, nothing, that he couldn't even speak the language, and look at him now, proprietor and manager of his own business, you should be ashamed to steal food at your age, I would rather starve than steal she shouted moralistically, and at a time when it is so difficult to get a good job, in the middle of a bad recession, and that there was nothing wrong, nothing shameful to work as a dishwasher, not in America, that it is of course temporary, that there are many people who started like that and became millionaires eventually and that in fact even her own father, though he is not a millionaire by far, but makes a decent living, well he too worked as a dishwasher when he first came from the old country, ask him she said proudly he'll tell you the story, he is not ashamed of it, and in those days it was really tough, even harder than now to get a job, especially for foreigners who couldn't speak the language, and that that yes her father rarely speaks about all that now but when he came to America from Poland (after World War One) because of the pogroms, it was much harder than now especially during the great depression when people were jumping out of windows and that that that indeed he should be glad and grateful to be able to earn a living and that it was not reasonable on his part and at that point a wave of anger came over him (I suppose because she kept bringing up her father as an example and that was a touchy subject with him) and though he knew that that would be the end of their romance he told her to shut up and go to hell and bug off fuck off you little prude, that she was a dumb cunt, that she was getting on his nerves, that she had no right to speak to him like that, who the fuck she thinks she is, that she didn't understand a damn thing about him and about his pride and his ambitions and what about human dignity does that mean anything to you, he shouted while raising his fist as though ready to strike her across the face in an ultimate gesture of impartial disgust, all those promises, all

those dreams, those beautiful dreams in the land of opportunities
and what do I get a dishwasher job (part-time at that) sticking my
hands day in day out in greasy boiling water to the point of being
ashamed of showing my hands in public, and by then his anger
had reached the force of a tidal wave, and he shoved her aside
while bombarding her with the foulest and most vulgar expressions he could muster out of his rather limited vocabulary (considering that he had only three years of experience with the
English language), using such expressions as (supposedly, for he
never reported directly the exact words he used) stupid dumb
broad pig's ass narrow-minded bitch conne salope tomate (a few
French words crept into the fury of his delivery) smelly cunt
blindfolded gooseneck pussy mule goody-goody lacteous vag-
inalized cockteaser

                              [of course he did not use]
                              [all these words and many]
                              [others that could not be]
                              [listed here he only used]
                              [them mentally he thought]
                              [of them in his mind in a]
                              [silent and discreet sort]
                              [of way to himself for in]
                              [those days he didn't yet]
                              [dare speak such language]
                              [aloud and in public even]
                              [with someone as close to]
                              [him as bernice he wasn't]
                              [sure enough of the exact]
                              [meaning of these curious]
                              [sounding words to permit]
                              [himself to use them in a]
                              [casual and native manner]
                              [this kind of specialized]
                              [language requires a long]

[time to be mastered by a]
[foreigner so that he can]
[handle it freely smartly]
[and deliberately without]
[self-consciousness yes a]
[long time to gain a full]
[mastery of such words in]
[all their subtle meaning]
[so that one can speak or]
[shout them to the person]
[with whom one has fucked]
[a few times even if this]
[relation is on the verge]
[of being fully cancelled]

and so he told her to go take a walk around
the corner and fuck herself in the brain and stop climbing up his
arms and down his back (figuratively speaking) and that she
could shove her crooked sense of responsibility and her American morality and even her Jewish mentality up her father's ass
and he threw her down the stairs!

And so, that day, just like that, to calm himself, he called Marilyn
in Brooklyn. He had been walking the streets for five hours and
was feeling somewhat sad and lonely, after that heated argument, sort of lost. And so he told her the whole story. The
humiliating job with his hands in the greasy boiling water. Bernice. Loulou and what he thought about life and reality and the
role of the artist in society and how he refused to compromise and
stayed in the room all day long except to go to the movies once in a
while when Bernice came over in the afternoon. The furnished
room in the Bronx for six bucks a week with the cockroaches
crawling out of the walls and how they exploded into sperm
when you stepped on them. The big salami under Bernice's skirt.
(He tried to laugh) Bernice (he felt a need to talk about her to

someone) and how suddenly she refused to pursue what had been for them such a lovely arrangement and a most practical situation. Told her about her crooked ideas. What she said about her father. About responsibility. Told her how ashamed he was of his hands and of the holes in his shoes. Told her about the pawn shops (on Sixth Avenue) and how even his saxophone was gone now. Told her about the noodles three times a day. The subway at six in the morning. Everything in other words. Even managed to sound suicidal on the phone. To sound as though he was crying. And she kept saying in a soft and delicate voice at the other end of the line poor dearest, oh poor dearest why didn't you call me poor darling why didn't you call me sooner? Come on over immediately. I can't he said shamefully. I don't even have money for the subway. What a life! Stay where you are dear one and I'll come and get you. At least Marilyn understood him. But before hanging up he told her in details the whole argument with Bernice or at least the climax of it. Word for word. Just to release tension! And so he told her in one breath how the two of them had fought like rag-pickers and how eventually he threw her out of his room down the stairs and told her to go screw herself in the brain that it was all over between them and that he was fed up with virgins and their darn sense of responsibility and their crooked morality and their twisted oedipal complex and that as far as he was concerned (and here he put on a forceful and knowing accent in his voice) he preferred women of experience women who have comprehension mature women who are capable of dealing with the facts of life and understand man's need of love!

How charming you are! And how I love your accent she said with deep emotion and lovely sighs. I could squeeze you in my arms right now!

And at that point he let out a whole tirade about human misery about the difficulties a man his age and with a sensibility as fragile and as acute as his has in finding a place in society and how life for a Jewish immigrant like him a displaced person who knows nothing about the American-way-of-life is a constant struggle and yet how hard how painfully he tries to carve a decent place for himself in this great land of opportunities but without sacrificing nor compromising pride dignity and the sense one has of having to accomplish one's calling!

Oh how right you are she said and one could hear her voice trembling at the other end of the telephone in Brooklyn. You said it so well! You should have been a poet darling. And who knows maybe you'll try writing all that someday just the way you said it to me. In poetry!

Yes I told that little bitch that she didn't understand a damn thing about life and that's why finally our love affair could not make it!

Did you really call her a bitch? (With Marilyn he could at least use this kind of language without self-consciousness. She was very open-minded). Yes that's exactly what I called her, even worse than that!

[Yes he knew a lot of those dirty words in English after three years]
[in America and sometimes he would even say them to himself aloud to]
[practice when he was alone in front of the mirror or in the dark or]
[in the bathroom blindfolding himself not to see himself blush since]
[he was so sensitive about language but it's really when he got into]
[the army that he began to learn and use such language freely and in]
[a regular and deliberate manner perhaps even too much and sometimes]
[these words would come out at the wrong moment and cause tragicomic]
[embarrassment for those who were involved wow how puritanic America]
[was in those days the days which are being alluded to in this story]

for instance one day during his first week-end pass after 14 miserable weeks of basic training at Fort Dix yes Fort Dix in New Jersey he had three days off to recuperate and so he decided to go up to New York but didn't really feel like calling Marilyn because of Benny who was eyeing them suspiciously already therefore he called Bernice (for old time's sake) and she was quite surprised to hear from him after all this time and to learn that he was still around and still alive and still well and how have you been what are you doing Oh you're in the army now I didn't know I'm proud of you etc etc it had been a good year since he had thrown her down the stairs a good year since she had been discarded like a useless object but nonetheless how happy she was to hear his voice and would love to see him again as a matter of fact why doesn't he come for dinner tonight her parents will be delighted to see him again REALLY they very often talk about him and even wonder sometimes why he no longer comes around her mother particularly likes him a lot and so during the meal he was in great form jovial and spirited as he told them his adventures in the army during the grueling 14 weeks of basic training and how tough such preparation is (just in case there is a war) but still how rewarding and advantageous it is from a physical and moral point of view for any man to go through such an experience (Bernice's little sister Solange was there too and she was the one who was laughing the loudest) and everybody was in a good mood and Bernice's father began telling some of his own army stories (during the First World War of course but without specifying which side he was on) explaining how it was something else A REAL WAR and not just make believe in basic training (Bernice was looking at her father with sad pleading eyes while her mother was looking at the guest of honor with gooshy-gooshy motherly looks) and at this point he leaned towards the father to ask him for the salt which was at the other end of the table (it was for the potroast which the mother had fixed and delicious it was indeed but which needed a touch of salt) and said with his mouth full COULD YOU PASS THE MODERFUCKIN' SALT PLEASE (which sounded even more atrocious with his French accent) and suddenly a dead silence fell over the family gathering as they slowly swallowed the shock of this linguistic enormity which came out of him so naturally and so unexpectedly like a reflex (a military-lingual reflex) therefore imagine the face of the father when he heard that foul punctuational word and that of the poor mother who was choking in her napkin and who motioned to the little sister to get up and go in the kitchen Bernice was red like a radish and couldn't decide whether she wanted to crawl under the table and make like she was picking up bread crumbs or run to the bathroom to vomit in the toilet bowl the father was marble white like a mortuary sheet he was a nice fellow usually in spite of his idiotic profession and even had a good sense of humor but at this time his sense of humor did not take too well to the situation parents do not like to be embarrassed in front of their children meanwhile the guest of honor went on masticating in slow motion the delicious piece of meat he still had in his mouth but he did not stick around for coffee he left immediately after dessert an exquisite and creamy (homemade) custard pie Bernice did not even follow him down the stairs as he thought she would eventhough he waited a few minutes in the lobby of the building just in case this time it was over between them (irrevocably) and all that because of a clumsy little word an inappropriate interjection (a malapropism) one sticks just like that in the middle of a sentence to punctuate its effect and also to better accentuate its meaning but without really doing it on purpose that's what army training does to you (what 14 weeks of basic training does to a man despite himself) it corrupts his linguistic purity and messes up his moral and sentimental life what just happened is a good example yes a quick stretch in the army and one cannot say three words after that without punctuating them with a fucking period no way out all the objects become fucking objects or cocksucking or motherfucking objects (and people too) and it stays with you for the rest of your life there in your mouth on the edge of your lips ready to come out at any moment and in the most touchy situations and mess up the most delightful moments of your life all of a sudden in any event after he left Bernice's lovely dinner party and found himself alone in the street with nothing to do for the rest of the evening and it was still quite early he decided to phone Marilyn and see if she was available.

Yes of course I understand darling!

But she was a bit surprised to learn that he was in New York City for already three months and had not given her any signs of life! She thought he was still in Detroit. And in fact, she had sent a letter to him there just about a week ago (AIR MAIL), to find out if he still thought of her, and was wondering why the letter came back saying that the person to whom it was addressed (you darling in other words) no longer lived at that address. (And it is true that he had not left a forwarding address given the fact that the poor guy never received any mail or once in a blue moon). But he had no idea where he was going to live he explained to her in

New York once he got there and this is why you understand it was hard for him to let her know and besides he had had such a rough (real rough) time since he was in New York. No job. No friends. Yes!

Yes of course she understood and forgave him   she wanted to see him immediately and why doesn't he come over   but he explained that he was broke that he didn't even have a dime for the subway (in those days the subway cost only a dime) and that he hadn't any means of transportation and hadn't eaten a damn thing in four days (he was of course exaggerating somewhat)   therefore she said   look stay where you are   and I'll come and get you   but then remembered that Benny was bringing somebody home for dinner   (a businessman with whom he was on the verge of closing a big lampshade deal)   you understand   but we'll meet tomorrow for sure   can you manage until then   do you have a place to stay for the night   yes don't worry about me   it's okay   I'll be alright

And so they met the following day in a swanky restaurant (Gilmore's Steak House on Lexington Avenue) a really fine restaurant (perhaps the most expensive restaurant he had ever been to and this is why he remembered the name so well so many years later when he told me that story he was really impressed   and even mentioned that sitting at a table next to them was Frank Sinatra with a group of foreigners it was the first time he had ever seen a movie star in person they had two stunning blondes with them)   so he was in a great mood and very proud of being with Marilyn who looked beautiful in her fancy Amazon hat but he was slightly embarrassed because of the holes in his coat (the sleeves of his sport coat were torn) and so during the meal and especially when Frank Sinatra looked his way he tried (without being too obvious) to keep his elbows below the table but when the steaks arrived rare and juicy and so thick and delicious he was amazed (yes quite shocked) that people who did not seem to work at all could eat that much meat while there were so many slobs out there who were starving but he soon forgot about these poor slobs and about his troubles because Marilyn had ordered a good bottle of wine to go with the rare steaks a 1948 Pommard (I remember the year because he specified and a damn good year it was for Pommards) so we can celebrate our reunion she said as they toasted each other with a loving mutual smile and reached across the table to touch hands!

Therefore
like an idiot
and I suppose under the influence of the wine
he started telling her all about his love affair with Bernice
how she was a virgin when they first did it together in New York
how she cried and bled and how later on they walked together arm
in arm on the Grand Concourse and how soon she started talking
to him about responsibilities the future marriage furniture even
and kids and respect for family life and bank accounts
and weekends in the country fresh air for the kids a good
steady job (8 to 5 or 9 to 6) savings investments et etc

Can you imagine me he said laughing while chewing an enormous piece
of steak and at the same time trying to hear what Frank Sinatra was
whispering to the platinum blonde sitting with him can you imagine
me in her father's delicatessen in the Bronx with a little white
apron around the waist slicing salamis all day long for life?

Poor love!

Oh am I glad to have dropped that Bernice and her kosher salami!

Things like that only happen to me he said giggling. But suddenly
he had a feeling Marilyn was getting angry. Had he gone too far
with the details of his relationship with Bernice? With women
(mature women especially) one never knows. They change mood
so quickly. And besides he should have known that when
telling a story one should never reveal too much. It's
one of the basic aspects of story-telling, always leave
something untold so that the listener's imagination can
furnish the missing details. But he was not a very good nor
an experienced story-teller at the time, he was too anxious to
get to the point (and too drunk too by then) and tell everything
without carefully working out the effect of what he was narrating!

And so later on, in the underground parking lot, after Marilyn had
slipped him 20 dollars under the table to pay for the lunch bill
as they stood next to her huge white Cadillac convertible with
electric windows power steering and power brakes (which from
time to time later on she would let him drive when they

went out together) she asked him with visible anger and
emotion in her voice why he could not have been patient
and waited for her rather than getting involved with an
imbecile little bitch like Bernice, especially after all the
promises they had made to each other in the Catskills and also
the love letters she sent in Detroit and even the lovely present
didn't you like it? Yes I did! It was beautiful and so precious!

He didn't mention of course that the beautiful and precious bathrobe had
landed in a pawn shop, but that did not calm her. She was still furious and
fuming as though ready to jump on him at any moment. He really couldn't
understand why she suddenly got so worked up. After all he had met
Bernice first. Had met her in fact the summer before he met Marilyn.
Therefore she should wait her turn. That's how one calculates these types of
relationships, as far as he was concerned!

You're a typical male chauvinist she screamed!
And suddenly BANG! she slaps him across the face without warning!
BANG and BANG again on both sides of the face! He was dumbfounded!
Just like that
in the underground parking
next to her Cadillac!
He quickly covered his face with his arms in case she decided to hit him
again. He was speechless. But she must have felt guilty about what she had
done (or something like that) because immediately after the two slaps here
comes a torrent of tears down from her eyes — ah the big beautiful black
eyes of Marilyn especially when she cried — and she grabs him passionately
and squeezes him against her clinging to him with her whole body (he feels
something leap inside his pants like a wild animal) he could taste the salt of
her tears sticking to his cheeks as they licked each other's faces and kissed in
quick and tender bursts each other's eyes and noses and necks twisting wet
and voluptuous tongues inside each other's ear lobes and then running the
tongues down the sides of their cheeks looking blindly (they both of course
had their eyes closed) for the other's mouth and suddenly her tongue
arrived first to his mouth and slipped in deep as it twiddled around. He
shuddered. Forced her tongue back into her mouth with a tongue-to-
tongue duel and when he had full possession of her mouth
he began to wiggle his tongue against her palate while grabbing
one of her teats with his left hand and letting his right
hand slide down gently along her thigh and then up
under her skirt to find its way all the way

up to her furry triangle
and all that   Two of his fingers move
with   into the moist region of her
perfect   privacy as she leans backwards
coordination   against the Cadillac arching back
without the least hesitation!   a little to better offer herself to
                                his greedy searching fingers! One of
                    her breasts pops out of her blouse
                    and he sucks on it especially the tip
                which hardens cockily between his teeth!
Meanwhile his left hand
(now free) is trying to unzip   The two fingers of
his fly but she says no no don't   his right hand are
not here not here darling as she rotates   so deep now inside
her abdominal region against his abdominal region!   of her that he is
                                                 afraid he might
Her large Amazon hat   hurt her but she
with its wide rim is getting   doesn't say anything
on the way of this delicate and   she just pants with her
difficult operation as their bodies   eyes closed!
continue their intimate and somewhat
suggestive contorsions in the underground parking!
They went on like that for a good 20 minutes with total abandon and ....

ZOWIE ZOWIE ZOWIE . . .?   [Two or three hands waving in the crowd]
Oh! You guys want to know if they slept together that day? No!

Suddenly she pulls away from him and says that she has to go but she will
see him again the next day for sure and that they'll talk about what to do
with him. Like perhaps have him move to Brooklyn so that they can be
closer to each other and perhaps even try to get a place for him to work a
good job not too hard in fact I'm going to ask all my friends no better than
that why not ask Benny if he can get you a job in his lampshade factory. I'm
sure he can use somebody like you I'll talk to him as soon as I get home you'll
see everything will be alright and meanwhile she gives him a twenty dollar
bill to keep him going as she gets behind the wheel of her Cadillac and he
leans into the car to give her another kiss on the mouth and touches one of
her breasts (the left one) she tells him to be patient as her tires skid away
hurriedly and he stands there alone waving good-bye to his love!

Well that evening he packed his suitcase and moved to Brooklyn to be ready for her the next morning. He left no forwarding address. And fortunately for him Loulou was out that night. Quite unusual but he did not question this curious absence. He just packed his suitcase!

He didn't have much to put in it. A [yes the same old black suit] few old clothes (three shirts two or [case with the leather strap] three pairs of socks two jockeys and [described in details in the] an extra pair of pants) half a dozen [other version of his story!] books in rather poor condition (the same ones mentioned earlier) and of course his jazz records (all 78s) which he packed in a card-board box but not his saxophone in its big black case because it was gone!

Yes the tenor saxophone which Charlie Parker
[yes the same old beat-up]
blew at the Blue Bird you remember the great [suitcase with which he'd]
historical solo on My Old Flame gone forever[landed in America almost]
for a lousy 50 bucks the bastards in a lousy [three years earlier same]
pawn shop on Sixth Avenue in fact it's quite [black suitcase described]
possible that's where Loulou is at this very [in the noodle story once]
moment in a pawn shop getting rid of another
[upon a time (passim) you]
piece of their clothing! Oh well he went on [guys don't remember? I'm]
packing his junk full speed because he was a [not going to go over the]
bit worried that loulou might show up in the [damn suitcase again that]
middle of his packing and ask to go with him [would be too repetitive!]
to Brooklyn and who knows he might even try to seduce Marilyn. Loulou knew nothing of Marilyn but Loulou was very smooth with women. [HEY WE'VE JUST MADE IT INTO VERMONT! YOU GUYS DON'T THINK I'M LOSING TRACK!] So as soon as his suitcase was packed he disappeared but without his saxophone however he didn't care because he had twenty dollars he was in love with a splendid mature woman who also seemed to be in love with him things were looking up!

upupupupupupupupupupupupupupupupupupupupupupupupup upupup
Life was beginning to smile upon him. And as he walked towards the subways with his suitcase in one hand and the card-board box in the other a feeling of relief came upon him and he started humming like a little bird (a French song he remembered from his childhood. Even told me the title of that song but I have forgotten it. I should have written it down. Very forgetful of me not to have noted the title of the song!) In the B.M.T. now he sat in a corner alone and contemplated inwardly the new horizon towards which he was now sailing. It was in February. Or March. Yes he had left Detroit three months earlier. End of December. It was cold that day and of course (this goes without saying) he didn't have an overcoat. Loulou had

already pawned all their winter clothes even though spring was still a good two months away. It was Loulou who had initiated him to the pawn shops (yes to do bizenèce with the pawn shops when the situation had reached the limit!)

0-0-0-0-0-0-0-0-0-0-0-0-0-0-0-0-0-0-0-0-0-0

He spent the night in a hotel room in Brooklyn. Cost him seven dollars for the room. Just around the corner from where Marilyn and Benny live in their deluxe apartment corner of Flatbush and Kings Highway. He had a rather bad night but no dreams to report. The next morning he called Marilyn early but not too early to make sure Benny had already left for work. He was very nervous.

Oh! You're already in Brooklyn! Well you don't waste a moment!

[If it goes on like that we'll be in Camp Drum by morning but that means that we have to drive all night and the damn road is getting more and more icy. Oh well let's keep going. Things are not that bad right now. Moving quite well in fact. Right on schedule. We have made a lot of progress since I got back in the driver's seat]

Okay! Listen you can move in with us. In the guest room. (I don't
think I mentioned the guest room before. Yes I don't think I said that they had a guest room in their apartment. Or if I said the contrary it was an error on my
With you? part)

Yes, I spoke with Benny and he agrees, he even insisted that I call you immediately to tell you, he's only sorry that he cannot be here to welcome you in person, I told him I stumbled into you by chance, while shopping downtown, and how difficult things are for you right now, you know, with the way the economy is going, and he understood and immediately suggested the guest room, nobody uses it these days he said, it's the least we can do for him after all, after all that suffering he endured during the war, a poor orphan like him, a poor displaced person, sole survivor from his entire family, it's a pity he said, and I agree with him, it's the least we can do for you, he even has a full time job for you already, in his lampshade factory!

Things were really working out well!
Even better than he had expected!
When luck comes along it comes
in huge packages he thought!
Si j'ai du cul he said to
himself reverting again
to his native tongue!

Listen Benny said to call him at the office as soon as you've moved in! He wants to have lunch with you. Wants to talk to you about the job in his factory!

Incredible! If it goes on like that the poor guy's going to faint! How much luck can a guy have in one day? A place to stay a woman a job and it's only the beginning hasn't even slept with Marilyn yet!

It's ESPLANADE 7-48-32!   What?   Benny's number!
Oh yes! In fact, call him right now, even
before you come here. He said he
would wait for your call. Do you
have a dime?
Yes I do!

[Maybe I should call Camp Drum to tell them I'm coming he thought while staring at the icy road for my money because of that goof they made the dumb bastards otherwise they'll wonder what the fuck I'm doing up there in the snows but at this time of night must be past 10 o'clock where am I going to find a phone and it's not moving very fast in this soup what a mess visibility zero doesn't pay at this time all the hillbillies are either asleep or else masturbating like a bunch of bulls in their khaki blankets better get my ass up there as quickly as possible double time]

And so he called Benny but not without some apprehension but immediately Benny tells him to meet him for lunch in a Chinese restaurant. So they meet at Lu Chang a rather fancy exotic Chinese restaurant on Avenue J (shit what a deal two free meals in two days!) and just before he was served his fortune cookies the deal was settled. Yes he starts working the next day in the lampshade business he moves in that afternoon in the guest room with his stuff his black suitcase and his card-board box and no further argument it's all settled you understand Benny says with a paternal tone of voice we American Jews it's the least we can do for people like you who endured so much during the war it's a very small payment for all that suffering

He agreed with him 100% and didn't even attempt to grab the bill for lunch and here they are in his Cadillac Coupe de Ville (they had two Cadillacs / his was black) on their way to pick up in the hotel where he had spent the night his suitcase and his box full of his jazz records and he was really enjoying the ride and they were having a most friendly conversation about this and that and how he was going to like the new job and how Marilyn was fond of him and how it's too bad he hadn't called sooner because in fact the guest room was available and he could have moved in any time

He slept rather well that night flat on his back in baby blue or rather sky blue sheets no distractions no dreams bad dreams like he had been having lately and the next morning at 9 o'clock they are on their way to the lampshade factory smoking Havana cigares after the delicious breakfast Marilyn had fixed for them Marilyn had gotten up to fix them breakfast and say goodbye and also wish him good luck with the new job (beginning of a most perfect day)

Not bad the lampshade factory a rather modern place (considering that we are in the early 50's) good lighting 30 to 35 sexy women working behind the machines four or five well stacked to say the least biteauculmettables if one made the necessary effort as for his job quite easy nothing to do with the machines right away he was promoted to foreman giving orders to others as Benny said to him he was in charge of the inside while Benny took over outside in fact he had been looking for someone responsible to take care of the running of the place so that he could devote more time to selling the stuff perfect arrangement therefore he showed up (so to speak) at the right moment in the most propitious conditions!

Part of his job consisted in checking the boxes in which the lampshades were carefully stacked before being loaded on the trucks and measuring the silk paper counting the frames used to make lampshades in other words he was the one who kept an eye on all the operations verified quantity and quality gave orders left and right and in general saw to it that everyone did his or her job smoothly and responsibly he was in charge

and three good home-cooked meals a day and in the evening the four of them (I mean with the kid) sat family style in the living room and watched television

she was six years old the kid polite cute and pretty like a doll and she loved him like a big brother he had a way with kids (the infantile technique one might say) he knew how to play games or talk to them on their level of mentality when he wanted to so they had lots of fun playing games together dolls and doctors cowboys and indian cops and robbers even hide-and-seek hiding all over the apartment under the table under the beds in the kitchen inside the broom closet under the sink in the pink bathroom

Sitting there in front of the television watching the dumb programs they showed in those days he was almost happy, almost, with the kid bouncing on his knees or climbing on his back, Benny smoking one of his huge cigares and dozing off surrounded by the aromatic smoke of his cigare, and close to them, usually sitting on the floor or else squatting on a large Moroccan pillow, dreamy and sensual in a loose house dress, Marilyn with her big black eyes lovingly staring above Benny's head either at the television or at the happy third partner who was really blooming in this peaceful familial environment. And
from time to time
he would manage to
    grab one of Marilyn's
        hands and squeeze it gently
            when Benny's head would wave to the side
                and Marilyn would squeeze his hand back so hard
                that he almost felt like screaming with pain and happiness
                as she pushed her long pointed nails into his skin in signs of love
                            what a sweet deal he kept thinking
                                it's like being in Paradise!

He only wished it would never end. That's what he kept saying to himself when suddenly his car started skidding on the icy road. He quickly put his foot on the brake and lucky for him the car came to a brutal stop on the edge of the damn gully. Wow! That was close! Better be careful and concentrate on the road! He stepped out of his Buick and out of his reverie there in the middle of nowhere in Vermont. It was cold like hell, but he took advantage of this unscheduled stop to take a piss. Damn is it cold! He said as he squeezed the last drops. And still snowing at a rate of two inches per hour (he estimated). Could be disastrous!

If it continues like that we may have to cancel the whole damn thing! Right now the snow must be a good two feet deep. Up to his knees and getting deeper! Hope we don't get stuck in this shitty landscape. I tell you it's not easy to keep going under such conditions. He walks back to his car and after several tricky maneuvers and some dangerous manipulations he is back in what he thinks is the middle of the road!
Well that's approximately
how the situation was before
he was drafted into the army
but still
he hadn't yet succeeded in screwing Marilyn
in spite of the ideal conditions under which
he was now living (this was so to speak the
only flaw in this otherwise almost perfect and
blissful arrangement) but since he was so
comfortable
so happy with them one
would have to be dumb and
ungrateful to complain in
such a case and if he was the
former he was not certainly not the latter that much can be stated, yes he was so comfy that he didn't even feel like going out at night, as he used to do in the past, when he lived in the Bronx, every night dragging himself in the muck of downtown in search of dubious pleasure, no he didn't even feel like seeing a good flick anymore on 42nd Street, and yet we know how passionate he is of movies especially cowboy and gangster movies!

This then was the situation as he described it to me up to that point . . . and summer was coming . . . and when summer came he told Benny that if he didn't mind . . . and since the lampshade business was quite slow during that season . . . he would like to go back again to that Country Club in the Catskills to work as a waiter . . . yes as a waiter now . . . and no longer as a bus boy because that summer he was hoping to get a promotion and graduate to the level of a waiter . . . and also in order to practice his tennis golf and swimming . . . especially swimming with his aquatic talent . . . and whispering into Benny's ear connivingly he also mentioned the cute counselors . . . that's what he said to Marilyn and Benny . . . one evening . . . and furthermore . . . he explained . . . it is a rather easy and pleasant way to make a few bucks . . . and Marilyn and Benny agreed . . . and moreover pointed out that it was healthy . . . especially for the lungs . . . to spend two three months in the country breathing fresh air . . . Benny was in total agreement especially since . . . he added . . . he was planning to send Marilyn and the Baby to that Country Club for five or six weeks maybe more . . . and he would be up on weekends because . . . even though business was slow . . . still he had to take care of it . . . yes maybe all of July and August . . . it'll be good for them . . . and this way you can keep an eye on them he said to his foreman . . . therefore everything was working out for the best!

Now that his car was back on the road he felt much better but still a strange premonition hung over his head and he had a feeling that this night would not end without his having encounter other adventures and perhaps even a tragic ending and so as he proceeded slowly he said to himself but aloud and with a trembling voice vas-y mollo mon vieux as if addressing an old friend sinon on va finir dans ce foutu de ravin!

Yes during the summer business was really slow and it's normal since people usually don't buy lampshades during that season so no problem he can easily handle the factory alone nobody really buys lampshades in the summer unless it is an emergency when a kid breaks a lamp and the lampshade cracks or else when a dog bites it you understand what I mean *visibility zero what soup out there and no place to stop what a way to discover America* so when time came for him to leave for the Catskills he packed his suitcase but by then he had bought a new one because Marilyn insisted that he gets rid of the old black one which was too ugly for words and he left by train *yes it would indeed have been smarter to take the train rather than take chances with such an icy road* Marilyn drove him to Grand Central Station but as they were kissing goodbye she made him promise that this time he would wait for her and not mess around with little virgins and this time you'll see *shit can't see a damn thing* we'll find a way and we'll make love and it'll be beautiful *keep America beautiful* two three weeks and she'll be up with him be patient darling *don't get nervous take it easy and hang on to the wheel* I understand how much you want me but me too *me too* I want you so much and It's not easy *damn right just because the dumb bastards goofed* you know what I mean and she promised and so he too promised not to get involved with anybody and that this time *yes* he would wait for her etc. etc. etc.

WHAT A STORY!
Are you guys still in-
terested or
do you prefer that I go into something else? Shall we skip all that and go directly to the rest of the journey? The Big Crossing! Just as he described it to me! Oh, you guys want a little more! Want to know if finally they made it together that summer! What sex maniacs!

Okay
here we go
but quickly
because me
I'm anxious
to get this thing
over with
however
if I don't set up
the basis
the fundamental basis
for the rest of this story
and if
I don't give you
the essential structure
for what is going
to happen next
you guys will get lost
and everything
will be confused
and superficial

Therefore
one must understand
the state of mind we
were in
and also
how much
we
members of the gutsy
82nd Airborne Division
had endured
and
of course
who we were at the time
how we functioned
how we supported
how we reacted
to life's little torments
etc. etc. etc. etc.

For
in order
to grasp
the tone
and the deeper meaning
of our journey
one must know
at least
what pushed us
(and MOINOUS too
for we have not lost
sight of him)
to volunteer
for the real thing
war in the Far East
even
at the risk
of getting
wounded
killed
or exterminated

Of course
much is being skipped
much is being summarized
and generalized
details
are being diminished
characters
are being left out
either completely
or partially
places
are given less importance
and
to a great extent
much of what he told us
is being rephrased
reshaped
for the sake of efficiency

For example have you noticed that there is very little description, in fact hardly any, in this recitation, I mean realistic and lively of people and places, this kind of stuff bores the shit out of me I tell you, therefore not the least physical detail about the people, or the places, in this story, except perhaps here and there a minor something about the softness of Marilyn's hands, or the sadness and blackness of her eyes, or the round-ness of her breasts, but me as a rule I don't allow myself to be carried away into detailed descriptions of the physical self, description is crap, useless, bores me! Not you? Particularly because of the adjectives, and nothing about the innerself of course, that's really useless, and besides there's no way one can get inside people, those who tell you they can, even though many have tried, are full of shit, they are just pretending!

Also have you
noticed how the
chronology of this
recitation often
falls apart and
mixes past and
present with fu-
ture virtual events

I know that normally in good story-
telling one must respect THE ORDER OF
THINGS so as to create a coherent sequence of events or at least permit the plot
or subplot if any to unfold logically and
rationally so that a semblance of continuity can be sustained

Ah, you guys approve! Yes for once you guys
agree with me! As soon as continuity is mentioned you guys start reacting! Well let me tell
you, me I prefer discontinuity, me I adore discontinuity, I wallow in disorder, my whole existence for that matter has been a JOURNEY TO
CHAOS (U.C. Press, 1965)!

I know what you guys are going to come up with next And what about representation? Yes what about it? Correct strict representation of reality! Words sticking to things! Meaning sticking to words! (Signifiant / Signifié), exact use of GRAMMATOLOGY (coucou) in order to differentiate speaking from writing and shouting from mumbling!

Yes I know what you think of writing and that for you guys it's an important (crucial) question, but we've already discussed all that and me in a sense (in LA LOGIQUE DU SENS if you wish) I don't give a damn about THE ORDER OF THINGS because me, I do not relate, I do not narrate, I do not recite in order to create order, rather not!

On the contrary what I do has to do with the problem of reading or listening. And not L' E C R I T U R E ! Me I speak to the senses and I'm not trying to make sense in any way. I deal in nonsense I deal in S U R F I C T I O N ! Or if you prefer I'm working my way toward unreadability, toward free reading, delirious reading, in a way I'm in favor of reading in flagrant breach of peace, caught in the act: F L A G R A N-
T E   D E L I C T O ! I don't fuck around!
But okay I'll stop this crap (single space, double space, triple space) and all that typographical masturbation. To tell the truth it disgusts me just as much as it might disgust you. But sometimes it is necessary to talk (or even write) about such things. Just to situate the problem correctly.
Yes, but what happens to language, you might ask?
What happens to meaning?
Good question!

Do you want me to answer
or do you prefer that I skip this one? One simply slides outside
and even
beyond language — HORS / TEXTE as a good friend of mine who
is well versed in the subject once said (she is a first rate woman /
intellectual of superior qualities who has published a great deal. I
really like her a lot).
But to go on with this a moment, me I think that one must
invent one's language on the spot (pure improvisation) or
else wait for the right circumstances, wait for it to come,
while practicing of course as much as one can, and therefore, write whatever comes out (at full speed) until one
stumbles on the proper tone (or as Sam used to say: It's
perhaps all a question of hitting on the right aggregate!) (By
the way, the same is true for talking, I don't make any
distinctions between the two. I used to, but no longer) And
there suddenly (and to the surprise of many) in the middle
of a page, in the middle of a sentence, just like that: coucou
le voilà votre langage! Mine came to me (or rather his) just
like that under a tree (or on the edge of a precipice leaning
against the wind) after many years of silence in the far past.
And his words, his pieces of sentences, his fucked up syntax, began to articulate themselves into an incredible discourse!
It quickly degenerated into a preposterous verbal mess
a torrent of exclamations
which I can only compare to a **long uninterrupted tenor
saxophone solo** and indeed it was pure improvisation
without shape
without form
without order
and to tell the truth without meaning

he was very much aware of it
and explained that it was like the reds and the blacks and the
yellows of Rebeyrolle
I had no idea what he was referring to
with sand and stones and pieces of woods thrown in it
and it was going full blast
wow did the two of us laugh that day
did we laugh to see and hear it flow like a torrent
the two of us
sitting there under that tree
but now we don't laugh as much
it's more serious
it's harder
it's hard work to reconstitute the whole thing
but careful
watch out
when I say serious that doesn't mean the other side of laughter
that doesn't abolish laughter
on the contrary
it simply displaces it
or if you prefer it merely makes it into FOURIRE (untranslatable)
In other words we speak in serious / laughter or laughing /
seriousness! We superimpose a serious and more recent self, or
to quote directly:

un moi sérieux récent —
le moi d'aujourd'hui
bibliographie énorme
type assez bourgeois
avec maison voitures
femme gosses et très
belle bibliothèque à
plusieurs étagères y
compris collection à re-
liure cuir pick up et collection jazz à peu près
complète en stéréo pro-
fesseur   de   lettres
titularisé à vie bon
salaire etc!

qui parle très bien

au moi riant & ancient —
le moi d'hier plutôt
pauvre con timide et
complexé sans boulot
régulier cherchant à se
faire une place y com-
pris famille pèze amour
amitié dans un pays
d'adoption plus ou
moins favorable à ce
genre d'ambitions à une
époque qui s'y prête mal
à   cause   de   crises
économiques à n'en
plus finir etc!

qui sait pas parler

and we confront them   and we merge them!
We make a single unique self out of them and call that being
MOINOUS for the sake of harmony and unificity! Of course you
guys may argue that all that is not very brilliant and that in fact
you do not give a shit about all our superimpositions and that
these are simply pure acrobatics which lead nowhere - - - - - a loss
of time and energy!

But what about you guys? Yes! - - - - - What about your acrobatics? At least me I work without a net, and at high altitude like a
flying trapezist! Whereas you guys when you do your intellectual
exercises and your mental gymnastics you make sure the nets are
well in place!
Well secured!   Just in case!
Yes I work without a net
bareass (figuratively speaking)
and in the dark
alone!
Well alright not ME
but THAT POOR GUY d
                      o
                        w
                          n
                            t h e r e   on that shitty icy road in Ver-
mont
lost in a snowstorm   in his beat-up Buickspecial on his
way to CAMP DRUM (12 miles per hour) to pick up his money $$$$ M
                                                    $$$$ O
                                                    $$$$ N
                                                    $$$$ E
                                                    $$$$ Y
                                                    ———-
                                                    000000

THAT'S WHOM WE ARE TALKING ABOUT
Well let's look at him
let's analyze him for a moment
yes let's psychoanalyze him carefully   or rather let's give
                                             the essential facts
                                             of his rather
                                             miserable
                                             life

born in paris parents poor father a gambler working class since
father an artist surrealist painter polyglot involved in marxist
politics starving his family wife three children of jewish origin
father mother sisters deported to auschwitz exterminated remade so
to speak into lampshades thus reason symbolic of course for working
as a foreman full time in a lampshade factory the circle is complete
the symbolic twist of events perfect even though simple sole survivor
twelve years old or so now driving madly in a 1947 buickspecial brutal
snowstorm after three years in america because of some typical error of
the army in the 82nd airborne division dreaming death or love to collect
his money even though the fact of dying is always a pure event which does
not verify anything asking himself therefore if death will cure him of his
miserable life because death is also the sneering of life's capital mistake

But nevertheless
and in spite of all

shy
stubborn
determined
brown hair
black eyes
strong nose
sensual mouth
slim (because of early undernourishment)
5'10"
141 lbs.
size 38 (or 36)
shoes 10-1/2
chest well developed (because of the swimming)
muscular nervous body
strong arms and legs (because of the push ups)
small scar on left knee
long unkempt fingernails
teeth white and well lined (few cavities)
average intelligence
great imagination
good sense of humor
suicidal tendencies
subject to manic depressions

This is, more or less (GROSSO MODO), of whom we are talking about!

But him, meanwhile, down there, in his Buickspecial, the guy whose
story is now being told (second-hand), and whom you may sometime
confuse with me, though I assure you was not me, but whom I
sometime try to make myself pass for, look at him, that
poor jerk, struggling like a clown, a court jester,
in the snow, and expecting that, at any moment,
something tragic will happen to him, and
that in the actual conditions of his
journey it is quite possible that
his car may leap unexpectedly
into the precipice
on his right!

Of course you're going to tell me that I exaggerate that
I dramatize the situation that I'm not telling the truth
that I'm joking that I'm simulating since it's me who is
telling the story and that therefore I can manipulate
the basic material as I move along

Quite true
I am the speaking-subject
and the thinking-subject of this story
thus also the inventing-subject of the details
of his journey which cannot seem to come to an end!

Evidently you're going to tell me that the two SELVES involved in this recitation
are simply DOUBLE SUBJECTS of the same being and that while ONE is being
told THE OTHER is telling and that as such inevitably the two of them coincide
merge and cannot be distinguished from each other

Well the only thing I can answer to this is shit in double and triple
form! Of course you guys would like me to identify the two beings
involved in the intramural development of this recitation, and I
suppose would also like to know the names of those involved,
that of the first-hand teller and that of the second-hand teller, I
mean their real names because I can always invent false names or
fictitious names for ourselves, yes you guys need names real
names to cling to, and reassure you of the authenticity and
validity of the story and of the people who people it, especially
double names, Jean-Louis, Jean-Daniel, Jean-Philippe (I'm
speaking now to the French contingent of my listeners), Jean-
Pierre, Jean-Paul, Jean-Peux-Plus, Jean-Ai-Marre, et ainsi de
suite et ainsi-soit-il, dammit haven't you finished bugging the
hell out of us with your bullshit about the subject and imposing
upon us your crappy system of personal nomination? I warn you,
if you go on like that with all your questions and interruptions,
me (this is the last time I tell you) I'm going to stop everything
right here, drop the whole fucking recitation, and you can go find
someone else to entertain you and tell you the rest of this story!

Because finally, subject or no subject (assujetti ou non assujetti) you yourself are but a bunch of shitty-subjects!

Which brings us almost to the end of our introductory material. Took us a long time to get there but we finally made it! We could now of course go on with the details (more or less exact) of his arrival at the Country Club in the Catskills that summer (49 or 50), or else we could describe what happened when Marilyn eventually came up and the two of them finally made it. We could also finish the many sub-stories we left unfinished along the way, or else simply jump nearer to the present and tell you how his BUICKSPECIAL .... no we shall let him tell that part of the story himself later on .... but of course one could if one wished start talking about anything directly or indirectly related (and why not?) to what has already been told. The leapfrog technique does allow it!

In short, I could, if I wished, situate myself at any point and any moment of his story (in time and in place), and begin reciting full speed anything that came to my mind, since between the functions of memory and that of thinking (between being-then and being-now or if you prefer being and non-being) there is but a perennial overlying!

To tell or retell, to make or remake works on the same principle of duplication and cancellation. Memory does not separate itself from imagination, or if it does it is only through a slight displacement of facts, a plagiaristic displacement which was once described by a friend of mine as playgiarism — imagination imagining it imagines!

Thus the entire past escapes us, or rather crumbles into lies which are reflected in the deceptive mirror of the present in the form of a molehill that substitutes itself for the real mountain. In other words, it is a process whereby the reality of an event and the fact of relating that event degenerates into self-mocking falsification!

All that may not be clear but at least it suggests the mountainous, and rugged aspect of the landscape in which we are now circulating, and also it permits us to take position, to set ourselves correctly in relation to the journey now in progress. It hasn't been easy, I admit this, but somehow we have managed to come that far all alone!

And in fact, we have also managed, after all these detours, and all these verbal contorsions, to get back to our journey and back again to our protagonist speeding along that icy road in Vermont where at any moment now something unexpected might happen to him. Therefore let us follow him as he concentrates on the road and listen to him!

XXI

critifiction: crap lie or die

Here I am then back on the road still forging ahead like a mule!

I still had pieces of memories flying in my head as I sped along (about 12 miles per hour maximum) on this crummy icy road in the middle of that snowstorm, but gradually the pieces faded away as I began calculating how far I had to go to reach my destination!

If my calculations were correct (but it was hard to verify), and I was still in the right direction, I had about 100 or 125 miles to go to reach my goal (Camp Drum that is Upper New York State)!

At the speed at which I was moving that could easily take from 9 to 12 hours or more. Without stops that is. It's not possible!

I've got to accelerate or else I'll never make it. But careful!

o-o-o-o-o-o-o-o-o-o-o-o-o-o-o-o-o-o-o-o-o-o

Okay I concentrate at the wheel and no more shitting around with mental images. Let's wipe out everything that flies in my head! It's useless anyway!

[For instance the calculations he was in the process of doing to find out how much money he would have after he collected his dough at Camp Drum that is to say his one month's pay in advance his travel expenses and whatever else the army owed him plus the 100 or 125 bucks he would get in New York when he sold his Buick whenever he got back there if he ever got back add to this another 20 dollar bill which (he hoped) Marilyn would give him as a farewell gift and he could

easily set out on the big crossing of America with 400 dollars in his
pockets (400 minimum) which is not bad with that kind of money
one could have an easy and cozy crossing particularly since he
had no intention of spending a penny on transportation (in
America one can almost go anywhere one wishes by simply
sticking out one's thumb if one has the courage at least it was true
in those days) so he said!]

o-o-o-o-o-o-o-o-o-o-o-o-o-o-o-o-o-o-o-o-o

400 bucks minimum!   Good I'm all set!
Therefore let's concentrate. Je roule pour vous he said smiling
ironically. But what soup out there! Can's see a fucking thing it's
worse than being in MOBY DICK! Have lost my way? Where am
I? Lost all sense of direction? Is it an illusion? A mirage? What the
hell is going on?
                              Who the hell is out there?
Suddenly   out of nowhere
there
not even ten feet from his car
in the middle of the road   (if he's still on the road)
a silhouette!   A phantom!
                       I tell you it scared the hell out of me
                       drops of sweat rolled down my nose. I
quickly stepped on the brakes
to stop the car
but not without
sliding
left and right!   The damn car was staggering
                         all over the place.   If the guy
                              hadn't jumped aside
                              I would have killed him

                        or else I would have had to steer
                        my damn Buick into the precipice!   Really
dangerous
that precipice!   And still following me on the right!
                        I don't want to exaggerate
                        the danger but my journey
                        could easily have ended
                        at the bottom of that
                        damn precipice!   Well the car did
come to a stop but only two fingers from where the guy was
standing!
That was close!

                        I open the window of the car
                        to curse the sonofabitch
                        but he greets me with a friendly
HELLO THERE PAREDROS! How do you do? What kind of a
joker is that?
The guy looks exhausted
                        half dead
                        eyes bulging out of their sockets
the look of a madman
                        long curly black hair
                        disheveled
                                    down to his shoulders
looks like an orchestra conductor
                        modern music
                                    shit hope the guy isn't going
                                    to give us a concert out here
                                    in the middle of that tempest
a three day growth of beard
                        at least
                        full of snowflakes

                              no hat but a huge coat
down to his knees
            fur coat
            makes him look like a teddy bear
                              what an energumen!
What the hell is he doing out here?
WHAT THE HELL ARE YOU DOING OUT HERE I ask?
Research! I am doing research!
Research? In the snow?
In the boreal whiteness my dear fellow!
                    Oh shit that's all we need
                              a madman!
Are you going to get in or not? I am freezing my ass I shouted
bluntly!
So here he is sitting next to me on the front seat of my Buick. He
went on telling me as we picked up the thread of his narrative. He
had a beige leather briefcase which he held with both hands
against his chest. I look at him sideways as I begin driving again.
In no time he seems to have fallen asleep. The guy looks ageless.
Could be 24 or 32 or 76. A rather used guy. Ancient one might say.
Not a recent guy. I mean not someone from the near past or the
present of this recitation. Certainly not. Definitely not in the
category of the two other visitors. The two delegates. Are you
sure I ask? No this one is real. Not a critispy therefore. That makes
us feel better and at the same time informs us that others out there
are as badly off as we are. This one really belongs in the period of
this story. In fact I wonder (he said to me) what you as my
second-hand teller think of this curious apparition? You mean
me? I really do not have an opinion at this time. But if the guy is
still alive he must either be in an insane asylum or else from the
way you present him rich and famous and semi-retired in some
more temperate climate minding his own affairs. What is certain
however is that he is not among the listeners of our tale I would
have recognized him by now!

That settles that!

After two minutes of silence I ask What kind of research do you do?

He jumps out of his sleep and stares at me like a zombie. Huumm! What . . . . Historico-literary with paracritical tendencies! Or if you prefer I dig below the surface for hidden facts and bring forth in my writings the pluralism of meaning. My method has often been described as playgiaristic. Or if you prefer I insert through the cracks in a written text that which was originally excluded for aesthetic or ethical reasons. In other words, I improve literature!

You don't say! That's tremendous. You and I could really help each other because once in a while me too I dabble in literature for fun!

You don't understand, it's a serious matter with me. Life or death!

Oh, I know I know. I didn't mean to be derogatory. I am as serious as you are. Some of my best friends have died because of literature and in fact just the other day I attended the funeral of someone who died because of an excess of literature. He wrote too many stories!

It happens sometimes if one cannot support the burden of creativity! This is why one must always be prepared physically and mentally when the time comes to face the act of writing. One must be in shape and for this reason do careful exercises prior to the act of creativity!

Ah, I understand now the reason why you're in this boreal whiteness!

Look here young man, it's not my fault if God decided to snow us in! The history of theology is full of such snow jobs. One must endure!

Endure I do, but I didn't insist. I didn't want to start some crazy theological argument with this guy. And besides I felt quite uneasy with him and somewhat intimidated by his way of formulating his rash opinions. So we fell back into silence. Me driving on. He asleep! Perhaps even dead! But then it occurred to me that I should perhaps not waste this rare opportunity and tell this guy a little anecdote! Just to pass the time and keep him alive. I could always unload the story of our friend Gugusse and his cock in the Automat. That story always goes well with strangers even if I have to change the ending!

Would you like to hear a funny little anecdote which a friend of mine once told me and which . . .

        NO! Absolutely not! (Quite sharply as my question shook him out of his sleep) I detest oral literature, young man! Particularly when it is improvised. I am for the written word! As a matter of fact I prefer silence to speech, but since you are not capable of remaining silent, whether or not you have something to say of any consequence, why don't I read you a few pages from my doctoral dissertation which I am currently writing, and which I hope to defend by the end of this academic year . . .

        YOUR DOCTORAL DISSERTATION!

                before the distinguished members of the English Department at the University of Wisconsin-Milwaukee!

        MILWAUKEE! I've never been there, but maybe in the future, during my big crossing of America!

Not much of a place, you know. In fact, it is often referred to as THE CROTCH OF AMERICA!

Oh, I thought it was THE ARMPIT OF AMERICA! One learns something everyday! But did I hear your right SIR? Read me from your dissertation? Wow I would be honored! (The guy's got nerves! Read to me, ME, of all the jerks in the world, from his doctoral dissertation! An occasion like this only presents itself once in a lifetime! Immediately acquiesce! And besides it might turn out to be interesting his thing and I might even learn something about history, literature, paracriticism as well as critifiction, and who knows, perhaps even about life, death, about myself too. Who knows! And also, can't vex the guy by refusing. So better grab the bull by the horns and ask a few pertinent questions!)
Heuh, Heuh, tell me, Sir, what's the subject of your dissertation?

It's about THE LIFE AND WORK of a great unknown writer. A foreign writer whose national and ethnic origins have never been confirmed (he never stays in the same place more than one week. Or rather I should say STAYED, because some people claim that he died recently but that too has not been confirmed). He left a rather considerable but totally ignored OEUVRE. Therefore, I'm trying to make his work known to the large public by explicating it using my playgiaristic method of critifiction which consists of echoing the plural voices of his writing. But more important I'm trying to establish the authenticity of his unpublished and lost manuscripts. Some of which, incidentally, are buried in this part of the country. Thus one of the reasons, as you can well understand, for my being here! But I am running out of time because I am gradually and hopelessly becoming blind!

Oh! That's terrible, I said with a lot of compassion in my voice!

Happens you know.

I suppose it's because you do a lot of reading and lots of special research for your work!

We are all born blind. Only a few remain so! He said, evasively!

Shit! Here he goes again. Better not pursue that subject. Heuh! What is the guy's name? I mean that great unknown foreign writer?

HOMBRE DE LA PLUMA! Though that's only a pen name. His real name is FEATHERMERCHANT, but he changed it for obvious personal reasons which I cannot reveal here.

HOMBRE DE LA PLUMA! Never heard of him. I once met a certain guy named HOMBRE DE LA CORNA, but I don't suppose it's the same person because mine was a saxophone player. Yes, tenor sax! And mine is still alive, as far as I know.

No, it's certainly not the same person. HOMBRE DE LA PLUMA didn't make music. But as I said before, he may still be alive. In fact this is another reason for my being here. It has been rumored (in various literary circles) that he was seen around here, just a few days ago. When I heard that I quickly rushed up here for it would indeed be a great pleasure for me to see him again. He and I were very close friends at one time.

Hey, that could really be something if we met him in the middle of the night! I have never met a great living author!

Have you met many dead ones?

Alright I didn't mean it this way. But you really put water in my mouth. Why don't you go ahead with your reading!

Okay, are you ready? I'll start reading, but pay attention. What I'm going to read is extremely complex and requires total and full concentration. Therefore I would appreciate it very much if you'd refrained from making any interruptions during my soloperformance!

He pulls out a little flashlight from his briefcase and an enormous yellowed manuscript (at least 800 pages) all messy all disorganized soiled with coffee stains or other such stains of blood booze sperm perspiration selects a few pages (hardly readable) and replaces the rest of the manuscript in his briefcase turns sideways toward me as he clears his throat (I'm still driving but I'm full ears) he's not kidding he's really near-sighted because he sticks his pages almost against his nose and with a loud and eloquent voice begins to read:

C R I T I F I C T I O N :   C R A P   L I E   O R   D I E
by
Cam Taathaam

Get it?
Got it!
Gooood!
The Court Jester

....

Hey! I like that title. It really goes well with our own situation!

No, you don't understand. It has nothing to do with that. As I move along you'll see the title will clarify itself. In any case, I would appreciate it if you wouldn't interrupt me as I read. Okay I'm going to start all over again! From the top of the first page. Here I go!

He moves the paper back in front of his nose clears his throat again places his index on the first word blinks as he illuminates his text with his little flashlight and this time he is ready to forge ahead:

Say? One more question. TAM TAM? That's a funny name. Where does it come from?

Not TAM TAM! TAATHAAM with 4 A's! Or as many as you wish. My name is very flexible!

Oh! With 4 A's! And what's the CAM for?

Irrelevant! Besides, I have rejected all notions of origins. First names and last names are interchangeable. Therefore I never discuss the origin and the meaning of a name. Mine could be French-Canadian for all I care!

Okay, okay. I didn't mean to probe.

Are you ready?   Yes!

CRITIFICTION: CRAP LIE OR DIE

by

Cam Taathaam

Introduction: Problems of Method

I'm only reading you the introduction to give you an idea of the rest.

CRAP: LIE OR DIE

(In other words, what happens next, I'd like to presume, that is to say, what follows, in a manner of speaking, will not be yet another article about the article I could not or would not, what's the difference anyway, write. The gimmick is overworked, undervalued. It's been done before, as they say, and better. The staple of fiction, these days. I've done it before myself, twice. The first article I wrote about the article I could not write was published, much to my bewilderment; the second article about the article I would not write was not published, understandably, since I did not write it. It's all a con-game, CONtinually CONtrived, and you've got to be either incredibly naive or incredibly clever to get away with it, the odds against success are disproportionate, readers being much too sophisticated nowadays. Really. The risk is too high, the stakes unworthy, the dice are loaded: one die(s) simply, without too much noise, if you please

— What crap!
— But notice how much space I managed to fill with it, leaning against the wind, facing the abyss and so on, the tired old words wordshit foirades whatever, anything's better than a blank page, after all, it's a fight to the death, me against the temptation to abandon the field, a struggle to fill in the blank, despite the risk that just one more word will cancel the entire performance with everything as yet blessedly unsaid.
    (Ah, I begin to understand what he means by paracriticism!)
(to be sure, writers real and so-called manage to get away with such as)
(this. name some, I dare you! well, there's Barth, Beckett & Borges. so)
(unds like a vaudeville team. and of course: Sterne, mustn't forget him)
(. and Sukenick, and Nabokov, and Barthelme, and Le Clézio, that guy is)
(fantastic, really, & ... & ... well, there's also: Hombre de la Pluma.)
    (Who the fuck are all these guys? Never heard of them!)

– *Who?*
– *HOMBRE DE LA PLUMA!*
– *Who's he?*

Hombre De La Pluma. b. May 15, 1928. Place of birth: unknown. Father's occupation: surrealist painter. Mother's occupation: unspecified. Two sisters. Family liquidated (X-X-X-X) at Auschwitz; Hombre De La Pluma escaped by jumping off a train. Spent remainder of World War II as a farm laborer in Southern Europe (perhaps France). Came to United States in 194? Brief period in army, c. 195? Married in 19??, approximately. Four children. Presently writer in residence (if still alive) in huge Department of English, major State University, location not revealed. Hobbies: sex, jazz, fiction.

– *So?*
– *There's more, all of it equally unreliable and improbable.*

Selected Bibliography: And I Followed My Shadow, 19?? (unfinished lost manuscript).
Mica, co-editor with H.B., 19??-19?? (small non-genre literary magazine).
Chaos, 19??
Sam, 19??
A.B. / P.M., undated (various multilingual poems it seems).
Don, 19?? (a real fictitious discourse).
Tioli, unfinished (trans. by the author and retitled El Am in French-Yiddish version).
Winner Take All, 19?? (project).
Dance, edited by Don Tioli, to appear in 198?

No more questions? Bon, alors, vous avez fini de m'emmerder avec toutes vos questions? You think (Hey, the guy speaks French!) it's easy to get on with this? It's embarrassing, believe me. (This thing is getting out of hand. How the hell did I allow this to happen?)

So. I'll tell you about this guy, Hombre De La Pluma. Maybe you've run across the type: you know, The Professional Foreigner, with an incredible accent, suave with precisely the correct mixture of appealing boyishness, poised posed impetuous spontaneous — women love it! Really, I should know. Sure, he even made a play for my wife once, all in fun of course, good fun, a game, a wager of sorts, but still: A PASS (made me angry as hell!). There we were, at this party, room filled with Poets & Artists & Writers & Critics (and me), and this guy (Hombre) corners my wife and goes into his act (well-rehearsed, believe me, I should know), and . . .

— ?

Shit! That's not important, I insist! Anyway, since then we made a kind of wager, double or nothing as it were, the details aren't that important I assure you

— Indeed?

Well, there we were, just the three of us, Hombre & My Wife (and me), and he challenged me to review one of his so-called novels, while winking slyly at My Wife, of yes, I saw that (made me angry as hell!), and he laughed in that incredible accent (*the guy is really the jealous type!*) of his, and I laughed nervously, and My Wife frowned and muttered something and went to bed

— Alone?

!!

Actually, I think I'd much prefer to tell you about this other guy,
Le Clézio
           but
                well
                     a bet is a bet
                     double or nothing
                     take it or leave it
                     WINNER TAKE ALL & DANCE

??

Okay, this guy (Hombre De La Pluma) (*The more he talks about him
the more I seem to know this Hombre guy!*) has written, more or less,
one book of criticism (average, unexceptional), one bibliography
(profitable, I'm told), three novels (four, if you count the ques-
tionable translation of the second, done by the author under a
fake name, yes with an accent aigu, no connection), not to mention the improbable collection of letters (what gaul) and various
poems stories essays unnamables. That much is established,
certainly. But for reasons as yet unclear unspecified uncertain, I
choose to play with review rewrite restate play (*That's what he
means by playgiarism!*) with the novels (mainly) — after all, this is
my game, I make up the rules, change them to suit my purposes
(as yet unclear unspecified uncertain) — take it or leave it (*He keeps
saying that and it sounds as if I've heard it before!*)

Everything happens (IN MY OPINION) pretty much at random.

For example: Was it really worth it while writing all that just like that? I mean, where was the necessity, the urgency of this book? It might have been better to wait a few years, perhaps, thinking quietly about it and saying nothing. A novel! A novel! I'm genuinely beginning to detest these threadbare little accounts, these tricks of the trade, these redundancies. A novel? An adventure, supposedly. But that's exactly what it isn't! All these efforts at co-ordination, all this machinery — this playacting — for what? Just so as to grind out another story. Hopeless dishonesty . . .

(The Book of Flights, p. 58)

(oh

god

comma

I

abhor

self-

con

— évidemment!   sciousness!)

The Story: (briefly, please) Hombre manages to escape the hor-
rors or war of extermination (X-X-X-X) displaying
such courage or just dumb blind luck works on a farm
for an indeterminate amount of time but not long
decides to come to America or the land of the free very
young naive stupid and so on only nineteen or there-
abouts meets girl from milwaukee of all places on boat
arrives meets polylingual uncle for the first time takes
subway to uncle's home looks up dress of fantastic
black woman fantasizes jerks off very embarrassing
moves to detroit goes to school (*The guy really exagger-
ates now!*) learns to play tenor sax works very hard
great determination or just plain dumb naiveté who
knows he doesn't that's for sure poor kid screws best
friend's mother (*This is getting frighteningly revealing!*)
excitement but also guilt of course that's normal
enough works in catskills during summers (*Hey, what
a coincidence! Me too!*) continuing sexual misadventures too confusing to mention eventually gets in the
paratroopers (*The guy is going too far now he's plagiariz-
ing my life! Or else just inventing facts on the spot!*) dumb
prick (*You too!*) really wants to fight in asia unbelievable gets a thirty day pass loses thirty day pass has
fantastic plan to travel across america but must first
drive to upper new york state to recover thirty day
pass stops in new york city has an unsuccessful sexual
encounter with married woman drives through new
england wrecks his fantastic 1948 chrysler (*well at least
the guy doesn't drive the same car I do that would really
have been too much!*) meets beautiful married woman
fantasizes incredibly erotic interactions and so on arrives at the place in upper new york state where his

thirty day pass is supposed to be but isn't of course
everything fucked up as usual gets out of the damn
paratroopers travels to west coast disappointments
variously arranged but not described heads back east
(I suppose that's where we part road!) stops in las
vegas for big CRAP game wins naturally enough to
lock himself in a room for one year (365 days) to write
novel DON (a real fictitious discourse) more travels
adventures disappointments vaguely referred to everything fucked up bien sûr learns that cristine whom
he loves (*Cristine*?) passionately it seems has finally
gotten her divorce drives wildly to los angeles to
marry her still dumb and as naive as ever at age thirty
and so on (*What a story*!) the same old story everything
fucked up ends up teaching major university (location
not known) condemned to stringing out the STORY
of his life endlessly in various novels that never quite
catch up to his encounter with their conception as
expected (0-0-0-0)

Sounds something like a QUEST of some sort, doesn't it? In
search of The American Dream, very Horatio Algerian. Lies, lies,
I assure you! Actually, the three / four novels form one endless
ESCAPE — a flight, detour digression evasion dodge. From
what? This and that; yes the past, present, future; most of all:
from language, writing (*I had a feeling he was coming to that*: l'écriture!). It's obvious. Just to CONfuse us, Hombre nearly admits as
much QUOTEthrough all the detours that one wishes, the subject
who writes will never seize upon himself in the novel: he will only
seize the novel which, by definition, excludes
himCLOSEQUOTE (Don, p. 146-1 / 2). See what I mean?
Hombre really writes like that, no kidding. Well, since Hombre

seeks to exclude or cancel himself precisely, avoid whatever it is that he is or might be more or less in his mannered speaking and incredible accent (*aigu*) he must escalate the internal space of the novel, disintegrate all forms in a language which cancels itself out at each instant. Wow! What a THEORY! This guy sure loves theories, believe me.

Four Propositions: 1. A STORY SHOULD BE LIKE A HUGE GIGANTIC ENORMOUS QUESTIO-NARY FULL OF OBSESSIONS (Don, p. 156).

Four Propositions: 2. TO WRITE IS TO PROGRESS, AND NOT REMAIN SUBJECTED (BY HABIT OR RE-FLEXES) TO THE MEANING THAT SUP-POSEDLY PRECEDES THE WORDS. AS SUCH FICTION CAN NO LONGER BE REALITY, OR EVEN AN IMITATION OF REALITY, OR A REPRESENTATION OR EVEN A REFLECTION OF REALITY, IT CAN ONLY BE A REALITY — AN AU-TONOMOUS REALITY WHOSE RELA-TION WITH THE REAL WORLD IS TO IMPROVE THAT WORLD. TO CREATE FICTION IS, IN FACT, A WAY TO ABOLISH REALITY, AND ESPECIALLY TO ABOLISH THE NOTION THAT RE-ALITY IS TRUTH (Tioli, p. 6)

Four Propositions: 3. RIGHT TO LEFT IN TOTAL CONFU-SION, TOP TO BOTTOM, AND THROUGH THE MIDDLE IN UTTER

INDECISION, LIKE SOMEONE WHO DOESN'T KNOW WHERE THE FUCK HE COMES FROM AND WHERE HE IS GOING AND WHO DOESN'T GIVE A DAMN IF EVENTUALLY HIS STORY DOES GET TOLD, DIRECTLY OR INDIRECTLY, IN A DISCURSIVE OR A NON-DISCURSIVE MANNER, FOR THE GOOD OF HUMANITY, AND THE PLEASURE OF ALL THOSE WHO MAY DECIDE TO LISTEN TO IT, THAT IS TO SAY THIS ORAL VOMIT, THIS ATROCIOUS DELIRIUM, THIS (ABRACADABRA) STORY, THIS VERBAL PROSTITUTION OFFERED FREELY ON THE SIDEWALKS AND ON THE PLATFORM (BETWEEN THE HEAD AND THE HANDS LIKE AN ACROBAT, LIKE A COURT JESTER) OF THE PAGES, IN THE FORM OF AN ANAL-YTICAL BLAHBLAH, OF A LINGUISTIC SCREWING OF ALL THE SEMIOLOGICAL RULES OF RECITATION, OF A CACACACOPHONIC JAWING, OF A XXXXXXX, NO HE DID NOT GIVE A DAMN IF HIS STORY WAS EVER TOLD OR EVEN RETOLD (Tioli, p. 64).

Four Propositions: 4. THAT'S WHY I'M STILL SEARCHING FOR MYSELF THAT'S WHY I'M FULL OF CONTRADICTIONS AND SUPPOSITIONS AND PROPOSITIONS IF I

KNEW WHO THE FUCK I AM AND
WAS THEN THERE WOULDN'T BE
ANY REASONS TO GO ON. I WON'T
GO MUCH FURTHER GOT TO GET
BACK TO THAT VANISHING POINT
OF FICTION WHERE NOTHING IS
EVEN LESS THAN NOTHING WHERE
LESSNESSNESS CRUSHES THE VOICE
OF THE ONE WHO WRITES. HOLY
SHIT . . . . (Dance, February 29, 19??).

:BLAblaBLAblaBLAblaBLAblaBLAblaBLAblaBLAblaBLAblaBLA:
-QUAquaQUAquaQUAquaQUAquaQUAquaQUAquaQUAqua-

— What twaddle!
— Oui.
— What crap!
— Take it or leave it, it comes to the same in the end; I'm as sick of
this as you are (*Damn right! Me too!*); there's nothing to say! —
Say nothing.
— How?
—   . . . .   =   . .   +   . . .

The THEORY of digressions: Hombre echoes Tristram Shandy,
although he (Hombre) denies that he's ever read him (Tristram).
Nonetheless, he (Tristram) insists that the essential value of
DIGRESSIONS (&tc.) to the Author (anyone) allows him to con-
struct the artifact "with such intersections, and have so compli-
cated and involved the digressive and progressive movements,
one wheel within another, that the whole machine, in general,
has been kept going" —— yet adds, slyly, "for in good truth,
when a man is telling a story in the strange way I do mine, he is

obliged to be going backwards and forwards to keep all tight
together in the reader's fancy —— which, for my own part, if I did
not take heed to do more than at first, there is so much unfixed
and equivocal matter starting up, with so many breaks and gaps
in it,——and so little service do the stars afford which, nevertheless, I hang up in some of the darkest passages, knowing that the
world is apt to lose its way, with all the lights the sun itself at
noonday can give it —— and now, you see I am lost myself!"

To be —
among —
such —
Lost Ones —
Ask SAM —

. . . .
    . . . . (wow! what a sentence! Hombre
        would trade his job wife and chil-
        dren just to have composed that
        one lovely (*normal*) logogophan-
        bombastic piece of discourse!)
    . . . . .

The theory suggests the paradoxical realization that any narrative
can be progressively displaced deformed decentered (the fluid
space between: difference / differance: AU / TO / BI / O /
GRA / PHY) to increase the improbable unlikeliness that the
narrator will ever be overtaken trapped engulfed by the tidal
events of his narration —— which is to say obviously that

— Are you still listening?
— Yes Yes but I'm concentrating on the road! Go on!

should the speaker ever coincide precisely with his speaking the wordmaker —— this part is very difficult therefore pay close attention —— I am —— with his words the writing with the written the result would be DEATH (X-X-X-X) —— so that clearly the only possible strategy the BEST BET is to cancel everything spontaneously instantaneously immediately to prevent forestall annul any final cencellation —— did you get that? —— yes I think so —— with the result evidently that everything becomes parenthetical so to speak ((((((très obscure)))))) which is to say incidental inconclusive incomplete so that no climax is called for leaving (   ) for THE NEXT TIME redeemed

Et maintenant . . . . eh? You don't understand? You have a question, perhaps?
— ?
I agree. It's all incredible, impossible, very obscure!

> Self-awareness: summons from self-awareness. Search. Truth is ceaseless movement, in distraction. Unity condemns. Plunged into disparity, in search of the anonymous.
>
> .
>
> .
>
> .
>
> Flight
> Escape
> Evasion

The art of traps   (*The Book of Flights*, p. 189)

To be ultimately anonymous, what ecstasy! What a joke!
— ?

And what am I perhaps escaping evading, what am I (ME /
MOINOUS) running from? That night, you think? That night
when Hombre and I / (*Moinous!*)
— I'm of course adjusting somewhat as I go along to make it
clearer.
—(*Well, good for me!*). Yes, of course, I understand. Otherwise . .

were smoking grass, that's right, POT, jiving each other, showing off shamelessly in front of my mistress
— ?
— What? Surely you didn't fall for that crap about My Wife? Let
me set you straight, clear it all up!

So. There we were, just sitting around, drinking too heavily, no doubt,
devising FANTASTIC ideas for this and that novel that Hombre De La Pluma
would write and I'd review, being all alone and all, nothing better to
do anyway, just rapping about l'écriture and so on, very impressive,
adolescent, who knows, Hombre dreamily dispersing his superb ego,
showing off as usual, I told him right out that he ought to
review his own work he loves it so much, he dared me to
try, so we made this bet, DOUBLE OR NOTHING, in a
manner of speaking, high stakes, WINNER TAKE
ALL, his lovely wife, whom I've never
met but intend to I assure you,
came into the room

— ?
— What? You mean to say you don't understand what all this has to do with
this article review essay (*Dissertation!*) wordshit so-called? You want me to
GET TO THE POINT? Ah, mon vieux, you simply fail to comprehend the
art of

                    distraction
                    evasion
                    traps
                    logospastics
                    cacacaphonics
                    holy shit!

In this first novel, Hombre juggles four 'voices': first, a rather stubborn and determined middle-aged man who decides to record word for word the story of another (second) man, rather paranoid and confused, who decides to lock himself in a room for a year (365 days, more or less), subsisting entirely on noodles (that's right), in order to write the story of yet another (third) young man, shy and naive, who comes from Europe (perhaps France) to America and who (if the second voice can pull itself together sufficiently to write and be recorded by the first voice) will experience various adventures and so on but who must for the time being wait until he is charactered — all of which implies a fourth voice managing the glorious, sacred, gimmicky confusion craftily jumbled. The essential weakness of his opening performance is the omission (alas!) of the fifth voice (THE TEXT) (*I was just going to say that!*), which interacts with the sixth voice (THE READER) (*Quite obviously!*) in order to evade the first four by contesting with yet one more voice, the seventh voice (the silent space between the fifth and sixth). Get it? (No, I didn't think of that one!)

In his second novel, Hombre advances tentatively by juggling the singled narrator's voice (varied and disguished, to be sure), which is rather stubborn determined paranoid confused shy crafty jumbled, with those of various unnamed but easily identifiable others (the TEL QUEL boys, some odd strangers, plus everyone Hombre has ever known or imagined), and so on. The weakness of this second act, aside from residual attacks of typographiphobia (a common ailment among modern writers, to which Hombre is particularly susceptible, rarely fatal however), consists of its omission of sufficient textual variety, as if the author so-called considers only literal-ly oral voices and overlooks the fantastic possibilities of distorted letters, graffiti, telegrams, dissertations, undecipherable scrawlings here and there, all of which jar against and seek somehow to evade / disrupt the purposive movement of the central text. Got it? (Almost, but not all of it!)

In his third novel, Hombre leaps courageously (following all my advice, naturally) by juggling not only all (each and every one) of the above elements (included, omitted, or merely imagined) but also a counter-voice (which includes, reversed, all the abovementioned elements) which reflects backward-wise on the hesitant progress of the central voice-text, displacement and denial being the technique here: displacing and denying its every move, and so on — with the incredible astonishing magnificent result that the entire work cancels itself out not only as it progresses, but also in advance! Good! (*Gooooood!*)

— What? Still not clear, you say?
— I didn't say anything!
— Too acacacademic? Merde!
— Vas-y Toto!
— Okay, okay. Let me set it straight, clear it all up.

For example,
in the first novel, Boris (the third voice) —— is he Russian? —— no! irrelevant the origin of names! —— undergoes various aborted frustrating guilt-producing sexual encounters (the girl from Milwaukee the woman on the subway Ernie's mother etcetera) experiences little satisfaction, less relief, coitus irrequitus being the trick of the second voice's trade, probably due (*to a great extent*) to some clumsiness, or proportionate frustrations on the part of the first voice in handling the climatic situation, or perhaps because of some unspecified confusion arising from the origin of the fourth voice, embodied appropriately in the passionate silence of the unused, fifth, sixth, and seventh voices. Which is to say: when it comes to fictionalizing sexuality, Hombre can get it up (imaginatively speaking [*Salaud!*], as it were) impressively enough but seems curiously unable to get it in to the narrative openings with conclusive satisfaction. Thus, in the second novel, in which the narrator quite skillfully manipulates the unnamed but easily identifiable (*A child's game!*) questioners in order to disguise, coitus interruptus being the mode of his manner, his disproportionately or real frustrating encounter with the first Married Woman (nothing much happens predictably), which then becomes the focus of his subsequent evasions, despite the fantastic or fantasized encounter with the second (beautiful) Married Woman (that is to say in the future) (everything happens obviously), which of course must be cancelled / annulled in order to provide the essential dissatisfaction which gives birth to the third novel, in which CRISTINE provides the juncture (*How does he manage that?*), front and back, for the

So. There we were, Hombre and I, strolling blindly through the seemingly endless night, gloriously lost not to mention high, and I noticed a book apparently thrown out with the rest of the trash, aha I cried melodramatically, The Book of Flight by J. M. G. Le Clézio, just what I was looking for, I said slyly, and I opened it more or less at random, who can tell in such circumstances, I mean, it being pitch-black, snowing, and so on, and read aloud, which I often find myself doing in such circumstances: "my counter-system consists also in breaking each rupture as soon as it has been achieved. No possible truth exists, but nor does any doubt either. Yes, everything opens closes again suddenly, and this stoppage is the source of thousands of resurrections"

— This guy Le Clézio is great, Hombre, I bet you wish you'd said that.
— Perhaps I did (he said, cryptically, with that incredible accent of his).
— What crap! Overmuch presence, that's your problem, mon vieux. Why not try Tiresias' advice, eh? In case of excessive identity and coitus irrequitus, make of withdrawal a second nature. Get it?
— What a joke!

She paused amid the kitchen to drink a glass of water; at that instant, losing a grip of fifty years, the next-room-ceiling-plaster crashed. So it goes, really.

It comes to this.

It's certain, one might say, that Hombre De La Pluma's fascination with gambling, the thread which links all his novels, stranded, motivates his incessant digressions.

But . . . he loses all the time, the central primal loss (X-X-X-X):

HURTS to lose all the time

Hurts like hell near the heart

near the guts too.

But he has to learn.

Doesn't help to feel sorry for him.

The only way to keep the game going, and what else matters, eh? and somehow evade either winning or losing,

The ONLY WAY is to inconsistently change the rules, disrupt the structures (*I knew it! I knew he would get to the STRUCTURES! Everybody does these days!*), backtrack, sidestep, lie, lie continually, with passionate convictions.

For example

THE ART OF TRAPS	S	THE ART OF FENCING AND STRATEGY
distraction	U	to find support on one's adversary
disparity	R	to rest upon that which attacked
anonymity	V	to find strength in what is destroyed
flight	I	to set the final period
escape	V	to end it all
evasion	A	to call the story finished
cancellation	L	cancellation

in fact, however,

there can

always

be

more words.

Words, yes, that's what I said, words. That's the real fear, no kidding: the FINALITY of syntax grammar sequence in fact all punctuation, stumbling inexorably toward some final period (X-X-X-X). Yet the writer can always go a little further down the road simply by saying that he can always go a little further down the road. Well, can't he? Of course, there's the risk of

And there's always the price. It's enough to make you cry or piss in your pants. Nothing can ever be allowed to reach its natural conclusion. All foreplay, no climax. I assure you.

So. There we were, Hombre and I, driving along in this car we found somewhere, what a fantastic car, a '48 Chrysler in just about perfect condition all things considered, can you imagine such a car, and Hombre began to get sentimental again in that incredible accent of his, unbelievable what he'll try, and he started talking about the bad times when he was a kid during the war (X-X-X-X), and it was snowing like crazy, and he started talking about the good times when he could still write (0-0-0-0), and we could hardly see where we were going, drifting all over the fucking road in that absurd car, it was one of those winding backcountry new england roads, and Hombre got into this story about noodles, NOODLES! shit! I didn't know what he was talking about, for christ's sake watch out where we're going you crazy bastard, and he was sobbing tears streaming down his face with that incredible accent of his, and I was pissing in my pants, and we were lost — that's right: LOST! —

So. There we were, unbelievable, lost in the middle of an empty page somewhere, and I interrupted him in mid-sentence and offered a wager, a bet, double or nothing / take it or leave it / winner take all.

......?

I suspect I should have written about the other guy, instead of all this whatever it is. Ah, then I might have said something profound. Imagine the possibilities, I might have produced a vast & profound & conclusive commentary on, say, the landscape of silence. "LE CLEZIO AND THE LANDSCAPE OF SILENCE." Impressive title, don't you agree? Yes! Yes I do! Yes, I might have written a fantastic article, I'm certain of it. As it is . . . . . (he shrugs)

Comedian! Ham actor! It is time to bring your pantomime to a halt! (*Who is saying that?*) It is time to stop your mumbling, time for your muscles to reabsorb their tremors; for all your roads to take to the air like drawbridges. Nobody is taken in by the performance any longer. You pretend that you are not there, but you are, you are! You pretend to be bigger than you really are. You wear the masks of masters such as you will never be, you want to imitate the gestures which you yourself could never create. Incapable of conquering the world, you reject it. But the figure who really occupies your skin, deep inside you, is the court jester. (p. 295)
I know, I know.

(*How do you know?*)

Yet nothing is decided.
That's certain, at least.
But wait,
The next time . . .
The next time . . .
The next time . . .
Then,
I'll . . . . . .   (what a joke!)

sisisisisisisisisisisisisisisisisisisisisis
lenlenlenlenlenlenlenlenlenlenlenlenlenlenlenlenlen
cecececececececececececececececececececececececece

The guy stopped! He was in sweat. Drenched! He nervously replaced his pages inside his briefcase. He had a wild look in his eyes. (Haggard)!

Wow, fantastic your thing! It's the most incoherent discourse I've ever heard . . . . I mean incoherent in the good sense of the word. It's really profound! It tells it all about this guy Hombre De La Pluma. And quite succinctly! I don't think there is another way to say it!

That's the whole point! To reach total unintelligibility in order to be understood peripherally by everyone!

Yes, you do write in the MARGINS!

How do you know that?

I peeked over your shoulder while you were reading!

Oh!

You know, the more you were reading the more it sounded like the tale of a guy I once knew.

It's not unusual. Many people have parallel lives!

Yes, it's true. But still there were a few things which escaped me!

That's because I only read you the introduction. Much remains to be clarified, obviously!

o-o-o-o-o-o-o-o-o-o-o-o-o-o-o-o-o-o-o-o-o-o-o-o-o

Nonetheless I was overwhelmed by his performance. J'en étais tout à fait BABA! (MOI AUSSI I must say, even though I did not participate in the performance, nor did I witness it first-hand. It was more or less reported to me). But it's not everyday that one has the chance to hear something that extraordinary!

Meanwhile he seemed to have regained his composure. He settled back in his seat breathing more easily. Then he took out a little bottle from his briefcase and took a long slow sip out of it as if gargling his throat wiped the top with his hand and passed it on to me saying TO YOUR HEALTH PAREDROS! I winked at him. So he moved closer to me and gave me a friendly tap on the shoulder followed by a cordial and typical embrace.

It was Calvados. And damn smooth. I took a long drink and gave him the bottle back. It's excellent, I said. My head is travelling way up in the clouds!

My dissertation? Yes, but also your Calvados! And you know it does throw quite a bit of light (somewhat diffuse, I admit it) on my very own situation. I mean by comparison. Especially those biographical details you give, and also your beautiful conclusion. SIR, I'm very impressed! I congratulate you! And to show my appreciation I offer him one of my cigarettes.

Thank you young man, you made my day! You are one of the few people I have met lately who appreciates what I'm trying to do. You see for me writing criticism is like writing fiction. I fable. I invent. Or if you prefer, I surfictionalize!

Exactly the way I cultivate my own garden, I said candidly!

I invent the truth from the false (and from exaggeration, I added with a smile). Yes. Exactly! Paracriticism is in fact a method of making something out of nothing! A way of inventing a subject out of a dying nature (Nature-Morte! I suggested). Yes. Exactly!

Now I understand the meaning of your title. CRAP LIE OR DIE! It does make sense once you've heard the body of your text.

Yes. Exactly! But stop now. Stop right here! I'm getting out! Yes right here!

HERE? But there is nothing! Total void! Not a soul in sight! Total nothingness! Only the white. The snow. The storm. Looks like hell!

STOP! I said. Doesn't matter. I have to pursue my research. I have to before it's too late!

I stop. My Buick doesn't even skid. I was not going to argue at this point. He grabs his briefcase gives me a little military salute opens the door and scrambles out of the car runs towards the gully stares at it for a moment and then jumps in.

Ni vu ni connu, I mumbled to myself totally amazed, dumbfounded, BABA! The kinds of people one meets while travelling! I must have sat in a state of stupefaction for a good 15 minutes before I was able to move again. I was alone again. Doing my usual 12 miles per hour. And it was still snowing like mad. But I felt good suddenly. Almost happy!

I reached inside the breast pocket of my field jacket (he was wearing his combat uniform. I don't think we've mentioned that before) where I knew I had a delicious Cuban cigare (there next to his wallet. Yes the leather wallet Marilyn had given him when he went into the army!) which I had bought in New York just before getting on the road for an occasion such as this one. But my hand stops full of anguish. For a moment it hesitates inside the pocket. The pocket is empty. What is going on? WHAT! Nothing there! The hand searches again. But! it's not possible! Further hesitation. Manual deliberation. It's clear! THE MOTHER-FUCKER! He stole my wallet! That dirty filthy. . . lousy . . . That intellectual fake . . . That Franco-Canadian . . . He was a thief . . . A pickpocket! I was red with anger. Foaming at the mouth. Talk to me about playgiarism! Wow I was so mad I could have demolished my Buick on the spot. Fortunately I held back. THE SONOFABITCH! he must have done it when he moved close to me to embrace me. POURRI! I wouldn't be surprised if he stole my wallet (with all his money and his papers and his pictures of Marilyn) to pay himself for his lecture. In lieu of an honorarium! He could have asked. If the guy was broke I would have given him a buck or two! But no! He took EVERYTHING! The dumb prick cleaned me out! Money identification pictures Cuban cigare and not even thank you! (Well, it's true he didn't have much money left! That's for sure. At most 12 or 13 bucks, from that 20 dollar bill he had gotten from Marilyn before departing, but of which he had spent a good chunk already for gas. Wow did his damn car eat up gas!) I take a look at the gasometer. About two gallons left (he estimates on the spot). Well I'll go as far as I can. No need to panic yet! Verra bien qui verra! Let's keep going! Mais ce salopard de foutu de critique de mes deux (as usual reverting to his native French as a sign of anger) il m'a bien eu! But the next time, the next time!

o-o-o-o-o-o-o-o-o-oooooooooooooooooo-o-o-o-o-o-o-o-o-o-o

XXII

the buickspecial

So. There he was all alone again. Broke now. But still on his way to Camp Drum. Hoping that . . . . .

Hey listen! Would you mind if I told this part of the story myself? I mean directly. Because you see we are now coming to the climax, I mean the real juicy part, and it would be better, and also much more suspenseful if I were to speak directly — first-hand!

I don't mind (I told him, when the time comes). But can you pull it off? Can you handle it by yourself? I mean, remember, I am the one who is supposed to recite this tale second-hand. And besides, it is not legal, you know! What will our listeners say when they discover I've handed you the narrative voice?

Please let me try! Just for a while. For this one part. It really means a lot to me! You'll see, I'll do it right!

Okay!   Look! I'll sit here in that
                                    corner and if you need me
                                    for anything just call

Okay! Here I go:

I was on my way to Camp Drum (Upper New York State near the Canadian border) 1952. February 1952 to be exact. In the middle of a brutal snow storm.

Hey wait a minute! I've already told all that . . . . . .

I know, I know, but if I don't go over some of the details once more I'll never be able to push forward. I've got to step backward a few steps to be able to jump forward. So be quiet and listen!

Okay, get your froggish ass in gear and cancel away! I'll be quiet!

I was on my way to CAMP DRUM. Upper New York State (near the Canadian border). 1952. February 1952 to be exact. In the middle of a brutal snow storm.

Quite unexpected.

I was driving my old beat-up 47 BUICKspecial. Black. Doing about 12 miles per hour on a potholed icy road. In VERMONT. The shortest way to CAMP DRUM. I was assured.

Four in the morning.

There was a deep gully on my right. Very dangerous I tell you. Real precipice. It had been following the road for miles now. Visibility zero! Bald tires on my Buick. Lucky the heater is working. What an enormous banana wagon my Buickspecial! A tank. Radio isn't working. To keep awake. To take my mind off my troubles I'm whistling jazz tunes to myself. Improvising. To pass the time. And also not to think about that damn gully to my right.

Already four days on the road.

I was driving up to CAMP DRUM. It was because my outfit (the glorious gutsy spitshined 82nd AIRBORNE DIVISION) had been sent up there in the snows of Upper New York State to practice parachute jumps in the snow!

But me. I had been left behind. FORT BRAGG (Fayetteville, North Carolina — of all places!) In the fog. I was being shipped Overseas. Yes to the FAR EAST. (Korea to be precise).

I had volunteered!

VOLUNTEERED! You're crazy man! All the guys in my outfit thought I was out of my mind. Some kind of a nut. A weak suicidal case. The nervous type. A psycho.

Bunch of hillbillies!

So when my outfit packed to take off on maneuvers (imagine that!) up in the snows of Upper New York State the Captain told me I wasn't going up with the rest of the regiment. To practice parachute jumps in the snow. Incredible!

No. Me, I had to wait for my travel orders. And then had 30 days (a whole month's vacation you might say) to get my ass to San Francisco. That's where you'll embark for the FAR EAST. The Captain explained.

And then they took off. The whole regiment. By trucks. In a cloud of dust at dawn. And I stayed behind (in the fog) at FORT BRAGG to wait for my orders. And finally my orders came. But they had goofed! They didn't have my travel expenses and also the one month's pay (the one month's pay in advance) they were supposed to pay me. Normal procedure. Those dumb bastards had sent my papers and my money (typical error!) up to the snows. All my payroll documents (that's what the fat sergeant at Headquarters called them) left for CAMP DRUM in that cloud of dust with the rest of the regiment.

I was screwed! The best thing to do (that fat nervous staff sergeant at Headquarters explained) is for you to get your ass up to CAMP DRUM man to collect your dough. If not might take a good week or two for them damn papers to get back down here.

At most I had twenty bucks left.

That really bugged the shit out of me. But I had never seen that part of the country before. A little detour North I told myself before heading West. Why not! With my twenty bucks and my old 47 Buick (special) should be able to get that far. After that we'll see. It would be dumb of me to try crossing AMERICA without my money. And a month's pay in advance (plus travel expenses!) in those days (I was a corporal) that's almost 250 bucks. With or without my Buick I could have a nice cozy trip seeing the country. A marvelous vacation! Discovering the whole lay out Up and Down and Across. AMERICA!

So there I was! On this shitty narrow icy road in VERMONT. Four in the morning or thereabout. After four days' driving (in the rain mostly and now in the snow) with a quick stopover in New York.

A little rest so to speak. In Brooklyn to be exact. To get rid of all my civilian possessions which I'd left with Marilyn. My civilian junk. My half dozen books my jazz records (mostly 78's) my tweed sport coat with patches on the sleeves and my two pairs of trousers my three shirts my jockeys socks etc. All that piled in that black suitcase I've been lugging around for years. And my typewriter. Portable Underwood. Used of course. A whole life to dispose of. To hock in fact. But for the time being all that stored away in Marilyn's closets.

Suitcases and closets. That sums up a life. And typewriters too. And ultimately pawn shops. But for the time being all that shoved away in Marilyn's closets with her brooms and her vacuum cleaner.

Ah Marilyn! What a woman! She was Benny's wife. My former boss when I worked (full time) in his lampshade factory on Flatbush Avenue before I got drafted into the Army. Marilyn! Wow what a gorgeous woman (29 years old). Beautiful body. Enormous boobs. Big black eyes. I was about 22 then. And quite naive.

What a set up we had. What a tremendous deal! Very sneaky. But I'll skip the details. A guy must have some decency. She was really sad. Even cried when I told her they're shipping me Overseas. But don't you worry I'll come back I swore to her. You don't think I'm going to let them shoot my ass full of holes! Be careful! She cried. And come back to me. She kissed me. Dearest love she said to me as I waved goodbye!

Anyway after that quick stop in Brooklyn just time to say goodbye (and all the rest) to Marilyn in a crummy motel room in Long Island there I was in the middle of the night in an incredible snow storm way up in VERMONT on my way to CAMP DRUM (near the Canadian border) to collect my money before heading out West across country across the Mississippi the great plains the rolling hills the Rockies the desert and California.

Wow what a vacation! Wow was I going to see things! Cowboys Indians perhaps gangsters in Chicago and rattlesnakes in the desert. Play crap in Las Vegas. See movie stars in Hollywood. Swim in the Pacific. Up and down and across. Discover the whole lay out. I had a hardon just thinking about it.

Okay I'll skip the details of all the adventures and misadventures I'd had since I left North Carolina. In my BUICKSPECIAL with my duffel bag. The unfortunate encounters and the unexpected incidents. Suffice to say that so far I had been robbed by an intellectual. Almost raped by an old pederast. Abused. Deceived. That I was dead tired and that my Buick was now dragging its ass on its last leg. At most I had a quarter tank of gas left (not even). And not a penny in my pocket. Out of cigarettes too and hungry like hell.

If I make it to CAMP DRUM I'll get rid of that damn jalopy. Should be able to get 25 bucks for it in a junk yard. After that we'll see. I'll bum rides along the way. Thumb my way across AMERICA like you thumb your way through a picture book.

Therefore everything is going well. So far! Except for the snow and the icy road. Visibility zero! Wow what soup out there!

Quarter past four. At least my watch is still working. No pawn shops around here.

So here I am on that stinking disgusting slippery road with twinkles in my eyes hanging on to the steering wheel with both hands. My windshield wipers screeching on the glass. Makes me nervous.

We'll go as far as we can. About three gallons of gas left. I estimate. Damn tank! Wow does it gobble up gasoline. And it puffs it farts burps like an old dying horse. Let's keep going though but without pressing too hard on the gas pedal. To save. To economize. I've got the steering wheel well in hand because this time it's really slippery. I'm almost out of control.

I'm going downhill now and there is a dangerous curve (that's what the sign said) can't see too well my Buickspecial (that old pile of junk) gets all excited and suddenly there she goes sliding sideways as I throw both feet on the brake pedal the damn boat hops to the left hits her ass against the snow embankment jerks rears bounces back in the middle of the road MERDE straightens up I've got my arms all twisted around the steering wheel trying to take the curve the rear tires skid and my wagon slides around in a full circle (almost a full circle) as though she wanted to go back uphill the motor whines into the night I give her a kick in the belly right there on the gas pedal she lets out a groan of pain the tires roar she lowers her front end and like a wild black panther there goes my BUICK leaping head first over the embankment diving full speed into the gully!

I had warned you about that dangerous precipice!

Here we go! That's it. I'm dead! I can feel my balls deflating. My blood rushing through my arteries for the last time. It's all over!

I wrap myself around the steering wheel fold my legs upward to protect my private parts. Normal reaction. My eyes are shut tight of course. So long life a little voice cries inside my skull!

CRASH!. . .BANG!. . .SPLASH!. . .SMASH! I feel atrocious pains all over. Blood pissing out of my mouth. Nose. Ears. I feel the taste of death under my tongue. A vision of my whole family (my mother weeping my father shouting my sisters screaming) flashes in my mind from beyond the grave . . . and everything stops!

But I'm neither dead nor at the bottom of the gully. I'm simply suspended in a dead faint. In a pile of apples. Coniferous apples. For in fact rising majestically from the bottom of the gully a giant pine tree an enormous pine tree had spread its boughs to receive my Buick in full flight and she had landed (head first) like an angel into the salutary branches of that big beautiful Christmas tree well rooted at the bottom of the gully.

At this very spot the gully must have been at least 100 feet deep. I'm not exaggerating though it was hard to judge exactly in the darkness and under the conditions of the present situation.

What a shock!

I had bells ringing in my head. Stars flying in my eyes. Butterflies whirling in my stomach as I slowly regained consciousness. The wheels of my Buick were still turning wildly into empty space. The horn was stuck howling its cry of despair into the night.

The windshield was in pieces. But the blow of the accident had jostled my radio back to life and for a brief moment a sad feminine voice sang a blues into the night I'VE GOT YOU UNDER MY SKIN and then went out. And now the gasping motor let out a final fart of vapor at the very moment when my headlights extinguished themselves.

My BUICKSPECIAL recoiled upon itself. Twisted itself into a last spasm of agony. Turned to junk on the spot. High in the branches of this miraculous pine tree!

And then all was silence and darkness.

I feel blood still running on my face and neck. I'm torn to pieces. Tattered. And my left shoulder is hurting like Hell!

But one must regain taste for life. Or at least one cannot remain there suspended like a jerk or like an acrobat or as my friend Sam

used to say of similar situations suspended in this NIGHTMARE
THINGNESS into which I am fallen (or in this case he would have
to say into which I am risen) at four-thirty-seven in the morning
(needless to specify though I did manage to glance quickly at my
watch just as my Buick flew over the embankment — but now that
good old faithful time piece is also crushed to pieces). NO! I cannot
remain there like some nocturnal bird perched on a tree branch.
The wind could perchance make us tumble down from the height of
this great perch into the depth of this immense hole beneath where
certainly this time we would indeed leave forever whatever is left
of life in us.

And already I can feel a vague oscillation!

Quickly through the broken car window on the driver's side since
the doors are jammed) I extricate myself from this twisted pile of
metallic junk.

I grab my big G.I. duffel bag from the back seat and find myself in
precarious balance like a night owl on a branch. An evergreen
branch heavy with snow and dry pine cones. My heart pounding
madly after this frightening accident which could have been fatal.

Can you visualize the scene? Can you imagine? Our story could
have ended there. The collecting of my money. The GREAT
journey West. The magnificent discovery of AMERICA. All that
(and more) could have ended in the bottom of that unfathomable
precipice! Way up in VERMONT. And you would never have
heard the rest.

Therefore suspended on this bough. Arms spread out to better
keep my balance I glanced towards my Buick for the last time. A

most affectionate glance towards that beautiful Buick which had served me so well up to this place but now reduced to a mere pile of buckled metal and broken glass recoiling upon itself like a crushed snail folded upon the remains of its glorious past existence as one of the fine proud American cars but now just a pitiful stack of GENERAL MOTORS junk (body by Fisher)!

The wind suddenly calmed down. And from behind the dark clouds the Moon sneaked out quietly to look over the scene.

For a moment I had a total vision of the situation and I will never forget it. My 1947 BUICKSPECIAL ass up in the air hanging in the evergreen branches stretched out like the arms of some saintly figure. Ah what a splendid tree I said to myself. What a divine tree! A true Pieta!

I managed to hook my duffel bag to a branch and slowly carefully painfully tiptoed towards the debris of my car like a tightrope walker on his wire arms outstretched. JESUS CHRIST! I screamed into the night. WHAT THE HELL AM I DOING UP HERE? And almost fell off.

When I reached my old Buick sprawled there like a clumsy baboon I gave her a kick full of affection and full of regret right there in the rear tire closest to me.

SO LONG YOU DEAR OLD BUICK I murmured with sobs in my voice. GOODBYE YOU BIG PANZER! FAREWELL SPECIAL BUICK! BARGE OF MY DREAMS! I sniffled a bit and then as I tiptoed away on my branch I said poetically: May angels guide Thee to Thy eternal rest in the Paradise of junk! FARE THEE WELL!

Well I'll skip the horrendous details of my ascension back up on the road where eventually I managed to scramble on all fours with my big duffel bag. My G.I. uniform torn to pieces. My teeth shattering. Blood stains all over. And where. Eventually. I sat down (collapsed rather) on a mount of snow with horrible pains all over my body. Pains which I hardly dare describe so horribly painful were they. My duffel bag rolled next to me at my feet like a wounded animal. It was full of blood and holes so much had it been tossed around during the accident. Torn pieces of pants shirts underwear socks were dripping out of it.

It was not a pretty spectacle! And even worse. Below me lost in the darkness now (her rear end up in the air) (tires torn to shreds) that heap of BUICKJUNK!

What a mess!

Alone on this lonely deserted road (up in VERMONT) Raped. Abused. Deceived. And now without any means of transportation. BUICKless. Pennyless. Arms and legs hurting. Frozen to the bones. Starving. Alone. And not even a cigarette left (the last cigarette of the condemned man). But nevertheless still on my way to CAMP DRUM. I almost wept. Yes! I almost allowed myself this moment of weakness. But I held back. It would have been useless in this solitude.

Around me only emptiness. Nothing! Nothingness! Nobody! Only the snow. The dark of night. And the cold. In other words Nature at its worse. And so I waited
    I waited like that. Hurting all over. For hours. Two. Three Four.
    I seemed to have lost the notion of time. And in fact I had lost it.

And also the notion of space. I was in total nothingness! In complete LESSNESSness my friend Sam would say where nothing is even less than nothing.

Yes I felt completely negated. If that's possible. That's approximately how I felt and where I was. I was (if I may say so — metaphorically speaking) in SHIT up to my neck!

Useless to try walking (I decided) with my heavy duffel bag and my terrible pains.

To pass the time. But especially not to freeze to death. I began hopping from leg to leg in the middle of the road. I did all kinds of gymnastics in spite of the pains and the bells still ringing inside my head and also in spite of my left shoulder which I could hardly move now.

I gesticulated. Capered about. Bounced around. Just to hang on. To survive. If not I would die on the spot. Yes I could feel life quickly abandoning me. Courage deserting me. And on top of that I was hungry like hell. Anything for a cigarette!

It's all over! Finished! I felt humiliated. Must have been ° below. I had a disgusting vision of myself frozen like a scarecrow in the middle of the road.

I was ready to give up. To renounce life when SUDDEN-LY   SUDDENLY in the distance   two beams of light gliding like fire on the snow probing the whiteness like the eyes of some giant monster rushing towards me   to devour me?

A CAR!

AN AUTOMOBILE!   I jump in the middle of the road wave to
that monster gesticulate shout scream stamp my feet enrage raise
my arms and legs (in spite of the pain and the fatigue) hop leap rear
roll myself on the ground crawl climb on top of a snow pile fall on my
ass pull out my handkerchief (full of blood) wave it furiously cuff my
trembling hands around my mouth to shout louder!

                                                    Stick out my thumb!

The car glides to a smooth stop in front of me without even skidding
on the ice. It's an enormous car. A Chrysler. Golden. I notice that
immediately. An IMPERIAL! I know my American cars. That one
must have at least 420 horse power. The window slides down
electrically and a head with splendid eyes appears (head of a
woman useless to say at the stage where we are). An incredible
beauty! Looks like a fairy queen or the heroine of a Victorian novel.
Sensual deep blue eyes full of compassion. Compassionate
enough to make you melt of love on the spot.

I lurch forward!

What is it young man? (A soft languorous voice).

An ACCIDENT! A TERRIBLE accident! Here come and see!

She steps out of her Chrysler wraps herself in a magnificent fur coat
(mink of course). She's tall slim and svelte. Gorgeous legs to give
you an erection on the spot. A delight to watch as she passes before
the car's headlights. She hardly touches the ground. As though the
snow did not exist.

She leans over the gully.

CAREFUL! I shout as I gently grab her arm.

Oh! is that funny! What's that in the tree? A car?

Yes . . . my BUICK!

She turns towards me and in the lights of the car sees that I'm wounded.

But you're wounded young man . . . young soldier! (She must have noticed my uniform. Or what's left of it). We have to take care of you immediately! Quick! Get in the car I'll take you to my doctor.

Blood must have started dripping again from my wounds. I suppose all that gymnastics I did to have myself noticed.

Hurry! Get in! You need medical attention.

I throw my duffel bag on the back seat (somewhat ashamed of its ragged condition) slide next to her on the front seat (the car seems perfumed) and she steps on the gas. The car floats on the snow like a speed boat on a smooth surface of water. She must have special snow tires because in spite of the speed (the female was doing 70 miles an hour) the huge car hardly skids.

My teeth were shattering like a pair of castanets.

You must be frozen poor dear one! How long were you out there?

I don't know. Hours! Maybe more. You know at this time of night and in such bad weather there isn't much traffic. Lucky you came along or else . . .

Poor boy! Yes lucky for you I was on my way home. I was playing
bridge at the house of some friends [at 4:37 in the morning! What a
sneaky broad! Must have spent the night with some guy — her
lover — but of course she didn't want to tell me and to be honest it's
none of my business] You're a soldier?

Yes. A paratrooper! 82nd Airborne Division!

Oh! A paratrooper! That must be dangerous. [damn right] . . . Are
you Italian by any chance? You have a charming accent.

Italian! Me? No, I'm French. [They always pull that one on me.
Because of my black hair I suppose and my big nose. They always
take me for a lousy macaroni. I ask you! Do I look like an Italian?]

Oh a French paratrooper! She said. But what are you doing out
here? What were you doing out there? In the middle of the night on
top of a tree? Did you fall out of a plane?

I giggle a little but the giggle turns into a groan of pain.

Sorry. She says. But what are you doing in the American army any
way if you're French?

Oh, it's a long story. I was almost ready to unload my whole sad
story but I was so cold the words froze inside my throat.

But you're trembling like a leaf! Listen. I live just a few minutes
away from here. Perhaps it'll be better if I take you home with me.
At this time of night especially. We can always call the doctor from
my house if necessary.

I was not going to argue with her. No. Especially since now (even though I was trying not to show it too much) my shoulder was hurting like mad. And then one never knows with such unexpected apparitions. Anything can happen.

Yes! Yes I think it's better. And quicker too. I said to this charming lady to make her understand that I agreed with her suggestion.

We arrive.

What a place! A castle! A palace! A fantastic mansion! This time I'm really in a dream. A fairy tale.

We go in.

I'm stunned. Dumbfounded by the richness the vastness the elegance the luxury the splendor of this abode.

You live here alone? I finally dare ask.

No. With my husband, of course. He's a banker.

That cools me off a bit.

He's on a business trip. In Boston. Until tomorrow evening.

That warms me up a bit.

Yes. In fact that's why I was playing bridge with my friends. I hate to stay home alone when Joseph is away. [At 4:37 in the morning or thereabout in a weather like this! Wow that bitch's got nerve. Lucky for me though. Otherwise I would certainly have died out there like a dog on this lousy deserted road]

Do sit down, please. She said with a lovely hospital smile. No. Not there! Here. On the sofa.

I collapse into a brown leather sofa of maddening softness and depth. She disappears for a moment and comes back with a whole collection of little vials and some hygienic cotton. In the bright light of the room she's even more beautiful. More stunning than before. I rub my eyes to make sure I'm not dreaming. Even pinch my thigh to prove to myself that I'm not asleep or unconscious. She's standing next to me now. If she touches me I faint. Wow! is she gorgeous! Golden blond hair. Eyes blue like the ocean. Yes the Pacific. Skin soft and white like sour cream. A real goddess! I'm ready to convert on the spot. About 32 at most. And so kind. So gentle. So full of warmth and delicate gestures. To give you confidence again in mankind.

She places one of her lovely hands on top of my head and with the other gently rubs my wounds with cotton. I let out a little groan. Does it hurt? Just a little I say. I know but I have to do it or else you'll get infected.

I give myself completely. She notices that my clothes are soaked and torn and that my left shoulder is bloody. You must take these off immediately she urges. I was not going to resist her.

Follow me!

We are in the bedroom now. She takes out a rich red silky robe from the closet. It's Joseph's she explains who is on a business trip in Boston. And she quickly unbuttons my paratrooper vest my shirt and all the rest and in seconds I find myself bare chested (but in my khaki G.I. drawers) standing in front of her. Trembling. I breathe deeply to expand my chest.

She's bandaging my shoulder now. Softly gently carefully and with a great deal of know-how. Funny! I don't even have a hardon. When she's finished with the shoulder she gives me a friendly tap on the back then leans forward and kisses my right shoulder softly kindly. It was as though a bird (a dove) had touched me lightly with the tip of its white wing.

I feel dizzy. Sort of split in half. No! That's not it. I feel soft and somewhat wobbly. She notices it because she asks don't you feel well? I say yes with my head.

Here. Why don't you stretch on the bed for a while.

No hesitation. I jump on top of the bed. KING size. An OCEAN of softness.

No no! Not on top of the blankets. Get inside. Rests for a while and warm up. I'll be right back. I just want to put on something more comfortable and then I'll bring you a nice hot grog to pep you up.

She disappears again and I sink into the waves of the delicious mattress and the current of the voluptuous sheets. In three minutes I'm snoring like a dolphin and feel myself floating drifting into the kingdom of dreams.

SUDDENLY   SUDDENLY
is it a dream a nightmare (or a hurricane) but a long greedy white hand is toying with my private instruments which take a leap upward into gigantic dimensions? White sails stretched to the point of bursting by the blow of a stormy wind. And now that mythical hand pulls my nautical tools toward a vague mass of rocky flesh trying to guide it all down the corridor of a pair of

narrow thighs at the end of which a gluttonous cave of fur gasps to swallow me. I hear a cry of distress inside my head. SHIP-WRECK!   I'm going down. Sinking!
HELP! ——S. O. S.   Though the water is tropically warm I struggle like a castaway body to remain on the sur-face.   MAY DAY!   I try to keep my eyes opened. And now I see her. Surrealistically. That beautiful charming blond siren soft and slippery (and naked) lying on top of me flinging herself about like a giant fishy creature in frenzy. She gulps shrieks whines howls sighs puffs. Lets out a stream of weird exotic cries: DO IT TO ME DO IT TO ME DO IT TO ME! A flood of fingers is pulling me down. GET IN she roars and I'm trying my best but the weight and furor of her slippery body is crushing me into the waves of this white sea of passion and its whirling foam. And now the nymph is pushing me down and under deeper and deeper with all her aquatic dexterity rowing paddling oaring slapping flapping the waters and eddies of this impromptu swim!

Half of me has disappeared inside the whirlpool of her cavity. And when she's almost finished caving me in she starts all over again with even more appetite: she gargles me up
                    drains me down
                    mashes me up
                    gobbles me away!
                    Wow! What a cannibal! What
a meal I make! Must have been shipwrecked for months and months on her deserted island of sexlessness!

I try to escape but now that flexible creature lifts me up into an arch (into a bridge) and slides my erected mast into her driveling porth-ole of a mouth swallowing it in one smooth stroke all the way down *to my inflated balloons. Then twisting her propeller-head in circular motions she bites & sucks & licks & chews (up & down & sideways & obliquely) with wet little groans and moans and whispers and when I let my material explode down her pipe she roars frantically and starts spitting like a water dragoness all over the flaps and flips of my hot belly and with her uncanny tongue she drags the sticky liquid all the way down (I am not exaggerating) to my feet along the shores of my legs and licks my feet my knees digs into my shivering thighs tongues up my hips gets inside my cute belly button up my chest and under my armpits. I start giggling embarrassingly while sinking ludicrously and hopelessly to the bottom of this desperate licking. I hang on to her with both hands as if she were a life buoy or a raft but she's the one who climbs* aboard *me again* (what the hell is going on?) *and with voracious fingers she grabs my loose paddle and stiffens it with jerky strokes. It's too much I don't want to swim any more! Thumbs up! Time out! Dammit it hurts like hell! Especially in my two blue sails. Again I try to escape by plunging (head first) into the swirls of the sheet to swim ashore but she grabs me firmly rigidly by the tip of the bow-sprit with one hand and hustles three fingers of her other hand into my stern I SCREAM (but in vain) as my poor splintered oar plunges into her stormy port! It feels as though I have just sank into a pool of honey.* (Must be dessert time!) *And now she screws my tail (or what's left of the bloody thing) in all directions until in a last stroke of rage and despair (a furious gasp of survival) I shout STOP! . . . STOP IT! . . . I CAN't no more!*

> *But she doesn't*
> *hear me or else*
> *pretends not to*
> *hear!* **True**

her head is buried shyly inside my shoulder (the good one fortunately). Suddenly she leans backward

away from me   and bursts
into hysterical inhuman laughter. I feel insulted vexed dejected
humiliated and quite repulsed. Get the fuck off! I scream as I try to
slide from underneath her. Get back down here! She replies as she
shoves me back into the water. Stop it! Please stop it! I plead.
We're going to capsize!
But she flops on top of me and wiggles herself into incredible
positions to sail the rest of me. What suppleness!
                    I struggle.   We struggle.
and SPLASH! We fall overboard onto the floor : me flat on my
back her sitting on top of me her buttock against my crotch her
back against my caving chest her long wavy hair (blond soft and
wet) drowning my face in its silky net.
                    We're like two swimmers doing a fancy
aquatic ballet. Like two water-wrestlers trying to drown the other
guy. If only there was a referee! No kidding! I assure you it's worse
than a match of catch-as-catch-can!

I can't take it any more. I'm washed out. Dead crippled worn out.
I'm empty crushed deflated. But she feels a remnant of an erection
(a bit bloody no doubt) still wriggling against her derriere puffed
like a pink cherub and she wants to take advantage of it. Gingerly (I
can't believe it!) *she tries to shove that scared piece of drift wood*
inside her rift. It won't go in. She crawls off me and dives across
the room in the bathroom and bounces back in a shiffy with a little
jar in her hand (just as I'm trying to slip under the bed) a pink jar.
She catches me by one leg and throws me back into the waters of
passion as she gets back into the sitting position on top of me. She
must think I'm some kind of a surfboard. (I'm on the verge of
cracking up). *She smears the cool goop from the jar (with two*
fingers) all over her anal passage (raising herself above me in an
acrobatic posture) and piles a glut of the stuff on top of my

frightened pinnula (what a mess) *and SWISH there goes the panic-stricken needle of my compass slithering into her North pole as if it were gooshy ice cream. This time it's not a joke we both howl in unison : me a sordid violent painful WHOOP she a roaring happy excited mewling of a WHAFF as we collapse together on the floor next to each other and roll on our stomachs limbs spread out like two bodies washed ashore by a furious tempest (it's all over I suppose)*

Minutes later we manage somehow to climb the sides of the giant bed and fall inside the hull where we lie sweating puffing breathing sputtering coughing like two athletes who have just broken the world record for the 200 yard dash - no, rather, the 1500 meter free style!

My darling
My treasure
My adorable paratrooper

how I adore you!   (Damn you!)
Wow you're delicious beautiful young strong superb and so juicy so hard so big so supple so delectable so voluminous so useful!

But me I rather feel ugly and small and weak and soft screwed up & down to the bone dried up useless abused deflated demolished pruned crushed!

But I'm not even listening to her any more as she goes on piling up her magnanimous mountain of adjectives on top of me. I'm drifting floating again downstream on my barge of exhaustion on my Medusa raft toward the kingdom of dreams wrapped in the chants of my snoring! ZzZzZzZzZzZzZzZz!

What would you guys have done in my place? I ask you! What a way what an incredible way to return to life after that terrible accident! What a resurrection! Call me Lazarus saved from the melting snows! I'm not kidding. What a swim! I ask you what would you guys have done had you to endure such a desperate such a brutal such an aquamonious salvation?

It was 4:30 p.m. when I woke up well tucked under the blankets of that king size bed. I had a lousy taste in my mouth and loud buzzing in my head. In fact my head felt like an empty box. A huge hole. A hollow sphere of darkness and forgetfulness. I felt rather weak (as if I had been blown out of existence by a stampede of buffalos!) and I couldn't remember a damn thing or at least it took me a good five minutes maybe more to realize where I was and what had happened to me in that storm!

In a moment of panic I thought of sneaking out through the window, but naked as I was it would be pure madness and this time for sure I would die out there in the cold of pneumonia. Better wait here and see what happens next. I looked around the room for my clothes. Just in case! Sonofabitch they're gone! A pain of anguish hit me in the chest. I'm kidnapped!

That's more or less how I felt and what I was pondering when the beautiful charming and smiling lady of the house walks in wearing a powder blue silky negligee and carrying a breakfast tray. For a moment (just in case) I thought of faking sleep but when I saw the sunnyside eggs & the bacon & the sausages the toasts jam (strawberry & marmelade) sweet butter coffee & two kinds of juices (orange & tomato) I propped myself against the fat pillows. What a feast! She had even brought me still unwrapped the Boston Globe. Not that I cared much that day about news of the world but it was a nice touch.

I eat the whole thing smartly dunking the yellow of the eggs with nice little pieces of toast. That's a good boy, she says as she watches me adoringly while sitting discretely on the edge of the bed her daringly sexy legs crossed outside her dishabille half opened all the way up to her perfumed crotch. I try to concentrate on my breakfast as she tenderly looks at me and from time to time leans towards me to touch with delicate hands the side of my face and then she kisses me with motherly affection on the cheek on the shoulder on the neck on the hands (as I steadily chew my delicious breakfast). She's really divine! Ah what femininity! No question about that. But we're not going to flop on top of each other again. Not at this unscheduled time of day. What am I? Some kind of amusement park? A toy? If she jumps me again, I scream! Or else I play sick and tell her I have horrible pains. I'm not going to let myself be abused (though after a breakfast like that . . . a guy could indeed . . .)

But if I were to talk to this charming hostess! Just to make a bit of conversation. After all we've hardly said three words to each other I must confess since she rescued me on the edge of that memorable precipice where indeed I should be lying dead now frozen (possibly devoured by wild starving animals) had she not appeared so unexpectedly to save me.

What's your name?
Mary!
Wow, you're beautiful Mary! And you have such lovely blond hair, such deep blue eyes!
It's because I come from the North. All my ancestors came from nordic regions. From Scotland originally. In fact do you know when they all came to this country? [No!] They all came on the

Mayflower. Yes way back at the beginning. That tells you how far back I go in the glorious past of our great country.
That explains why you're such a fine navigator!
Yes, in a way they were all pioneers!

Shit! That really blew me off. Pioneers! Like me. That explains it all. You guys realize. Me. I had just fucked (or been fucked whichever way you look at it) what's best, what's most respected in America today. ME. Poor lost paratrooper, poor wandering French Jew (perhaps I should have mentioned that earlier) I had just wallowed in bed without any scruple with all the glorious history of America. This lovely WASP! This perfect WASP. This 100% American had landed her most distinguished ass, her historical ass on my guilt-ridden circumcised dick without being aware of it. How proud! How alive I suddenly felt, how relieved too! What luck! What fantastic luck I had! Faced with this incredible revelation I suddenly felt good and much better, tremendous in fact. I really felt great, relaxed, secured, accepted, at home and free as I grabbed one of her teats and reached subtly for her cunt her sophisticated ancestral cunt. But she giggled (even blushed a bit around the eyes) as she pushed my hands away gently saying NONONO dearest love! We have to hurry because she had to go and pick up Joseph [Oh yea] at the train station and with such bad weather (it was still storming out there) it might take a good 45 minutes to drive there. Therefore my dear wild naked little ape hurry up! Let's take a quick bath together and get dressed.

But what about me! What do I do? What happens to me now? I asked anguishly.

You! I'll drop you at the train station with your duffel bag and you can go on wherever you have to go.

[To CAMP DRUM . . .]

It's the most practical, my dear! There's nothing to do.

Just like that? And we'll never see each other again? Never!

I doubt it. But one never knows. Perhaps someday . . . by chance.

Yes . . . perhaps! In another journey. Another story. Yes! I would
like that very much.

The train! I hadn't thought about that. Not a bad idea. Especially
now that I'm carless. Buickless. A quick snapshot of my
BUICKSPECIAL resting in the arms of that pine tree flashed
through my mind and I felt a little pang of sadness.

Yes! the train. It's a good idea. Especially since I have to go to
CAMP DRUM (because of my money) and CAMP DRUM mustn't
be very far from here?

No. It's just about two hours from here by train. Direct in fact!

Things really work out well!

Yes, it's perfect. She says somewhat absentmindedly already
thinking I suppose of Joseph's return.

Yes, but, I hesitate, the train, that's fine, but, you see, me, I'm, I'm
completely broke, you understand, it's not my fault, it's because
that old intellectual, yes a French-Canadian intellectual, he stole
my wallet, and also a fine Cuban cigar I had bought in New York,
for the trip, that was while I was driving through Massachusetts,
way back, in another part of this story,

Why didn't you tell me before?

I didn't have a chance. And besides it's a very long and compli-
cated story. Do you want me to tell it to you?

Okay! If you want to but quickly while we're taking a bath.

And so while we're taking a bath and she's scrubbing my back with
soap I tell her the whole sad story of my journey since I left North
Carolina a good four days ago in the rain and in the snow in my old
47 Buickspecial black from beginning to end to this very moment I
tell her about the chicken-shit 82nd AIRBORNE DIVISION and
all the lousy hillbillies and the fat sergeant and the push ups give me
20 give me 25 give me 30 and on the double and the parachute jumps
and the butterflies in the stomach as she rubs my belly and the FAR
EAST and how I volunteered and the fucked up system and the
goof they made with my documents and my travel expenses up in
the snow of Upper New York State (near the Canadian border) and
my duffel bag and Brooklyn and my civilian stuff my jazz records
my half-dozen books my socks my shirts etc. my typewriter and
my black suitcase shoved away in a closet (nothing about Marilyn)
and my ambitions my dreams my hopes my desires my departure
and the lampshade factory and Benny (but nothing about Marilyn
of course) as she shampoos my hair and that sneaky French-
Canadian intellectual who read me the introduction to his doctoral
dissertation right in the middle of night as we drove through Massachusetts and how after he left I found out he had lifted my wallet
and my Cuban cigar (that sonofabitch!) and then I plunge into the
past my lousy childhood as she tickles my feet with her little
bathbrush and the war the occupation the Germans the Jews yes of
course I'm Jewish do you mind and the camps my father mother
sisters uncles aunts and all the cousins the whole family remade
into lampshades exterminated (X-X-X-X) and the farm where I

worked so hard in the South of France and the Liberation Victory V-DAY and the black market to survive and the French ah the French with their acute sense of patriotism LIBERTY EQUAL-ITY FRATERNITY (Bullshit!) and then AMERICA HERE I COME and my suitcase the black one and loneliness homesickness starvation and the search for love and despair and always broke and so on and so on . . . .

In other words I tell her the whole fucked up story of my life as she keeps scrubbing me with her delicate hands and tears are running down her cheeks and at the last moment just before she dries me off with a thick towel she kneels at my feet to give me a farewell blow-job (but this time gently kindly sadly even and with a great deal of compassion in it because of all my sufferings) so that I won't forget her she tells me and don't worry about the train I'll buy the ticket for you it's the least I can do for you after all.

You couldn't do any better I was going to say [like 20 bucks or something] but I didn't. I didn't because after all even though the broad had screwed the hell out of me I had some decency left in me. And besides. Besides I had slept well in her king size bed (their bed) and even wore Joseph's lovely robe and she had fixed me a delicious breakfast. Even scrubbed me all over. A guy should be grateful for that much attention. Especially at the stage where we are for if one were to examine the situation carefully (in retrospect) it is quite obvious that at this very moment I ought to be dead. Yes frozen in the snow. A moribund lying alongside a deserted road way up in VERMONT had she not appeared in the picture to bring me back to life and thus permit me to continue my journey (by train now) and of course my story. Truly. Without her everything would have been finished. Don't you agree?

And so here we are again in her big golden IMPERIAL on our way to the train station both staring straight ahead at the road not talking to each other just staring blankly ahead beyond the road toward our future. Hers rich and happy. Mine still quite uncertain but certainly poor and doubtful.

We were both a bit sad now.

She had cleaned and mended my uniform nicely (though it was obvious that she was not very gifted for those sorts of things) while I slept I suppose. Therefore I looked decent. And in fact one could say that I looked rather well. Healthy. Indeed I felt quite cheerful in spite of the brutal accident and the desperate storm I had endured during the night but through which I had survived. Nonetheless.

What time does Joseph's train get in? I finally asked just to say something.

6:15.

What do we do if he sees us together?

Nothing! He won't see us because we'll arrive at the station before he does. A good twenty minutes. And your train leaves at 6:00 sharp. I called to make sure.

What a perfect hostess!

Things really work out well I said. But she was already somewhere else. In the arms of Joseph (figuratively speaking).

And at six o'clock sharp after touching but brief goodbyes there I was stretched lazily on the seat of an empty railroad car on my way to CAMP DRUM at last somewhat pooped I must confess but well fucked. Broke. Carless but nevertheless happy to be here. Happy to be back on my way. Anxious to push forward!

XXIII

crucifiction & cancellation

The train was completely empty. A ghost train he thought! And he was asking himself, half asleep and half dead of fatigue, what the hell he was doing here? He couldn't make sense of everything that happened to him since he left Fort Bragg!

Two hours later, however, he arrived at Camp Drum. Little hicktown of nothing lost in the wilderness and in the snow. And it was time! Yes because you guys must have been wondering, I suppose, if he ever would get there. To that damn Camp Drum way up north, lost in the middle of nowhere, near the Canadian border!

Well! I made it, finally, he said! As he found his way, knee deep in the snow, towards the camp. Two soldiers were standing guard in front of the gate. He asked them where his regiment was [Company C—Third Platoon]? And here he is with his duffel bag on his shoulder, walking bowlegged like a mule, on his way to Captain Cohen's office.

He was there — Captain Cohen! In his little temporary office. Alone in fact, practicing his golf swing and his putting (at about twenty or twenty-one hundred hours! The guy must be a fanatic!) He had a green piece of carpet on the floor to do his putts. He watched him a moment from the door. The Captain hadn't seen him come in. Not a bad putter he thought! But he could have given him a few pointers! But suddenly the Captain noticed him!

FRENCHY! What the F**** are you doing here? We thought you were . . . .

It's because of my money, SIR! A little error — typical! Sir, you understand? They told me . . . .

But everybody thought you were already on your way to . . . .
Oh yes, I know! Your money . . . . We found your papers when
we got up here. It was an error. But everything was sent back to
Fort Bragg!

WHAT! To Fort Bragg, in North Carolina? But I just came from
there when they . . . .

Yes, but it's not our fault! You could have warned us or something! Write a letter. Send a telegram. Make a long distance call.
After all doesn't take much brain to think of that! Ones does not
jump out of an airplane without a parachute! (He giggled at his
own joke but Frenchy found it rather poor). One does not under-
take a journey (to the end of nowhere) like this without . . . .

Oh! the mother . . . . But they told me at Headquarters that
. . . . WHAT! I had come all the way up here, had endured all
that suffering, that humiliation, loneliness, fear, had been robbed, abused, almost raped and dishonored, could have died
frozen in the snow, been killed, yes devoured by wild beasts,
assassinated, been crippled for life, could have been disinteg-
rated, and all that for nothing! NOTHING! Just a dumb joke: One
does not jump out of an airplane without a parachute . . . . For
the birds! But . . . . Sir! It's not fair! . . . . It's not fair!

Nothing I can do now, Frenchy! But don't worry. Everything will
be settled tomorrow morning. Besides it's quite a coincidence that
you are here because a telegram came for you just this afternoon,
and we didn't know what to do with it. From New York City!

A telegram?   For me?   From New York?

[Telegrams, he explained to me, always scared the shits out of him!]
[Telegrams, he explained to me, always bring bad news. At least in]
[his case. Somebody died. Or else somebody is not coming back, or]
[decided to marry somebody else. And for once, he was quite right!]

The Captain gave me the yellow thing and I opened it with frightened fingers. It
was from Marilyn [obviously] and it said in large black floating letters:

DO NOT COME BACK STOP!
BENNY KNOWS EVERYTHING
STOP! I LOVE YOU STOP!

Goddammitmotherfuckercocksucker! That's all I needed! What a
blow! What bad luck! (Everything was falling apart now!) No
more car, no more money, no more love, no more nothing!
Everything gone! Alone! Finished Marilyn's beautiful black eyes!
Gone too! He was ready to let the tears roll down from his eyes,
but realized where he was, or to tell the truth it wouldn't have
mattered because Captain Cohen at this point went back to practicing his putting, though he did ask in a somewhat concerned
manner, over his shoulder: Is it very serious?

No! (He hesitated) Not really! . . . . Just a friend who is . . . .
sick and wants the name of my doctor!

Ah, fine! . . . . Listen why don't you go to your old platoon say
Hi to the boys find a bunk for yourself and get a good night's rest
and in the morning we'll discuss the situation. I'll see what I can
do!

Yes, because, me, you know, I'm dead tired, and also I'm broke.
Not a penny left. Nothing! And I don't see how I'm going to get

back. Yes back to Fort Bragg I suppose? North Carolina? From
where I just came a few days ago. To collect my money. And get
going to the West Coast across country!

So he left the Captain's office totally dejected after he was told (in
a rather offhanded fashion) where to find his old platoon: in
barrack Charlie, there in that direction ⇥⇥⇥⇥⇥⇥⇥⇥⇥⇥⇥⇥⇥⇥⇥⇥⇥

He knew in advance what those dumb hillbillies would say when
they saw him pop up like that but he had to face the music. So here
he is once more with his duffel bag on his shoulder trampling
through the snow in a dejected mood feeling empty humiliated
furious chewing insults as he prepares himself for the confrontation with his former fellowsoldiers!

He walks into barrack Charlie!

Most of the guys were half naked either lying on their cots staring
at the ceiling dumbly or reading comic books or simply con-
templating with anticipatory delight the moment when the lights
would go off and their masturbation session would begin or else
sitting on the floor around a footlocker playing poker. Everybody
turns around when he walks in and with a single collective voice:
FRENCHY! FRENCHY BABY! WHAT
THE FUCK ARE YOU DOING HERE?
HEY YOU ALL LOOK WHO IS
HERE? YOUSE GUYS IT'S FREN-
CHY? AND WE THOUGHT THE
MOTHERFUCKER WAS ALREADY
IN CHINA GETTING HIS ASS SHOT
FULL OF NICE LITTLE HOLES! YOU
CHICKENED OUT?

FUCK OFF you bunch of creeps. He said to them collectively. GET OFF MY BACK you bunch of miserable assholes! He shouted angrily with his incredible accent. I didn't come here to discuss my social life with stupid bastards like you! And besides I'm in a bad mood! Youse guys can go jump in the lake! Leave me alone, or I'll knock the shits out of you one after another!

What's wrong Frenchy Baby? You got screwed? They didn't want any of your dead meat? You're too skinny? Too nervous? You don't know the gook lingo? You gotta learn Inglish first? Your dick is too fat and too sloppy? You caught the clap? They found out you eat pussy? Hey they found out you're a yellow kike?

DROP DEAD! He screamed at the fat little guy from Maryland (for that was him again who was bugging the shits out of Frenchy) and he turned away from him to stretch fully clothed on an empty cot and feel sorry for himself. He was hardly stretched out with his hands over his eyes so as not to see this hillbilly brothel when the ferocious mean voice of the fat sergeant who used to bug the hell out of him screams a rather unexpected TENNTIOONN! They all jump to their feet like wild puppets and stand there chest out like wooden pickets in a fence. He too, as a military reflex, jumps up! But not too happily.

It was Captain Cohen. At ease MEN! We're jumping in the morning, at zero six hundred sharp! Reveille will be at zero five hundred and no fuckoffs! Everybody'll be outside the barrack in full pack, armed to the teeth, in combat uniforms. Everybody! Is that clear?

Yes SIR! They all screamed back like one man. GERONIMO! Up & Away!

But then just as the Captain was ready to leave the little bastard from Maryland asks: Sir? Excuse me Sir? Does Frenchy jump too? I mean if he's here he should participate?

NOT ME! He shouted defensively. NOT ME! Officially I'm not here. No I'm absent! On leave! 30 days! And besides I'm on my way to the West Coast! To the FAR EAST [en passant par San Francisco]! Therefore, I'm not here legally, and theoretically also!

No, No, No! They all shouted like a chorus. Yes, Yes, Yes! He's here so he jumps too!

Shut the fuck up you bunch of creeps! The sergeant ordered.

Captain Cohen thought for a moment. Okay! Frenchy jumps too, since he is here in body! And turning towards him: Zero Five Hundred! In full combat uniform. You'll be there with the rest of the platoon!

But SIR! . . . . Captain! . . . . I . . . . But . . . . It's not normal . . . . I . . . . sonofabitch!

It's an order!

Ah! If it's an order!

And besides it'll do you good! It'll keep you in shape! 'TENNNNTIONNN!

Everybody went back to doing what they were doing before this interruption. Back to poker comic books staring at the ceiling yawning &tc&tc!

Dammit! What a day! But deep inside he really didn't care because he rather liked jumping out of airplanes. Gave him a feeling of freedom! And in the snow could be fun. Can't get hurt in that soft stuff. And also might perk him up. Morally and physically. Because at this time his moral and physical states of being were rather low. Below normal!

So. The next morning at zero five hundred (it was still dark outside) after an abominable night full of bad dreams and the disgusting noises of the hillbillies jerking off (full blast) under their khaki blankets to get rid of the butterflies which were butterflying in their bellies as soon as they heard about the jump there they were in full pack knee deep in the snow in front of barrack Charlie clinking at the teeth and at the knees of fear and cold shit all over their asses and 15 minutes later there they were packed inside a huge C145 parachutes tightly on their backs huddling close to one another the straps of the parachutes cutting into their shoulders and under their crotches (in his case the left shoulder particularly was hurting him because of the car accident a few hours ago) all of them pale like moribunds and not saying a word simply breathing heavily like a herd of calves going to the slaughterhouse not a very pretty spectacle this pack of pissors in their combat uniforms eyes squinting like cockholes lost in the loud buzzing of the plane's engines which was taking them toward the drop zone perhaps for some of them to drop dead at last but it goes quickly before they know it the green light already tells them it's time to get ready everybody jumps to his feet and quickly checks to make sure the parachutes won't fall off then the red light now says THAT'S IT and they all rush madly toward the opening of the door that leads to the sky hesitate a moment while waiting for the sergeant's kick in the ass that tells them to go :

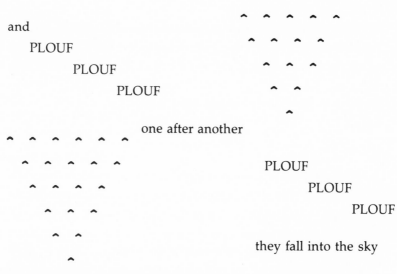

and
        PLOUF
                PLOUF
                        PLOUF

                                one after another

                                        PLOUF
                                                PLOUF
                                                        PLOUF

                                        they fall into the sky

A tremendous slap of cold wind hits me in the face as I
tumble backward like a sack of potatoes I am flying upside
down
but I shout ONE THOUSAND . . . .

                        TWO THOUSAND
                                        THREE
THOUSAND . . . .
Nothing happens!
I panic!
Quickly I open my eyes! I'm falling . . .
I'm finished! I'm dead . . . Just a little
parcel of human flesh rushing down-
ward to its extermination! Can't breathe
anymore can't move anymore can't go
                        back anymore!
I'll be buried six feet below the surface into the whiteness below ni
vu ni connu little bloody pieces of crushed human body buried
alive à fond!

So long life! Surface life! I open my eyes one more time. Dead and buried all in one blow!

Around me dozens of other little human packages are also being expedited to the ground!

And me too I am one of the dumb packages on its way to its final destination!

Falling like a firm piece of shit from the plane's asshole into the toilet bowl of the big blue sky to be flushed down the drain of Mother Earth!

But suddenly it feels as if I have been hit by a tank speeding out of control squarely into the stomach! An enormous punch!

Yes as if my jacket suddenly and quite miraculously got caught by the collar on a giant nail stuck firmly in the middle of the sky!

Way up there in the blue yonder!

Everything stops! I'm suspended like a puppet in midair gesticulating in the emptiness! My shoulders neck crotch private parts feel like raw flesh!

Never has a human body been so humiliated physically!

But above me the big mushroom is beautifully deployed and I float in the sky!

Wow is it gorgeous what a sweet sight! Fantastic! Wow the sky is big! Lots of room up here to float around!

I feel like staying up here forever! Never again come down to set foot on that bitch of an Earth!

Never again! On that bitch of an Earth which forces you to

walk & run
live & love
piss & crap
suffer & die
and even forces you to tell all kinds of stupid stories!   lie & die!

The sun had just climbed over the horizon and the top of its orange head appeared behind the clouds. All around me a field of mushrooms sprouted under the sun's nose. We recognized each other and gesticulated to each other like marionettes to draw each other's attention. Hey Frenchy, the fatso from Maryland shouted at me from under his own mushroom! What the fuck are you doing up there? Shitting in your pants? Drop dead I cried back you dumb prick! But he was already drifting away in his own corner of the sky. Hello Frenchy, another guy shouted at me just as his convex mushroom passed below me. Ain't you glad you made this one? Isn't it a beaut? Drop dead too! But this one also had drifted away past my feet!

I looked down finally. And shivered! The ground was climbing toward me and my mushroom at full speed! It looked like the ass of a giant monster which was ready to fart in my face. And it was coming up fast even though I felt like I was standing still. Dammit it doesn't last long the pleasure. It's too quick! And already I can feel in my stomach the butterflies moving in!

I get ready to land there in that soft cushion of snow that clean padded smooth mattress of snow nothing to worry about it's a cinch an easy one!

I bend my knees in the proper position for landing which we have been taught so well to do by reflex look straight ahead into nothing and I wait I wait I wait I wait shit I wait you mustn't cheat and look down or else I wait I wait shit just a little peek no wait wait so I won't break a leg so I look straight ahead into the empty sky hanging there like a dumb prick because me I'm careful I don't want to fuck up this one I hold on tight to the parachute straps above my head just as the book says you're supposed to do pulling down slightly ready to let go and release the weight as soon as the feet touch the ground to soften the shock and bounce up before rolling over into a perfect P.L.F. and so I wait I wait good perfect landing position very supple relax wait wait for the little blow when the feet touch the ground and quickly I rehearse in my head the perfect parachute landing fall and already in my head I can see myself flat on the ground (in this case in the soft snow) resting peacefully and happily after the perfect landing and so I wait I wait I wait ignoring the butterflies concentrating carefully on the up-coming little blow . . . .

VLAN! CRACK! BOUM & PATATRAS!
Talk to me about the soft cushion of snow or that smooth clean padded mattress of snow! I land squarely on top of a huge rock! Jagged and sharp rock hidden under the surface of the snow — à fleur de peau et de neige — and therefore invisible to the naked eye. And Vlan Crack Boum & Patatras, my whole body falls to pieces. I can feel it in the legs arms neck head. In the ass too. As if I was being crushed into the ground by a giant hammer! I collapse into the vicious snow twist myself into spasms of pain while howling like a calf being hit on the head in a slaughterhouse. I don't see any blood running in the white snow but I tell you I was really suffering like hell! Yes unbearable!

Two of my fellowparatroopers come rushing toward me when they hear me screaming and start laughing at me: Hey Frenchy! Does it hurt? Did you break something? How the fuck can you get hurt landing in a soft bed of snow like this? What a clumsy frog?

Does it hurt? You motherfucking jerks! Don't you see I'm in pieces! All broken up! Demolished! Half dead! And they ask if it hurts, if it hurts when I'm literally dying on the spot! You meatheads! Don't you see I can't hardly talk? Call the fucking medics!

The queer medics arrive full speed with their stretcher pick me up by the legs and arms and swing me on top of the stretcher. I scream and moan like a pig. Allez-y mollo you big brutes! Murderers! Salauds! Undertakers!

What the fuck is he talking about? Must be raving? Delirious? Shit looks like he broke a leg. And his neck too. And also look here, it looks like both his arms are out of place!

Stop handling me like a piece of meat, you bunch of butchers! What's the matter with you? Don't you see I'm wounded to death?

Full speed they throw me into the ambulance which skids on the ice as it goes into gears and almost hits a tree but finally it swirls on to the road and takes off full speed toward the camp's military hospital some 30 miles away. There three military doctors after a brief examination and consultation rush toward me to fix me up. Me I pass out!

After four hours and fifty-seven minutes of surgery (that's how
long it took to fix him up he was told later) there he is all plastered
up from neck to toes
v
e
r
t
i
c
a
l
l
y and fingers to fingers h o r i z o n t a l l y

in a neat little human

                    c
                    r
          c r o s s
                    s
                    s

both legs broken (one at the talus the other
at the femur) both arms broken (one at the
humerus the other at the radius) neck out of.
joint plus several other less serious broken
bones bruises cuts etc. in other words a
               complete human mess!

You should have seen him! It was not a pretty spectacle!
Lying there on that white hospital bed both legs in one huge
cast (the doctors thought it would be better to squeeze both

legs together in the same cast to prevent him from moving) hanging from a bird perch and both arms stretched out in another cast which went all the way across his chest his neck squeezed inside some kind of a metallic contraption and the rest of his body wrapped up in some white tape which made him look like an Egyptian mummy. A ghost!

Look at me! He thought. ME the SUPERMAN of the 20th Century! Don't I rather look like an UNDERMAN? UN SOUSHOMME? A human garbage pail?

He was pondering all the possible degrading images adequate to describe his present condition when Captain Cohen walked in.

CHRIST ALMIGHTY! What happened to you Frenchy?

He asks what happened to me? As if it wasn't obvious! Is he blind the old fag? I fell out of the plane, Sir! I tried to say smiling but the very act of smiling was a real torture.

Looks like it's going to be a while before you're back on your feet, at least that's what the doctors say! Three to four months! At least for the legs! The rest might be sooner!

Three to four months! But what about my 30 days? What about my leave?

Your 30 days you'll spend them in bed, and even more! We are shipping you back to Fort Bragg in a few days! Yes by special convoy!

But what about the FAR EAST? California? The big journey?

CANCELLED!

And what about San Francisco? The discovery of America?

CANCELLED!

And the OVERSEAS DUTY? And . . . And . . . And . . . And
. . .

Cancelled! Everything is cancelled! Annulled! Once and for all!

But Sir! Why? Why? Cancelled? Why can't everything be temporarily postponed until I get back on my feet? And then I can go
on with the rest of my journey [and me with the rest of this damn
story]!

Cancelled I said! Permanently! You are no longer in condition to
do your duties! No longer in condition to serve your fellowmen
and your country properly! You are a medical case! Disabled!
Bodily and who knows perhaps even mentally incapacitated!
Unfit in other words! Or if you prefer in a state of suspense!

Suspension! I would rather say, Sir, with my legs up like that!

Say what you will, Frenchy, you have rendered yourself useless
to the military service in general and to the 82nd Airborne Division in particular. Therefore we are shipping you back to Fort
Bragg! You will be in reprieve!

[I would rather say that he was in shit up to his neck, or plaster up to his ass, to be more precise!]

Therefore, everything is cancelled for you! And on that, without any further explanations, Captain Cohen leaves the room giving him a curt cynical and flippant military salute and a SEE YOU LATER FRENCHY when you're back in shape!

I didn't even return his salute! [How could he?] I simply cursed the hell out of that pederast as soon as he had left the room! But I had a strange feeling inside that this time I had really been screwed!

So here he is in pieces. Arms and legs in pieces. Broke. Fucked. Alone and without any means of transportation. His Buickspecial in a state of junk up in the branches of a pine tree some 150 miles or so away. Without love. Marilyn now faithfully back in the arms of Benny some 350 miles away. Without friends. That's for sure. And everything else cancelled. And now they were going to ship him (by special convoy whatever that means) back to North Carolina where it all started. But what about my things? My possessions? My duffel bag and also the stuff in Marilyn's closet? What are they going to do with all that?

Don't ask me I said to him! I'm only here to report. I don't have any control over such things! I merely tell it as it is! It's not part of my job to keep track of your things! But nonetheless as he went on with the rest of his story I could tell he was disturbed by the state of his affairs!

Cancelled! The damn Captain walks in here and tells me point blank it's all cancelled! But doesn't he understand that I'm fed up with all that connerie! Fed up with the Army the 82nd Airborne Division the Dumb Hillbillies American Life! I can't take it anymore! Can't go any further!

What the fuck does he want from me with his cancellations? J'en ai plein le cul plein le dos plein les bras et les jambes c'est pas de la blague ah c'est bien le cas de le dire (all that in French comme d'habitude) of their Army Country and Fellowmen! I've nothing left not a damn thing! Nothing! Hardly a rest of life! A rest of hope also! Everything has been taken away from me! Gone! Obliterated!

No more love
No more money
No more Buickspecial
No more lovely vacation
No more discovery of America
No more beautiful war to die at last
No more big trip across country to the West Coast
No more adventures unexpected encounters and stories to tell
No more friends no more moinous either no more nothing nothing nothing

Except the jerks from the regiment who are certainly going to come and see me in a few minutes to make fun of me to laugh at me to mock me to curse the hell out of me to tell me what a stupid ass I am to crush me

X X X X X X X X X X . . . . ! [Hey! Everybody is gone! Where the hell did you guys go? Dammit! Don't you want to hear the rest of the story? Come back you guys!]

I'm all alone now and I begin crying like a kid there on that hospital bed arms and legs in pieces all plastered up into a cross suspended in the air cancelled from all sides and not even able to wipe away to dry up the tears rolling down my cheeks
♪

   ♪

      ♪

       ♪

          ♪ into my contraption!

Finished . . . it's finished . . . foutu . . . america . . . the great journey . . . the great discovery . . . the great plains . . . north south . . . east west . . . through the middle . . . the rockies and the plateaux . . . the mississippi . . . the grand canyon . . . it's all finished . . . rattlesnakes in the desert . . . the big sky in the far west . . . the beautiful landscapes out of sight . . . las vegas and the crap games . . . indians with feathers . . . and the naked movie stars in hollywood . . . gangsters in chicago . . . up and down and across the middle . . . oil wells in texas . . . reno l.a. frisco . . . all the beautiful dreams . . . finished . . . wide open space . . . the big factories where they make funny gadgets and giant salami . . . foutu tout ça . . . fini . . . all the little hicktowns with exotic names . . . these united states of america and the land of opportunities . . . all the detours . . . down the road . . . the unknown . . . wild animals . . . one-legged birds and golden buffalos . . . the never-seen before by a human eye with or without binoculars . . . the never-heard before by human ears with or without hearing aids . . . chance . . . luck . . . and maybe even unexpected love . . . coincidence . . . and moinous . . . alone and on foot . . . eh yes . . . poor moinous . . . with his music and his duffel bag on his shoulder . . . with his detours . . . on his way to florida . . . with his aunt

augusta . . . apple pies in the sun . . . what's going to happen to
him . . . is he going to reach san francisco . . . are they going to
assassinate him . . . with a knife in the chest . . . we'll never
know now . . . never . . . will he make it . . . we'll never know
the end . . . the whole story is finished . . . cancelled . . . across
country . . . we'll never know if the story was true . . . the
whole lay out . . . it's finished!
We'll never know the rest!
If it really happened the way he said it!
Or at least not in the present version of this recitation!
Because now it's all finished
                        finished
                        finished
                        o o o o o o o o f o u t u !

And so he folded himself upon himself like an old wrinkled piece
of yellow paper there on that hospital bed as I took leave of him
[on the edge of the precipice] closed himself like a used torn book
which nobody needs anymore a useless book to be thrown in the
garbage as he thought of the trip the big beautiful journey he
could have made cross country coast to coast and which someday
he could have told like a beautiful story or retold with all the
exciting details to a friend or to some gathering of interested
listeners with all the passion necessary to tell such a story directly
or indirectly but now it was finished cancelled cancelled and so
empty of his last drop of courage and the last words of his story
which is now cancelled cancelled since they were shipping him
back to where it all started he said sadly to himself
no need trying to go on
no need . . . .
but perhaps the next time . . .
yes . . . the next time . . .   [*So long everybody!*]

o o o o o o o o **FINISHED** o o o o o o o o

ABOUT THE AUTHOR

Raymond Federman was born in France. He came to the United States soon after World War II. Totally bilingual he writes both in French and in English. Presently Professor of English and Comparative Literature at the State University of New York at Buffalo, he has published numerous articles, essays, poems, stories, translations in various magazines in the U.S., Canada, England, France. In 1966-67 he was awarded a Guggenheim Fellowship. His novel, DOUBLE OR NOTHING, was awarded the France Steloff Fiction Prize, 1972.

FICTION COLLECTIVE

books in print:

The Second Story Man by Mimi Albert
Searching for Survivors by Russell Banks
Reruns by Jonathan Baumbach
Things In Place by Jerry Bumpus
Take It or Leave It by Raymond Federman
Museum by B. H. Friedman
The Talking Room by Marianne Hauser
Reflex and Bone Structure by Clarence Major
The Secret Table by Mark J. Mirsky
The Comatose Kids by Seymour Simckes
Twiddledum Twaddledum by Peter Spielberg
98.6 by Ronald Sukenick
Statements, an anthology of new fiction